MW01134452

NEVER TELL

NEVER TELL

Larry Sydow

© 2017 Larry Sydow
All rights reserved.

ISBN: 1547052953
ISBN 13: 9781547052950
Library of Congress Control Number: 2017909017
CreateSpace Independent Publishing Platform
North Charleston, South Carolina

Acknowledgments

Dedications, credits, and thank-yous given to other people by authors all sound a lot alike. However, I now know how important that support can be. It is what kept me going, and without that support, *Never Tell* might never have been completed.

First of all, I want to thank my wife, Jean, and my sons, Travis and Andy, for their encouragement to complete *Never Tell*. Their opinions matter the most, and they are the ones I seek to impress. My wife is the only person who has heard brief parts of my Vietnam experience over the years, and she has always said that I should write a book.

A special thank-you goes to Cindy Cutts, who prodded me to get started. Her encouragement and advice throughout the process gave me the confidence to complete *Never Tell*. She is an accomplished author who has helped many other authors with their work.

My sister-in-law, Darlene Ellis, read each blundering first attempt at each chapter, and her positive encouragement and advice inspired me to revise, revise again, and continue.

I would also like to thank another group of people who were intrigued enough by the story that they volunteered to be the first to read my next-to-last revision and offer their critical advice. My daughters-in-law, Amy Sydow and Jessica Sydow, along with Doug Kosti and Steve McGrew, provided the final support for *Never Tell*.

Introduction

Never Tell is the story of how eighty-three men made a promise to keep a secret. It all happened over a ten-day period in early 1971. The men were on an important assignment in the jungle of Vietnam at a critical time during the war. Ten days was a mere fraction of the US Army's one-year tour of duty.

It has been over forty years since I returned from Vietnam, and I spent most of those forty years trying to forget. The nightmares and phobias have subsided, and the last fifteen years have been free of troubling thoughts of Vietnam. That was until a little over a year ago, when one small incident triggered a flood of forgotten memories and had me worried that I might be crazy.

At the time, my life was progressing smoothly. You might even say that I was on a roll. I was semiretired, and I was out for a midday walk. Usually I tried to cover about three miles as I wove my way around the neighborhood. On this particular day, I turned a corner to head up a wooded hill, and suddenly, without warning, I had a vivid—absolutely realistic—flashback to Vietnam. A squad of Viet Cong was jogging across my path just one hundred meters ahead of me, and they were carrying AK-47 assault rifles. I flinched and started for the ground, searching for a place to hide. The image lasted for only a split second. I knew exactly where I was. I knew I was standing on a sidewalk in my neighborhood. I knew that I was out for my exercise walk, and I recognized the impossibility of such a sighting. But it was real.

I didn't make it to the prone position. The flashback didn't last that long, but it had been too realistic to just shake off. I looked around to see if anyone was in the area and had observed me. I continued to walk, and my emotions ran wild. At first I was scared, and that progressed to shock, and finally I was questioning my sanity. It had been forty years! Forty years had gone by with nothing like this happening to me. I had experienced nightmares and phobias after I initially returned from my tour in Vietnam, but this hallucination was on a totally different level. The vision had taken place while I was fully conscious, and it had come out of the clear blue.

When I returned home, I made the mistake of telling my wife what had happened. It had been such a shock and such a random event that I didn't pause to think about any ramifications. We talked it over, and I laughed it off. After that I considered the matter closed.

I walked the neighborhood for each of the next several days, and nothing out of the ordinary happened. The tree-lined street on the wooded hill remained just that. I spent a lot of time thinking about why I might have a flashback now. Years had gone by. This was the least likely time for that kind of incident to take place. I was sleeping well, and life was good. However, in the meantime, unknown to me, my wife was on the computer researching. She had e-mailed some of my friends I had served with in Vietnam and told them about the flashback. She then informed me that they wanted to meet to renew our friendship.

We planned a meeting, and seeing my friends again was an emotional reunion for each of us. Our conversation was serious in nature, and we talked a lot about what might have caused my flashback. It was most comforting to know that each of them had experienced similar incidents.

As we reminisced about different events that we had shared in Vietnam, one particular mission came up, and all I said was "That would make a great book."

I was shocked by their reaction. They said, "Go for it." I was encouraged on the spot to attempt it.

"What about the promise to never tell?" I asked them. The promise had been part of my life ever since Vietnam, and now they were downplaying its significance.

I was again told to write it if I wanted to. After all, it had been over forty years since it happened. They had never worried about it. I was the one who had taken all of the risks.

At this point, our conversation was adding years to my life. I felt a wave of relief and realized how much greater the significance would have been if this meeting had taken place thirty-five years ago. Now that it was forty years later, some of the stress and pressure had lessened over time. It's amazing what time can do. I could now share some of the secret that I had been guarding all of these years.

At the time of our reunion, I had no intention of writing a book. However, only a short time passed before I told some other trusted friends about an idea that I had for a book, and I was encouraged to get started. At this point I still hadn't given anything away.

The men of Bravo Company who promised to never tell can be compared to a sports team that has lost its star player to an injury. Eighty-three men stepped up to do the job of 225 men. Like members of a team, each of the men took on more of the responsibility of running the company.

Americans who served within the borders of Vietnam number 2,709,218, and 58,202 of those lost their lives. Another 303,704 were wounded, and for ten days, eighty-three of those defied the odds. Those eighty-three men are the only ones who know exactly what happened during those ten days.

Once the mission was underway, Bravo Company, without knowing, became the focus and talk of the entire division. Bravo Company was undermanned and lacked the leadership of trained officers, yet they were assigned a particularly dangerous mission. The men stepped up and formed a bond, as so many other men in combat had done throughout history. They resolved to keep one another alive for as long as they could. The secret of *Never Tell* was the result. What makes this story unique and even more remarkable is the fact that there were no officers present for what amounted to a major mission. The company was led entirely by NCOs, and the highest-ranking NCO was a staff sergeant who served as the company commander. That would be me!

1

"We beat the odds, we beat the army, and we survived even when we weren't supposed to. Now we must never tell." The mission had concluded, and the men were awaiting the arrival of a new CO (commanding officer) to lead them to a new AO (area of operation) and the start of a new mission.

The sun was intensely bright, and the morning chill had already abated. It was just after 0800 hours, but it felt as if the temperature was already closing in on ninety degrees. Today was going to be hot, and by the time the new CO (commanding officer) arrived, it would be much hotter.

The speech wasn't short because of the heat. It was ingrained in the minds of the men, who had been in-country for a while, to avoid groups or clusters.

Keep your interval. Keep your distance. Spread out so one grenade can't get all of you had been constantly stressed to the men throughout their training. There were no FNGs (inexperienced troops who were new to Vietnam) in Bravo Company. Everyone was fully acclimatized to the heat, and today promised to be hotter than usual. The fact that there wasn't as much humidity made it seem hotter, although no one probably even noticed.

The time in the open had to be limited, and all of the men were to some degree aware of being in the open and exposed. It wouldn't take long before the men would instinctively start to begin edging back, each giving himself some space between himself and the next person.

The gathering of a group this size—seventy-six men—wouldn't have bothered me three, four, or five months ago. But in the past ten days, my life had changed. I had been forced to be much more alert. My senses had become more acute. I worried more. I used to think of myself as easygoing. Now my life was seriously intense. Yet, because of the situation, I felt I had to force myself to appear in total control of my emotions. I was the decider.

I gave the men a brief moment while I looked down at the ground trying to sort out my private thoughts. I would have to trust each man. My future depended on the ability of each member of the group to keep a secret forever. It was time, and all I could think of was "Here goes."

I raised my can of lukewarm Falstaff beer into the air and spoke to the rest of the company. "I will never tell."

Each member of the gathering joined the ceremonial toast and simultaneously raised a canteen cup containing cocoa or coffee, a can of soda, or a can of beer. In one soft voice they each repeated, "I will never tell." Then they drank.

The last words were spoken as I added, "Thank you, each of you, for helping to pull this off."

Seventy-six men who were thankful to still be alive at the end of the mission had just made a promise to keep a secret.

Without another word being spoken, the men quickly dispersed in every direction as they headed back to their posts and platoon areas. There was no discussion, nor would there be. What was done was done, and what was said was said. The events of the past week would never be spoken of again.

Only one soldier, Tommy, a sixty gunner who appeared too small to be carrying such a large weapon, spoke to his sergeant when they reached the shade. "Don't mean noth'n." This phrase was the infantry man's colloquialism for "I won't let it bother me."

Tommy would never tell.

I didn't realize it at the time, but I was probably the only one who would continue to worry. The uncertainty of what could happen would continue to haunt me for years after returning from Vietnam.

I was the focus at this assembly—me, SSG Jerry Miller. The meeting had taken place in the center of an encircled company of APCs (armored personnel carriers) in South Vietnam. We were surrounded on three sides by rubber trees. The rubber trees were part of an old French plantation, and the trees covered thousands of acres. What was impressive was how incredibly straight the rows of trees were. The company of APCs was loggered up, or camped, at the very southern edge of the rubber plantation. To the south was a large basin of virgin jungle that provided plenty of cover and concealment for enemy troops.

I had just met with what was left of Bravo Company, fourth of the Twenty-Third Mechanized Infantry assigned to the Twenty-Fifth Division.

I was the highest-ranking member of the company and had been assigned the duties of company commander on the sixteenth of February. Today was the twenty-sixth of February, and the company would finally be getting a new commanding officer (CO).

At daylight I had met with the six soldiers who were missing from the gathering. They were out on observation posts (OPs) as part of the company security. Even though we would be leaving the area soon, we were still in no-man's-land, and we needed to protect ourselves. The six men and I had ceremonially toasted and sealed the same affirmation before they left the perimeter at daylight.

I lingered in the center of the perimeter after everyone else had left. I was trying to control my runaway imagination. When the new CO arrived, I would be back with second platoon as the second's acting platoon leader, a lieutenant's slot. I looked forward to being back with second platoon. I should have been feeling some degree of relief, but it wasn't there. My mind was racing at warp speed, and I was having trouble controlling my thoughts. I changed tactics and tried to think about my wife, Kate, back in the world. I longed to be with her and could picture her next to me, but, I couldn't hold those thoughts either. There was too much yet to do. The company was more vulnerable now than we had been since the twentieth of February. We were in the process of preparing to move, so the perimeter security had been picked up, which meant the entire number of trip flares and claymore mines.

I was acutely aware of the heat. The sun was going to punish us today. There was no dew. The vegetation's foliage was dry in spite of the normally high humidity. There was no evidence of the recent late-afternoon rains. Where the earth was bare, the soil was dry and dusty.

On the other hand, nights, no matter how hot the days got, were always cold and uncomfortable. Trying to sleep when the temperature drops fifty degrees or more from the previous afternoon can give the body quite a shock and can be incredibly uncomfortable. The light jungle fatigues designed for the tropical climate dry out quickly but don't retain much heat. With only a poncho liner to wrap in for warmth, nights pass slowly with a lot of shivering.

There was nothing for me to do now except wait, but the waiting was raising my anxiety level. Once again I tried focusing my thoughts on my wife and the fun that we had had on R&R in Hawaii, although it wasn't called R&R here. The men referred to R&R as I&I (Intoxication & Intercourse). The once-comforting thoughts of time spent with my wife were not currently working. All I was remembering was the terrible sadness when R&R was over and I had to return to Vietnam.

Too much had happened in the past ten days. I had plenty to think about and plenty to worry about. I wondered whether I could ever forget as I turned and strode toward the APC that served as the command track. Most of the time, the men referred to the APCs simply as tracks.

"Today is the twenty-sixth," I was thinking as I walked, "and it all started on the sixteenth, my birthday. How ironic! I didn't even remember that it was my birthday until late that night amid one of the worst days of my life, and I had no idea that there were more such days to come."

I can remember the moment. I really needed something to do that would hold my focus. My mind was full of random thoughts. I couldn't keep my thoughts from straying. I was almost desperate to escape to another train of thought, a simpler subject. It was like a song that you hated, yet you couldn't keep from replaying it over and over and over in your mind.

By now I was concentrating on the down ramp of the command track. I needed to monitor the radios.

Andy, the command-track RTO, was motioning me to the shady side of the track. The PRC-25 radio with the extended whip antennae was sitting on the top of the track and leaning against the jeep seat that I rode in when the track was in motion. This radio was tuned to the battalion frequency. Another radio was on the ground leaning against the track. This radio was tuned to the company frequency, and this one was rarely out of arm's reach of Andy.

Andy, back in the world, was Andy Schmidt, a middle linebacker from the University of Texas. He was big and muscular, at least 6′ 4.″ His athletic ability was obvious. For his size he was cat quick and had a knack for unnoticeably appearing in a spot that had been vacant a split second previously. His most endearing qualities were his good-natured personality and his perpetual smile. It was hard to imagine him playing the combative sport of football. Even though he had the size, the build, and the speed to be a great football player; it was his personality. He seemed way too easygoing to be a football player, especially a linebacker.

I had gotten to know Andy well during the last ten days. We had spent each of the twenty-four hours of each of those days in close contact, and I had come to rely heavily on Andy.

As I rounded the track to step into the shade, I asked Andy, "Any news yet?"

"Not yet, Sarge. How're y'all doing?"

"Andy, to tell the truth, I am glad this is about to be over with, and I am ready to go back to being the second platoon's leader. It will be good to get back to second platoon."

"Well, hey, we got used to y'all. You're gonna be missed here. I like bein' your RTO, and I kinda wish I could go with y'all. But that would mess up Art. He's been the second-platoon RTO for as long as I've been here."

"You and Ron will be busy enough taking care of the new CO," I told him. "You're both good at what you do; besides, we'll still be just across the perimeter and be able to see each other during downtime. And we'll work together on future missions. Hopefully, there won't be a high stress level involved."

Neither of us was pressed to do anything at the moment, so we enjoyed a quiet pause in our conversation.

I finally broke the silence. "Andy, thanks for being here. I am really stressing, and I don't know why."

I felt I had the men's respect. I was completely confident with second platoon, which was my platoon. I tried to be a positive leader. I frequently complimented my men; not just for a job done well, but to acknowledge jobs done correctly. I thought it was important to maintain a positive attitude. I felt that this approach went a long way toward getting things done. You never ask or order anyone to do something that you yourself wouldn't do. No doubt my elementary teaching background had taught me the value of positive thinking and positive reinforcement.

Most people—and it was especially true of second platoon—would rather work for someone who appreciates them. In fact, by now I was confident that I could ask the members of second platoon to do just about anything, and they would comply.

For the last ten days, I had been dealing with the entire company. Realizing that ten days isn't a very long period of time, but because of what we had been through, I had the same confidence in each member of the rest of the company as with the members of second platoon. And now I had to trust them.

I would have much preferred that I be the one keeping a secret for the rest of the company, but that role was reversed. Eighty-two men were keeping a secret for me. I trusted each of those eighty-two men of Bravo Company, but I feared what the future might bring.

Another one of Andy's attributes was that he was a good listener. He had heard me say that I was stressed, and now he was going to take care of me.

"Wait there in the shade for a second, and I'll be right back." Andy ducked around the corner of the track. He circled the track and was back with a familiar object.

"Here, you have time to sit for a while."

He was unfolding a battered old—really old, really battered—folding garden lounge chair. The chair was referred to as the company commander's throne. It was known by several names: the captain's throne, the commander's throne, the CO's throne, or simply the throne. Where the chair had come from, no one knew. It had been with Bravo Company for as long as any of the present members could remember, and it had been repaired so many times that it didn't seem to have any of the original parts. The webbing was a mixture of rubber cords and old rucksack straps. The metal tubing was spliced and replaced with bamboo and lengths of angle iron. Where the angle iron came from was anyone's guess. Most of the tubing was obscured by tape, leather wraps, and small-diameter cord or rope.

The chair had held more than a few Bravo Company commanders. It had its own tradition and was a testament to the respect that the men of Bravo Company had for their commanders.

Only the company commander ever sat in that chair. There was no envy or jealousy on the part of the men. The throne was a tradition that we all supported. I was humbled to realize that I had earned the right to sit in the commander's throne as I thankfully sank into the chair. It was comfortable, and, as Andy had said, I didn't have anything that needed my attention until the new CO arrived. That is, assuming that nothing drastic or unexpected would happen in the next couple of hours. After all, we were still in Charlie's backyard, and he would decide what would happen next.

It dawned on me that this was my first downtime since the sixteenth of February, when all hell broke loose. I had a chance to relax if I could. I could feel tense muscles start to unknot. The tightness in my back was disappearing. It was as if I were melting into the commander's throne. My body continued to stand down and relax, but my thoughts were a different matter.

I was flashing back to the first time that I was shot at since coming to Vietnam. It happened on a thick jungle trail, and the contact was a close ambush. You weren't supposed to survive a close ambush, but amazingly, our patrol suffered no casualties. The VC unit that opened up on our patrol was only twenty meters away.

I had survived two close ambushes. I had survived a grenade landing close to my position, and I had pulled off several ambushes against the enemy. I had even experienced a four-hour firefight. Our company was supporting an ARVN (South Vietnamese army) unit led by MAC-V advisors. The ARVNs were in hand-to-hand combat with VC or NVA dressed in ARVN uniforms less than fifty meters right in front of us. We didn't know whom to shoot.

I had been in country just shy of ten months, and there I sat trying to count the number of times that I had been shot at; however, the secret that the eighty-three men of Bravo Company had just toasted must be kept, or the consequences could be much scarier than anything that I had already been through.

2

While sitting in the commander's throne, I appreciated the fact that I finally had some time to myself. The past ten days had gone by slowly. Even though there had been times that I had to myself, it wasn't the same as this moment. There had always been something to worry about or a problem to be worked out, but now, finally my mind could wander. So why was I having such a hard time relaxing?

The more comfortable I became sitting there in the throne, the more I relaxed. As I unwound, I reminisced. I was thinking back to how I had arrived at this spot in time, in the position of what I liked to think of as "the decider."

How I had acquired the skills that had led me to my current position, the present situation, and to this location, was less complicated than one might think. I loved sports, and sports had been a big part of my life. I had been fortunate to be able to play football at a small college.

I met my wife early in our college careers, and we married before either of us graduated. Upon graduating with a degree in elementary education, I taught sixth grade for one year before being drafted. That first year of teaching had been exciting, fun, and very rewarding. I wasn't able to anticipate or look forward to the upcoming school year, since I received my draft notice at the end of February during my first year of teaching. I was, however, allowed to finish the school year before reporting for basic training.

It all seems so strange to me now. Both my wife's life and my life changed drastically in a very short time. My first teaching job was in a small rural school district in Oregon. I was twenty-four years old and had been married for three and a half years when I received my draft notice. If you made it to twenty-five, you were considered too old to be drafted.

I was usually the oldest person within any of the military groups that I was assigned to in the army. Field-grade officers and senior NCOs were the only ones older than I was, and few of them had assignments where they spent time on the ground in the jungle.

I was a lot older than the eighteen- and nineteen-year-olds who made up the majority of the forces serving in Vietnam. In fact, I was older than most of the captains and lieutenants I came in contact with. I had just turned twenty-six a few days ago. I was older, I was married, and my former teaching job had all made me naturally a very responsible person.

Once in the army, I approached my training just as I had sports and life in general. I gave it my best effort.

As I sat in the shade with Andy, my short journey back to my stateside duties was over. My thoughts were taking me back to the sixteenth of February. The more I relaxed, the more my mind seemed to wander. It was as if my brain were doing back flips. I wasn't able to escape my unpleasant thoughts, but I was aware of the stored-up tension leaving my body.

The sixteenth of February began on a Tuesday morning that promised to be just like any other Tuesday morning. My platoon and I were all up and about. The dawn was breaking, but the sun hadn't yet emerged. We hadn't been on one of the night ambush patrols; instead, we had shared the company's perimeter security with the mortar platoon and the elements of first and third platoons that weren't on patrol. The patrols were due back just after daylight. The evening before, the CO briefed the platoon leaders that we had marching orders and had been assigned a new AO (area of operation). We would be pulling out sometime in the morning.

The second platoon was packed and ready to roll just after daylight. The fact that we were ready early meant that my platoon medic and I were going to enjoy another cup of cocoa. Marcos Ramirez, the platoon medic, had just lit the dime-sized ball of C-4 that we used to heat water for cooking and coffee or hot chocolate. At that instant the radio crackled with a call from the company first sergeant.

The company's first sergeant was a sergeant first class, or SFC, who was on his second or third tour in Vietnam. His ambition was to attain the rank of command sergeant major. The first sergeant, being the top sergeant in the company, was simply called Top. He ran the company headquarters in Long Binh, which was also our battalion and brigade headquarters.

Top was at his best taking care of the company from the rear area. He was very shrewd and skilled at what he did. He made sure that the company ran smoothly. He took care of all of the paper work. He made sure that each member of the company got his R&R leave and an in-country leave. When someone was getting close to his DEROS (date of estimated return from overseas), Top would get him out of the field. But most importantly, he was able to keep the company resupplied.

In early January Top's jeep had an accident. An APC that was escorting Top's jeep and some other vehicles hit a mine. The mine was big enough to flip the APC on its side. Even though the mine didn't directly impact Top's jeep, the jeep driver swerved drastically. The combination of the jeep's sudden change in direction and the concussion of the mine blast caused Top to fall out of the jeep. He said he flew. Anyway, when he landed, he broke his leg.

It was now the sixteenth of February and Top was still on light duty.

Top was well-liked by all of the men in the company. He was also one of the most interesting individuals I have ever met.

Top was fluent in three languages. He spoke Spanish due to his Hispanic background, and he spoke English from growing up in the United States. He was also fluent in German since he had met his wife and married while he was stationed in Germany.

I knew that Top had joined the army just out of high school and served a year in Korea as well as a year in Germany before being sent to Vietnam. For this being at least his second tour, he appeared remarkably young. I would have guessed Top's age to be in his midthirties.

Top had some unusual, outstanding traits that set him apart from everyone else. He could swear! I mean he took profanity to a new level, and he swore in three languages. He went from English to Spanish to German and back and forth. Top's swearing could stop the most rancid and rankest sailors in their tracks speechless. Top didn't swear out of anger. It was just part of his normal conversation. To think what he might sound like if and when he was really angry was hard to imagine.

I had seen Top angry only a few times, and it was hard to keep a straight face. When Top was upset, he mixed his metaphors. I remembered witnessing Top dressing down a clerk who had made some minor mistake in the rear area. Top was nose to nose with the young soldier. It didn't matter what the clerk had done. I had just come upon the scene and instantly was feeling sorry for the clerk until Top said, "You buttered your bread. Now you have to lie in it."

Top came up with some real hilarious combinations. "You can't have your cake and wipe your butt with it too!" I will never figure out how he put that one together.

On the sixteenth of February, at the company logger site that we would be vacating shortly, I was sipping my cocoa and trying to make it last when Top radioed that he would be picking me up in about thirty minutes.

It was Top's idea that within our company, the platoon sergeants and sergeants acting as platoon leaders took turns visiting the men from our company who were in the hospital and taking them their mail.

I grabbed a bandolier of loaded M-16 magazines and set them next to my rifle so I could be ready as soon as Top got there. Doc Ramirez and I were still relaxing with our hot chocolate and enjoying the moment.

The company logger site where we were camped was right next to a well-traveled single-lane dirt road. The dirt road turned south off of Highway 1 between Long Binh and Xuan Loc just before Highway 1 reached the coast and turned north toward Cam Ranh Bay and continued all the way to the DMZ.

The dirt road that we were using ran north and south and connected several rubber plantations with Highway 1. The maps that I was using didn't show the area to the far south, but it seemed likely that the dirt road continued all the way to the delta and terminated at some port city from where the rubber latex could be shipped.

Top arrived in a little more than thirty minutes. He had been following the engineers, using them as an escort, as they swept the road for mines.

This was a daily occurrence before traffic was allowed on the road. The road had to be cleared all the way to Fire Support Base Georgia, near the end of the road. Fire Support Base Georgia was one of the many temporary six-gun artillery bases that were strategically located throughout Vietnam so they could fire artillery support for infantry and ground operations in the area.

As usual, Top was in a hurry. I grabbed my rifle and the loose bandolier and jumped into the back seat of the jeep. Top, amid a stream of profanity, hustled over to the captain's APC to confer with him before we would be heading back to Long Binh.

I looked forward to visiting the men in the hospital. We didn't always have people in the hospital, so it wasn't a regular rotation. But today it was a great privilege to ride in a jeep and get away for the day.

On this particular day, there were two men from our company in the hospital. One was from first platoon and had been wounded by a booby trap. The wound was serious enough that he was probably going to Japan soon and then home. The other member of Bravo Company who was in the hospital was Junior, a 6'7" bean pole of a man from somewhere in Oklahoma. He was a member of the third platoon, and he injured his back when he fell off his moving track.

Junior hadn't been a dust-off. The first sergeant drove him to the Twenty-Fourth EVAC Hospital in Long Binh in his jeep. Maybe it was more serious than I thought since he had already been there for five or six days.

Top returned to the jeep smiling amid another flurry of profanity. It was hot! This was near the end of the dry season, and red dust was swirling as we jolted and bumped our way onto the road and headed north toward Highway 1 and then Long Binh.

Before Top had arrived, I briefed Sergeant Ralph Moore. Sergeant Moore was next in the chain of command in second platoon. He would be in charge in my absence and had needed to be informed about the order of march when the company moved out.

3

We headed north on the dirt road to Long Binh without an escort. The road had just been cleared of mines, and the sun was starting to climb into the sky. We hadn't gone far when the radio mounted on the side of the jeep behind the front passenger seat began to sputter. The radio was tuned to our company frequency, so we were hearing Captain Cooper's orders to the rest of the company. The company would be in a hurry now. The night ambush patrols had all returned, and I thought I could hear the APC's engines starting to rev up.

It took a while to sort out what was happening. We were finally able to determine that Fire Support Base Georgia was taking sniper fire. Someone at Georgia was trying to estimate the number of snipers. The guy obviously didn't know much. He went from two snipers to maybe a dozen. No one had seen a sniper, but two of the artillery crew had been shot.

The fire support base (FSB) was stocked with artillery personnel and REMFs (a derogatory term used to describe the support personnel who ate hot meals, slept in sheets, and had maid service and air conditioning). No one apparently had the expertise—or more likely, the will—to go after the snipers and chase them away.

By now I could accurately picture what would be happening back at the logger site. All of the APCs were running, and some would be starting to move. Everything would happen quickly now.

Even though second platoon was ready to go first, it wasn't their turn. The second platoon would be last in the order of march, with the mortar platoon in line in front of them. The lead platoon, or point, was at a higher risk because of mines, booby traps, and ambushes, so the platoons took turns on point. Today it was third platoon's turn to go first and be the point. They would be followed by the captain's track with all of the attached personnel. First platoon would be next in order, followed by the mortar platoon and then second platoon as the rear security.

There would be no stopping the company now. Each APC would be rolling into position, and as soon as the CO's track was in position, the speed would increase dramatically. APCs can max out at over forty miles per hour. However, in Vietnam, on a dirt road and fully loaded, the speed can, surprisingly, still approach forty miles per hour. It could put a lot of pressure on the mortar platoon and the rear security to quickly get in position and up to speed when the rest of the company was already flying down the road. There should be no gaps in the column as the speed is maintained toward Fire Support Base Georgia.

Bravo Company just happened to be the closest unit to the fire support base. Thus, they were the most obvious ones to be tapped to react to the sniper fire.

In the jeep, the driver, Top, and I were all mesmerized by what we were hearing over the radio. Finally Top spoke to his driver. "You don't need to go any slower. The company can handle this candy-ass mission. Those snipers are long gone by now."

Top's jeep driver had been an APC driver for third platoon. He was short, meaning that he had little time left to serve in-country before his tour was up. He actually had less than a month to go before his DEROS date. Top had gotten him out of the field and made him his jeep driver. When he finally went home, Top would take the next shortest member of the company to be his driver.

I was suddenly alerted to the sound of an approaching helicopter flying straight toward us, following the road that we were on. It was a dust-off on its way to pick up wounded, and I was assuming that it was headed for FSB Georgia to pick up the two wounded artillery men.

The radio was silent now. I had lost track of the time, but I had to think that the company was getting close to the FSB. My thoughts were rewarded when I recognized Captain Cooper's voice directing third platoon to come on line to begin a sweep around the FSB. He had just started to direct first platoon to link up with the third platoon when the radio traffic went crazy. There was more static, squelch, yelling, and unintelligible noise than I had ever heard over a radio. Something was terribly wrong!

The uncertainty of not knowing what was happening was clawing at my insides. I was looking at Top, and he was tapping the driver on his shoulder in order to slow the jeep down.

The radio continued to crackle. I couldn't make out all that was being said, but I heard enough of the transmission to know that my company was in real trouble. The first thing that registered was "three KIA."

"Oh, shit! Turn this son of a bitch around!"

The driver didn't hesitate. In fact, he had started the maneuver before Top and I had even gotten the words out. Top was ashen-faced, staring straight ahead as we headed into the dust that we had just kicked up. Then I spent the longest thirty-five minutes I can ever remember.

As we sped down the road, I saw the second dust-off. It was low, lower than the first one, and flying straight down the road. It had come from behind us now that we were headed in the other direction, and it was doing well over ninety miles per hour. The helicopter was quickly out of sight. A few minutes later, a third dust-off appeared following the same route, flying a little higher with the familiar, unmistakable wamp, wamp, wamp of a Huey.

Maybe no more than four or five minutes had passed when a fourth Huey, following the others, wamped overhead.

I knew this could not be good at all. There would be no rush to pick up the KIA. It registered heavily that three dust-offs in addition to the one for the men wounded by the snipers would mean multiple wounded.

What could possibly have happened? I was sweating guilt for not being there.

We came over a rise in the road, and as we topped the hill, we were speeding directly toward the returning engineers who were headed back to Long Binh or Xuan Loc. The jeep driver quickly veered to the right. He was able to keep two wheels on the road, which had no shoulder, in order to pass the engineer's vehicles.

Our vision was instantly impeded by the thick cloud of red dust left in the wake of the engineers' passing. The dust was thick enough to chew, and I tasted and smelled the mud that was forming in my mouth and nostrils.

We were incredibly lucky that we hadn't crashed the jeep and created our own disaster. The rise in the road was probably the only place on an incredibly straight road where you were blinded from the oncoming traffic.

I couldn't help but wonder how all of Bravo's APCs had gotten past the engineers. Some of the dust that hung in the air was probably left over from the company's passing. At last the dust was beginning to thin, and we could once again see the horizon.

"I think we're getting close," exclaimed Top. "I'm sure that little speck is a medevac lifting off." Top was pointing straight down the road. Being in the front passenger seat with me in the back, he had a much better view.

At that point I grabbed the radio mike. There was still too much chatter, and I didn't want to interrupt communications with the medevacs or the company and battalion.

A few minutes later, we were able to make out the fire support base in the distance. There was a lot of dust and a lot of things happening. Missing were the gunships in the air and the sounds of artillery. There was something very strange about what had happened. I tried to analyze the situation. There were casualties, but there had been no firefight. The most logical scenario was a booby trap or mine. As I went over what I had heard on the radio, a booby trap seemed unlikely. The tracks had been moving when whatever happened had taken place. The men were most likely riding on top of the tracks. If a track was disabled, that would have come across over the radio. I was just as confused and curious about what could have happened now as when we had first turned the jeep around. But we were getting closer, and I would soon learn the details.

As we approached the fire support base, the jungle on the right side of the road had been cleared for two hundred meters back from the road. However, it had been a while. Brush had grown back to about waist high and higher. At the edge of the cleared area, the jungle rose to over one hundred feet or even higher. In the cleared area, where the brush had grown back, growth was very uneven. It was as if some of the vegetation had gotten fertilized and other plants remained stunted. Here and there were small groves of trees, with some of the trees being as tall as twenty or thirty feet.

Starting two hundred meters from the FSB and on the right side of the road as the jeep was headed south was Bravo Company. The APCs were sitting in some strange modified echelon formation. None of the APCs were running.

Between the jeep that we were riding in and the entrance to the FSB sat a Huey with its blades barely turning. The Red Cross on the nose was unmistakable, and it appeared to be shutting down.

We were almost parallel to the company as the jeep began to slow down. I grabbed my M-16 and bailed from the jeep before it came to a complete stop. I then sprinted for the nearest track, which happened to be one of the mortar platoon's.

The mortar platoon was sitting by itself less than fifty meters from the road. In the first few strides of my dash, I was able to identify all four of my platoon's tracks. The mortar platoon had been dropped off when the rest of the company began to form an on-line sweep around the fire support base.

I recalled listening to the radio in the jeep when Captain Cooper instructed the mortar platoon to their current position. It was a moment later, when the CO was instructing third platoon to come on line, that whatever happened had taken place.

Something definitely wasn't right. The first three dust-offs had arrived and departed, and they hadn't flown over us on their return trip. They weren't headed for Xuan Loc, but were on a more westerly route to the hospitals in Long Binh. The last dust-off was shutting down right next to the road. It was too quiet, and I still couldn't fathom what might have taken place.

As I ran, I didn't stop at the mortar platoon. I veered between the first and second tracks from the left. When I cleared the mortar platoon's position, there in front of me was my platoon. All four APCs were on line, with most of the men standing beside their tracks.

Someone saw me coming, and everyone moved to the rear of my track; it was the first one on the left. I was even more perplexed as I studied the faces of my platoon. There was none of the fear or excitement that I had expected to see. The only way that I could think to describe the expressions on the faces staring back at me was depression, disappointment, and heavy sadness.

A weak voice in the back mumbled in a barely audible tone, "We really fucked up."

I turned to address the man I had left in charge of second platoon. "Ralph, tell me."

Sergeant Moore began slowly. "Sarge, third platoon and one of first platoon's tracks rolled into an old minefield. When the tracks entered the minefield, they triggered some of the mines. When the first mines went off, the guys riding on top of the tracks thought they were being shot at, so they jumped down. Only they were jumping right into the minefield. This caused some more mines to detonate. It was one big chain reaction. It's some sorry shit. Some of the guys are still trapped in the minefield. The captain is wounded, but he's still here. His track didn't go into the minefield; instead, it's sitting right on the edge. The first platoon track that was in the minefield wasn't in very far, and they backed out before third platoon was told to stay in place."

I stopped Sergeant Moore, figuring that I had heard enough for now. I just had one question for him. "Can you give me a head count?"

"Yah, that's the first thing that the CO told me to do. Second platoon is all present and accounted for except Doc. Doc ran into the minefield to help third platoon before the CO could stop him. He made it, too. And he's still there. The dust-off landed right on top of the track and took the two guys that Doc was working on."

Sergeant Moore paused again and briefly looked around. Seeing that the situation hadn't changed, he continued his report. "Sergeant Hawkins and Tommy are pulling security over there." He pointed to the northwest, toward the jungle. "We're supposed to stay here until things get sorted out. And the captain wants to see you."

"OK," I said, "I'm going to check with the CO."

I walked the fifty or so meters to the CO's track. He was sitting on top of the track in a jeep seat talking to some clean uniforms who were standing alongside. I assumed they were from the FSB, and I was right. It turned out to be Lieutenant Duff, the battalion liaison or tactical officer stationed at the FSB. The other two, a captain and a lieutenant, were artillery officers also from the FSB.

As I approached the CO, he saw me and began immediately. "Sergeant Miller, I need to talk to you. You are now the senior in command. That means that you will be taking over the company. Top has to run the rear area and hasn't fully recovered yet."

The other three officers quietly slipped away and headed for the FSB without excusing themselves.

I remembered that the first sergeant's jeep had avoided a mine, but Top had been thrown out of the jeep. He had sustained a slightly broken leg, if there was such a thing. Currently, he was still walking with a limp.

Captain Cooper continued talking as I listened intently. "I've got ti ti shrapnel in my lower legs. It's not that bad, but they're trying to get me on that dust-off over there." He pointed toward the road.

I took a closer look at the captain's legs. His boots were unlaced and open, and his trousers were pulled up above his knees. Both legs were bound in gauze bandages from the ankles to just below the knees. There were at least a dozen red spots that were showing though the gauze bandages, and there were an equal number of red stains on each leg.

"Sergeant Miller, you're going to be here all night. The engineers don't know what kind of mines they're up against, so they won't be here until tomorrow to clear a path out of the minefield."

The captain continued. "We just missed them on our way here. In fact, we passed the engineers on the road going the other way. As soon as I figured out what had happened, I radioed them to try to get them to come back, but they insisted that they needed different personnel and some equipment that they didn't have with them.

"Sergeant, there are still three tracks stuck in the minefield. It is all of what is left of third platoon. There are eleven men on those tracks. A couple of them have some minor wounds, but they say that they're OK. Doc Ramirez agrees."

Third platoon only had three tracks. One had been sent to the rear for repairs over a month ago, and no one, not even Top, knew when we would get it back.

Captain Cooper still had more to tell me. "Your medic did one hell of a job; probably saved two lives. I had just figured out what was happening, and here he came. He ran full speed by us and right into the minefield. He claims he didn't understand us. That was lucky for the two guys he dragged over to the track on his way in. They had been wounded by the same mine that Lieutenant Herbert stepped on. Doc Ramirez had to administer IVs and everything. He's still in the middle track there."

Marcos Ramirez was the newest member of the company, and he was assigned to second platoon as a replacement for the platoon's former medic, who was lazy and unreliable. We had been in some action in a rubber plantation up north of there, and Sergeant Moore caught the medic taking a handful of pain pills. He was roughed up pretty good. His medical bag, his rucksack, and everything he had was taken away from him. We sent him back to Long Binh on a resupply helicopter for the first sergeant to deal with. He was yelling and bawling and begging, but it didn't matter. He hadn't done his job, and more importantly, he wasn't dependable. Sergeant Moore carried the medical bag plus all of his own gear for three weeks until Marcos showed up on a resupply chopper.

Marcos was short and stocky. He really didn't look the part. When Marcos arrived, Ron, the command track's medic, brought him over to introduce him. All I could think was, here we go again. Sometimes it was sure great to be wrong.

Marcos was a Mexican national who had joined the US Army. His English was bad, to say the least. He probably didn't know what "stop" meant when he ran into the minefield.

I was like a sponge trying to absorb everything that the CO had to say. However, I was distracted when I saw three body bags being carried on stretchers toward the FSB. I knew one was Lieutenant Herbert. I would learn who the other two were soon enough. All three had been from third platoon.

The captain wanted a more private conversation with me, so I climbed up on the track and sat on the edge in front of him, feet dangling, right behind the driver's hatch. The CO was in his jeep seat next to me, where we could easily see and hear each other.

What Captain Cooper said next put things in perspective and set me up. This was my wake-up call.

I hadn't realized that I wouldn't see him again. More than once I would continue to be mentored by him in his absence. The thought of what Captain Cooper would do in certain situations helped me to make decisions and continue to move forward.

"Sergeant Miller, I probably won't be coming back. Don't say anything; just listen. The minefield isn't on our maps. Get Top to get you some updated maps. You'll get a new CO real soon. The army won't wait for me to heal, so until...keep everyone together, keep them busy, security first, and always watch your back. You'll be fine.

"Oh, Lieutenant Jones is in the fire support base with his artillery buddies. No need for him here."

Lieutenant Jones was assigned to our company as an FO, or forward observer, to assist in calling in artillery strikes.

With what he wanted to say concluded, Captain Cooper climbed down from the APC and began limping toward the road. After much arguing and protesting, he finally settled on a stretcher to be carried to the waiting dust-off.

As I turned back from watching the CO's departure, I was surprised to see Andy Schmidt with a radio standing next to me. "Where did you come from?"

"I've been here all the time. You need to check in with battalion."

Battalion was waiting for my call. I was talking directly with Major Anderson. I told him that we had to spend the night in the minefield until the engineers arrived the next day. I let him know that my first order of business was to set a night perimeter so we could cover the APCs that were still trapped in the minefield. He didn't say anything in response to the company's situation. All he said was that the battalion commander was coming to FSB Georgia tomorrow afternoon.

I was thinking that our company might be getting a new company commander as soon as tomorrow.

4

We had radio communication with each of the three APCs stuck in the minefield. Extra time was spent explaining to them what was going to take place over the next fifteen to twenty hours. The eleven trapped men were given more information and specifics than the rest of the company. They wouldn't be pulling any guard duty during the night. All they would be required to do was monitor their radios.

Sergeant Pomeroy was now the platoon leader for third platoon, and he would decide who would be listening to the radios during the night. Third platoon was to wait out the night as comfortably as they possibly could.

After talking with Lieutenant Duff and the artillery captain at the FSB, it was decided to move the mortar platoon's tracks into position just to the east of the fire support base's main northern entrance. There they parked their APCs in a slightly crescent-shaped arc facing out at the rows of rubber trees 150 meters away.

On the west side of the road leading into the FSB was 50 meters of bare red packed soil that was void of any vegetation. This area served as the base's helipad.

A makeshift road circled to the right as you were headed south around the west side of the FSB. The road was 60 meters out beyond the wire and trip flares. It eventually linked up with the main road at the south entrance to the FSB.

The bare ground of the helipad extended 200 meters to the north and gradually tapered toward the main road until there was just the road. On the east side of the road, starting 170 or 180 meters north of the FSB, the rubber trees were planted right to the edge of the road, and they continued to the north for as far as you could see.

Fifty meters farther west of the helipad, the new-growth vegetation began. This vegetation was just tall enough to obscure the minefield, which was marked with a single wire fence. I had noticed this just after the captain's dust-off departed, when Andy pointed out the markings.

Three-inch yellow inverted metal triangles hung from the wire every six or eight feet, indicating the boundary of the mined area. The problem was that the vegetation had grown up and hid the warning fence that marked the minefield.

Later, we would learn that the minefield had been one of ours, laid as a joint operation by the Big Red One, or First Division, to teach the ARVN engineers how to lay a minefield. As far as anyone knew, this minefield was mostly antipersonnel mines of the bouncing Betty type that were used in Korea. The army cartographers had made a huge mistake, since no one could find the minefield on any of our company's current maps.

With the mortar platoon all set up at the FSB and in place, it was a matter of minutes before second platoon and first platoon formed a half circle facing east toward the road. The CO's track remained in place. This enabled us to provide better security for the tracks of third platoon. By leaving the command track where it was, it marked the edge of the minefield. One track each from first platoon and second platoon, those closest to the minefield, were angled toward the minefield in order to provide better cover for third platoon.

By now it was getting late in the afternoon, and the men were ready to stand down. At least they were ready to eat something and relax for a brief time before they prepared for the night to come. There would be little opportunity for the five of us on the command track to relax, even for a little while.

The radios were constantly barking Captain Cooper's and my call signs. This was at first confusing until I called battalion headquarters to inform them that I now had the company commander's call sign. I gave them Sergeant Moore's line number and told them that Sergeant Moore would be answering my old call sign. That problem appeared to be solved.

There were a lot of directives and orders being given. Andy and I both were writing everything down while Ron was monitoring the company radio frequency. At one point, when there was a ten-minute break in the radio traffic, Andy remarked that he had already compiled a book. Ninety percent of the orders had to do with preparing for night security. With Andy and Ron's help, we were more than competent. The orders had already been anticipated and were in place before they were actually received.

Over at the FSB, the mortar platoon was positioning and preparing their mortar tubes to be able to cover the area around the minefield. With the close proximity to the FSB, I had more confidence in Sergeant Finley's crew for a danger-close fire mission, which meant that the shells would be exploding close to our position. Nevertheless, I called in several predetermined artillery targets, just in case.

I had plenty on my mind to keep me busy. Guard duty throughout the night, radio monitoring, and the new chain of command all needed to be gone over with the remaining company NCOs. The fact that there were no officers present didn't enter a single member of Bravo Company's minds. Back at Fort Benning, the NCOs of Bravo Company were trained at the NCO Academy to be able to run a company.

Without even realizing that it was happening, I quickly transitioned into Bravo's company commander. At 1800 hours I visited each track that wasn't still in the minefield. I would get to the mortar platoon in the morning. I explained what I knew and answered questions. The suggestions and concerns that the men had were greatly appreciated. The men's biggest concern was for the welfare of the men who were still stuck in the minefield.

Communications with the men confined to the APCs in the minefield could easily have been by voice. But a normal speaking voice was a very loud voice in Vietnam. Noise discipline was so ingrained that the radios were used so the conversations could be whispered.

As it started to get dark, I was certain that the company was ready for the night. The only thing different from any other night that I had spent in Vietnam as a member of Bravo Company was the fact that three APCs and the men on board were in peril by being forced to spend the night confined to their tracks in a minefield. As I thought about the company's readiness for the night, there were just a few things left to do. There was really only one more important item that needed my attention before we were operating in the dark. That last detail could be taken care of now.

With the exception of third platoon and the mortar platoon, the other two acting platoon leaders were summoned to the command track by Jerry to plan the events that would take place in the morning and to go over the new chain of command, which had the most effect on second platoon and third platoon.

Sergeant Lee was the very competent platoon leader of the first platoon. Sergeant Tui Lee was from Hawaii. He had an upbeat, good-natured personality and was very popular with his men. What made him stand out was the fact that he wanted to make the army a career.

While Sergeant Ralph Moore of second platoon had been one of my squad leaders, now he would be taking my previous call sign. The recent turn of events had elevated Ralph to acting platoon leader. Most recently, I had served second platoon as both platoon sergeant and platoon leader. If and when I ever got back to second platoon, Ralph would continue as the platoon sergeant.

It was common in Vietnam for line companies to be understaffed. The minefield incident left Bravo Company with the bare minimum number of bodies to be able to function as a company, and third platoon was dangerously understaffed. The company had no officers and was short of NCOs. Most of the NCOs were doing double duty, and now, I was the company commander.

The lack of personnel created a hardship on the company's operating proficiency. Third platoon was down to just ten men. Fact of the matter was that we only had other line companies in Vietnam to compare ourselves with, and I was aware that there were many units operating with fewer personnel.

A good friend of mine from my experience at Fort Benning was SSG Larry Sydow, who was also assigned to the Twenty-Fifth Division with the

First Wolfhounds battalion. Larry had been at the top of the class with me and had also graduated as an E-6 staff sergeant. Being in the same brigade, we had occasion to see each other in passing while coming from or going to the occasional company stand-down. The last time we spoke, I learned that Larry's platoon at one time had gotten down to only eight men, counting him. (A platoon should consist of over forty men.) At this point I couldn't concern myself with being short of personnel. Keeping everyone safe and in one piece was the task at hand.

As darkness descended, the radio traffic also eased up, with just an occasional situation report from some far-off patrol. This was an opportunity to call the FSB and then battalion headquarters to try to pin down when the engineers would be arriving, but first I needed to dismiss Sergeant Lee and Sergeant Moore. Instead, I asked them to wait a little longer.

On the call to battalion headquarters, the only person who was available and was willing to offer any information at all was a battalion clerk who happened to be on his scheduled radio watch. He implied that he had overheard a conversation earlier when he had been working in the orderly room. He remembered that the engineers would be arriving at our location around 1000 hours. I wrote the time down even though I didn't believe it. The engineers usually had the road cleared to the FSB way before 1000 hours. Now I could finally dismiss the two sergeants so that they could return to their respective platoons.

Sergeant Lee and Sergeant Moore left, and Andy, who was still lugging a radio; Ron; and I moved to the top of the command track. The night's radio watch for the command track had yet to be scheduled. The command track had to listen to the battalion radio frequency as well as the company's frequency. Andy, Ron, and I agreed to split the watch three ways so that one of us was always awake. The track's driver and TC (track commander) would double with the early morning watches.

The driver and TC slept inside the track. That left Andy, Ron, and me to settle into the jeep seats on top of the track. The air was still, very still, and at that time the perfect temperature. It was just the right degree of warmth, so if you let yourself relax enough, you might pee your pants, like sticking your hand in a pail of warm water while asleep.

I had just settled into the mounted jeep seat and wriggled myself into a comfortable position when it hit me. This was my birthday. I was now twenty-six years old, and what a shitty day it had been so far.

I kept my thoughts to myself and amused myself with one of the army's nighttime gadgets. I was playing with a starlight scope. It was the handheld mini version. I checked the battery—good. I then positioned the eyepiece to my right eye and pushed to depress the eyepiece. It activated, showing a glowing green as the landscape to the southwest appeared in a light snow storm. The moon wasn't up yet, or the picture would be daylight bright but still with the green glow.

I was thoroughly enjoying the moment. My muscles were relaxing. I was muscle tired but not sleepy. All of a sudden there was a brilliant flash of light around the eyepiece of the scope. I jerked the starlight scope from my eye and held it in my right hand. I reached across my body and covered my right eye with the palm of my left hand.

Off in the distance, miles away to the southwest, a Puff the Magic Dragon had located enemy troops on the ground. Puff was a C-130 cargo aircraft modified with side-door-mounted miniguns. Firing at a rate of four thousand rounds a minute, the tracer rounds produced an intensely bright solid stream of light when viewed though a starlight scope. The starlight scope amplified light many times; thus, the blinding flash that I experienced.

Ron was the first to speak. "Are you OK?"

"Yes, I see spots, but my sight is coming back."

"I love watching Puff the Magic Dragon put on a show. Puff is doing a J. O. B. on someone." Ron sat dreamily staring at the C-130 off in the distance. Then the show was over. It ended as abruptly as it had begun. Two passes of less than twenty seconds each was all that it had lasted. Then you couldn't see or hear anything. It was curtain dark, since the moon hadn't shown itself yet. The only light was the twinkling of the stars.

I leaned toward Andy. "We're coming up on the hour. It's time to get a report from each platoon. Be sure to include the mortar platoon, even though they're over there. I only needed to gesture in the direction of the FSB. Use the standard secure procedure by pressing squelch."

"Roger."

Then, as Andy called the first platoon, he whispered, "If you have a negative sit rep, press squelch twice."

In first platoon, whoever was monitoring the radio complied, and so it went with the second, third, and mortar platoons.

Things had finally settled down and were starting to smooth out. The men of Bravo Company wouldn't dwell on the deaths or the wounded men lost to the company. "There it is." This phrase was spoken to remind the infantry soldier that his number could come up at any time. An overtly callous statement, it reminded soldiers to avoid close attachments. When things went wrong, those who remained standing needed to be able to move on. "There it is."

Ron, Andy, and I took turns dozing. We had all agreed to be awake most of the night, so we stayed on top of the track. We each had a poncho liner for warmth when the late-night chill set in.

It was a little after midnight and Andy had just finished the third situation report when I was jolted to full consciousness and sat straight up. "What the hell is that?"

A light was radiating from the cargo bay of the middle track in the minefield. Andy already had the track on the radio and in his easy Texas drawl was ending his conversation with "Out." The light was gone, and darkness prevailed again.

Andy had a funny little grin as he explained. "They were hungry and were going to fix something hot to eat. They're eatin' it cold now."

I was wide awake, and my stomach was growling. "That reminds me, I haven't eaten yet. Are either of you hungry?"

Both Andy and Ron mumbled that they had eaten.

I remembered that this wasn't my track. "Andy, what do you have to eat here?" I was hoping for a can of C-ration fruit.

"The CO has some lurps…I don't think he's going to miss them now." With that, Andy disappeared.

I continued talking to Andy even though he wasn't in sight. "If you can find one…" I was going to give him my favorites to look for, but I cut myself off when Andy appeared from below with a green canvas-like package and a gallon-sized soft canteen of water.

I cut the bag open with my fancy Gerber knife that my wife had sent me and examined the contents. "Chicken stew; it's my favorite." I then proceeded to open the plastic bag, which was mounted on a thin slab of cardboard, and carefully poured an unmeasured amount of water over the freeze-dried contents. "That should be about right." I then carefully folded the plastic package so that it wouldn't leak, and I placed the entire package inside my shirt and under my arm.

"In about ten minutes it should be warm enough." In the allotted time, I produced a plastic spoon from my jungle-fatigue shirt pocket and ate in silence.

So far the night had been like so many other nights in Vietnam. The majority of nights were uneventful except for the occasional artillery fire, Puff the Magic Dragons, distant firefights, helicopter noise, and so on, all directed someplace else.

At 0214 hours the battalion radio began to buzz with excitement. It seemed that Charlie Company, one of Bravo Company's sister companies within our battalion, was being probed and taking sporadic fire as well as mortar rounds.

A very loud explosion erupted as the battery of 105 howitzers at the FSB began to adjust fire. There was no danger to us, but it meant that we wouldn't get any rest either. The rounds seemed to be going directly over us to the northwest. So Charlie Company's position was north and west of us on the other side of the strip of jungle that spread out to the north and the south next to our immediate position.

After the third shot from the 105 howitzer, all six guns began firing, indicating that the target had been pinpointed. Off to the north, it sounded as if another artillery battery was joining the battle.

The battalion radio was very busy, and Andy was on it, listening to the action. I took the opportunity to use the other radio, which was tuned to the company frequency, to check with Sergeant Finley of our mortar platoon. There was nothing that he could do because Charlie Company was out of his range.

The artillery battery's fire mission lasted a little over ten minutes. That seemed to be about the average length of a fire mission, but then, for the rest of the night, they would fire again once every forty or fifty minutes just to harass the enemy and keep him moving.

In Vietnam the morning daylight couldn't come soon enough. Night crept ever so slowly along with the Puff the Magic Dragon, the outgoing artillery, and the radio chatter; they were all a regular nightly occurrence, but not a comfortable routine. The company needed the comfort of a normal routine, and this was about as normal as it could get. No one could predict what would happen tomorrow, so you accepted the surrounding distractions. You lived entirely in the moment.

An hour before the first light announced the impending sunrise, there was a false dawn. It wasn't really discernible. It happened just before the first noticeable streak of light appeared in the eastern sky. This had become my favorite time of the day. It occurred sometime after 0400 and sometime before 0500. It was a quiet time, at least for me, where nothing out of the ordinary had happened yet. It was a good time to think, because there were so few distractions.

I shivered in the jeep seat as I adjusted the poncho liner to cover my arms for a little more warmth. I could see Andy's silhouette in the jeep seat on the other side of the track and could tell that he was also awake. Normally, Andy sat behind the CO so that he could hand him the radio handset at an instant's notice.

I wouldn't have my cocoa or coffee until it was light because I wanted it to be hot. I couldn't heat food or drinks in the dark because light from the heat source would give my location away. I had discovered that the best way for me to ward off the morning chill was a hot cup of either cocoa or coffee, so as I waited for the sky to lighten up, I used this time to think.

What would this new day be like? The engineers were arriving this morning. Once the minefield was cleared, where would we go? Who would be our new CO? All I had was questions, so I would have to wait to be told the what, when, and where yet to come. The army didn't answer the "why" question. There were no standing orders, and there were no long-term orders to fall back on. One thing was for certain: the company was going to get a fresh set of orders sometime this morning.

Realization struck suddenly with the force of a sledge hammer. I was now the company commander, not the CO, since that stood for commanding officer. They were just words. I was being asked to do a captain's job. I had now been the company's leader for over twelve hours.

Captain Travis Cooper had been the company's CO. Everyone liked Captain Cooper and had great respect for him. I wondered what would happen to him now. I made a mental note to try to find out. I remembered what the captain had said—that the minefield wasn't on the map. It would be just like the army to try to blame someone for the minefield screw-up. I truly hoped that Captain Cooper would not be the army's scapegoat. Damn army.

Ron and Andy were both stirring. The last situation report was in, and it was fast getting light. It was now safe to light a flame; it could no longer be a target for enemy fire.

"Ah, finally, it's time to make some coffee."

There was also some stirring on the tops of all three APCs that remained in the minefield. Hopefully, they won't have to wait long.

Two of the men in third platoon were urinating off of the top of the APC farthest to the right. One of the men was speaking to his sergeant. "Sarge, pee can't set off a mine, can it?"

I grinned ever so slightly as I shook my head involuntarily from side to side.

The cup of coffee was slowly consumed, along with a coveted can of peaches. Peaches, it seemed to me, were the single most popular item of all of the C-rations. Peaches used as barter could almost guarantee a successful trade for whatever you wanted. Toilet paper, beer, and sodas were some of the items that were frequently traded.

5

Where were the engineers? It was after 0930, and still no word. Everyone was getting impatient. There seemed to be a lot going on at the FSB. Every so often you could hear voices. There was the sound, every once in a while, of metal hitting metal. Add to this the sound of the artillery fire from the battery of 105s, and one could assume that they were busy at the FSB.

The artillery was just finishing another fire mission. Again they were shooting right over the top of us, only a little farther south than last night's barrage. Andy said it was support for the 199th Light Infantry Brigade working the AO (area of operation) next to our battalion's AO.

With all of the action going on around us, all we could do was wait quietly, and the waiting wasn't easy. I was absolutely churning inside, yet I was the person who had been elevated to being responsible for the men's well-being at the moment. I thought about having the tracks back out of the minefield following their own tracks. I realized that wouldn't work, since the drivers couldn't see behind their APCs. Someone would have to direct them and be exposed, either behind the APC or on top of it. In the event that another mine was set off, the risk of being wounded was too great. So that idea was quickly abandoned.

At the current time, the men had been in the minefield for over twenty-four hours.

Things were becoming increasingly uncomfortable for me, so I could only assume that the guys trapped in the minefield had to be getting stretched to the limits of their self-control. Yet as I carefully studied the men for signs of impatience, they were instead a picture of contentment. All eleven men were relaxing on the tops of their respective tracks as if they were sunbathing. The picture would have made a great poster for

Coppertone suntan lotion. Some had their shirts off and eyes shaded. Some were reading, and others were just sitting and visiting. In no way did they appear stressed. I could forget my stress theory.

Andy was the first to notice the dust. It had to be the engineers, since no one else was allowed on the road until it had been swept for mines. They weren't just late. They were a couple of hours overdue. At this point you couldn't find a single member of Bravo Company who wasn't ready to take a bite out of the engineers.

Sure enough, it was a procession of three vehicles: an APC, followed by a deuce and a half (a two-and-a-half-ton truck) pulling a jeep trailer, followed by a three-quarter-ton truck.

I waited anxiously, guaranteed that I was prepared to ask them what had taken so long.

The three-vehicle convoy of engineers came to a stop and parked outside the FSB main gate just across the road from the helipad. They were right next to the mortar platoon's end track.

We could see the engineers moving around. Several men from the FSB had joined them. I was sure that one of them was Lieutenant Duff. They appeared to be getting equipment from the back of the deuce and a half and the trailer.

After what seemed like a long time—but it had only been ten minutes—several men loaded the truck and headed our way. It was a good thing that they were finally coming in our direction. A moment later and I would have been going after them, desperate to speed things up. It wasn't that the engineers moved slowly. They were in fact indicating that they were hurrying. It was just that I was out of patience.

It was easier for me to relax a little after I glanced back at the third platoon, and they hadn't moved or even appeared to notice the engineers' arrival. On each one of the three tracks, the scene was the same tranquil setting.

The engineers came out to our position in just one of the vehicles. They drove the truck right up to the rear of the command track at the edge of the minefield. They had apparently been directed by Lieutenant

Duff. A captain, a lieutenant, two E-5 buck sergeants, and a specialist 4 disembarked from the truck.

I was finally going to have my say as I hurried to step in front of the captain, but I only managed to blurt out "Sir..." when he was all over an apology for not getting here earlier. They were delayed because they had discovered a mine in the road right where the road to the FSB turned south off of Highway 1. The mine had been planted where the paved road ended and the dirt road began. The captain assured me that he was aware of the urgency to get to us. However, they were forced to move slower than usual to sweep the remaining section of road. It was common for antitank mines to be deployed in pairs.

The engineers would have been even tardier, but it seems that Charlie Company had moved to the road early this morning after last night's contact. They loggered up on both sides of the road about two klicks to the north of us. When the engineers reached Charlie Company's location, they geared up and increased their speed in order to get to us quickly.

I was satisfied with the captain's explanation, even though it had little effect on calming me down. While the captain was explaining his reasons for being delayed, the lieutenant stood close by and said nothing, and one of the sergeants and the specialist were putting on flak jackets, knee leggings, and steel pots. The other sergeant was assisting the two of them and testing batteries and equipment. These guys were efficient, and they weren't wasting time.

It was my turn now to brief the captain. I started by informing him of the number of men still on the three APCs. This seemed totally unnecessary, since all were on top of their tracks for him to see, but he needed to start with an official head count. No doubt, he would have to submit a written report to his superiors.

The army kept records of everything imaginable and was in love with paper work. The only other thing that I could tell him was that we thought the mines were all US antipersonnel mines called bouncing Bettys. The captain confirmed this when he volunteered that he had done some research yesterday evening after he learned of our predicament. He then produced a map, and the map, upon examination, proved to be at least several years old, because the FSB wasn't even on it. Superimposed was an overlay outlining the minefield with little triangles that I assumed represented the mines. I was ready for this and produced the map that Captain Cooper had been given; and, of course, it showed no minefield. The captain finally added that he really wasn't sure that the entire minefield was antipersonnel mines. The history of the minefield that he had researched was incomplete. There could be some larger antitank mines also.

My thoughts went back to what Captain Cooper had said. The minefield wasn't on the maps that our company was currently using. Later the engineer captain would disclose that there used to be an ARVN training center nearby, and the First Division and ARVNs laid the minefield as a joint operation to teach the ARVNs how to do it.

By now the sergeant and specialist had secured their gear and appeared ready. Each carried a handheld metal detector with huge earphones that pinched around their necks at the ready. The lieutenant took over and explained the procedure. They would follow the trails left by the APC tracks into the minefield and clear a path as they went. They would clear the way for each APC, one at a time. Then each APC in turn could back out the cleared path. They were to clear the center area between the tracks, as well as a path two feet to the outside of each track.

The other sergeant had a handheld radio that he was using to communicate with the two sweepers. The sergeant and the lieutenant stood side by side next to the command track, while the captain had moved back to the second platoon's APCs and well behind the truck. He was ordering everyone back with himself, and that included me. When I last glanced in the direction of the third platoon, there was no one visible on the tops of the APCs.

It took most of forty minutes before I heard third platoon's number-one track start its engine. Here it came, backing out of the minefield, and then it was out. The track kept rolling until it was twenty-five or thirty meters into the half circle perimeter that the rest of the company had organized for last night's security.

My attention was diverted to the engineers, who were having a lively discussion at the edge of the minefield in line with the next third-platoon APC to come out of the minefield. The captain walked briskly past me headed for the group. Without asking permission, I followed. Just before we reached the others, he turned to address me. I was so sure that he was going to order me back that I blurted out, "I'm the acting company commander." Nothing else was said. He merely turned and resumed his pace to what was becoming a heated conversation.

The sergeant with the handheld radio was the one who seemed to be the most agitated. He wanted the mines that were found to be blown in place. He didn't like the idea of having to maneuver around them. The lieutenant was saying that the troops were in too close a proximity to the mines to blow them in place. The risk of someone being wounded was too high.

The next statement I didn't need to hear. The sergeant with one of the detectors spoke next and confirmed that they had identified and marked three mines. I was stunned to hear that one was in the middle, between the tracks. The APC had straddled it when it had rolled into the minefield and again when it had backed out. The other two mines had been located on the left side of the trail toward the FSB within twenty-four to thirty inches of the crushed vegetation left by the APC's tracks.

I saw no reason why the mines couldn't have been blown up. Most of the men in the company had worked with explosives. It was no big deal. Blowing up the mines would take extra time, and I wanted to get away from the minefield as soon as possible. So I listened and waited.

The captain listened without interrupting. Finally, when it appeared that the sergeant and the lieutenant had no more to say, they both turned and faced the captain expectantly.

The captain's reply was curt. "Flag the mines and leave them in place as long as there is room to get around them." He turned, and we proceeded back to the second platoon area. On the way back, he kept glancing sideways at me. He was, no doubt, wondering how an E-6 staff sergeant had come to be commanding a company of APCs.

I was curious as to how the engineers were marking the mines that they had already discovered, so I focused my gaze into the minefield, following the path left by the third platoon track that had just been freed.

There they were. Standing out and easily seen were three tiny red flags of engineering tape that were tied to three one-foot-high wire stakes.

All attention now was on the second path being cleared into the minefield. The men on this track wanted to watch the action and had to be told to stay below, down in the hold. I didn't blame them for being excited at the prospect of being freed. Nevertheless, they still needed to be safe.

I positioned myself this time so that I could have a direct line of sight to the engineers who were clearing the path. I hadn't been able to see when they had found the first mines and marked them. I was a little embarrassed and still felt foolish. Attention to detail was an important trait for a sergeant. After all, I had a need to know. The company was now on my shoulders. This time I followed every move much more closely.

Watching the engineers and their movements reminded me of a class in road-clearing security that I had taught to infantry AIT companies that were headed for Vietnam. After I graduated from the Fort Benning NCO Academy, I was stationed at Fort Ord, California, and assigned to the patrolling committee group as a principle instructor for teaching infantry subjects. This was my OJT (on-the-job training) before going to Vietnam.

As I observed the two engineers doing the sweeping, it was evident that the classes that I had taught in road-clearing techniques had moved way too fast. We had the security part right, but we were way off on the operation of the mine detectors themselves. The sweeper determines the speed of the whole operation, and there appeared to be a lot more technique to operating a mine detector than I had ever imagined.

Suddenly, in unison, both of the sweepers froze in place. It was as if they were bird dogs on point. Then each of them in turn passed his detector over the spot between the tracks. They were maybe only ten or twelve feet from the APC. The specialist reached inside his flak vest and produced one of the little marker flags. The sergeant pointed to the spot where he wanted the flag placed. It was obvious that the two worked well together.

Fifteen minutes later, having found only the one mine, they proceeded to back the second track out of the minefield. The APC backed across the company perimeter after exiting the minefield.

It was almost comical the way the men were all reluctant to get down off of the top of their track. Everyone was all smiles and making jokes, but it was more than a few minutes before the driver lowered the ramp and they walked out the back.

The engineers were now meeting at the path of the third track where it had entered the minefield. They needed a break. Andy produced some sodas for all of the engineers, who took them eagerly. The specialist and sergeant who were doing the sweeping were almost entirely drenched in perspiration. Not only were their shirts and trousers wet, their faces and arms were heavily beaded with sweat. They definitely needed more liquids.

While they were drinking their sodas, the captain spoke to me. "If I could be sure that all of the mines were antipersonnel and not antitank mines, the APCs could have driven out. But we don't know that, so here we go. Are you guys ready?" He was addressing the sweepers.

They were already in position, and the rest of us moved back toward second platoon for the third time.

Andy was on the radio talking to the last APC still in the minefield. He was explaining why there had been a delay, and after just a few clothing and equipment adjustments, the engineers were ready to do it again. By now we knew the routine and were back to our previous positions.

I had some things that I needed to talk to Andy and Ron about, but I didn't want to jump the gun. It would have to wait until everyone was safely out of the minefield.

This trip into the minefield turned out to be a free trip. No new mines were found. The third APC had set off several mines when it had unknowingly entered the field. This had been Lieutenant Herbert's track. When he had jumped down from the APC, he landed on a mine, which started the second chain reaction of explosions that brought us to the present.

As soon as the third APC was safe within the perimeter, I looked around for Andy. There he was, standing just to my right and two steps to the rear.

As I made eye contact, I told him, "I want to thank the engineers and see them off, and then find out where battalion wants us to go next."

The engineers had already stowed their gear in the truck. The specialist and the sergeant sitting in the back were shirtless, and each had a five-quart canteen of water. The captain was sitting in the front passenger seat again. So much for protocol, as the other sergeant was the driver and the lieutenant was in the back seat, where the ranking officer should be.

Oh well, I wasn't going to say anything, but I was trying to keep a straight face in spite of my humorous thoughts. Protocol requires that the lieutenant's position in the vehicle get saluted, but this wasn't stateside. This was Vietnam. I was able to brush those thoughts aside and address the captain.

"Sir, thank you."

"You're welcome, sergeant." He was looking at me, and his eyes sparkled with understanding. I had gained his respect, and it showed in his gaze.

The truck started, was eased into gear, and began to pull away. The captain turned a bit more to face me and said, "Sergeant, good luck." And with that, they drove to their other waiting vehicles and were soon just a cloud of red dust headed north.

6

I was standing alone after watching the engineers depart, but I hesitated for only the slightest moment as I glanced around to check on what was happening. Most of the company was gathering around the men from the three third-platoon tracks that had just been rescued, and everyone was congratulating the medic, Marcos Ramirez, who had run into the minefield and saved lives.

I was anxious to get moving, but no one had yet supplied me with any information indicating where the company was to go next. Since I was now "the decider," I wasn't going to wait to be told where and when to move. I was going to act on my own initiative. This could take some getting used to. I was now the one who was going to make things happen, since I was the acting company commander. I was feeling no fear. I had no second thoughts, nor any doubts about how I should proceed.

I didn't fully know all of the responsibilities and duties of a company commander, a captain's slot. Still, I had been in-country long enough to have learned the company's operating procedures while in the field. Now was the time to act and put some distance between the company and the minefield. I wasn't going to wait for battalion to call and tell us where to go. No telling how long we would have to wait until they got around to us.

I made my first conscious decision as company commander, even though I had been running the company since yesterday afternoon.

I looked for Andy. As I turned to my left, there he was, not far away, grinning broadly.

"How do you do that?" I didn't wait for an answer. "I need to call battalion and tell them that we're moving to the road."

"It's already done. We received the call from battalion while you were saying good-bye to the engineers. We're supposed to logger up in front of the FSB. Elmer Fudd is coming to the FSB today, and I was told to be in place…not me personally, the company."

"Is there anything else?"

"Nope, not yet. So far, that's it."

I gestured toward the command track. "All right, let's get out of here."

We climbed to the top of the track and settled into our jeep seats, and I asked for the radio. Andy reached forward and handed me the handset attached to his radio, which was tuned to the company frequency. It was time to call Sergeant Moore and instruct him to call in Sergeant Bernie Rios and Sergeant Doug Hawkins, who were out on OP guard duty as part of our security, and bring them back for the move to the road.

I then called Sergeant Finley of the mortar platoon and told him to leave his platoon's APCs in place in front of the FSB. The rest of the company would establish a perimeter around them. Rather than wait to be told, I planned to place the company in a defensive position outside the fire support base.

I had a definite plan as to where I wanted each of the platoon's tracks placed. Mortar platoon's four APCs were already to the right of the front gate of the FSB on the rubber plantation side of the road and on line facing away from the FSB. Between the mortar platoon and the FSB was about fifty meters of concertina wire, trip flares, and a row of claymore mines that were placed closer to the FSB perimeter. It was a generic set up for a fire support base's security, and our company had to be on the outside of the wire.

The third platoon's three tracks would be facing the west at the edge of the road. Then the first platoon's four tracks would be linked to the command track, which would be placed between the third platoon and first platoon. The second platoon's four tracks would be linked to first platoon, forming a closed half circle that completed the perimeter.

As the tracks began moving, I was able to direct each track to its assigned position, and the perimeter was formed just as it had been rehearsed many times.

There was no balking or hesitation. All of the men pitched in and were busy, with each member of the company contributing to the setup. The engineer stakes were being driven into the ground; and screens, which were sections of chain link fence, were being fastened to the stakes. The theory was that an RPG (rocket-propelled grenade) that was fired at a track would explode on the screen and thus not disable the APC. In reality the exploded RPG produced lethal shrapnel. Men could be eliminated, but the armored personnel carrier would be saved.

Another standard operating procedure (SOP) during setup was to put out trip flares and command-detonated claymore mines. We were used to a routine of night ambushes and deployment of mechanical ambushes as part of the company's security. Wherever the company had been previously, this SOP had been followed. However, at this point, I held off on doing anything beyond the RPG screens until I could talk to the battalion tactical officer at the FSB. FSB Georgia had been there for a while, and I was curious to know whether there were any security devices beyond the perimeter wire or out in the rubber trees.

It wasn't a long walk, but rather than leave the company perimeter and enter the FSB, I used a radio to contact Lieutenant Duff. He was a first lieutenant with a contingent of clerks and jeep drivers that comprised our battalion command at the FSB. This was particularly confusing to me because here was a lieutenant issuing tactical orders to the battalion companies and possibly the artillery battery, which were led by captains—or at least they were supposed to have a captain in charge. It was hard to imagine how this could work in an army built on the chain of command.

After talking with Lieutenant Duff, I was amazed to learn that there was no added security in front of us in the rubber trees, not even trip flares. Depending on how long our company would be there, that would change. Each day that passed, our company system of security would become more and more intricate.

I didn't hesitate to tell Lieutenant Duff that our company would be placing trip flares and claymore mines in the rubber. We would also be sending night ambush patrols out into the rubber plantation.

He merely said, "Go ahead, but make sure you pick everything up when you leave."

"Roger. That won't be a problem."

"Sergeant Miller, you know that the battalion CO and XO are coming to the FSB today for a battalion tactical meeting with all of the company commanders?"

"I am aware." I paused awhile in order to mull over the thought of how the company would be affected by the visit before I signed out.

There were a number of ways the company could be affected by the visit. My first thought was that we might be assigned a new CO. My next thought was that the new CO would need to be briefed and brought up to date. An inventory of the company's weapons and personnel would need to be prepared. These were all things that I could take care of, and there appeared to be plenty of time for the task.

I was back to regarding Lieutenant Duff. The guy didn't impress me. I hadn't known him very long, but he seemed to have no sense of command. Here he was, right next door, and we had hardly heard a word from him when we were stuck in the minefield, and we were within spitting distance of each other. With no officers left in the company, I would have at least expected him to offer some advice or assistance.

The reality in Vietnam was that many people chose to avoid being involved, no matter what the situation. Even people in positions of command followed this premise when they could get away with it. When you could be killed, taking care of "number one" became a top priority. In the army you were taught, beginning in basic training and in each stage after that, to never ever volunteer, and another practiced rule was to neither be the first nor the last.

With a number of thoughts to consider, my next order of business was to do a quick check of the perimeter to see that everyone was correctly in place. The placement of claymores and trip flares had been approved, so I assigned the first and second platoons to do the installations together. They all needed to know where everything was. I was also planning the night ambush patrols. Generally, there were two patrols out at night, and I was debating with myself on whether there was a need for two night ambushes.

I had started my inspection with the third platoon, and I was standing behind third platoon's position when Andy interrupted me by pointing out an approaching officer. He was a ways away yet, so I continued my inspection of third platoon's setup. Since the third's APCs were facing the road and right next to it, there hadn't been a need to put up the RPG screens—plus, the other side of the road was the helipad and cleared of all vegetation. Beyond that there were two hundred meters of cleared jungle and the minefield.

I stepped out from behind the third's middle track and came face to face with a 6'4" lieutenant. He had a very stateside military manner about him, and that was the most obvious thing that I noticed. He was self-assured, almost cocky, as he asked to see Sergeant Miller.

"That would be me," I said, and I couldn't help but think that I was going to have to do push-ups for not saluting.

I was studying the lieutenant as closely as I could without being noticeably rude. His uniform was clean and just short of being starched, and a crease had been ironed into his trousers. His shirt had also been ironed wrinkle-free. His fatigue trousers were neatly folded at the ankles and bloused in the OCS style into his boots. I half expected to see airborne Cochrans on his feet, but he wore the issued jungle boots, toes polished! His name tag was still intact, and it had actually been blackened to avoid fading. My guard was up, and my thoughts were that this was the true definition of a lifer.

It was apparent that he was from the artillery battery since he even wore the artillery insignia on his lapels. His speech was short, clipped—even staccato—and I couldn't believe what he was saying. It was as if all of Bravo Company was being punched in the gut. I was speechless and completely unprepared for the orders he was giving me.

Andy took a couple of steps back so the lieutenant would notice his displeasure as he stared daggers at the lieutenant.

We were totally blindsided when he barked out, "Sergeant Miller, you will send twenty-six of your men—and four must be NCOs—to the artillery command bunker at 2000 hours for perimeter guard duty. Have the men report to the second Quonset hut." The bunker that the lieutenant referred to was a metal prefabricated building with a double row of sandbags stacked five or six feet high on the outside.

"What are those gooks doing here?" He pointed to Bey and Coe, who were squatting by second platoon's position.

"They are our Kit Carson scouts, sir."

He just stared and didn't say a word.

He had given me a lousy order, and now he was being disrespectful. I was angry, and I didn't mind that it was showing.

The lieutenant paused a little longer, as he was studying my expression before adding, "That's an order. Be prompt."

He turned just as abruptly, not quite an about face, but close, and he stepped out for the entrance to the FSB. Andy and I both kept our eyes on him all the way until he was out of sight inside the gate.

I was absolutely stunned. This was the worst possible scenario for the company. There were only eighty-three of us, counting me, in the whole company, and he had just taken twenty-six men away from us for the FSB perimeter guard duty. That didn't leave us enough men to adequately protect ourselves. It would leave the company with an average of less than four men per APC, and there couldn't be a night ambush patrol. I was sure that the artillery lieutenant hadn't made any inquiries. He was merely going to exploit us. We were being used to give the artillery personnel a rest, and we were getting no consideration for what we had just been through.

To say that I was furious would be a gross understatement. How could this be happening? Wasn't anyone paying attention? Artillery shouldn't be able to command us. The only thing the lieutenant had going was that he outranked me. The only common thread was that we were both assigned to the Twenty-Fifth Division, and we were both working in the same area. I was trying desperately to figure out a procedure to get his order rescinded. I would first use the chain of command, starting with the company first sergeant. I was willing to dedicate every waking moment to trying to get out of the FSB guard duty. Little did I know that I would become even more upset before the day was over and that the guard-duty issue would become much less important compared to what was yet to come.

I had been infuriated when the artillery lieutenant called our company's Kit Carson scouts gooks. Bey and Coe fought at our side. They took orders just like the rest of the men. They were Hoi Chanhs. Both were former VC who had chiew hoied (defected).

I knew the most about Bey, since he was assigned to the second platoon. He was my platoon's Kit Carson, and the men appreciated, respected, and depended on his skills.

His family had lived near Tay Ninh City in a village to the west near the Cambodian border. His VC squad, platoon, or whatever they called their units got into a firefight with one of our US units. The VC dispersed and ran. It took Bey too long to report back to his unit. He made a large circle into Cambodia. Here he was safe from the Americans, but the Cambodians also needed to be avoided, and that took time. When he returned to Vietnam, he went to see his family first.

It was hard to imagine what he went through when he arrived home and found that his entire extended family had been murdered by the VC. They must have thought that he had defected. As near as I could tell, Bey had a wife, a son and a daughter, his parents, his wife's parents, and an elderly grandfather—all killed.

In the middle of the day, Bey walked up to the army's main gate at Cu Chi, the Twenty-Fifth Division headquarters and base camp. That he was able to infiltrate that close without being noticed was absolutely amazing.

Instead of putting his hands straight above his head, he positioned his arms more to his sides, forming a V with his palms facing forward. The guards at the gate were MPs and had to be shocked when Bey appeared from nowhere and walked toward them shouting, "Chiew Hoi, Chiew Hoi, Chiew Hoi..."

After his indoctrination and training, Bey was assigned to our company, and, even more fortunately, second platoon. Bey had joined second platoon and Bravo Company at least a year before I showed up.

Bey was totally fearless. All he wanted to do was kill VC. He insisted on walking point when we were following a trail. He was invaluable at recognizing booby traps. He knew all of the signs that marked booby traps, so the local civilians recognized them and didn't set them off. I was sure that Bey had set his share of booby traps before he defected.

The men had enough respect for Bey that they shared things with him such as their food, and they paid close attention to Bey when they were in the field.

Coe, the other Kit Carson, was more tolerated than respected. The men of the company joked that Coe was a VC cook and got kicked out of the Viet Cong. Coe was assigned to the first platoon and Sergeant Lee.

Once Coe had been on patrol with first platoon and was walking along when suddenly he began firing his M-16 into the ground on full automatic. Not knowing what was happening, everyone dove for cover. When they finally recovered, there was Coe, standing in place, shaking, his M-16 rifle lying on the ground at his feet. Sergeant Lee determined that Coe had his safety off as he was walking along and had unknowingly pressed the trigger.

Under normal circumstances Coe would have been gone, sent to wherever. But Coe had one very helpful redeeming quality. He had a sixth sense, or built-in radar, that alerted him when VC were present or nearby.

Coe had an unusual ritual that he went through every time he suspected that any VC might be close by. He stopped, froze in position, and put his hands together in front of himself with his fingers extended and the tips touching. His expression changed to a wide-eyed stare, and he moved his hands to the top of his head as if he might be indicating the conical hat that the Vietnamese wore. Sometimes he would squat down in this position, but usually he remained standing. All of this took mere seconds to do before he whispered "VC" as a warning.

In nearly a year since joining the company, Coe had never been known to be wrong. However, Sergeant Lee had to check Coe's M-16 safety regularly.

The artillery lieutenant had upset everything. Andy and I just looked at each other. Damn army! The system allowed things like this to happen. I had to calm down and think this through and then act. I had to start with Lieutenant Duff. It was my conclusion that Lieutenant Duff had probably rubber-stamped the order that had our company pulling guard duty for the fire support base. My next move would be to go to Top. I was confident that if anyone could get us out of the guard duty, it would be Top. Maybe I could go to battalion or even brigade—as if I really thought that would work. It was really hard to think and calm myself down at the same time. I was close to the melting point, and I seriously needed to be in control more than ever. An entire company was depending on me to look after their best interests.

7

It was midafternoon, people were beginning to arrive at the FSB, and I was anxious to talk to two of the arrivals. First, Top showed up in his jeep pulling a trailer. He had two extra men with him in the back seat.

My first thought was that we were going to get two new replacement troops, but I was mistaken. They were cooks, and they were going to cook steaks for the men tonight.

Steaks, beer, and sodas—and that shitty guard duty; somehow the combination of the two didn't go together. I was sure that when the twenty-six men found out their assignment after I decided who they would be, they would experience the same emotions that I had just been through—anger, disgust, and downright loathing. The men would be aware that the guard duty would be giving the troops at the fire support base the night off. I would not be very well thought of at that time. I seriously considered putting my name on the list. Then I would only have to pick twenty-five others.

I met with Top while the cooks and the jeep driver set up the barbeque in front of the mortar platoon's position. It was the first time in memory that Top had let me down. He turned out to be no help at all. Regarding the guard duty, his opinion was that we were probably going to have to pull it as it was assigned. He did give me the name and call sign of a master sergeant friend of his at battalion headquarters who might be able to help.

Top and I were through talking for the moment, and Top wanted to supervise the cooking and hand out beer and sodas. It gave him a chance to visit with the men. If Top didn't have a way to get us out of the FSB guard duty then I gave us little hope, but I was still going to pursue the matter to the very end. This was my first big challenge after taking over for Captain Cooper. All I felt was helplessness. I had little faith that I could get the guard duty changed now that I'd talked to Top, but I wasn't willing to give up just yet.

I moved over to the jeep trailer and was about to fish a cold beer out of the icy water when I heard a helicopter approaching. Sure enough, it was going to land at the helipad. Four people disembarked and ran hunched over as the helicopter was shutting down. This was a helicopter with the doors still in place, which was a dead giveaway that it was transporting VIPs.

A slender red-haired man wearing a baseball-styled soft cap got out first. He was followed by two more men carrying several black briefcases and as many portable files.

Finally, the fourth person stepped down. As he to bent at the waist and hurried to clear the rotors, I noticed that this person was short and stout, not a protruding belly, but no waist either. He wore a flak vest and a steel pot (helmet). This had to be Lieutenant Colonel Dumford. The red-haired man had to be Major Anderson, the battalion's second-in-command (the executive officer, or XO).

Lieutenant Duff was there with three of his subordinates to meet the arrivals. Once again I was surprised. Lieutenant Duff and his men actually saluted the major and the lieutenant colonel. It didn't take long to clear the helipad, and soon they were out of sight and inside the FSB. The rotors of the helicopter were making the last erratic turns before stopping. The helicopter pilot and his Peter pilot (copilot) remained in the helicopter. I yelled at Sergeant Moore to take them each a soda or beer and invite them for steaks later.

I made my list of twenty-six men who were going to pull the guard duty for the FSB. The count was very heavy on second platoon, and the rest came from the mortar platoon, including Sergeant Finley.

That done, I thought I would have a second beer. I was still stewing over having to do the guard duty for the artillery crew. It had taken a good deal of time to come up with the names of the twenty-six men. It was getting late in the afternoon, close to 1700 hours. I still had to break the news to the men. This would mean that there would be no night ambush patrol, because the company would be too shorthanded after the men reported for the FSB guard duty. I decided to wait until the men had eaten before breaking the bad news.

Again I heard the noise before I saw it. In a cloud of dust, a lone APC stopped between the helicopter and the front gate of the FSB and parked off of the road on part of the helipad. I recognized the track as that of Captain Jim Sorenson, the Charlie Company CO. I had been awaiting his arrival. Since this was the only road to the FSB, I knew that Captain Sorenson would eventually show up here. I was hurriedly striding toward the APC before the captain could get down and inside the FSB. I really didn't need to hurry as fast as I did. He saw me coming and met me on the road.

Captain Sorenson spoke first. "I'm so sorry about what happened to Bravo Company. Travis was a good friend of mine and a good CO. He knew his stuff."

I greeted the captain with a nod and got right to the point. "I know that you, sir, and Captain Cooper were good friends. He spoke highly of you, and I need some advice. There is no one else I can turn to, and I can't find anyone who will talk to me and give me a straight answer. I just can't get the information that I need to keep Bravo Company running efficiently. You know that I'm the ranking NCO. Top can't run the company in the field. He's still recovering from that mine blast north of Xuan Loc. He will probably go home with a disability, except that he is trying to extend his career. We are already being unnecessarily jerked around."

"Hold on a second, Sergeant Miller." He paused, took off his hat, and repositioned it. "Jerry, there is not a lot I can tell you. What you are experiencing is actually what Travis and I go through regularly. Your worries may be unfounded. Bravo is going to get a new CO ASAP. This I am sure of. The army won't wait on that. You may have a new CO today. I'm here for our tactical operations meeting. All of the battalion COs will be here, I've got Lieutenant Highlander as my first platoon leader, but he hasn't been here long enough yet. Alpha Company has Lieutenant Koenig as their second platoon leader, and there are a half a dozen others in the battalion and brigade who qualify. Fact of the matter is that the new Bravo CO could even come from Cu Chi." That was the Twenty-Fifth Division headquarters.

The captain paused again. "In the meantime, I sense that there is something else on your mind."

Captain Sorenson walked to the jeep trailer and helped himself to a Pabst Blue Ribbon beer. I handed him my B-52 beer can opener, and then I began explaining the guard-duty situation.

"They're only doing that to you because they can. If you were me or another officer, it wouldn't have even been considered. When you get a chance, see if you can talk to Major Anderson. He's OCS and a straight shooter. This is what you tell him. You are already undermanned. You are planning your night ambushes. Remember, that's part of your company training—staying in practice. If you can't do the night ambushes, your training lags. My guess is that he will get you out of the guard duty, or he will at the least provide you with a good reason that you can share with the men. In fact, the best advice I can give you, Jerry, is go to Major Anderson with problems that you can't solve."

"Thank you, sir" was all I could manage to get out. There was hope again that the FSB guard duty could be scratched.

"Come on; I'm Jim, or at least Captain Sorenson, to you—not sir, especially here. You embarrass me."

Captain Jim Sorenson excused himself to report to the battalion bunker. He said that he would be back to see if there were any steaks left after the meeting, and I was much more optimistic now that I'd had a chance to get his advice.

Alpha Company commander arrived from the south and was already there. His track was parked on the other side of the FSB.

Delta Company was a completely different matter. Way back when I had just arrived in Vietnam, Delta was ambushed somewhere near Xuan Loc, and many of the tracks were destroyed or disabled. The majority of the company survived, but most were wounded.

Delta Company was dismantled and reorganized. The tracks were turned in to be repaired and then redistributed to other companies. The new Delta Company was made up of mostly administrative attachments. There was a supply section, a special intelligence section that no one knew anything about, a group of snipers who could be attached to other companies outside of our battalion, and the recon platoon. The recon platoon was the only element of Delta that I knew anything about.

The ambush that caused the dismantling of Delta Company was a hot topic of discussion in all of South Vietnam. It was hard to believe that the small VC elements that were operating in the area could combine to launch such a precision attack on a full company of APCs with their .50-caliber machine guns and their tremendous firepower.

Since the time Delta was ambushed, a South Vietnamese army basic-training facility was overrun, and a regional force (Ruff Puff) outpost was also overrun. The attackers left enough equipment behind for intelligence to determine that the attacking unit was a unit of North Vietnamese regulars. Hence, the North Vietnamese 199th Phantom Regiment was the talk and focus of most of the southeast area of Vietnam.

After the 1968 Tet Offensive (an all-out VC attack on all major cities and military installations in South Vietnam), the VC ceased to exist. North Vietnam countered by sending its regular army troops south to continue the fighting and to rebuild the Viet Cong infrastructure. The 199th NVA Regiment was believed to be hiding in the area just to the north of the Mekong Delta and east of Saigon. It was a large area, and we were right in the middle of their AO. Since the 199th NVA Regiment was believed to be operating in the Twenty-Fifth Division's sector, every effort to get information on the 199th Regiment's location was pursued.

8

As I looked around the company area, the men were in small groups visiting. They would soon be eating steak. Steak dinners were usually reserved for stand-downs when the company was in a rear area for a change of clothes, refitting, track maintenance, and resupply. Because of the mobility of the APCs and the need for refueling, we seemed to get more stand-downs than the nonmechanized straight-leg outfits. We did have the tracks to take care of, and a good deal of the stand-down time was spent working on the tracks.

Sergeant Moore, his RTO, and Tommy were getting ready to head up the road to relieve Sergeant Rios at the OP (observation post). Unless the company was in a totally secured area, we always had security out.

Ralph Moore had made a point to talk to me before he departed. "Sarge, I've got the night 'bush. It's all planned, and the first platoon and third platoon have the LPs." Listening posts were the nighttime equivalent of observation posts.

Ralph, Bernie, and Doug were more-than-competent NCOs; they anticipated and were prepared. I was proud of them and could trust that they had things covered.

Now it was time to talk to Major Anderson about the guard duty. I arrived at the tactical operations bunker and was surprised at the number of people occupying the space inside. I asked the first clerk I encountered if I could see Major Anderson. And I could tell right away that he was going to blow me off. I interrupted him, stating my name, and was about to further impose my urgency to talk with the major when he held up his hand indicating my plea wasn't necessary, and he motioned for me to follow him.

Major Anderson was hovering over a table covered with maps and other documents with Captain Sorenson and a lieutenant I didn't know.

The clerk mumbled my name to the major, and he said without looking up, "Good. Sergeant Miller, we just sent for you."

Captain Sorenson was looking at me and not smiling. He was staring a hard stare. I was confused, since he had been so friendly and personable just moments earlier. He shifted his expression to a sadder look, yet very serious. Sometimes I am really dense; I wasn't getting his message. Instead, my feelings were hurt by his lack of recognition. Priding myself reading faces and situations, I instantly was on alert as a wave of uncertainty swept over me. At the time, I wasn't aware that Captain Sorenson was trying to warn me.

Major Anderson stood, straightened himself, and spoke to Captain Sorenson. "We're almost ready. Take your places, and we can get started now that Sergeant Miller has arrived."

He then turned to me. "Sergeant, I need to brief you before we go in." He was referring to the open area with the folding chairs, charts, and blackboard as a separate room. He was also studying me very closely, looking me up and down as he spoke. His eyes were steel blue, and they accented his red hair.

"Sergeant Miller, the purpose of the meeting is to assign each of our companies a new mission and a new AO. You have been asked to join us, obviously, since you are temporarily commanding Bravo Company." He gave the word *temporarily* extra emphasis.

"Once you are seated, you are not allowed to speak. Do I make myself clear? Now take your seat in the front row."

I quickly interceded. "Sir, may I take notes? And…I have a pressing problem that I need to discuss with you as soon as possible."

The major actually showed a slight grin, with a little crinkle around his eyes to give the grin away. "How long will the pressing problem take?"

"It will only take seconds."

"Shoot."

I hurriedly explained the guard duty that was being forced on us and started to explain how that would leave the company.

He waved his hand to dismiss any further discussion. "I'll take care of it. And, yes, you can take notes."

It had been almost too easy. I couldn't have felt better. I was ecstatic. The guard duty had been taken care of, and I was eager to tell Top.

I headed for the only front-row seat available, the one on the end nearest me. I was the last to be seated. There were six chairs in each row and three rows of chairs. I was instantly aware of everyone looking at me. There was something about the stares. What I expected to see was some flicker of curiosity. Why was a sergeant here? There was none of that. It was eerie, to say the least, and I was feeling more and more nervous. The stares weren't fleeting glances that would then focus on something else. Everyone just kept looking at me. I was becoming more and more uncomfortable. Every single person's expression was deep concern and as serious as could be imagined. Even Captain Sorenson had the same stare as all of the rest. Something was up, and I should have been warned. But I was incredibly naive at the moment, and I failed to recognize the warning signs.

Another big hint that should have been a clue that something was wrong was the way that Major Anderson had briefed me with the fact that I wasn't allowed to speak. What was that all about? By now I was unnerved and trying to sort it all out.

The sound of a throat clearing came from the front of the room. The stares left me, and everyone turned to look at Lieutenant Colonel Dumford.

I didn't know a lot about the colonel, and all of my information had come from other people. I knew that he was not taken seriously by the men in the field, since most of them referred to him by his nickname, Elmer Fudd. He looked a lot like the cartoon character, with his bald head and high forehead and short, stocky body, but that was where the similarity ended. When he spoke, he was very articulate, and he had a reputation as a hard-ass.

Captain Cooper had referred to Lieutenant Colonel Dumford as Elmer, without the Fudd, which made me think that Elmer really was his first name.

Anytime that he was out of the battalion base camp and headquarters at Long Binh, the lieutenant colonel was seen wearing a flak vest and a steel pot.

The facts about Lieutenant Colonel Dumford that I found the most interesting were that he was from my state back in the world. He was an ROTC officer who had volunteered to come to Vietnam to get his ticket punched so he could be promoted to a full-bird colonel. His day job in the world was that of a high school principal. That was the most intriguing bit of information, since back in the world my boss was also a principal.

After clearing his throat to get everyone's attention, Lieutenant Colonel Dumford looked directly at me. There was a pause that put me on edge and made me even more uncomfortable than I previously was, and now I was guardedly suspicious.

He finally spoke. "Bravo Company has been through a harrowing ordeal. This is Sergeant Miller, who is filling in for Captain Cooper until a replacement is available."

I had expected the replacement to occur at this meeting, but the colonel sounded as if I would be leading the company for a while yet. I needed to pay closer attention to what was being said.

Then the introductions were given. I stood, turned, and faced the rest of the room so I could see everyone as they were introduced to me. Apparently they already knew one another. Not everyone was introduced. The second row of personnel included the artillery officers, with the lieutenant who had tried to stick me with the guard duty. Lieutenant Jones, our company's FO, was there with the artillery officers. Lieutenant Duff and several others I didn't know were also seated in the second row. The first row was all that was introduced. The introductions started with Lieutenant Koenig of Alpha Company; then Alpha Company's CO, Iron Mike Brown; followed by Captain Sorenson and then Lieutenant Maxwell of recon.

I sat back down as Lieutenant Colonel Dumford continued. "Bravo Company has been through a lot recently, so we need to keep them busy. We don't want them to have time to dwell on the past."

So far, I was listening and could support all that was being said, but what came next was the shocker of a lifetime. The lieutenant colonel read a lengthy intelligence report about the location of the NVA 199th. The 199th NVA Phantom Regiment was supposedly not far from our present location. They were thought to be just a few klicks to the east of the FSB.

There was a large rubber plantation to the north and east of us that extended northward all the way to Highway 1, and to the south of the rubber plantation was a huge jungle basin of double- and triple-canopy virgin jungle. The basin extended almost to the Pacific Ocean and drained into the Mekong Delta to the south.

At this point I was fascinated. Then it hit! The next words out of Elmer's mouth were "We are sending Bravo Company to verify or disqualify this intelligence."

Without thinking, an involuntary reflex caused me to shoot up out of my seat. "Sir, we are severely undermanned, and—"

"Sergeant, sit down! You will not speak, or you will be removed and receive your orders in your company area."

Stunned, I sat back down.

No one can come close to imagining the emotional impact on me at that moment. I forgot to take notes, and it became hard to focus on what was being said. All kinds of what-if scenarios were flooding my conscious thoughts.

It felt as if a fire were burning inside me. It took a while, but I gradually was able to regain my focus. In actuality, only a couple of minutes passed before I was able to recover and return to the reality of the moment.

The next zinger that hit me was that Bravo would be departing the FSB for the new AO the very next afternoon. This was suicide. It would be impossible to be refitted and ready for a new mission in only a half a day.

If this was really going to happen, I had questions. I had requests for supplies and equipment. Yet I was forbidden to talk. It hadn't dawned on me that I had been set up from the beginning. It would be much later when I would finally figure out that my company and I had been discussed as one of the topics at the meeting before I arrived.

I now clutched my notepad and began to write furiously. I composed and wrote a general statement of the mission, adding in my own words, "We are the bait for the 199th NVA Regiment." I then wrote the questions that I had regarding specific details on how the mission was to be carried out. I wasn't finished, and I continued to write as Alpha Company was assigned to move farther east of where their current AO was to the south of the FSB. Then Charley Company was assigned essentially the same area that they had been working. I missed the recon platoon's assignment. By now I was focusing on supply requests for the mission.

People were on their feet and moving toward the exit. "Sergeant Miller, Sergeant Miller." Then, louder, "Sergeant Miller!" It was Elmer. He seemed pissed, but I couldn't care less at this point. I looked up and must have given him a death stare because he came right back. "You would be wise to temper your emotions. Your insolence will get you into more trouble than you want."

He then continued. "Lieutenant Jones is being reassigned and will no longer be with Bravo. Now, I suggest that you meet with your company and begin planning for your departure, and be sure to pick up a copy of your orders before you leave."

He had infuriated me all over again, but now there was a difference. As angry as I was, I could still think clearly. Somehow I would turn this back on Elmer. Instead of leaving, I sat back down. I didn't slump in my chair in defeat. My back was ramrod straight, and I continued to write.

I had noticed Major Anderson glancing at me and studying me. The uncontrollable thoughts that were sneaking into my consciousness between relevant thoughts were a distraction for me and were interfering with what I wanted to accomplish.

I had lost track of time while I was recording what I wasn't allowed say or ask. In fact, I had gone way beyond the questions that I had about the mission, and now I was aware that the clerks, the major, and the lieutenant colonel were packing to leave. I jumped to my feet, notepad in hand, and rushed to the major.

I hadn't needed to be in such a hurry. The major was preoccupied with some paper work. I stood motionlessly by and waited to be recognized. When the adrenaline is flowing—and I had just received an overdose—a short wait can seem like such a long wait. Finally, he looked up as if he were expecting me.

"Sir, there are some logistical problems that will prevent us from moving out in the morning—or, in fact, at any time tomorrow."

"What logistical problems are you talking about, Sergeant?"

That was my opening. "One, our maps need updating. The minefield that we ran into wasn't on any of our current maps."

I was reading from my notepad. "Two, it is brigade policy to allow the prescouting of a new AO. I am requesting an aerial reconnaissance of the area before the company moves out."

I could tell that I had his attention now. "Three, I want my men to rehearse patrolling for close-quarter action."

I knew that I was making an impression at this point. "Four, I am requesting some special equipment for this mission. I will need starlight scopes, extra batteries, and gas grenades to be used for breaking contact."

The major stopped me by raising his hand. "Sergeant, you are very persuasive. I'll see what I can do. I have to leave now. The helicopter is warming up. How long do you think it will take you to be ready?"

"Depending on the availability of the requested items and the flyover, I think five days should be sufficient."

He didn't bat an eye. "I will let you know in the morning."

Major Anderson then motioned to one of the clerks still packing the maps and paper work. The clerk immediately produced a blue loose-leaf folder from the file box that he had been packing. It took the clerk just three exaggerated steps to reach the major and hand him the folder with flare.

"You need to initial each page and sign at the bottom of each page where it says 'received.'" The major then spread four pages on the table next to me and produced a pen from his breast pocket.

Normally I would take some time to study the pages more closely, but the major was in a hurry, and I really didn't have the patience at this point to check the paper work more closely. As I initialed and signed "SSG Jerald M. Miller," I realized what I was signing my name to—I had just signed for Bravo Company's equipment, including all of the weapons, the radios, the APCs themselves; everything. That had to be worth several million dollars. On top of everything, there was no explanation because the major and his contingency were in a hurry to depart the FSB. The same clerk handed me two more sheets of paper. These were a shortened form of my orders regarding the company's new mission and AO.

"Good-bye, Sergeant, and good luck. I will talk to you in the morning." With that, the major was out the bunker door and heading for the helipad.

As I stepped out of the bunker, Lieutenant Duff was standing a short distance away talking with Lieutenant Jones, the FO (forward observer). As I stepped toward the main gate, Lieutenant Jones motioned me over to where he and Lieutenant Duff were standing. It became obvious that they had been waiting for me.

I could tell that Lieutenant Jones was agitated. "Jerry, it wasn't my idea, being reassigned. The lieutenant colonel said it would be awkward for me, being an officer and all..."

"Thanks, but I'm thinking that if we ever needed you, it's now." I was still upset and immediately regretted my tone.

Lieutenant Jones's voice softened to almost a whisper. "I hear you, and I'm sorry."

I then turned my attention to Lieutenant Duff. "I have a list of requested items. Do I turn them in to you, or do I order them through the rear area?"

"That depends. If we have what you want here at the FSB, they are yours."

I read the list to Lieutenant Duff, starting with the starlight scopes; I wanted three of them plus the extra batteries, and I ended with a request for a case of gas grenades.

The answer that Lieutenant Duff gave me was expected. "We don't have any of those items, so you'll have to get them from the rear area, either Cu Chi or Long Binh. Good luck getting any of those items."

At last I could head back to the company area. I wasn't in a hurry because I had nothing but bad news to share when I returned. As I left the TOC (tactical operations command) area, I was surprised that the sun was still quite high. The temperature was pleasant and as close to perfect as it ever got. However, I was unable to enjoy any of it. It wasn't anger that controlled me at this time. I was only concerned with how to break the news to the rest of the company. As I walked, I tried to recall different parts of the recent meeting.

I was thinking, "Let me get everything right and in the correct order." By now I had made it to just outside the gate of the FSB. "I've been ordered to take my company on a suicide mission, to be used as bait to lure an NVA regiment out of hiding, and for every piece of equipment lost, I will owe the army. How fair is that?" Damn army!

As I walked, I was pacing myself and taking as much time as I could. I dreaded having to tell the company what was in store for them. I was aware that I was dragging my feet in the dust, but as I got closer to my APC, a clear plan began to take shape, and by the time I was almost to the track, my step had picked up a bounce. I was thinking that maybe, just maybe, I could make things right.

When I reached the command track, my destination, Sergeant Moore was waiting with Ron and Andy.

"Well, we might as well get this over with," I was speaking to Andy, "Get Finley, Lee, and Pomeroy. We have to talk."

Ron had heard me, and he waved Andy off and took off to fetch the men himself.

The nightmare was growing, but I would wait until the rest of the NCOs were present to tell them about losing Lieutenant Jones. The lieutenant's FO skills could be an extremely valuable asset for this mission. This left the company with only two attached personnel, and I was confident that we would get to keep our Kit Carson scouts.

While I waited for the NCOs to arrive, I tried to plan what I was going to say. I couldn't come up with anything that wasn't going to be unbearably painful.

9

Sergeant Lee was the first to arrive, followed by Sergeant Finley. Ron was leading Sergeant Pomeroy and was in sight and headed our way. Sergeant Moore of second platoon was already here.

Top came over to say good-bye. He and the cooks had to be back in Xuan Loc before it got dark. Captain Sorenson was going to escort his jeep to Highway 1.

The steaks had been a hit and were greatly appreciated by the men, especially now that we didn't have that FSB guard duty. I had yet to eat, but I wasn't hungry or even felt that I had missed anything up to this point. I had a lot to go over with the company NCOs.

The men of the company had been spared the news of the on-again, off-again guard duty for the artillery at the fire support base. I was glad that I had postponed telling them.

The first sergeant handed Andy a stainless-steel metal container that contained some leftover steaks. Top's last words were "Jerry, check with me every day. We'll figure out the best time. Just keep me informed. I'll let you know tomorrow when your supplies can be delivered."

With my parting words I informed Top, "I'm asking for an aerial recon of the new AO in addition to the supply list you received. I'll talk to you tomorrow."

Top had been impressed with my efforts to get the guard duty rescinded, and he told me so.

The plan that I had hatched since leaving the FSB was more of a wisp of hope than a plan, but another thought now occurred to me. At first I was upset that Lieutenant Jones had been taken away from us, but that could end up being an asset. One little piece of the plan was falling into place.

I now turned my attention to the group of NCOs I had summoned. They were all of the company's platoon leaders. We sat on ammo cans and an assortment of make-do seats. We were positioned at the rear of the command track with the ramp in the down position. Andy was at the top of the ramp just inside the APC, monitoring the radios, and Ron had moved to the top of the track in order to read.

As I looked around the group studying the NCO's faces, there were no surprises. They all wore solemn expressions, as if they knew what was coming. In reality, they had no idea. Just by studying their facial expressions, I could tell that each of the sergeants knew that I had some serious news to convey to them. However, I also knew that they were unable to prepare themselves for what was coming. They were about to be shocked, stunned, and flooded with anger, just as I had been when I first received and processed the order for Bravo Company's new mission.

I eased into my report by addressing Sergeant Moore. He was the only one who knew about the guard duty outside of Andy and me. I was careful to backtrack and tell the whole story so the other NCOs could be brought up to speed. When I finally got to the part where Major Anderson got us out of the extra guard duty, there was a lot of air being exhaled. At this point everyone had been expecting the worst as, step by step, I gave them the details that had led to Major Anderson canceling the orders.

The relief on the faces of the sergeants and their instantaneous relaxed posture made me think that they thought this was going to be the bad news. With the important news yet to come, I hadn't foreseen the men's mood swing to such a high note. This made what I had to say next more difficult.

I paused just briefly and then cautiously started with "Now we have a more pressing problem." With the NCOs' attention refocused, I began again by telling them about the battalion tactical meeting with the battalion commander and the other company commanders. I omitted the part about not being allowed to speak and the verbal reprimand that I had received from Lieutenant Colonel Dumford. I went into all of the details that I could remember about the intelligence report and was confident that I had covered it well. I had my extensive notes to aid my recall. After sharing the details of the intelligence report, I was able to spend less time on the special orders for the company's mission.

As I studied my notes I noticed some gaps and I remembered that I had quit taking notes at one point. However, I was confident that I was able to remember all that was pertinent to our company.

I had predicted the sergeants' reaction to what I was going to say next, and that reaction came as soon as I repeated Lieutenant Colonel Dumford's words: "We are sending Bravo Company to verify or disqualify this intelligence."

Everyone began talking at once. It took a while, at least fifteen to twenty seconds, to get everyone's attention again so that I could continue.

I spoke into the din without raising my voice. The NCOs were pretty keyed up by now, and I wasn't going to add to their anxiety by yelling louder in order to get their attention back.

"Wait, wait." I paused. "Listen to me. Hear me out. There's more." I paused again. "I have a plan." I hadn't meant to say that. "I have a plan" had just slipped out, but it worked. The moment that I said I had a plan, it instantly became quiet again. And once again, just that quickly, I had each of the sergeants' attention. I immediately regretted mentioning that I had a plan, since it was more of an idea to be developed than a well-thought-out course of action.

I had anticipated that this meeting was going to take some time, and now it was time to tell them about my second conversation with Major Anderson. I left out having to sign for all of Bravo Company's equipment and started with the supplies and equipment requests. I showed some enthusiasm as I told the NCOs about the requests for special equipment such as the starlight scopes, a ninety millimeter recoilless rifle and special flechette rounds of ammunition, the request for aerial reconnaissance, and the request for the gas grenades. I knew there would be questions about the gas grenades.

I slowed my speech down for effect and for the men to gain full understanding. "These requests are in line with what Captain Cooper would have done. However, we need to buy some time. Our orders were originally to move out tomorrow around noon. I asked Major Anderson for five days to prepare, rehearse, and receive supplies. He's going to let us know in the morning."

As I looked into the eyes of the men I was addressing, I looked for signs of understanding.

There was still much to cover, so I continued. "Top is working on the supply list, and Lieutenant Duff is arranging for an over flight of the new AO tomorrow. As long as we are here, we will run a riff"—a search-and-destroy mission—"into the rubber trees each day. This will keep us in practice and keep the lifers off our backs. Let them see how busy we are."

I hoped that focusing on the supplies first would divert the NCOs' attention from the real mission until I was prepared to discuss the elements of a plan that was still taking shape in my imagination.

I left out the fact that I was trying to delay long enough for a new CO to be assigned to Bravo Company. That was my first and foremost thought when I had asked the major for five days. Not that time for the extra preparation wasn't important and necessary, but three or three and a half days would have been sufficient preparation for the company to be able to depart, provided that we would be able to get the requested special equipment.

Another thought that I kept having was the presence of an officer such as Lieutenant Jones, the artillery FO who was assigned to the company as attached personnel. He wouldn't have bonded with the company, and that could create problems. It had become evident to me that if Lieutenant Jones were still assigned to the company, I wouldn't even be considering the course of action that I was preparing to explore. I could pursue my idea for at least a little longer. I knew I was on shaky ground, and I realized that I probably didn't have the guts to go through with my idea.

I was operating on the assumption that we would have five days to prepare, but in present time, it was now late in the day, and the NCOs and I needed to prepare for the night's activities. I needed to keep the meeting moving along.

I knew it was coming, and it came from Sergeant Lee of first platoon. "Sarge, what are the gas grenades for?"

I began. "On this mission, I figure we will need every option that we can come up with to survive. My intentions are that every patrol leader who leaves the company perimeter be armed with some of the gas grenades. They're for breaking contact, so you can *di di*"—Vietnamese for "hurry"—"back to the company perimeter.

"Captain Cooper and I talked about incorporating gas grenades as part of our mechanical ambushes by taping them to the front of the claymore mines. It seems like this might be a good time to try it.

"Oh, one more thing while we're on the subject, and then you can get back to your platoons. When we get to our new logger site, anytime we have a patrol outside the perimeter, we will have a reaction patrol waiting, on full alert, inside the perimeter in order to be able to assist quickly if something happens."

I couldn't resist by following up with "Our real mission is to keep everyone in one piece. If there are no more questions, let's get ready for tonight, and we will continue this meeting tomorrow."

I asked Sergeant Moore to stick around for a moment as the other NCOs were quickly departing for their respective platoon areas. "Ralph, I want you and second platoon to do the first riff into the rubber tomorrow. Sergeant Lee will be the reaction force back here, and I will be working with him.

"We have to put on a show for the FSB personnel. We need to appear busy so they won't mess with us. I don't care, once you get far enough away, if you want to sit tight and relax. Let the men write letters or read, and if you get back late, it's OK. Anyway, keep your guard up, and make it real enough. Charlie has to be keeping an eye on the FSB."

Ralph departed for second platoon, and Andy and I were alone again to plan for the night. Ron was there to volunteer for anything that needed to be done. Ron was the company medic and rode on the command track. He was rarely idle. When he wasn't helping one of the drivers change oil and fuel filters, he was making cocoa or coffee for someone in one of the platoons. He scouted the company for things to do and people to help, and when he wasn't on his feet working, he was reading. He read more than most of the men and was always trading books. He insisted on sharing radio watch with Andy and me. We had agreed to one hour on duty and two hours off throughout the night.

The command track's driver and TC (the track commander who manned the fifty-caliber machine gun) were part of the guard rotation on any given night, but with my approval, they pitched in to help third platoon with their guard duty, since they were so shorthanded. They both liked Sergeant Pomeroy, and he made every effort to accommodate their needs.

The night passed at the usual slow-motion speed. It was now the next day and coming up on the predawn hour. Andy had just done the company situation reports and was trying to gently awaken me for my next turn at monitoring the radios. Anyone serving in the infantry in Vietnam was sleep deprived, and I had been awake and under pressure for most of the last forty-eight hours. Until last night after midnight, I had not been able to rest for more than an hour at a time. Now, with a two-hour stretch of time, I had dropped into a deep sleep. Andy was carefully shaking me. I was almost conscious as I stiffened and opened my eyes with a start. No words were exchanged, as I silently was able to convince Andy that I was awake and functioning.

Andy had an orange soda waiting for me. He handed it to me and disappeared around the track. Before opening the soda, I rubbed my eyes and looked around, trying to adjust my night vision. Before long I would have an adequate supply of visual purple and be able to see well into the darkness. I pulled the poncho liner back up over my left shoulder, and I leaned to my right as I awkwardly fumbled for my B-52 can opener so I could open the soda.

After a long sip, I checked my watch under the poncho liner. I still had fifty minutes plus before the next situation report. I sat back in my jeep seat to do my thinking.

The first thing that I thought about was just exactly where I was. I considered myself to be fortunate to have ended up in the Twenty-Fifth Division, and I felt equally fortunate to have been assigned to the Tomahawks Battalion, and especially Bravo Company. The only blight tarnishing my good fortune had been the TOC meeting yesterday afternoon.

I truly and genuinely liked the men of Bravo Company. There were only a few slackers and complainers, and they were all basically good-intentioned people. The company attitude was a tribute to Captain Travis Cooper. Even though the captain was gone, I felt compelled to not let him down or disappoint him, and I knew that others felt the same way I did.

Bravo Company, like all infantry units in Vietnam, was diverse in every way. The men's education ranged from high school dropouts to college graduates. At least a half dozen racial and ethnic backgrounds were represented: Polynesian, Asian American, Native American, African American, and Marcos Ramirez, a Mexican national. But there were also some commonalities. Ninety percent of the company was between eighteen and twenty-one years old. At twenty-six I was now the oldest member of the company—except for Top, who, of course, was older, but Top wasn't out in the field. The complex backgrounds of the members of the company had no meaning or effect on how they got along and were able to operate as a unit.

Had anyone else in the company at this point known what I was thinking and planning to do, they might not have considered themselves as fortunate as I did to end up in Bravo Company. There was still time to plan and adjust. Most of all, I needed the men's support for any course of action to be successful.

My thoughts now shifted to the approaching morning. Looming big was the awaited call from Major Anderson. Then there was the call from Top about the chances of procuring the supplies I wanted. Third on the list but no less important was the reconnaissance flight. Timing was important. The flight couldn't take place before I talked to Major Anderson. The more I thought about it, the more I realized that I had nothing to lose. I surmised that if the recon helicopter was here and waiting, I would have the perfect reason to call the major. I was sure that I could make things work with few delays.

Looking to the east, I could see that it was just starting to get light. The thinnest streak of light was like a hair part on the horizon. Thirty minutes later it was getting light quickly, and men were starting to move about. Around the entire company there was the stirring of activity.

10

I was anticipating a hot cup of cocoa this morning. After I heated the water and mixed the powdered contents in my canteen cup, I sat in the captain's throne. I held the canteen cup in both hands and was shivering slightly while I glanced around the company perimeter.

My gaze swept the area and settled on three dogs that were milling around and sniffing one another in the center of the company perimeter directly in front of the mortar platoon's position. Since I had been in-country, all of the Vietnamese dogs that I had seen were about the same size, maybe fourteen to eighteen inches at the shoulder. They were for the most part light colored. Their color ranged from a creamy white to blond to orange to light brown and all shades in between. The tails were straight or curled over their backs. They were all short-haired and had pointed snouts. I was reminded of the dingoes of Australia.

The dogs showed up around our base camps and some fire support bases looking for handouts. Some of the REMFs (derogatory term for rear-echelon troops) kept them as pets.

One of the dogs began undulating and gagging. It was trying to vomit. When it was finally able to regurgitate, it had attracted at least a dozen stares from the men nearby.

A small, weak voice from the back of one of third platoon's tracks was the only other sound that carried. "So you're the one that I had the beer chugging contest with." That had to be Harlan. He was known for his off-the-wall comments, and they never failed to surprise us. I looked to third platoon, and there he was, sitting on an ammo can and holding his head in both hands. Apparently Harlan had drunk too much beer with his steak last night. He obviously had quite a hangover, but he had been allowed to drink since the third platoon was being protected with light duty. The light duty was ending today.

As I thought about last night, I also couldn't help but wonder where Harlan came up with his one-liners. He had made it hard to focus on last night's events. I had to first get Harlan's projected picture out of my mind before I could concentrate on anything else.

The base's artillery had only one short fire mission early last night. No wonder I had slept so soundly. There had been none of the usual interruptions.

I felt a shudder pass through me, and my eyes involuntarily widened in order to focus a little harder on the person who was coming across the perimeter from the front gate of the FSB. I identified Lieutenant Duff, who instead of calling me on the radio was coming to see me in person. No matter what his message was going to be, I couldn't help but be impressed.

Lieutenant Duff greeted me with a pleasant "Good morning, Sergeant." He gave no indication that this was going to be bad news. The lieutenant's demeanor seemed unusually lighthearted and casual. He showed no trace of the stiff, abrupt officer that our company had encountered when we first arrived at the FSB, and, as it turned out, the lieutenant had a great report for me.

"I just got off the horn with the aviation group stationed in Xuan Loc. They have an LOH"—light observation helicopter—"available for your recon flight on standby right now. In fact, they can be on their way as soon as you want them. On my request they agreed to make themselves available for the next few days. All that is holding them up is they are waiting for me to call them back and schedule some times."

"That's great news...definitely good news." I was having a little bit of good luck at the moment. Maybe things would continue to favor the company and me. We needed every advantage that we could get. I was going to get my recon flight, and I was ready to go at that very moment, except that I had to wait for the call from Major Anderson. The company's immediate future depended on the outcome of that call. I had to wait for the major's call.

I took time to explain to Lieutenant Duff what Major Anderson's decision on the company's departure time meant in terms of preparedness. I omitted the fact that I believed the longer we waited in place, the more likely it was that we would be assigned a new CO. The lieutenant agreed with me that the call meant a lot, but he made no move to leave. Either he wanted to be there when the call came through from Major Anderson, or he already knew something that I did not.

Andy was offering the lieutenant anything and everything. The lieutenant finally settled on a soda. Andy opened an orange soda and handed it to him.

Sergeant Lee returned from patrol and reported to me before heading for the first-platoon area. The nighttime LPs had been replaced thirty minutes earlier by the daytime OP guards.

The day was beginning to accelerate in activity. Exactly on the hour at 0700, the call from Major Anderson came through. Andy was monitoring the radio and took the call. He identified himself and handed me the handset, but my hand and arm were already extended to receive it. I immediately identified myself and was silent as I listened with nervous anticipation. I actually had butterflies in my stomach. I was thinking positively and working to contain my expectations.

I was aware that the palm of my hand that held the radio was sweaty as the major spoke. "You can't have five full days before your deployment." My heart sank. All of the men around me were watching and waiting as my expression and body language showed my disappointment. It was so obvious, because everyone, including Lieutenant Duff, followed my lead and also deflated and became extra concerned.

The major paused ever so slightly and continued. "However, in view of what you outlined for your preparations, I can justify three more days." Now my expression and body language showed elation. Like puppets being manipulated, the crowd around me followed my lead and also instantly perked up.

The major hurriedly finished. "You have today and tomorrow, and your departure from the FSB is to be noon on the day after tomorrow. I will be monitoring your progress. If you have any questions, ask them now. Over."

"I have no questions at this time. Over."

"Then I'm out." And with that the major concluded his report.

I handed the handset back to Andy. He couldn't suppress his smile as he eagerly relayed the news to the not-so-small gathering that we had gained some preparation time. By now the group at the rear of the command track had grown considerably to include not only Lieutenant Duff, but Sergeant Lee, Sergeant Finley, Sergeant Pomeroy, and almost all of third platoon.

It was time to move on, and I was already making plans about how best to use the time available. I turned toward Lieutenant Duff to address him. "Lieutenant, I am ready for the loche." This was a light observation helicopter.

Lieutenant Duff turned toward the FSB and began stepping out without saying a word.

"Wait a second," I called after him. "See if you can schedule a flight for 0900 tomorrow and on the same time the next day."

"Roger," replied the lieutenant as he turned back toward the FSB.

I tried not to show as much positive emotion as I felt, but I was pleased with the way things were progressing. In fact, I realized that I had just given an officer an order. That was a first for me. More importantly, things were finally going the company's way. The message from Major Anderson had turned out in my favor. I would have my three reconnaissance flights over the new AO. That was better than I had hoped to get. All that remained was the call from Top about the availability of the extra supplies that I had requested.

I had two maps laid out and was studying them intently as I waited for the arrival of the LOH. Today I would recon to find a suitable logger site for the company. The logger site was important because it was the company base camp and all patrols radiated from that location. And, most importantly, the site had to be defendable. Tomorrow I would scout the entire AO, and on the following day, the third planned flight would be a diversion.

I was certain that Charlie would be aware of the recon flights. If too much attention was given to a particular area, the VC would realize that the Americans were going to show up in that location. In order to confuse the VC, I planned to use the LOH to create a diversion. On the third day I would have the pilot fly lower and appear to be looking more closely at an area farther to the south. My hope was that if the VC were aware of the LOH's presence in the area for three days, they would make the assumption that the Americans would be showing up in the south. It was a gamble, but at this point I had nothing to lose and everything to gain. It was definitely worth a try.

As I waited for my recon helicopter to arrive, I reviewed some of the things that I had picked up since coming to Vietnam. I had learned a lot about the army and army subjects in my short career. I was aware that the army tried to operate with a conservative approach. It had taken a long time for the army to adjust to the close combat tactics of jungle warfare in Vietnam.

It hadn't taken me long after joining Bravo Company to realize that we didn't have access to all of the weapons and equipment that I had been trained to use when I was schooled in infantry subjects at Fort Benning. Now that I had the chance and the authority, I was going to request all of the weapons and equipment that I had been trained to use stateside and were currently missing from the company's inventory.

None of my requests were out of line. The company would be able to use five times the number of starlight scopes that I was requesting. The company could also use a ninety-millimeter recoilless rifle. Since we were mechanized, we had the ability to transport such a bulky weapon. In fact, I didn't think it would be out of line to have one for each platoon.

Tactically, the army had slowly adjusted to the close combat of fighting small hit-and-run units in the jungle.

The tactics employed involved two schools of thought that were practically opposites, but each had its place. The first tactical action was based on keeping your exact position unknown to the enemy for as long as possible. When the enemy appeared, you first blew your claymore mines. In the ensuing confusion, you next threw your grenades. The last resort was to fire your M-16s or 60 machine guns. The muzzle flashes always gave your exact location away. This tactic was practiced by infantry companies when they deployed ambushes, especially the night ambushes.

The second tactical action was called recon by fire, which meant putting down a wall of fire or bullets. Mechanized units such as Bravo Company frequently used this tactic during daylight hours. For example, if the enemy was even suspected of being in a wood line that the company had to pass through, there were several options available. First, an artillery strike could be called in, or napalm could be dropped by jets. Another option was to call in gunships to prep the area with rockets and machine-gun fire, or, in our case, the APCs could come on line and pepper the area with fifty-caliber and M-60 machine-gun fire. And we also had a mortar platoon.

I was willing to use the tactic that would give my men the best chance of survival.

As I checked my watch trying to estimate when the LOH would arrive, I felt the added pressure of being responsible for an entire company. I remembered when I had been promoted to leader of second platoon. The feeling was one of stepping up to fill a responsibility. However, I realized that the same feeling had been multiplied by many times since becoming responsible for the entire company. This was much more pressure.

Life wasn't easy, but I was sure I could do this. I would look after the men of Bravo Company and somehow accomplish the mission.

I still didn't know whether I had the guts to go through with what I was planning. The army had forced me to consider an action that went against my training and my ethical beliefs.

I could revisit my dilemma at a later time. I needed to get ready for the recon flight. I was going to take my M-16 and a bandolier of ammunition. I also needed the maps that I had been studying and extra pens and pencils. With the exception of the M-16 and the ammunition, all the rest of the items could be stuffed into the cargo pockets of my trousers.

There was nothing left to do but wait for the arrival of the recon helicopter.

11

I was waiting by the third platoon's APCs, which were parked just across the road from the helipad. I actually heard the LOH before it came into view. I was hoping to have heard from Top by now, but he still hadn't called me about the extra supplies, so I briefed Andy to take the call.

As the LOH got closer, someone from the FSB threw out a green smoke grenade. This was completely unnecessary. It was a clear day, and the pilot would have no trouble identifying the FSB. The medevacs from two days ago hadn't needed smoke. Even Elmer's helicopter hadn't needed smoke. Oh, well.

The LOH landed, and I scooped up my rifle and bandolier of ammunition, bent over, and hurried to the waiting ride. I opened the passenger door and gave a nod and a mock salute as I climbed in. The first thing that got my attention was the presence of the lone pilot. There was no Peter pilot, no crew chief, nor door gunners. Previously I had only ridden on Hueys. This was to be my first ride in a light observation helicopter.

I searched for the helmet with the dangling cord that would allow me to communicate with the pilot. I finally spied it in the back seat behind the pilot. When I hesitated, the pilot gestured me to take my place in the back seat where the helmet rested. Briefly confused, I awkwardly reopened the door and maneuvered to my assigned place in the rear seat. Then I positioned the commo helmet on my head as I simultaneously plugged in the jack. I wondered about balancing the aircraft with both of us on the same side.

When I was ready, I merely said, "Hello."

The pilot's reply was loud and clear. "Welcome to Vietnam Tours. This is your pilot speaking, and we will be flying over an especially scenic section of this enchanting country.

"Actually, when you want to say something, my name is Rock. There are no radio-telephone formalities in this cockpit as long as it's just the two of us. By the way, the reason I had you sit behind me is so that when the craft banks, we both are seeing the same thing at the same time. Now give me a briefing while I get us airborne."

I told Rock that I was looking for a place to park a company of APCs somewhere due east of our present location.

From that point on, Rock was all business. We engaged in some of the usual small talk, such as where we were from back in the world and who was going to win the next Super Bowl. But most of our conversation was about the maps, the lay of the land, and the various types of terrain in the area.

We had gained altitude while circling the FSB, and we seemed to be flying quite high. I guessed our altitude to be approaching four or five hundred feet as we headed straight east of the FSB. After less than fifteen minutes in the air, I saw what I had been looking for. Coming into view was a large clearing in the rubber trees. Either it hadn't been planted, or the trees had died out. What appeared before me was a grassy meadow a little less than an acre in size, or roughly the size of a city block. I had discovered the location of the site on the photo map that I had looked at first, and I then located the position of the clearing on my topographical map. I had picked out the spot just minutes before Rock's arrival. It had looked promising on the map, and now I would be able to verify the information in person.

I told Rock that the clearing was exactly what I was looking for, but to keep going so as not to call attention to the site. No way did we want to appear interested. I got the topographical map out of my pocket and located the spot, which I had already circled. This was too easy. The center of the clearing was exactly where two grid lines crossed. I got out the aerial map, or photo map, in order to double-check the location. I confirmed the location by comparing the grid coordinates, since the maps were printed with two different scales. The clearing showed up as a light spot amid the uniform yellow-green of the rubber trees and the darker green of the jungle. It was a little short of the hypothetical position that Elmer had indicated for the company position on his big map. But it was close enough, and it put the company within the boundaries of the newly assigned AO of the company's next mission.

Rock kept us on course to the east for another ten minutes. We had covered enough distance from the clearing, so I instructed Rock to turn back to the north a half a klick (five hundred meters) and fly a parallel route back to the road to the FSB. He complied without speaking. When we made our turn to the north, I thought I could see green open areas to the east indicating rice paddies, and beyond that the slightest glimpse of the Pacific Ocean on the far horizon.

I wanted to see the clearing from another angle and also check out the series of ravines shown on the map that cut into the rubber trees like little fingers of jungle from the south.

The rubber plantation was huge. Even seen from the air, it seemed to go on forever, but I had to direct my attention to the terrain to the east of the clearing. There were several deep ravines running north and south. They were much wider at the south end, where the rubber plantation ended and the jungle continued. The ravines continued to the north for a couple of klicks before they gradually tapered to a point and finally disappeared.

When we flew back by the clearing to the north as we were now heading west, it looked even better to me. It appeared to be on a slightly elevated ridge that ran north and south. I needed to view the site again from the south. I wanted to confirm a feature shown on the maps that I had failed to see on the first or second pass over the area.

When we reached the road—that is, as soon as we could see it—I instructed Rock to fly the same east-west pattern five hundred meters (half a klick) to the south of our first pass. This route would take us over the continuous heavy jungle to the south of the rubber plantation. Heading back to the east again, when we passed the clearing that was to the north of us, and on my side of the helicopter, I was pleased with what I saw. It was just what I had expected and hoped for after studying the maps. There was a sheer rock face bordering the south side of the clearing. It didn't look very high, but I really couldn't tell from this altitude. I guessed that the rock face was maybe twenty or thirty feet, or it could be as high as forty feet. Here the vegetation dipped downward. That is, the tops of the trees indicated to me that the ground beneath them angled sharply downward from the rock face and went for some distance. There appeared to be a significant change in elevation as the jungle spread out to the south. It was hard to be precise because the vegetation was so thick.

On this same pass to the east, I let Rock go a little farther. I was able to confirm what I had suspected on the first pass. It was the Pacific Ocean off in the distance. We turned north, this time farther to the north, to line up for a return pass back to the west. I searched the rubber trees for terrain changes and changes in elevation or any abnormalities. I was marking up my maps. I had circled numerous areas that might warrant further inspection. By now it had become obvious to me that the series of ravines that we had just scouted could very easily be travel routes for anyone hiding in the large jungle basin that lay to the south.

When we arrived back at the road to the FSB, we had been in the air for quite a while, and it was time to return to the FSB. We flew south following the road just as the dust-offs had done several days earlier. When we landed at the helipad, I told Rock about my plans for the next morning's recon.

Rock said, "That would be me. Pick you up at 0900?"

He made that a question. It was clear that Lieutenant Duff had done the scheduling for all three days.

I confirmed the time at 0900 hours, took off the commo helmet, unplugged the jack, opened the door, and jumped down and out in order to clear the skid. Bending at the waist, I hurried across the road. When I reached my stopping point I turned to wave, but the loche was already gaining altitude and headed north.

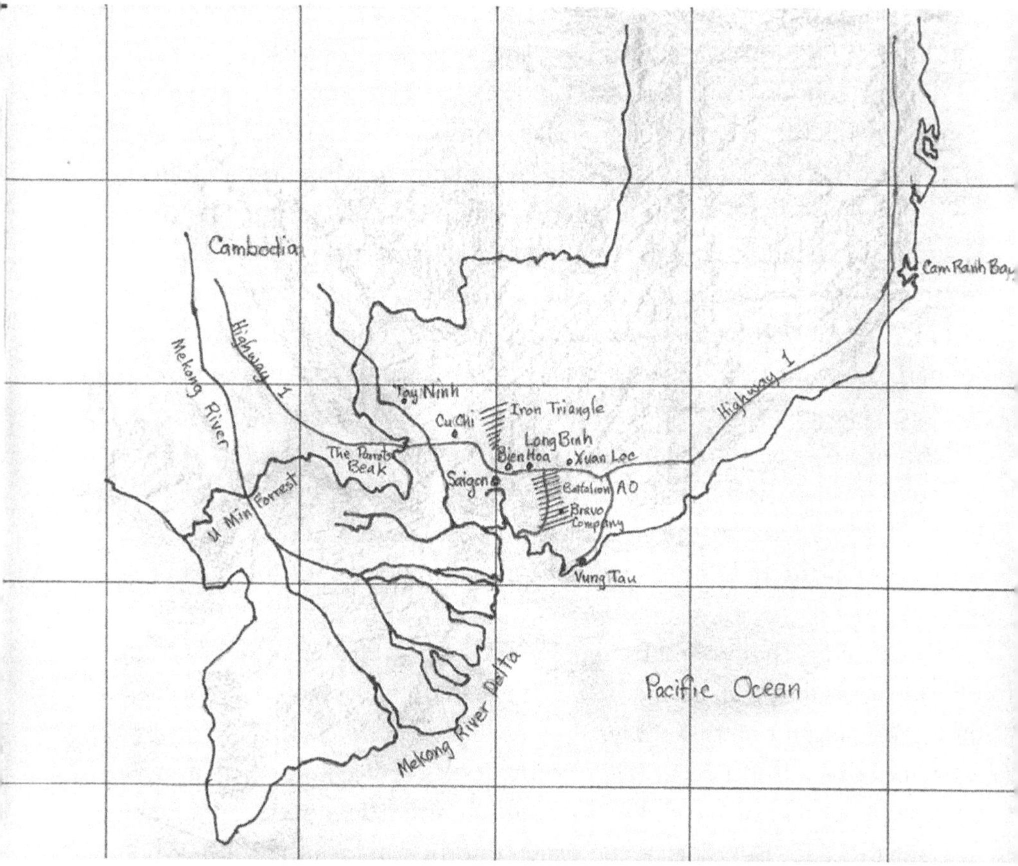
Cambodia
Highway 1
Mekong River
Tay Ninh
Iron Triangle
Cu Chi
Long Binh
Bien Hoa
Xuan Loc
The Parrots Beak
Saigon
Battalion AO
Bravo Company
U Min Forrest
Vung Tau
Cam Ranh Bay
Highway 1
Pacific Ocean
Mekong River Delta

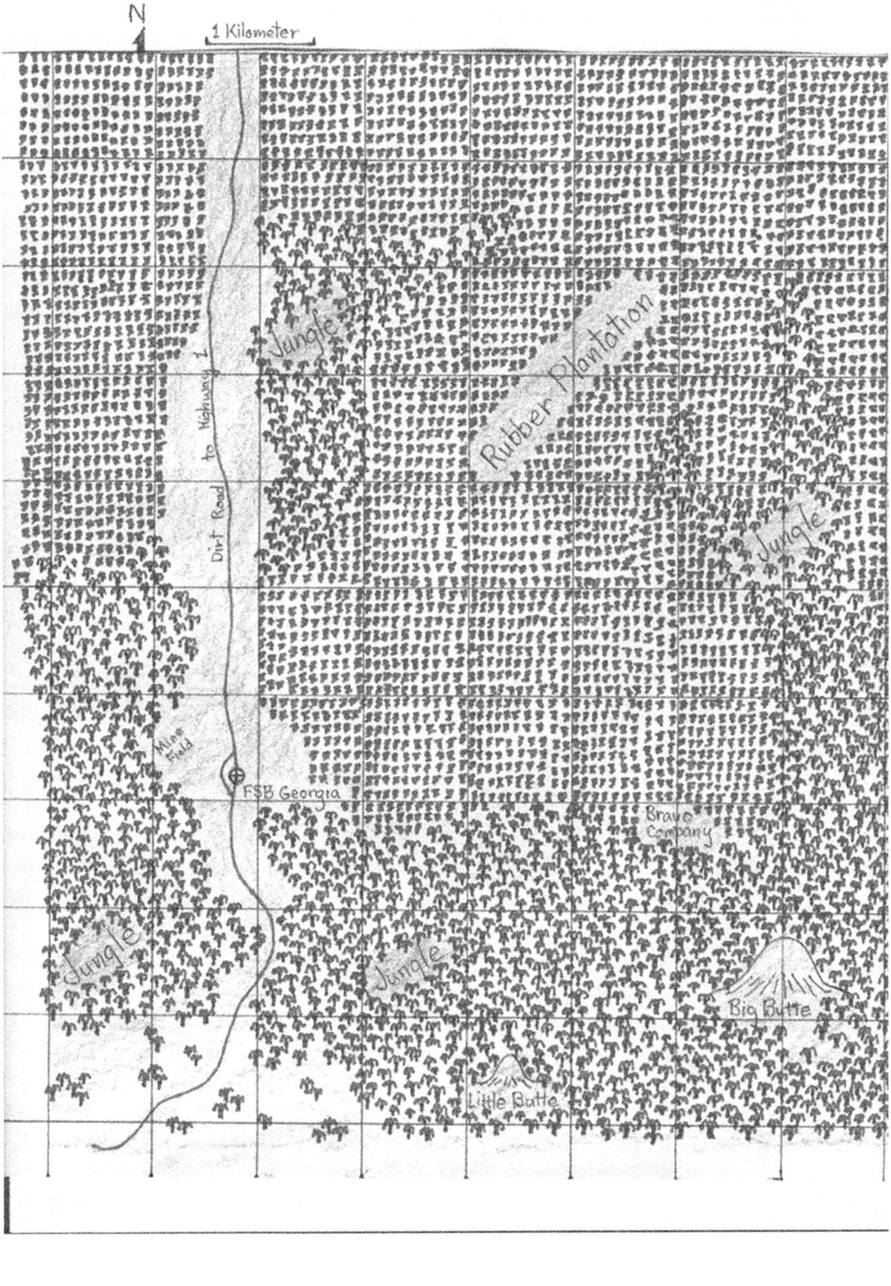
N
1 Kilometer
Jungle
Rubber Plantation
Dirt Road to Highway 1
Jungle
Mine Field
FSB Georgia
Bravo Company
Jungle
Jungle
Big Butte
Little Butte

12

Andy had heard Rock and me returning from the recon mission and was waiting for me at the road. Seeing him waiting reminded me that Top should have called by now. I anticipated more good news and felt that I was on a roll. I had plenty of information gathered from the recon flight to share with the company NCOs this evening. I was thinking that I should include all of the company's NCOs and not limit the information to just the platoon leaders. I was still edgy and nervous about the company's orders and the newly assigned AO, but I was going to have the company supplied and ready when the new CO arrived. It wasn't the first time or the last time I wished that I had not told the men that I had a "plan."

I turned back to Andy from watching Rock's helicopter fly up the road. It was easy to tell that Andy had good news. His smile and his body language all conveyed his eagerness to report to me what he had learned in my absence. As I had guessed, the message from Top was good. All but one of the items that I had requested would be arriving at the FSB first thing in the morning. A deuce and a half carrying our supplies would be following the engineers to the FSB.

I could hardly contain myself. We were actually going to get three more starlight scopes, bringing the total in the company to four. The scope that we were currently using had belonged to second platoon and me. It had been ordered several months earlier, just after I'd figured out that if you wanted something, you had to ask. Each night ambush patrol would now be able to have its own starlight scope, and the company would still have a couple for use on the perimeter. I had ordered enough extra batteries to power the scopes for over a month. I had also ordered a month's supply of radio batteries. Along with the batteries, we would be getting four cases of smoke grenades, two cases of fragmentation grenades, three cases of hand-activated parachute flares and star clusters, extra sixty machine-gun ammo, and extra M-16 ammo. We had plenty of fifty-caliber ammunition and M-79 grenades on hand. We were a mechanized infantry company, so we would have no trouble transporting the additional munitions.

I had a surprise for the company coming with this supply shipment. I had requested a ninety-millimeter recoilless rifle. The ninety-millimeter recoilless rifle was a large bazooka-like weapon. In fact, it was nothing more than a large bazooka. It loaded from the rear, and the back blast escaped through the rear opening of the tube; hence, no recoil. I had fired one on a range at Fort Benning. It would be a great addition to the company's arsenal as an offensive or defensive weapon. The ammunition that I ordered for the ninety-millimeter rifle consisted of six HE (high explosive) rounds and six flechette rounds. The HE ammo was the normal high-explosive rounds designed to disable tanks, and in our case to neutralize fortified bunkers. The flechette rounds were a new antipersonnel item loaded with thousands of one-inch darts. When the flechette round was fired, the darts spread out sixty degrees when they left the muzzle and could nail a person to a tree at over one hundred meters.

I was gloating over Top's success, and I hadn't yet thought about which item was missing from the list. Andy patiently waited as he watched me process the information that he had just given me. "Day after tomorrow," he finally continued, "the gas grenades will be here. Top says they won't fly them here by helicopter, and they have to come all the way from Cu Chi."

Now I knew what was missing. "What about the maps?" Top had been told that the minefield wasn't on our current maps, and we needed our maps updated. It wouldn't have been a problem to get more copies of the map we were using, but I had specifically told Top to get newer versions of the maps of the AO as well as an aerial map.

Andy could only tell me what Top had said, and Top was working on it.

After considering our good fortune, I concluded that there wasn't much on our supply list that I would give up for newer maps. The ones that I had used on the recon flight had been sufficient. I made a mental note to pick up more of the current map copies from Lieutenant Duff before we moved out.

A look at my watch indicated that noon was a ways away yet, so Andy and I returned to the command track. Sergeant Finley and Sergeant Lee were there, sitting on ammo cans and visiting. They stayed there as I rummaged through a pawed-over case of C-rations trying to find something suitable to eat. My hand closed on a can of fruit cocktail. I hadn't expected to find that. Fruit cocktail was second only to peaches on the hierarchy of preferred foods.

I avoided the captain's throne and tipped an empty fifty ammo can on end and sat down. It felt like sitting in a little kid's chair, with my knees almost even with my ears. This was only a slight exaggeration. In a country where everyone squatted instead of sitting, I guessed it was OK to use a position that was somewhere between sitting and squatting.

I opened the can of fruit cocktail with the P-38 that I carried on the chain around my neck. The chain also held a St. Christopher medal. My dog tags were on my boots, held in place by the laces. I ate the fruit cocktail, and it was gone long before I wanted it to be.

We talked and joked for a while until I became uncomfortably aware that I still had work to do. I excused myself by saying that I needed to see Lieutenant Duff. It wasn't urgent that I see him at that moment, but I wanted to thank him for getting the reconnaissance helicopter for me. I was also thinking that maybe I could use the TOC bunker to do some planning.

As I walked toward the FSB entrance, I was acutely aware of the heat. We had been sitting in the open, no shade, each of us covered with tiny beads of perspiration on all of the exposed skin. Sergeant Finley, Sergeant Lee, and Andy were still there talking.

After entering the bunker, it took a while for my eyes to adjust to the dim light. It wasn't that it was so dark inside; it was because the light outside was so intensely bright. As soon as my eyes adjusted, I located Lieutenant Duff. He was talking on the radio, seated with his back to me.

One of the clerks also with his back to me was the first to turn around and notice me standing there.

The formalities were over quickly, and I was given a clean table to work at. I placed my notepad on the table and carefully spread my map out. I noticed that the map was becoming worn. When the lieutenant could spare the time, I would share with him what I had discovered on my recon flight.

I was lost in deep thought. I had roughly sketched how I wanted the company perimeter placed in the clearing that I had scouted this morning. For the task of finding a suitable logger site, at this point, there was only one plan, plan A. I had also traced a route on my map from the FSB to the clearing.

At that point I became aware of lieutenant Duff peering over my left shoulder.

I scooted my folding chair back and stood next to the lieutenant so both of us could bend over the table. I briefed him with as much detail as I could recall. I included the time slot that Major Anderson had given me until our departure from the FSB.

It was cooler in the bunker, and this made for comfortable working conditions. I asked the lieutenant to estimate the boundaries of our AO by drawing them on my map. I expected him to hurriedly sketch the lines; instead, he went to his desk and returned with a clear overlay. He placed the overlay carefully on my map, and, by lifting the corners and edges of the overlay, he scribed a series of dots. By connecting the dots, he was able to provide a precise outline of the area where we would soon be working. The shape of the AO was four-sided. It reminded me of a lopsided, upside-down kite. It didn't matter. I was relieved to see that the clearing was a full klick (one thousand meters) inside the boundary.

I then discussed the position of the clearing that I had chosen as the company logger site. I didn't ask any questions. I merely spoke to what I had already decided. Lieutenant Duff was interested in all that I was telling him, and he was agreeing with each of my decisions.

I explained to the lieutenant that maps were one of the things that I still needed. Forget the newer, updated map that I had requested. What I needed was a fresh copy for each of the NCOs who would be leading patrols. In addition, I would need one for myself and one each for Andy and Sergeant Finley.

"You know, sir, I really need a new aerial map of the AO. I hope I can get one with enough detail."

Lieutenant Duff was scratching the side of his head as he studied the aerial map that I had laid out on the table.

"Give me just a minute. I may be able to help you." He headed back across the room to his desk and began leafing through a file drawer. "Ah, yes, here it is." He lifted a large folded document out of the file drawer to the height of his face. As he turned back toward me, he closed the file drawer without looking with a push of his right knee.

Lieutenant Duff returned to his spot at the table and began unfolding a very large aerial map. It was an aerial photograph of Fire Support Base Georgia and the surrounding area.

The FSB was close to the center of the map, and the detail was amazing. I could pick out the six gun pits and make out the individual 105s that swiveled in each pit. As small as they appeared on the map, they were clearly there and identifiable. The two Quonset huts covered with sandbags and serving as bunkers for the artillery and the one that I was in stood out even more. After a quick study of the FSB, I let my eyes wander. The minefield wasn't indicated on this map either. I then looked to the right, which was east on the map, and the direction of our company's assigned AO.

Something wasn't quite right. It occurred to me that the map wasn't oriented. I commented to the lieutenant that I needed to orient the map and gave it a quarter turn so that what had been east was turned toward us and north on the map was now to our right. At last both the map and the ground we stood on aligned with true north.

It didn't take long to realize that this map didn't cover all of the company's assigned AO. The clearing at the southern edge of the rubber plantation that I was searching for was in the center of the map directly in front of us. The clearing was quite close to the edge of the paper. The eastern 25 to 30 percent of the AO was missing. The east edge of the map bisected a butte that was located in the basin to the south and slightly east of the clearing.

This was a great map, and I was sure that I could use it. The map wasn't designed to show elevation, but because of the shading or changes in the vegetation, I could see the side of the butte and could make out a smaller butte or rise in elevation farther to the west and south. The variations in the vegetation from rubber trees to jungle stood out with good contrast. Within the shades of greens and yellows, thin blue lines indicating small streams and drainages snaked their way across the map generally in north-south direction. Some of these drainages were quite large and developed into deep valleys and ravines.

I stood up straight in order to stretch my back, and Lieutenant Duff followed my lead.

"How can I get a map like this one?" I asked.

The lieutenant couldn't remember where the map had come from, but given some time, he thought he could come up with one. I was thinking that every other photo or picto map that I had seen was a little fuzzy. None of the maps came close to the detail I had just seen. If Lieutenant Duff wasn't able to produce another picto map, I would ask for his copy.

He had only a half dozen topographical maps on hand, and he gave me all of them on the spot. He assured me that he would have more within a day or two.

I felt as if I had accomplished a lot, and I was ready to meet with the company NCOs and share with them what had been done that day. I still held out hope that we would get a new CO before we had to leave the FSB. The company was going to get all of the supplies and special equipment that I had asked for. We also had received an extra three and a half days to prepare for our departure. With the details of preparing the company for the upcoming mission, I had all but discarded the radical idea that I had thought of immediately after leaving the battalion tactical meeting. The idea was still fresh in my mind, but it was fading fast. My initial thought that I didn't have the guts to go through with such a plan was proving true. So I immersed all of my energy into busily preparing the company for the mission. I didn't like it, but that was the way it was.

When I stepped out of the bunker, I was shocked at the time. I had spent the entire afternoon in the bunker. I was left with a lot to do in a short time. I hadn't needed to worry. The company NCOs had already gotten together and posted the perimeter guard duty. The command track driver and TC would again help Sergeant Pomeroy and third platoon. Sergeant Rios was going to do the night ambush patrol in the rubber trees, and he was being more ambitious than I wanted him to be. He had picked a spot for his ambush next to the road where the rubber trees veered away from the road and a patch of jungle began. I was concerned because of how far away it was from the company's position. If his patrol got into trouble, it would take a while for the company to be able to reach his position.

Sergeant Moore, Sergeant Finley, and Sergeant Lee joined me as soon as I cut between the mortar platoon and third platoon. I was informed about the guard duty and the ambush patrol as we walked. Sergeant Rios and the patrol were already headed out and walking up the road before they would angle into the rubber trees.

This would be the best time to meet with the company's NCOs. I felt it was necessary to include more than just the acting platoon leaders. We met at Sergeant Finley's mortar track. I didn't waste their time with any unnecessary details. I outlined the supply shipment that we were getting in the morning. Sergeant Pomeroy was assigned to intercept the supplies. I handed him a copy of what was coming so he could verify everything. I spent the most time on the three planned reconnaissance flights. I was able to confirm that I had located a suitable logger site. I went into some more details about how the site could best be defended. After that I explained what I had in mind for the third day's recon flight. I would have the pilot fly low all over the southern end of the basin. I wanted it to look as if we were interested in LZs and logger sites in that area. Before the meeting ended, I promised new maps and reminded them that the gas grenades were coming later.

The meeting hadn't taken as long as I had thought it might. I was hungry and needed my own downtime.

I ate a cold can of pork and beans while I wrote a letter to my wife Kate. Wow! Did I miss her. I had no trouble thinking of what to say. The words flowed easily as I reminisced about our time together. I had time for a second letter to one of my aunts in Minnesota. My Mother and Father moved to Oregon in 1944 leaving all of their families in Minnesota. I was born in Oregon but returned to Minnesota for family reunions. I got to know my aunts while I was growing up, and now I can't begin to express how much I appreciated my aunts' letters and what they meant to me. It took some time for me to realize that my aunts had done this before.

My father was the youngest of a large family. When he was a small boy, his parents died, and he was raised by his older sisters, who were married and had children his age. My father's sisters absolutely doted over him at family reunions. My father was affectionately referred to as Little Lawrence, even as a grown man. When Little Lawrence's son was drafted and sent to Vietnam, my aunts were there to support me. They were master letter writers and corresponded regularly.

In our letters the war was never mentioned. My aunts wrote about what was happening in the family. In return, I tried to tell them about news that I had received from my wife and father. I also described the weather, wildlife that I had sighted, and some of the life of the Vietnamese civilians.

The company seemed to get along fine with or without my presence. The driver and TC were headed for third platoon to check in with Sergeant Pomeroy. Ron was washing his hands trying to get the grease off. During the day Ron had been helping a driver and TC from the third platoon work on their APC's engine. Andy had been writing a letter.

The mail had arrived by helicopter around 1100 hours, and we were aware that during the last few days we had all gotten behind in our letter writing, especially me. Letters were our main link to the world and friends and families back home.

The night was fast approaching, and I had gotten through another day. The temperature had cooled just enough and was very pleasant. It was starting to get dark. Everything was quiet. The insects and jungle night sounds were just beginning to increase in volume. No lights or noise of any kind emitted from the company area. One had to look closely to even see any of the men, but each track had one or more men sitting on top. Today there were a few hammocks strung between some of the tracks.

Ron, Andy, and I were all sitting on top of the track with the radios, not talking, but just listening to the building crescendo of the humming of the insects. Far out in the rubber trees, some animal or bird was emitting a strange call.

This was the third night since Captain Cooper had left us. Both he and Captain Sorenson had predicted we would have a new CO by now, so why didn't we?

I could taste the acid in my stomach as I recreated the memory of the tactical meeting with Lieutenant Colonel Dumford.

At that moment I had a revelation.

Bravo Company wasn't going to get a new CO until that NVA regiment was smoked out. My company really was being sacrificed. The force of the realization hit me with such a jolt that my heart rate quickened, and I was drawing my breath in short, quick gasps. I had missed all the signs. How could I have been so dense? It was finally glaringly obvious that Captain Sorenson had been trying to signal me, to warn me. They all had been trying to send me a signal. I was ashamed of myself now, as I recalled having hurt feelings because I thought everyone's reaction to me was because I wasn't an officer, that I was merely out of my element and not to be accepted. I was embarrassed now that I realized how wrong I had been.

The company commanders and the others who were present had already had the real meeting. They already knew what was in store for Bravo Company. Worst of all, they had been forced to sit and listen to me and my company getting the shaft. I could clearly picture Captain Sorenson's expression. I remembered the others' unwavering stares. They were all trying to warn me. I remembered the stiff body language of the men seated around me and how they all seemed so angry. Well, now I realized what they were angry about and why they acted the way they had.

It was crystal clear to me that I had been set up from the beginning. The stares, the removal of Lieutenant Jones so the company would have no officers, not being allowed to speak at the meeting were proof. The meeting was already over before I made my appearance, and the rest had been a charade to keep me in the dark.

Well, I knew now! I was convinced that I had figured it all out and was seeing the big picture.

It was time to start worrying again. With the detailed intelligence report and the nature of our mission, I was more convinced than ever that there really was an NVA regiment in the area.

The idea that I came up with when I was walking back from the battalion tactical meeting, as unrealistic as it was at the time, now became more than a serious consideration. I thought I might have the guts after all.

I was surer than ever before that I could follow through as I began considering all of the what-ifs.

Andy was tapping me lightly on the shoulder for radio watch. I was already fully awake. My mind had been elsewhere, and now it was time for my last radio watch of the night.

Sergeant Rios's ambush patrol was going without a hitch. I had the predawn radio watch, and I was freezing. The poncho liner had slid off to one side. Once I had the liner readjusted, I hoped that I could get warm again before daylight. The morning was progressing smoothly. I had managed to trap some heat and had regained a degree of comfort as light appeared in the east and grew until it was time to heat water for coffee.

Sergeant Rios radioed that he had just picked up his mechanical ambush and was headed back.

Yesterday there had been a few fluffy clouds in the sky late in the afternoon. It wouldn't be long before we could expect regular afternoon showers.

I was finishing my first cup of coffee with some peanut butter and crackers. At the same time, I was gathering the gear that I would take with me on the recon flight. It was impossible for me to relax. I knew that before this day was over, I was going to have to make a decision as to how the company was going to operate in the new AO.

A blast of automatic M-16 rifle fire came from up the road. The sound was that of just one rifle, but on full automatic. It had been a long burst of over half a magazine. I was well aware, as was everyone else, that it had to be Sergeant Rios's patrol.

Andy was on the radio and hustling toward third platoon and the road. I was right behind him and moving just as quickly. Sergeant Pomeroy and most of third platoon were standing in the road and staring up the road to the north.

Harlan was the first to say anything. "Well, at least Coe ain't with 'em."

The patrol appeared, angling out of the rubber trees and onto the road. They were well over a hundred meters from where we were standing, and it took a while for them to reach us. I studied the patrol as they came closer, and they looked relaxed. There seemed to be nothing wrong or out of the ordinary, and by the time they reached us, there was quite a group waiting in front of third platoon.

I knew that it was nothing serious when I saw that Sergeant Rios was grinning.

Bey and half of the patrol turned in to the perimeter and headed for their tracks, and half of the crowd went with them.

"Norm shot a cobra, and it was a big sucker, at least ten feet long."

Norm interrupted. "I was on point, and it rose up right in front of me. It had its neck all flattened out and was swaying a little back and forth. It happened so fast. I stitched it. Got a good look at it and went around it, and here we are."

Norm and Sergeant Rios, as well as the other members of the patrol, would be telling the story over and over to anyone who would listen for the rest of the day.

A glance at my watch indicated that the LOH and Rock would be arriving soon for my recon, and so would the engineers. Sergeant Finley told me not to worry, that he and the mortar platoon would assist Sergeant Pomeroy with the supplies when they arrived. However, neither the handling of the supplies nor the recon flight was what I was worrying about.

It became apparent that the supplies would be there soon and would beat the LOH that I was waiting for. The engineers were coming. I could see dust in the distance up the road. There was nothing for me to do but wait, worry, and think.

13

The dust indeed was stirred aloft by the engineers. Each day it seemed to grow worse and hang in the air longer.

There was the deuce and a half with our supplies following the engineers. Sergeant Pomeroy and Sergeant Finley had six or seven men with them. They had things covered, so I could concentrate on my map study. I mentally sketched in the routes that I wanted to fly today. Special points of interest such as the buttes and the larger waterways were circled on my map. I wrote some of the coordinates in the map's margins.

I was thinking that my M-16 would just be in the way, but it went everywhere with me. It was like an added appendage. I wouldn't leave it behind.

I was as ready as I could be, and it still wasn't 0900 yet. Sergeant Pomeroy and Sergeant Finley's crew had everything unloaded, accounted for, and neatly displayed at the mortar platoon's location. I especially noticed the ninety-millimeter recoilless rifle. It stood out because its size and its shape made it unmistakable.

The engineers had turned around and were already headed back up the road to the north. It still perplexed me that we were given a 1000 hours ETA for the engineers on the seventeenth of February, yet on most days like today, they had the road cleared of mines and were on their way back before 0900. It didn't make much sense to me, but there was no use being upset about that. I would never find out the why. Damn army.

The clock was moving slowly, and I still had some time. A lot had happened since the morning of the sixteenth of February. My revelation of the night before was clearly embedded in my preparations for the company's upcoming mission. Who knows what I might have decided to do if I hadn't figured things out when I did. Now my preparations were full speed ahead. I knew exactly what I was going to do. There would be no hesitation or rethinking at this point because I had made my commitment. All that was left for me to do was convince the NCOs and men of the company. My only uncertainty at this point was when should I present the plan and inform the company. I didn't have much time left, but it seemed to me that the best time to inform everyone would be tomorrow close to noon. That would correspond with our departure time.

Sergeant Moore was heading toward the command track. I had already briefed Andy and him about my recon flight. In my absence Sergeant Moore would be in charge of the company, so he needed to operate from the command track. He showed up with a book. That was about right, since neither of us expected anything to happen while I was gone. I planned to be busy when I returned from the recon flight. I would have more information to process, and this time tomorrow, the company would be making preparations to leave. Again I reminded myself of how little time I actually had.

About thirty seconds before 0900, the sound of an approaching LOH coming from the north could be heard. This pilot was punctual to the second. Rock came straight in and landed without circling, so the helicopter was facing the FSB. The skids barely touched the ground and were slightly shimmering back and forth less than an inch or two over the packed earth.

As soon as the LOH touched down, I was on my way. With my pockets crammed full with maps, notepads, pens, and pencils, I clutched my M-16 and the bandolier of ammunition and ran to the LOH. I had more gear with me today than I had yesterday.

I was relieved to see that Rock was piloting the LOH. After our first flight together, I felt that we had a rapport, and I liked working with Rock. He greeted me with a huge smile that showed almost all of his teeth. He yelled above the engine noise, "Welcome. Today we will be continuing our aerial tour of lovely South Vietnam." He then added, "It's the same procedure as yesterday." He pointed to the rear seat where the commo helmet rested.

Like a Jekyll and Hyde, he switched to his other persona and projected the businesslike seriousness needed to accomplish the job at hand.

By the time I had the commo helmet on and adjusted, we were already airborne. I began to outline what I wanted to accomplish and what I wanted to see. As Rock gained altitude, he circled to the west of the FSB, and we headed south as he digested what I had to say.

I felt I was giving him too much information as I told him about finding the logger site yesterday. I knew we had talked about the site, but I let him know that a final decision had been made. I wanted to be sure we didn't go near there today, because I didn't want Charlie to think that we had any interest in that area at all. Rock understood exactly what I wanted to do.

At his suggestion, we would start even farther to the south of the AO and work our way north. That way, when we decoyed tomorrow's flight, we would be covering some of the same areas twice. I was satisfied; we would go with Rock's suggestion.

We flew south for what seemed like quite a while before we turned east. The terrain here in the south was much more open. There were rice paddies on the low land, and at the higher elevations, with the characteristic red soil, a variety of other crops had been planted. Tapioca fields dotted the area; it was one of the crops that I recognized simply because it was a favorite of mine back in the world. The farther to the east we went, the thicker the jungle became. It really wasn't important for me to pay such close attention to this area since we weren't going to be in this part of the battalion AO, yet it was still fascinating.

At last, the land below us turned to mostly jungle with an occasional agricultural plot. Rock circled the open areas and would then dip down for a lower pass. He was making it look as if we were interested in the area. Every time the helicopter descended, I hoped we wouldn't be a target for some zealous Viet Cong. The area that we were flying over seemed to be a likely place to find Charlie. The area was remote, with many places to hide and escape routes in practically every direction. It was close to food sources and population centers. I was alert knowing that this was Charlie's element. I knew that we were well within the range of the FSB's 105s in the event that we should take fire. I could assume that Rock would call in the coordinates and that would be it.

Back and forth, back and forth, circle and dip, circle and dip as we worked our way north. Just a few more passes, and we would be close enough to begin observing the southern boundary of the company's AO. There were several good LZ clearings right at the south edge of the battalion AO. I was pleased with myself for already locating the LZs when I had met with Lieutenant Duff on the previous day. The information that I had scribed on my map was coming in handy, and we wouldn't have to waste any time on tomorrow's flight to deceive Charlie.

After we dropped in altitude to circle the clearing located farthest to the east, we were approaching from the east with the sun at our back. Rock was flying at treetop level when he turned abruptly and quickly gained altitude. We had both seen the same thing at the same instant. What we saw was a flash of light from a reflection. Not sure exactly what we had seen, and not wanting to go trolling for enemy fire, we decided to notify the artillery personnel when we returned. Lieutenant Duff or the artillery people could decide whether or not to fire a blind fire mission. I was actually hoping they would decide on a fire mission. That would give my decoy idea more validity.

The farther to the north our passes took us, the thicker the jungle became. No water could be seen where the maps indicated waterways or streams. The jungle vegetation was too thick.

The terrain that we had just flown over oozed Charlie. I was happy that the company's assigned AO wasn't to the south of the FSB. I can't explain why the area that we had just flown over had spooked me so much. It felt as if there could be a VC behind every bush. I was also thankful that I had found a defendable logger site at the edge of the rubber trees to the north. I was more than a little relieved that we weren't being sent into the area that I had just observed.

I remembered that Alpha Company was south of the FSB and somewhere to the west of where we were flying. I couldn't worry about Alpha Company, but I did have a new respect for them.

The territory that we were flying over currently was directly adjacent to my company's AO. We were also getting close to our last few east-west passes. It had been a while since we had dipped down and flown at treetop level. We were flying at altitude now.

I tried to be more focused on the terrain here. With the sun at mid-morning height and still in the east, I was getting the best look that I could of the south sides of the buttes. I wished that I had a pair of binoculars. How had I overlooked that? Artillery had binoculars, and I could definitely have used a pair at the moment.

I was noticing something, but I just couldn't be certain. I was concentrating on the larger of the two buttes. Its proximity to the logger site on the map put it less than two klicks away. What I thought I was seeing was less vegetation on the southeast slope. That was why I needed a pair of binoculars. There appeared to be less vegetation in the understory. After I discussed my suspicions with Rock, we both took one last hard look on the last pass going west. He couldn't say for sure, but he thought that I was onto something. It made a lot of sense to me that the southeast slope of the butte would be an ideal place for a bunker complex. The slope provided drainage, and it received the morning sun and afternoon shade.

The fuel situation necessitated that it was time to head back. We returned to the FSB by coming around the south side and circling around the west side to the helipad. This time when Rock set the helicopter down, it was facing north and parallel to the road. This was just the opposite of his arrival.

Rock agreed to be there at the same time on the next day. We were beginning to know each other better, and we had much more to talk about today as I gathered my maps and M-16. Placing the commo helmet in the same place that I'd found it, I opened the door and jumped down. I had had just enough time to shut the door and begin my hunched-over sprint clear of the rotors when I heard Rock taking off straight north.

Standing on the road, the company looked the same as when I had left. Of course, that was exactly what I had expected to see.

My plans were to first check in with Sergeant Moore and Andy. I would then double check the supplies that were still stacked by the mortar platoon. How they would be dispensed could be handled later. As soon as that was done, I would have something to eat and then head for Lieutenant Duff's bunker. That thought was my reminder. I had almost forgotten. I was still standing on the road, but instead of heading into the company area, I dashed directly to the bunker to report the glint of light from the reflection that Rock and I had seen. I had eight-digit coordinates for the lieutenant. I hurriedly gave my report and left, telling the nearest clerk that I would be returning shortly.

Back inside the company perimeter, I was with Sergeant Pomeroy, Sergeant Finley, and Sergeant Moore looking over the ninety-millimeter rifle when the artillery battery opened up with a fire mission. The timing and the direction that the guns were shooting indicated that they were targeting the map coordinates that I had just given Lieutenant Duff. I couldn't suppress a smile. They were actually doing it. I had to be sure to tell Rock in the morning.

Tomorrow's recon flight could be much more dangerous if things had gotten stirred up by the fire mission, because I was convinced that there were VC in the area.

I told Andy and the three sergeants that the company NCOs would be meeting much earlier today. They needed to make sure that none of the NCOs were scheduled for an OP guard duty so we could have everyone present. I had some things to talk over with Lieutenant Duff, and I would like to meet as soon as I returned from the bunker.

At today's company meeting, the NCOs would learn the details of movement to the new logger site. I planned to do some things differently than the company was used to. The defense and security of the location would be covered in detail. As soon as we arrived at the clearing, there would be an immediate need for a couple of scouting riffs to check out the surrounding terrain. There would be no need to wait before scheduling those patrols or the night ambush patrols. The other thing that I wanted to cover was how to incorporate the gas grenades into a mechanical ambush.

It wasn't yet noon, but I was hungry. I was also anxious to get to the bunker and get my planning started. I found a can of pork slices in the box of C-rations. The command track shared one case of C-rations at a time.

With five of us, a case got picked over pretty fast. The individual meals were opened for the chewing tobacco and toilet paper, leaving the individual cans loose in the box. The idea of eating the pork slices cold was unbearable, so I heated them along with a cup of coffee.

It didn't take me long to eat, and then I was headed back to see Lieutenant Duff. The lieutenant had become an unexpected source of support. He didn't seem like such a bad guy now.

When I entered the bunker, it took the same amount of time for my eyes to adjust to the artificial light. I worked at the same table. Right away, today was different from yesterday. Lieutenant Duff and both clerks were at my table as soon as I was opening my map and setting my notepad down.

The fire mission had them excited since I had initiated it, and all three of them wanted more information. Without waiting, Lieutenant Duff asked for a briefing of the recon flight.

I went into as much detail as I could remember. With the notes that I had written in the margin on my map, I was confident that I hadn't missed anything. I showed them the spot on the map next to the clearing where Rock and I had seen the reflection. I took some time to describe the view from the air and the surrounding area.

The lieutenant asked, "Did you get to see your entire AO?"

I was feeling good as I answered, "Yes, sir." I then pointed to the larger of the two buttes on the map that I had also circled. It took more than a few seconds to explain my suspicions. It took extra time to explain what I thought both Rock and I had observed on the slope of the butte. A lack of undergrowth vegetation created a strong likelihood that there was a bunker complex at that location. I just couldn't be 100 percent sure.

The lieutenant then made an assumption that with the area now covered by the reconnaissance flyover, this should conclude the reconnaissance of the AO.

"Have you informed the LOH pilot that he won't be needed tomorrow?"

I was taken a little by surprise. I quickly explained the decoy plan.

The lieutenant wasn't having any of it. He argued that today's flight had accomplished enough of a decoy. We went back and forth for a while, and he finally relented when I said that I could assess the results of the recent fire mission. He did want the area of the fire mission checked out. That little glint of a reflection had saved the third day's flight.

I outlined details of my scheduled meeting with the company's NCOs. I made my outline on my notepad at the same time that I was verbalizing the information for Lieutenant Duff. All of the information pertinent to the beginning of the mission was covered. I needed his input in order to make sure that I hadn't left anything out.

The lieutenant was most intrigued with how I planned to use the gas grenades. He had never heard of such a thing, because at least three times he remarked, "That's so simple."

I had everything that I needed for my meeting with the company NCOs except the maps. Once again the lieutenant had come through. He produced one dozen crisp new maps. They happened to be the latest artillery maps. After a quick examination, I noticed that the clarity was good and the necessary detail was there; however, I also noticed that the minefield wasn't shown on this map either.

First impressions obviously didn't work for me. The first time I had met Lieutenant Duff, I wasn't impressed at all. At the present time, however, things were different. Lieutenant Duff had become a major contributor to the company and an advisor to me. I had grown to like him and respect him. He had become an unlikely source of support.

I was ready to begin the mission. All that was left was to inform the company and begin preparations for our departure, and I was on my way back to the company perimeter to inform the NCOs of the marching orders and details for the start of the mission.

As I cleared the FSB entrance, Andy intercepted me with news from Top. Some maps and the gas grenades would be arriving in the morning with the engineers. Now we would have everything that I had requested. Even if we didn't use some of the items, it was reassuring to have them available.

I no sooner arrived at the command track than the NCOs came. Each had been instructed to bring his M-16 and a bandolier of ammunition. I planned to patrol a short distance into the rubber trees and demonstrate how to incorporate the gas grenades into a mechanical ambush.

The meeting started at the mortar platoon, where the supplies were still neatly stacked. I began by giving each NCO one of the new maps. I then informed the men that we would get to the maps in a moment.

Starting with the ammunition, I laid out how it would be distributed to the platoons. The grenades, star clusters, smoke grenades, and radio batteries I also divided among the platoons. The starlight scopes and the ninety-millimeter rifle would ride with the command track so they could be shared by all. I emphasized that each night ambush would have a starlight scope available to them, and they were encouraged to use any and all of the equipment that the company could now provide for them.

The next item on my agenda was the maps. I had each of the men open his map. I then showed them how I had folded my map in order to show the company's new AO. I made sure that each person saw my map with the company AO outlined. It wasn't necessary for them to have the AO outlined on their maps, but I wanted them to see our proximity to the FSB.

We were finally ready to discuss orders for the mission. There would be no mention of the 199th NVA regiment in the area. That was already a well-known rumor. All of my references to the enemy would name Charlie, the army's nickname for the VC.

The men were already studying their new maps as I gave them the coordinates of the clearing that would serve as the company logger site—the same one that I had discovered on my reconnaissance flight. Next I went into detail about how we would defend our position, pausing often to allow for questions.

The mortar platoon would park on the south side of the clearing just back from the rock face that dropped sharply to the jungle below; because of the terrain, we had only three sides of our perimeter to defend. The platoons would align from the west toward the FSB, with the first platoon on the west side. Third platoon would be next to the first platoon and in the center of the formation, facing north into the rubber trees. That left second platoon to cover the east side of the perimeter.

When the company moved to a new location, the men rode on top of the tracks, where there was plenty of room since all of our company's platoons were well short of the forty-plus men that a platoon was supposed to contain. The order of march would be second platoon on point, followed by the command track. Then would come the third platoon, followed by the mortar platoon, and first platoon providing the rear security.

The company would depart our current location by heading north up the road for one and one-half klicks. We would then enter the rubber trees and proceed east until it was time to turn right ninety degrees and head south.

I wanted to be able to approach the clearing as quietly as possible. I was hoping that the rubber trees would mask some of the APCs' engine noise.

When we approached the clearing, I wanted the tracks to shut down and wait in line back in the rubber trees while Sergeant Moore with Bey and enough men for security scouted the clearing. When we moved the tracks into place, there was to be none of the usual engine revving and knocking trees over as each track adjusted its position. We would ease in one at a time as quietly as we could.

A lot depended on how quietly we could move into place, so I instructed the NCOs to wait on deploying the RPG screens. We would consider putting up the screen after everyone was in place. I was afraid the noise of driving the stakes could be louder than the tracks themselves.

Immediately upon our arrival at the logger site, we would need two riffs to scout the company's flanks. That assignment would fall to the first and second platoons. They should each scout the area in front of their platoon's position out at least one klick. Each patrol would be following the edge of the rubber plantation where the jungle began. They should also be checking for places to set up night ambushes.

Sergeant Pomeroy was protesting, saying that third platoon wasn't pulling their weight. I assured him that they would have plenty to do, and the workload would quickly even out.

I was, at last, ready for my planned demonstration patrol into the rubber trees. We weren't going far; however, the patrol was still organized. It wasn't going to be a cluster.

"Sergeant Pomeroy, you have the point and slack." I was referring to Sergeant Pomeroy's lone squad leader, Sergeant Turner.

"Then first platoon, Sergeant Lee, is responsible for left and right security, and second platoon has rear security."

I carried four claymore mines, two to a bag, the straps crisscrossing my back and my chest. I also had four smoke grenades and a roll of tape. The smoke would represent the gas grenades for my demonstration.

I motioned for Sergeant Pomeroy to head out and indicated the direction with the same motion of my arm. After we had gone two hundred meters, I stopped the patrol, and we formed a fairly tight circle with me in the center.

I was able to place the claymores in a tight array without directly hooking up the battery that was carried in one of the bags along with explosive white det. cord, which looked like clothesline. I then produced the tape while I explained that the gas grenades that I had mentioned yesterday would be arriving in the morning.

The demonstration was a success, and we reversed order back to the perimeter. I was thinking hard, trying to remember if I had covered everything that I had wanted cover at this meeting. For the moment I was satisfied. I would explain the plan in full to this same group tomorrow just before we left the FSB.

As it turned out, it was later than I anticipated. I hadn't planned for this meeting to take as long as it did. Sergeant Moore and Sergeant Lee informed me as soon as we entered the company area and the rest of the NCOs were excused that they would take care of the LPs' guard duty schedule, the night ambush, and perimeter guard duty.

Sergeant Finley and Sergeant Pomeroy were lounging at the command track, just wanting to visit. I had an insistent urge to tell them my plan—at least run it by them. It was very hard for me to keep my mouth shut, but I was able to repress it. Tomorrow would be soon enough for everyone in the company to know. The two of them hung around for most of an hour. We weren't talking as much as we normally would. Our entertainment was Ron, who was making a chocolate cake. He was making a paste from several packs of cocoa that would be the frosting for a C-ration pound cake. The pound cake wasn't chocolate, but the frosting was. The cake had been delicately placed on a piece of the corrugated white paper that lined the cracker cans. After the decoration was complete, the cake was admired for only seconds before Ron devoured it.

Ron eating the cake signaled that the entertainment was over, so Sergeant Pomeroy and Sergeant Finley returned to their platoons.

Temperature-wise, it was once again the most comfortable time of the day, and we were taking advantage of the situation by lounging in the jeep seats on top of the track. I searched the sky for clouds. I could see a few fluffs of clouds in the west, where there was a lingering glow of light. I had been aware that there were more clouds this afternoon than the day before. The afternoon rains were coming. It could happen any day now.

When it began raining, we wouldn't be sitting on top of the track enjoying the weather. I vowed to take advantage of the moment for as long as I could.

The darkness of the night was soon fully upon us, and the insects seemed unusually loud. The sound of the insects was comforting, like the gurgle of running water or the gentle lapping of waves. When the insects became quiet, it was time to be on full alert.

While I had been working in Lieutenant Duff's bunker that afternoon, a group of Vietnamese civilians had come down the road in Lambrettas. They were vendors selling sandwiches, sodas, and beer, all for a dollar each. In comparison, we paid twenty cents apiece for a soda or a beer. One vendor had a selection of souvenirs that included some really gaudy artwork painted on black velvet, along with some metal bracelets, headbands, bead necklaces, and some embroidered sew-on patches that had obnoxious messages such as "Viet Cong Hunting Club."

I hadn't seen the vendors, as Ron and Andy were filling me in with all that they could remember. According to them, the sandwiches were really good. They consisted of white bread with mayonnaise, lettuce, tomato, a dark meat, a light meat, and cheese. Ron mentioned that Bey claimed that the dark meat was duck and the light meat was rat. I was sorry that I had missed out on a chance to have a good sandwich.

We were quite a ways off the beaten path, so the Lambrettas showing up at the FSB made me highly suspicious. You never knew whether any of the vendors could be affiliated with the Viet Cong and on a scouting mission.

The afternoon visitors had raised the hair on the back of my neck, so the night ambush would be up the road. Sergeant Lee had left the perimeter and headed directly toward the center of the rubber trees and was angling away from the road. The patrol would then circle back to the road at a point about halfway to where Sergeant Rios had been the night before. One of these nights, something was going to happen.

As the night progressed, there was the usual helicopter traffic in the distance. The sounds almost always were to the north of us. Sometime before midnight there was the sound of a distant firefight far to the west. We could see the familiar red tracer rounds of an M-60 machine gun arcing in the sky above the jungle. There was also one brief trail of green tracers crossing the red ones going in the opposite direction. The tracers disappeared. The firefight was over, and it remained quiet. Only the insects continued to hum. I had expected an artillery mission, but none occurred. The firefight was over in less than three or four minutes. Seeing the tracer rounds and judging their distance apart, the firefight most likely wasn't a close ambush. To my way of thinking it would have been a great opportunity to use artillery support. I kept looking in the direction of the distant firefight expecting at least for some gunships to show up, but no artillery and no gunships appeared. I was just about to lose interest when a parachute flare lit up the sky above where the firefight had taken place. From my viewpoint, the parachute flare drifted in the breeze just above the jungle. Then there were two flares in the sky. A third flare appeared just as the first flare burned out, and that was it. The show was over. Since there hadn't been any gunships or artillery in support of the contact, I could only assume that the firefight had been in some no-fire restricted zone.

The rest of the night went on without a hitch. The artillery battery remained quiet all night. I was pulling my usual guard duty as streaks of light began to appear in the east. As the sky got a little lighter, I noticed some tints of red. Were there distant clouds out over the Pacific, or was it smoke?

I was remembering my childhood and the many times when I had gotten up early to go fishing. I regarded my childhood as being as close to perfect as any life could be. I had a bicycle, a fishing pole, and a BB gun. What more could a boy growing up in a rural community want?

Dawn arrived, and it was now as light as it could get with the sun still below the horizon. On the west side of the road, in the direction of the minefield, several thin layers of fog were suspended, about head high. Being only a foot or two thick, the air beneath the fog was as clear as a bell, and so was the air above the fog, as I could see the jungle above it in the distance. The sight of the thin layer of suspended fog made me shiver and at the same time try to capture the moment as an artistic memory. It was eerie and beautiful at the same time.

More people were stirring now. Andy took over the radio and informed me that Sergeant Lee was already on his way back. It was earlier than usual and his patrol wasn't that far away, but today was departure day.

Well, this was going to be a big day, and I was confident, much more confident than I had been at any time during the last three days.

14

The early morning of February 20 mirrored the previous day. For someone viewing the company, there wasn't even a hint that Bravo Company was going to leave the FSB. Preparations to leave would begin after I had left for the decoy reconnaissance flight over the south end of the battalion AO and the jungle basin where it began to thin out and became agricultural land. My departure was the company's signal to begin making preparations, and by the time I returned, the APG screens and the stakes that supported the screens would be tightly rolled and fastened to top of the APCs, across the rear just above the ramp.

Today it wasn't necessary for me to closely study my map in preparation for the flight, but I studied it for another reason. I was focusing on another area. I went over the company's travel route to the next logger site, tracing the route that I had chosen through the rubber trees. I spent even more time studying the terrain on both sides of the logger site. The east side looked to be the most challenging. A valley of jungle starting to the northeast of the site continually widened as it dropped in elevation as it spread out to the south. This strip of jungle separated a southward projecting finger of the rubber plantation farther to the east from the rubber trees surrounding the logger site. The map contour lines indicated a series of gullies angling into the larger depression of the valley. This strip of jungle lined up almost directly north of the larger butte, and I had strong suspicions about the larger butte. As I continued to study the map, it was easy to see that the area to the east of where the company would be located posed the most obvious threat. I could picture NVA soldiers moving freely through the area. It was a hauntingly scary thought. It was OK to be scared, but at the moment, I couldn't afford time to dwell on being scared.

There was a lot to think about. My thoughts returned to what I was about to propose to the entire company. I had better be right, because there wasn't much time left. Was I crazy to be developing such an idea and actually thinking that it would work?

I had played team sports in high school and college. You go to practice. You practice hard for your playing time. You work to improve your skills because you want to be a winner. You do what the coaches say. Playing time is earned in practice; hence, your success depends on your ability to conform. The army was the same way. I did what I was told, and I always tried to do my best. So now, why was I putting myself out on a limb and sawing it off? How had I gotten to this point?

I hadn't chosen the army. The army chose me when they drafted me. With my background and personality, the sports analogy worked to sort out what I was feeling. I felt that my army experiences to this point closely paralleled my sports experiences, at least in the way I chose to participate.

There was a lot more that I needed to know and wanted to know before I told the company what I had in mind, so I was back to looking at the map again. The line on the map where the rubber trees met the jungle was fairly straight. The terrain was similar to the west all the way to the FSB. This area warranted being watched closely also. The area to the west of the site wasn't as steep, and a series of gullies provided easy travel routes out of the basin and into the rubber trees, which provided for fast travel with overhead cover.

My only concern was that I had to be right when I made a decision, and I had to get it right on the first try. Once again, I turned my attention to the route the company would take to get to the new location from the FSB. I was trying to judge how far the sound of sixteen moving APCs would carry. It was an impossible conclusion.

Charlie might hear us and know we were coming, but we would be much quieter on this mission than any previous one.

The sound of an approaching LOH snapped my attention from the map, which I was now folding to put back into the leg pocket of my trousers. I was searching the sky as I stepped from the corner of the third platoon track to the middle of the road and waited.

In seconds the helicopter was in sight, and I glanced at my watch. It was a habit that I couldn't help. I had this need to coordinate the time with whatever was happening, and, sure enough, it was a perfect replay of the day before. The LOH landed the same way. Without circling it was facing the FSB, and the time was exactly 0900.

As I bent at the waist and shifted my M-16 to my left hand, I leaned into the stiff breeze created by the force of the rotors. Today the air was warmer than I remembered from the previous days, as I was getting blasted by warm air; yet it was still relatively early in the day. With a slight nod and a grin as I made eye contact with Rock, I slid into my usual seat and put on the commo helmet.

I initiated the conversation with a "Good morning, Rock."

Rock returned my greeting with "Hello, Jerry."

This time Rock didn't do the Vietnam tour routine. I liked Rock, it goes without saying, and I was sure that he liked me also. I was aware that today would be the last time we would see each other.

In Vietnam you made friends and you lost friends. Close attachments were avoided. There was no need for promises that couldn't be kept. Rock and I had become friends, yes, but we were also just doing our jobs.

The helicopter rose and turned west, making a wide circle around the FSB as it gained altitude before heading south. There seemed to be less to say today. Together Rock and I had previously planned what we wanted to accomplish on this flight.

I finally found an opportunity to tell Rock about the fire mission as a result of our sighting of that reflection from the day before. We were both somewhat eager to view the results of the artillery barrage.

Today Rock wanted to talk about baseball. He was a Boston Red Sox fan, and he vacationed in Florida every year during spring training. Spring training would be just getting started. He insisted that this would be the year that the Sox would beat the Yankees and overcome the Bambino's curse. I wasn't going to get involved in this discussion, at least not very deeply. Rock was a very passionate fan!

Rock mentioned that he could never forget his DEROS, since it was the same time as the all-star break in July.

We were turning east now, and it was time to get serious. We would soon be circling and dipping.

I was searching the rice paddies, the dikes, the groves, and the fields for signs of life. The agriculture was laid out neatly using all available space. What I finally noticed was that there were no people visible. There were no civilians working the fields or paddies. Someone had to maintain them to their present state. This was indeed strange, and it seemed to have only one answer: Charlie had to be somewhere nearby. The civilians would know when Charlie was around, and they would want to avoid being caught in a cross fire.

When I told Rock my suspicions, he said that he had been thinking the same thing. He randomly circled some of the fields. He was careful to stay away from the patches of vegetation on the knolls and hilltops. When we dipped to the treetops, Rock increased the helicopter's speed and made sure that there was jungle on both sides of us.

We had logged several east-west passes and were slowly working our way north. It would be a while yet before we could get a good view of the clearing adjacent to where the artillery barrage had been directed the day before.

The agricultural land was giving way to jungle as the LOH continued circling the clearings and increasing speed for a treetop run. I could see the breaks in the jungle where the northernmost clearings were. I remembered that there were three potential LZs in an east-west line. The opening in the jungle farthest to the east was where we had directed the artillery strike.

We were headed east into the sun when I got my first good look at the most westerly of the openings. The westernmost clearing was the largest of the three and oval shaped. I couldn't tell why no jungle grew there, but I suspected that under the yellow-green tall grass were basalt rocks. The rocks could be as large as watermelons or larger. The grass would hide the rocks. The clearing appeared to be slightly elevated as if it was the top of a knoll or a small hill.

Two hundred meters to the west of the clearing that we were studying, we could see the remnants of an old road or trail cutting through the vegetation. This section of jungle was more brush than trees. There were none of the tall, stately trees that formed the double and triple canopy jungle that I was used to seeing. If the taller trees were in place, we wouldn't have been able to see the trail.

The trail had to fork or turn off of the dirt road that continued south of the FSB. This was a very likely spot for an American combat unit to show up. The access was there. Flying the same area today as yesterday put my nerves on edge and had me being extra vigilant. I had the same feeling as the day before. Add to that the fact that the civilians had left the area. This area scared me because it had food and cover to support a large enemy force.

Rock and I talked about the probability of this spot as Rock made some extra passes. He then gained altitude and continued to circle the area. I was more convinced than ever that Charlie was watching us and was taking notes. The VC would be waiting in the area and expecting an American unit to show up for a surprise party.

It was finally time to move on, and we continued flying east into the sun. When we arrived at the next clearing, we spent less time circling and flying at treetop level. This clearing also appeared to be a small hilltop. It was steeper than the site we had just left. The slope was easy to see and much more pronounced than the previous site. This opening in the jungle was only one-fourth the size of the first clearing. I didn't need to be so analytical, but this site was too small to park a company of APCs.

Heading east again, we were going to see if the artillery had done any damage to the spot where we had seen the reflection. I looked at my map, searching the margin where I had written the exact coordinates. We were circling high above the clearing and were hopefully out of range of any ground fire. I located a section of jungle that looked as if it had been recently damaged. It was the spot, and it matched the coordinates exactly. It was easy to see where the artillery rounds had exploded in the clearing. There were numerous brown earthen patches marking the small craters left by the exploding shells. In the jungle the damage was harder to assess. There were a lot of broken tree limbs and wilted vegetation, but the ground below remained hidden under all of the growth.

We continued in a straight line to the east as we came out of the circle patterns that we had been flying. Rock asked if I was ready to head back yet. I had no reason to delay. Rock made a sharp turn to the north, and we were headed back to the west. This was a low pass at treetop height over the jungle just to the north of the clearing that we had just inspected. When we passed the pockmarks left by the artillery, the helicopter gained altitude and continued west. Rock did one last high circle of the first potential LZ before heading for the FSB.

If anyone had been watching us—and I was certain that Charlie was watching—they would know exactly where an American unit was going to show up.

When we reached the FSB, Rock once again landed facing north. There were no good-byes. A couple of good-lucks and a see-yas covered the parting. As with the previous flights, Rock was gaining altitude and heading north, and I was once again standing in the road looking around.

None of the APCs had moved, but, as I had called it, the RPG screens and the engineer stakes had been pulled, rolled, and secured to the tracks. The men were lounging near their individual APCs and looking relaxed.

I was thinking that there were just three things left to do and the mission would be underway. As I mentally outlined the three things and counted them off one by one, Andy showed up, and it became two things to do. Andy informed me that the gas grenades had arrived. Both the canister style and M-79 rounds had been sent. I hadn't known that there was such a round for the M-79 grenade launcher.

I was now on to the second order of business. I needed to report to Lieutenant Duff and brief him on the artillery strike. It had turned out to be nothing. The best information that I had was that the strike was right on the coordinates I had given him. At least Rock and I hadn't been able to see anything from the air that would indicate someone or something had been there. I really hadn't expected to find anything or see any evidence that there were any casualties. Charlie was good at cleaning up after an action. He didn't often leave bodies or equipment behind.

Lieutenant Duff was glad to see me and anxious to get a report. As uneventful as the report was, he seemed satisfied. It was turning into an awkward moment as I was about to excuse myself, and Lieutenant Duff did it for me. He handed me his aerial photo map and said, "Looks like you're about ready to pull out."

We said no good-byes or good-lucks—just a "Yep" from me as I left the bunker.

15

Now it was time for the third and final item on my list of things to do before the company departed. I was ready to meet with all of Bravo Company's NCOs in the middle of the perimeter. I was surprised that I wasn't more nervous than I was. The fact that I had finally made a decision had a calming effect. I had been thinking about this idea off and on since the thought first came to me on February 17, and today was February 20. After all, there were only two possible options, and I would go along with whichever option the men chose. I would present the sergeants with all of the facts that I had gathered and recorded. I would then lay out my version of plan A. If anyone didn't like it, or even had reservations, the company would go to plan B, and plan B was the army's plan. Plan B was the mission orders as I had received them. I had a huge problem with plan B, because I couldn't help but think it was a suicide mission if it was carried out as ordered. Plan B was sure to get people killed; in fact, it had the potential to get a lot of people killed.

I couldn't put it off any longer. It was time. I studied the faces of the sergeants as they began showing up. It still wasn't too late to back out. I could just present them with plan B and go for it.

I couldn't imagine going against any of my football coaches and doing something that went directly against their wishes. I had come up the sports analogy relating to my army career. I had appeared before my draft board to try to appeal and get a deferment, but once there was no getting out of the draft notice, I had embraced the army. I was positive that with a college degree, I would have a safe job in the army. Was I ever wrong! It required a very high level of intelligence to be an infantry soldier. I was not aware of the fact that performing well on all tests and phases of training only served to increase the odds that I would be in the infantry. I had been trainee of the cycle when I graduated from basic training. At every step of the training, I had been at or near the top of my class, and the army had rewarded me at each step.

I was faced with a monumental decision. Up to this point, I had thought that I was under control and that following through wasn't going to be so tough. This event was turning into a major crossroad in my life. In fact, as I faced the young sergeants gathering for their briefing, I was wavering with indecision. Maybe I shouldn't go through with my plan. How much longer could I stall?

As the last of the sergeants arrived, my last thoughts were that I was the decider. These men depended on me, and they looked up to me. I had their respect, and more importantly, I was expected to keep them alive. I didn't need any indecision, especially now. I once again made the final decision to stick with the plan.

Once I started talking, it was easier than I had anticipated. I started with the intelligence report as it had been given to me by Lieutenant Colonel Dumford. I didn't hold back anything as I read parts of the report directly from my notepad. I couldn't hold back any information; the men deserved to have all of the details that I could provide. The company might as well know that the 199th NVA Regiment was who we were going after. I read aloud my copy of the battalion orders. I wanted the men to hear the directive to run patrols into the jungle to the south of the rubber plantation.

By now there wasn't a single person who hadn't grasped the seriousness of the mission. At this point I was pausing to gather my thoughts. I had to keep my emotions low key so each man could make an informed decision. I wasn't going to charge the situation further by telling them that we were bait or how I had figured out that the army was using the company and everyone in it. They could figure those things out on their own. I expected no less than an honest decision from each man.

So I began. "Listen carefully. What if we don't set foot in that basin to the south of the rubber plantation? Instead, what if we protect ourselves? We patrol outside of our perimeter. We run our night ambushes, and we set out our mechanical ambushes."

I was now ready to divulge the idea that I had come up with when I was returning from the battalion tactical meeting. I looked the men straight in the eyes as I began talking once again. I was going from face to face. "The day riffs could be phantom patrols that we can do over the radio from inside our perimeter. Keep in mind that battalion will be monitoring the company radio frequency, and we will be working as far as they are concerned." I had to pause, because I was having trouble reading some of the men's expressions, but I was into my idea and I needed to finish. I blundered on. "It won't be a cakewalk. It isn't going to be easy just protecting ourselves being so shorthanded, but we will protect ourselves. Nothing will change after dark. We will still do what we have always done." I stopped talking again briefly in order to assess how my idea was being received. There were a few short whispers back and forth and a lot of up-and-down head nodding.

"Not just us, but everyone in the company has to go along with the plan. They need to understand the implications. We need consensus. There are eighty-two of you, and all of you need to agree. I don't want any of us getting court-martialed, especially me. If you think about it, my neck will be the one that's on the line. I will be the one taking the fall if we get caught."

Sergeant Moore spoke up first. "Sarge, I'm with you. I'm all for it. The way I see things, you are the only one who will end up in LBJ or go home to Leavenworth. I will do whatever you say if it's going to keep me alive."

LBJ was the maximum-security prison run by the army. Long Binh Jail had the same initials as the president under which it was established.

I remembered passing by LBJ when the company and battalion moved from Cu Chi to Long Binh.

LBJ had such a reputation that most of the troops stationed in South Vietnam would rather be captured by the enemy than sent to LBJ. One, it was probably easier to escape from the enemy than from LBJ. Two, if you did escape from the enemy, you were a hero and you could still go home. If by some miracle you managed to escape from LBJ, there was absolutely no place to go. You couldn't go home. Your life was over, completely and utterly ruined if you were ever sent to LBJ.

No one else seemed to have anything to say or add, so I asked the question that had to be asked. "Is there anyone who isn't totally, one hundred percent sure they can do this? For Pete's sake, have the guts to say so if you disagree. It won't be held against you. Now is the time to say something."

There were no words, just positive nods.

"When we finish here, you need to take it to the rest of the men before we leave. Respect everyone's decision. If anyone doesn't want to go along or has questions, send them to me. If anyone doesn't like the plan, or has a problem, we won't do it. If this isn't going to work, we all have to know before we leave here.

"There's one more thing. When we get the new CO, it's business as usual. All bets are off, and the subject is closed. This is your last chance for questions. OK, run it by the rest of the company, and I'll wait. If I don't hear from anyone in thirty minutes, we're out of here."

I was committed now. I really didn't want to have any regrets, so I waited while the sergeants told the rest of the company the orders for the mission and the plan to run phantom patrols. I waited and watched and waited some more. I could see small squad-sized groups assembled all around the perimeter. Some were standing on the ground, and some were standing on top of their APCs.

In the next moment, an engine roared to life and then another. A chain reaction had been initiated. I took it as a sign of support. By now almost all of the tracks were running, and no one had come to see me. I had given the NCOs thirty minutes, and it had only been fifteen. I wanted to be absolutely sure that I had the total support of the company. I couldn't help it, so I sent for the NCOs to meet in the center of the perimeter one more time. With the tracks running, they showed up quickly and confirmed that everyone favored the plan.

I hurriedly reviewed. "Yesterday you got your marching orders. Remember how the logger site will be organized, with first platoon on the west and second platoon on the east. We want to idle into position one track at a time. It will take longer, but I can't emphasize enough to be as quiet as possible."

"Let's go."

They all dashed for their tracks, and second platoon was headed for the road. Still no one had come to me to question or talk about the plan. I was aware that everyone had time to think about the situation from now until tomorrow morning, when the first riff would take place. Someone might change his mind, then or anytime in between.

The instant that I had verbalized my plan to the NCOs about faking the mission, I put myself in jeopardy. It no longer mattered whether I did or didn't follow through. I was in big trouble for just saying what I did.

I was anguishing and second-guessing myself again.

16

All of the tracks were moving, and the second platoon, the command track, first platoon, and half of mortar platoon were idling up the road. Soon third platoon would also be on the road. The mission was underway.

There was no urgency for speed on this trip north up the road. It didn't matter that we were moving slowly. The red dust was suspended heavily in the air. It was a little after noon, and the midday heat was almost suffocating. The dust was turning to mud where it clung to the damp perspiration stains on our fatigues.

As the command track followed second platoon onto the road, I noticed Lieutenant Duff standing at the entrance to the FSB just inside the gate. He cared enough to see us off. He didn't know that I was aware that he knew where we were headed and what we were in for. He had no idea that I had been able to put enough clues together to know as much as he did, even though some of the information was purposely kept from me.

I couldn't wait to get out of this dust and into the rubber trees, and at that point I was actually looking forward to the rainy season. I also knew that the first night that I spent soaked and shivering, I would be wishing for the dry season and the dust to return.

As the APCs rumbled up the road, radio communication between the company tracks was very light or nonexistent. Sergeant Moore picked the spot on his own where he decided to angle into the plantation's precise rows of trees. Each track turned at exactly the same spot as the company left the road and wove its way into the rubber trees. When third platoon's last track left the road, Sergeant Pomeroy radioed the command track to let me know that the last track had entered the rubber trees and the company was clear of the road.

Once in the cover of the rubber trees, the company moved even slower. The distance between the rows of trees was just wide enough for an APC to pass. Much too often an APC would bump or nick a tree trunk as it passed. As the branches above the track shook from the impact, the men riding on top of the tracks were likely to get a shower of stinging red ants. Sometimes giant black-and-yellow spiders fell onto the tracks, and once a snake dropped onto one our company's tracks from a tree being bumped. You never knew what would happen when a tree was jarred. It could just be a few, none at all, or hundreds of the ants. It seemed that the more there were, the madder they were. Every tree bump put the men on that track ready to react, and you always knew when a nest of ants had been dislodged by the way the men jumped around and slapped themselves.

I checked my watch again. The action was half habit and half necessity. We had been on the road for twenty minutes, and we had been moving in the rubber trees for almost thirty minutes. It would be another twenty-plus minutes before Sergeant Moore would direct the column to turn ninety degrees to the right and head to the south. Last night Sergeant Moore and I had tried to calculate how long the company needed to run to the east before we turned south. If we missed the clearing, then all of the stealth and need for noise discipline would be lost, but if we guessed our distance based on our speed, we should be heading straight for the logger site.

It was a long half hour heading south before second platoon stopped. I had been looking at my watch frequently, and I figured that we should be getting close. I stood up on top of the track to look for the clearing, but I couldn't see anything. I could sit back down and wait for Sergeant Moore to report on the radio, or I could dismount and walk forward. With the second platoon directly in front of my track, I jumped down, M-16 in hand, adjusted my boonie hat, and started forward.

Ralph; Art, the platoon RTO; Bey; and three others were adjusting their rucksacks to their backs. I was still searching for the clearing, and I couldn't locate it. Ralph finally pointed me in the right direction. We had missed the clearing by a little to the west. It was probably good that we weren't coming straight in.

I desperately wanted to go with that patrol to check out the logger site, but I would stay with the rest of the company and let Sergeant Moore handle it. While I waited, I had the APCs shut down, and it became quiet. The insects and birds had grown quiet with our arrival, and it took several minutes before the sounds began to build back.

Sergeant Moore had stopped the company's progress at about two hundred meters from our destination. I was having trouble keeping the reconnaissance patrol in sight. They were moving slowly, and the tree trunks were getting in the way. They were being careful and taking their time. I judged that they were about halfway there and still moving.

Here I was, waiting again. I couldn't remember ever having this much trouble waiting. In the army you were always waiting. We even had a saying, "Hurry up and wait." I should have been used to it by now, but I waited as I continued to study Sergeant Moore's progress. I was standing on the ground next to the second platoon's first track when it finally dawned on me that I could see better from on top of the track. I should also have access to a radio.

As I pivoted to return to my track to get a radio, it was no surprise to see Andy already standing there. Even though I was startled, I didn't want to give him the satisfaction of being surprised, so I hurriedly climbed up the front of the track and stepped to the rear, past the track commander's hatch where the fifty-caliber machine gun was mounted. This provided a much better view, and I could see that the patrol was almost there. In less than two minutes, Sergeant Moore's patrol was at the edge of the clearing. I was straining to see the men at that distance, as there appeared to be some kind of commotion. Something was happening. My heart was racing, and I was preparing to react. There definitely was too much movement coming from the men at the edge of the clearing. As near as I could tell, the patrol had come on line and was facing in toward the center of the clearing, where I could see flashes of movement. I was anticipating the sound of gunfire, but none occurred.

Something had definitely left the clearing, moving quickly to the right and disappearing.

Before I could jump down off of the track and organize a reaction party, Sergeant Moore was calling on the radio. He quietly whispered that they had surprised a flock of wild peacocks that had flown off to the west; that had been the movement that I had seen leaving the clearing. Later that day Sergeant Moore would tell me that there had been at least fifteen or twenty of the large birds, and when they flushed, the patrol was completely taken by surprise.

Sergeant Moore's group was methodical and thorough as they cleared the area. They found no evidence that anyone had been there recently, and they concluded that it had been quite some time since any humans had been in the vicinity of the clearing.

After radioing the report, the patrol made good time returning to the company. Now it was my turn to take over. Second platoon were the only ones who started their engines. I instructed Sergeant Moore to get second platoon in place as quietly as possible. As the platoon approached the site, I told him to move them into position one track at a time. He called me on the radio when they were in place, and I could now move the command track into position. After the command track was in place, I took charge of positioning the first platoon tracks. Only the four first-platoon tracks were running as I had them idle into position one at a time. Then came the mortar platoon, one track at a time, and finally the third platoon completed the perimeter. There had been only four engines running at a time, and they were idling back in the rubber trees as one track at a time came forward to take its place. As I moved around the perimeter personally directing each track to its position, I was wondering how far the sound was carrying. I was pleased with how quietly we had accomplished setting the perimeter, and because of the thick vegetation surrounding us, I guessed that the sound of our arrival hadn't carried beyond a couple of hundred meters.

With everyone in place, we still had over five hours of daylight left. As the last of the third-platoon tracks was put in place, it was time to check out the surrounding area. Sergeant Rios and Sergeant Hawkins were getting ready to patrol to the east, and Sergeant Lee was going to do the same to the west. After two hours they were to return regardless of how far they had gotten.

Sergeant Pomeroy and Sergeant Moore were assigned to place some claymores and other security measures outside the company's perimeter.

The clearing turned out to be smaller than I had first thought. All of the second platoon tracks were completely in the rubber trees. Sergeant Moore had done a good job of judging how much room would be needed for the rest of the company in order to form the perimeter. His judgment had made it possible to get it right on the first try. There had been no need to reposition any of the tracks. Three of the first-platoon tracks were also two or three trees in. The rest of us were only partially into the rows of rubber trees, exposing the rear of our tracks to the sun. Mortar platoon was the exception. They were on line across the south side of the clearing and completely in the open. That was fine because we didn't want them firing their mortars up through the tree branches.

Both the east and west scouting patrols were out, mortar platoon was on standby, and third platoon was ready as a reactionary force should one of the patrols get into trouble. Sergeant Pomeroy and Sergeant Moore were out in the rubber trees working on security while the drivers and TCs were digging shallow foxholes between the tracks. I was walking the perimeter and rechecking the placement of each track. When I reached the mortar platoon, I tried to joke with Sergeant Finley about his position having a view. With the steep rock face directly in front of his position to the south, the mortar platoon tracks had an unobstructed view of the basin. There were only a few trees that were a few feet higher than the ground that we stood on. My attempt at humor fell flat. In fact, it was pretty lame. I was now clued in that the men were tense and probably a little scared.

Well, we were finally here, and the first thing we had to do was make ourselves as safe as possible. At the moment, all of our energy would be focused to that end. If we could be ready to defend our position, and if we could just make it through the night, then and only then could we afford to worry about tomorrow.

I remained at the mortar platoon looking out over the basin to the south. I tried to organize information that I had learned about mechanized units and their probability of an enemy attack. A mechanized company had tremendous firepower with its fifty-caliber machine guns and their mortars. The biggest danger was hitting an antitank mine. Most enemy contact was by men on the ground out away from the APCs on patrol. When attacks did occur on mechanized company perimeters, they were usually small-arms fire or probes of the security, and the probes usually took place after the company perimeter had been in place for several days or more.

Our company's situation was uniquely different. I could discard and forget all of the statistics about the probability of enemy contact that I had just mentally reviewed. Hadn't Delta Company of our battalion all but been wiped out by the same NVA regiment that we were supposed to be looking for? The attack on Delta Company had happened while they were on the move.

We had to protect ourselves above all else.

Both patrols had been gone one hour. We would wait for them to call us to check in. I wandered back to the command track. I was aware of Andy's constant presence, because he needed to have a radio available for my use at any given moment. I would try to be more considerate of Andy and not make him wait for me just because I was lost in thought somewhere away from the command track. When I was spacing out, he might as well be able to eat or write a letter, or just be able to relax.

Pretty soon the radio was receiving a call from hotel Zulu two three. That would be Sergeant Hawkins. So far everything was negative, and the patrol was still continuing to the echo (east). Almost immediately after Sergeant Hawkins's report, Sergeant Lee, hotel Zulu one six, called to report the same message, except that his patrol was continuing to the whiskey (west).

Sergeant Pomeroy and Sergeant Moore showed up to report their progress in securing the perimeter. They had placed a claymore mine in front of a tree one row in front of each APC facing out into the rubber trees. They placed the clackers at the driver's hatch with enough wire to be able to move it to the ground or to the top of the track. A clacker was the trigger device that was depressed to set off the mine. It was called a clacker because of the sound that it made when depressed. Next they were going to randomly string some trip flares thirty to fifty meters farther out in the rubber trees. They would flag two trails for the men to follow to the OP guard-duty positions on each side of the perimeter, one to the northeast and one to the northwest.

Directly to the north and sixty meters in front of third platoon's position was the start of a slight depression that angled to the northeast. As the depression angled away from the company, it became deeper and deeper. Sergeant Pomeroy wanted to put a mechanical ambush that would be triggered by a trip wire in the depression since it was out of sight of his platoon, and it provided a likely approach route for the enemy. I approved the mechanical, and it would be deployed just before dark.

I had decided to not have any listening posts (LPs) outside of the perimeter at night. We would be on higher perimeter alert, and we would also have two night ambush patrols out as well as three mechanical ambushes.

The day was progressing, and in three hours it would be starting to get dark. I laid out all four starlight scopes and an extra battery for each of the ambush patrols. I was checking the batteries that were already in the scopes for their remaining life when Andy showed up to report that Sergeant Hawkins's patrol was no longer headed east. They had been following the edge of the jungle almost due north for thirty minutes. I could visualize the map and remember what I had seen on my reconnaissance flight. If the patrol was headed north, they were following the large ravine or valley that funneled south directly to the larger of the two buttes in the basin. The patrol was ready to return, and they had found what they thought was a good place for a mechanical ambush.

I asked for the radio handset from Andy, called hotel Zulu two three, and identified myself simply as hotel Zulu. It turned out that Sergeant Hawkins's patrol had found recent trail sign. The mechanical would be anywhere from three hundred to five hundred meters from the night ambush. I authorized the mechanical and planned to have it rearmed with the gas grenades the next day.

Fresh trail sign was not something that I wanted to hear.

Sergeant Lee's patrol hadn't found anything out of the ordinary, and he too was on his way back. He informed me that he had chosen both a site for his mechanical ambush and the position of his night ambush. He would set the mechanical on his way back.

I approved Sergeant Lee's request also and then scolded myself for not being able to incorporate the gas grenades into the mechanicals. At least the night patrol leaders would be able to carry gas grenades with them, and if either patrol had an M-79 with them, they would have more gas grenades.

By the time both patrols were back, there wasn't a lot of daylight left. Sergeant Pomeroy and Sergeant Moore were still working on the perimeter security, so I instructed first and second platoons' night patrols to get something to eat and get loaded up. There was a lot to do in the time that remained before it was dark. I needed to meet with the platoon leaders before the patrols left the perimeter for the night.

It all came together like clockwork. Sergeant Pomeroy and Sergeant Moore showed the first and second platoons where the claymores and the trip flares were placed. They were careful to explain how to get in and out of the perimeter without setting off any of their devices. After each of the patrols had returned, Sergeant Pomeroy and Sergeant Moore completed the ring of security by placing the last of the trip flares in front of both first and second platoons.

There was just enough daylight left as the night ambush patrols were ready to move out. At my suggestion, each was going to be a six-man patrol. There were only six because they were going to be only two hundred meters from the perimeter. It might be even less. There needed to be at least six men so that two of them could be awake at all times. They could do as we did on the command track—one hour on and two hours off. With the size of the patrols and their locations decided, all that was left to cover was the reporting times. The situation reports would be ten minutes after the hour, starting at 2110.

At last the night patrols were on their way. The platoon leader meeting had been shortened purposely so the ambush patrols could be on their way while there was still enough light. The last preparations for the night security were being taken care of as Sergeant Pomeroy took Sergeant Finley with him to place the mechanical that he had requested to the front of his platoon's position. That left Sergeant Moore and Sergeant Rios with me to discuss the next day's riff. I had saved one of the artillery maps just for the daylight patrols. After a brief discussion, the three of us decided to wait for Sergeant Pomeroy and Sergeant Finley. I wanted as much input as I could get for what I was about to do. When they finally arrived back at the perimeter, the sun was just beginning to set.

I told my small group of sergeants that I wanted to discuss details about what we should include in the fake patrols. Again I was emotionally struck and fighting not to show it. I really was doing this! There was none of the shame or guilt that I expected to feel at this point, only commitment to making it work.

From what I had seen of the basin from in front of the mortar platoon that afternoon, it was a huge area to cover. When I looked at it from the ground, the area seemed even larger than when I had flown over it. I was determined to avoid the basin for as long as I could. To my knowledge, our only support was the battery of 105s at FSB Georgia, where we had just come from. The nearest aviation group was stationed in Xuan Loc, which was just off of Highway 1 some distance to the north and at least a twenty-minute helicopter flight to our logger site. I didn't know what was in Vung Tau, to the west. All I knew was that Vung Tau was an in-country resort on the beach, and it was quite some distance away from our current position. I remembered from the mission orders that the only support mentioned was FSB Georgia's 105s, so with the apparent lack of support for our company and the fact that medevacs would be difficult through the heavy jungle canopy, I found it hard to order men into the basin.

In the days to come, I learned that Vung Tau had a battery of 175s, and there was another FSB that housed a battery of 105s in range of us to the northeast. It was perplexing to me that all possible support wasn't included in the orders. It was easy for me to conclude that there was too much territory for a small patrol to cover. How long would a small patrol be able to hold out against a larger group of NVA regulars?

I was back to the business of keeping everyone alive. I told the sergeants that I wanted to script the morning's riff into the basin. Sergeant Pomeroy and Sergeant Finley were positioning themselves on ammo cans, so I got started as soon as they had arrived.

I laid out the map and asked, "Do we start on the west side or the east side?"

Before the question was answered, Sergeant Finley spoke. "You need two maps. You need one, and the patrol leader also needs one. After all, both of you will need to be on the same page." It was a hint at humor, but more importantly, it was sound thinking and good advice. This had come from a mortar sergeant, but I wasn't surprised. I had long recognized Sergeant Finley's intelligence.

The least likely place to find Charlie, and the least threatening, was to the west, back toward FSB Georgia. Here the edge of the jungle and the rubber trees was almost a straight line.

I had the two maps ready but was thinking that before we riffed into the basin on the west side of our perimeter, we should have Sergeant Lee's input. He had scouted the edge of the rubber already today and was currently unavailable, since he was leading one of the ambush patrols. Without the presence of Sergeant Lee, we made the decision to go east.

I drew a light line in pencil on one of the maps. The line went straight east and turned ninety degrees to the south and into the jungle. The line continued curving around to the east, then to the north, and eventually angled back to the company location. This was called a cloverleaf pattern. The first fake patrol would be a cloverleaf into the jungle just to the east.

The battalion headquarters and Lieutenant Duff would all be listening to us on our company frequency. It would look as if we were gung ho and jumping right into the mission.

Radio talk is short, with no wasted words. Nevertheless, I found it difficult to script the fake patrol. I had never thought about what was said before, and every patrol was different. We needed to be authentic, yet we didn't want to find anything or create suspicion.

With the sergeants' input, we figured that the riff should take five hours. We would have a situation report every hour. That meant that there would be four of those plus the announced departure and return. Sergeant Moore would radio the company twice between regularly scheduled reports to describe game trails and minor terrain changes.

Before the sergeants left to attend to their regular platoon duties, I reminded them that there would be no LPs out tonight. The night ambushes were so close that they could view into the rubber trees, and since each patrol had a starlight scope with them, they would be able to observe a greater area.

At daylight we would put two OP guard posts out in the rubber one hundred meters on each side of the perimeter.

We would have three mechanical ambushes out and were going to leave them in place. I had the script of the first riff in the morning. I just had some minor touch-ups to take care of, and we would be patrolling from the perimeter.

It was time to dismiss the sergeants. It was starting to get dark, and I was looking west, searching for the disappearing sun, which had just slipped below the jungle horizon. I was looking through the rubber trees when I felt the first huge scattered drops of rain. A small, dark cloud moving west had sneaked up on me. I had been scanning the sky all afternoon, but I had been caught off guard. The shower was a deluge, and the downpour lasted for ten or fifteen minutes, and then it was over. Everyone and everything was soaked. Ponchos came out of the tracks, but there wouldn't be enough time tonight to make any watertight shelters to sleep in.

All I knew was that it was going to be a miserable, cold night before I dried out. There was one errand left for me to do, and that was to distribute the remaining two starlight scopes to tracks on the perimeter. I gave the second-platoon track parked next to the command track a starlight scope and an extra battery. I then took the other starlight scope and an extra battery to the last third-platoon track to the west.

Ron, Andy, and I had our radio watch already set. It hadn't changed since that night in the minefield, and the command-track driver and TC seemed content to be helping third platoon.

The brief rain shower had been warm. The rain itself was cool, but the air had been warm. Now that the sun had gone down, it had turned quite a bit cooler. We wouldn't be lounging as comfortably on top of the track tonight. All of us would be starting the night wrapped in our poncho liners, and I could only hope that we wouldn't get another shower during the night.

I came up with one positive thought in regard to our current location. The FSB, the area that we had just left, would be a muddy mess by now, and that was the only reason I could think of to not still be there.

As we shivered, we got through the first situation reports, and Andy checked in with the FSB and battalion headquarters. The sky had cleared, the stars were very bright, and there was a thin crescent of a moon low on the horizon. I hoped that it was rising and not setting, because the light from even a small moon would greatly enhance the starlight scopes.

I tried not to think about any negative situations, but I still didn't sleep well at all; a few short catnaps between situation reports and reports to the FSB and the battalion were all I could manage.

It was a cold, shivery night, and by the predawn time for me to take over the radio watch, I had steam dried while rolled in my poncho liner. My poncho liner and my clothes were still a little damp, but I was significantly warmer.

Even though I had no expectations beyond what I knew the men could handle, I still had to anticipate future events. The longer we went without something happening, the more likely something would happen. We had only been here a short time, and I felt the odds going up.

My other thought was, what could battalion and the brass in the rear be thinking? They had sent us here, and what were they going to do if we didn't find anything? What was more troubling was, what would they do if we did find something? There had been no mention of a reaction force to come to our assistance should we get into a firefight. It appeared that we were entirely on our own. The orders had stated that we were to verify or disqualify the intelligence report. My plan was to disqualify the report and not find anything. I wanted to draw a big blank. Somehow we would have to be convincing enough to be able to eventually get out of here.

The history of company orders was no help to me as I tried to determine how long we might be at this location. Once we had been assigned a new AO and were there for only four days; another time, we were in place for nearly a month.

This time of day was my time to think, and my thinking wasn't going well on this particular morning. I hadn't come up with any decision-making ideas. Instead I only had coffee on my mind.

The dawn was breaking very slowly. There were no clouds in the sky. The day's beginning was a promise of direct sun and warmth in a few hours.

Finally the last situation reports were covered, and the patrols would soon be on their way back. Third platoon would provide the OP duty during the day. When it was light enough, I planned to review the script I had written for the phantom patrol. I was wondering if anyone in the company was getting cold feet. I looked around, and everything appeared normal. It wouldn't be long now before we reached the point of no return, and I could put the plan into action. There was still time to back out.

17

It was now the morning of February 21. The day was beginning just like so many other days began. Viewing the company from any angle showed that there was nothing out of the ordinary, with one exception. Very few men could be seen, and you had to search hard to find them. It appeared that everyone had grasped the seriousness of the mission and was being extra stealthy.

This morning I had more than a little weight on my shoulders. I was worried, as worried as I had ever been in my life. My plan to run phantom patrols had to be the right decision. It had to be the best option for the company. For the last several days, I had thought long and hard about what I should do. My decision was made, and I continued to fret and worry that it was the right decision, because if it wasn't, then I could expect the worst consequences.

The morning riff had been scheduled for 0830 after the script had been prepared the evening before. Sergeant Moore, Bey, Art, and five others would make up the patrol. You always had to have a head count for the army. In the event that something happened to the patrol, you had to be able to report the line numbers of the people involved.

I was reviewing my plan and sipping on my second cup of coffee while I organized and studied my notepad with the script and the maps that went with the script. I was trying to memorize the script. It wasn't a lot to learn.

I was interrupted by a familiar faint sound in the distance. I knew immediately what the sound was the instant I heard it. What was surprising and somewhat annoying was that the sound was getting louder. Eventually, a lone Huey passed just to the north of us and within sight. The four mortar tracks were there in the open, but the rest of the company was at least partially in the trees and harder to notice. The Huey was angling a little southward as it flew toward the coast. It occurred to me that it was probably headed for Vung Tau. So why was I worried about our own forces knowing where we were? Was I that jumpy? I finally concluded that the realization that there could be regular air traffic over us meant that we needed to keep the fake patrols out of sight and hidden within the company perimeter. It wouldn't be a close-quarter cluster, as I had first envisioned. We would get more separation and space ourselves across the perimeter from one another as we acted out what was on the script. Now we really would need two of everything—two maps, two scripts, and two radios for sure.

Sergeant Moore and his RTO, Art, as well as Andy and I were going over the last-minute details of the script. Sergeant Rios would also be with Sergeant Moore and Art, since he had been with Sergeant Hawkins on the previous day's scouting mission and had knowledge of a portion of the area to be covered in the riff. Andy and I would be sitting in the command track with the ramp down, while Sergeant Moore's group would be positioned near the last second-platoon track to the east of the mortar platoon's position. They would be in the shade and be comfortable. The distance separating us was a short forty meters diagonally across the perimeter. The rest of the company would be on extra strict noise discipline until the patrol was completed. No one was to bother either of us for any reason short of a major disaster.

The phantom patrol started at 0830, when Sergeant Moore called hotel Zulu to inform me that hotel Zulu two six was departing the perimeter. We now had our planned hour to wait until we spoke again. It was time to call the FSB and give them coordinates for possible fire missions along the route sketched on our maps.

I knew without a doubt that our company radio frequency was being monitored. It was more than an assumption that the battalion headquarters would be listening to our every move. It was OK to move around the company area and do things until it got close to the next reporting time. As I looked at my watch, Sergeant Moore would be calling in less than fifty minutes. I was nervous and had no desire to move around. I was tied to the script for the next five hours, when the patrol would be concluded.

The next report came at 0930, but not right on the dot. It was closer to 0932. Sergeant Moore reported that they had entered the jungle, and the patrol was descending a steep grade with heavy undergrowth. The going was slow since they had to cut their way through.

At 0955 I was holding my copy of the script and waiting at the radio. Sergeant Moore made the first of his two scripted "unscheduled" calls. He reported that the patrol was crossing the blue line. The blue line meant water on the map, in this case a stream bed. According to the report, the stream bed was just a trickle, and they were able to step across it. The terrain was more open, but the wait-a-minute vines were keeping the pace slow.

So far, our sham sounded like a real patrol. It was realistic enough that both sets of actors reading their lines were tensing, as if they could subconsciously sense the scene in reality. I felt the emotion in our conversations, and I wondered if battalion was picking it up also.

There was the unmistakable sound of helicopters headed our way again, and there was more than just one. My first thought was that they were coming to our location for some reason. I couldn't help thinking that way, but my worries were unfounded. First of all, I knew that I would have been notified of any arrivals in advance. It turned out to be four Hueys flying in loose formation, headed on the same line as the previous Huey.

Andy was using the time between radio reports to read a Louis L'Amour paperback that was being passed around the company. I thought for just a second about what I could be doing between radio reports. I was totally engrossed in my present situation, so the short answer was to continue staying focused on the script.

Time was passing quickly, and soon it was 1030. Sergeant Moore reported that he was heading east and was now going uphill. I was having second thoughts about what came next in our script. I was regretting that it might be a little too cute, but here goes. I keyed the mike, identified myself, and asked if there was any sign of trails. Sergeant Moore's reply was that they hadn't yet discovered anything that stood out; however, the area next to the blue line was open enough for speedy travel. The report was concluded, and that was it.

The next lines of the script would air at 1110, when I would receive the second unscheduled report. As it was getting close to 1110, I was waiting by the radio and ready. In fact, I hadn't moved since our last conversation. I was seated in the same spot and in the same position. It had been over thirty-five minutes since I had last spoken with the patrol, and I couldn't remember how I had spent the time. The only thing that I was certain of was that I hadn't dozed.

At last it was time, and Sergeant Moore was on the radio. I had watched the whole process as he reached for the hand set of his radio and started speaking. I kept watching the sergeant as I identified myself and said, "Go." That was his signal that it was his turn to talk again.

He informed me that the patrol was headed north. They were on a hill-side on the west side of the large ravine and were traversing at the same elevation as they headed to the November (north). With that message concluded, Sergeant Moore was out.

We just had two more conversations, and the patrol would be over.

The command-track driver and the third-platoon drivers all had grease guns, and they were inspecting the tracks and track pads while they were greasing the road wheels and the idler wheels of each of third platoon's APCs. Ron was right there helping the drivers in any way that he could. They would be servicing the command track just as soon as we were done with the scripted patrol.

I was feeling some hunger pangs, and I couldn't remember whether I had eaten anything for breakfast. All I remembered was the two cups of coffee.

I had just decided that I hadn't eaten yet today when the 1130 call came. This was a brief exchange and didn't take me by surprise. Again, I was watching Sergeant Moore as he went through the motions. I watched him holding the script and reading that all he had to report was that the patrol was still headed north. He was out, and we were down to just one more report. Only one hour to go.

We had carefully studied the map and knew how steep the sides of the valley were by the closeness of the contour lines. Sergeant Rios and Sergeant Hawkins, on their scouting patrol the day before, had peered down into the jungle, and they verified the steepness and thickness of the undergrowth. What we really didn't know was what was in the bottom of the valley and what was on the other side.

It was noon, and Andy was calling the FSB and battalion for our midday report. He was early with his call as he reported that one patrol was still out and everything was negative. Everything negative was correct, but it had a different meaning for me.

I reminded myself that I would eat something after the next report. I was feeling a little more confident now that we were close to the end of our charade. In fact, at this point I was sure that this patrol had been believable. The uncertainty of not knowing what was in the bottom of the valley and on the other side was eating at me. I was rationalizing that I needed to have that information for the company's protection, and perhaps we could run a patrol to check it out in the near future. I would think about it some more and then discuss it with the NCOs.

I shuddered at the thought of getting close to the buttes, which were the prominent terrain features in the basin. I would stall and fake the patrols for as long as I could to avoid going that far into the basin. I also knew that one of the next riffs would have to do just that. How hard would it be to prepare a script for that patrol? Our company was expected to find something. How could we satisfy battalion and still avoid a disaster? We could call in artillery, but if gunships showed up—and they likely would—they would require us to mark our position on the ground with smoke. We wouldn't be able to pop smoke if we weren't there. I had thought that I had everything figured out, but things kept cropping up. All I could do was take things one day at a time. I would wait and hope that nothing happened until I could think of something.

It was 1230 and time for the final situation report from the patrol. Sergeant Moore was again brief. The patrol had turned west and was crossing the valley to climb up to the rubber trees and return to the company perimeter.

At last I could eat. Each track carried cases of C-rations, and it was practiced procedure to open one case at a time. The men would eat from that box until it was gone and then open the next one. The next case was usually opened before the already-opened one was completely gone. The box that our track was currently working on appeared to be about two-thirds full, when in reality it was the remnants of several previous cases.

I started searching through the case. There was no toilet paper, no fruit, and no Beechnut Chewing Tobacco. I couldn't find anything that appealed to me. I considered opening the next case. I could say that I needed the toilet paper, but the guys would see through that.

So I closed my eyes and grabbed a can, and it turned out to be "ham and claymores." I set it back and blindly closed my fingers around a second can. When I opened my eyes, it was again a can of "ham and motherfuckers." The same thing had happened twice in a row. I put the second can back, and, once again, trying not to peek, I lifted a third can of ham and lima beans to my eyes. That was it. This would have to be the one.

Andy had been watching me out of the corner of his eye and was amused. I had just been a source of entertainment for him.

I had to say something. "Well, that's all there is."

Andy surprised me with "Hand me one. Let's get 'em used up."

Ham and lima beans were impossible to eat cold, so we took the time to heat both cans, and we each applied a generous helping of hot sauce. I must have been really hungry, because I was able to keep them down. I was even able to chew a little.

After eating the C-rations' most obnoxious meal, I found my canteen, which contained unsweetened Kool-Aid. All drinking water in Vietnam had a horrible chemical taste, and the water that we didn't get from the army came from muddy streams and scum-filled bomb craters and required purification tablets.

Andy was getting comfortable with his book when at 1355 Sergeant Moore radioed that he had the company in sight and soon would be entering the perimeter. I was looking across the perimeter at Sergeant Moore, and he was eyeing me as he was saying that he had us in sight.

At 1403 Andy radioed the FSB to report that all patrols were back. He also informed them that there would be two night ambush patrols. We would call artillery later in order to register the usual predetermined targets.

18

It was still early in the afternoon. The first phantom patrol was over, and how did I feel? I wasn't feeling guilt, but I was scared. Fear is easily recognizable if your mind is open. I was sure that our location in the area of a NVA regiment had to be shortening my life-span through my elevated stress levels. The added stress had more to do with where we were and all of the unknown factors of the mission. Most of my apprehension stemmed from the intelligence report that indicated the NVA presence in the area. Granted, the VC had been doing the fighting in the south for a long time, but the NVA were trained soldiers, just like us. They were less likely to abandon a fight, and they were likely to be more aggressive. All of this information contributed to my anxiety.

I hadn't lost confidence in the plan. I just wasn't as confident that I could pull it off now. The orders had been to run patrols to the south of the rubber plantation and into the jungle basin that contained the two ominous buttes.

I couldn't share the feeling that something bad was going to happen. It had been hovering over me since our arrival at this spot, and it was getting stronger with the passage of time.

I needed to keep my emotions in check. I didn't want any of the men to detect any doubt or weakness on my part. In fact, the entire company needed to reflect a defensive posture that showed no weaknesses. I could fake the patrols, but I couldn't predict what Charlie would do. He could very well come to us, and our survival could depend on our defensive preparations.

The anticipation was eating away at me. I might not be able to entirely shake the feeling that something was about to happen, but I could make myself busy. Staying busy was my antidote for hiding my emotions, and there was still plenty to do. I would use the available time to make preparations for the night, so I went directly to Sergeant Pomeroy to ask him how we could strengthen our security beyond the perimeter. He had some ideas, but he didn't want to elaborate just yet. He wanted to talk to Sergeant Moore first. Then he would get back to me.

I was thinking way too much, and I was scared. The stress of suppressing my fears and the responsibility of leading the company caused me to dig deep within myself. I needed to hold together long enough to see this mission through.

Sergeant Lee and Sergeant Hawkins had scouted the area beyond the perimeter, so I wanted to talk with them before I decided on the location of tonight's ambushes. My thought was that the night ambushes should move out into the rubber trees beyond the OP's positions where the patrol still had vision to the edge of the jungle.

I didn't want the night ambushes going to the same spot every night, because it would only take one VC observer, and Charlie would be waiting when the next night patrol showed up. By moving the ambushes out into the rubber trees, the patrols would be able to visually recon more ground, and if they were just close enough to the edge of the jungle, they would be able to observe any movement there.

Inside the rubber trees, the ground wasn't completely flat. The trees had been planted on gently rolling hills. There were small, subtle changes in the terrain throughout the rubber plantation, and here at the south end, the dips and valleys were more pronounced. The maps that we were using showed most of the slight changes in the terrain and elevation; however, with a contour interval of twenty feet, not all of the dips and high spots showed. The one consistent feature was that most of the high ground ran primarily north and south.

By now I had pretty much made up my mind about how I would move the night ambushes around. I still needed input from sergeants Lee and Hawkins before making the final decision.

The sun was still high in the sky, but it had shifted to the western sector. There were numerous patches of white, cottony clouds forming in the east and south. It looked as if we could be in for another late-afternoon or evening shower.

The night before had stirred about a fourth of the company to action. Every third or fourth track had erected a poncho shelter to keep the rain off. The men sleeping in these shelters slept on stretchers, so they were off of the ground. The drivers and TCs stayed with their tracks and slept on top of the ammo stored in the hold of the APC.

The command track had kept one of the inside seating benches intact, along with several radios, each tuned to a different frequency, positioned above the bench. Andy and Ron frequently took turns sleeping on the bench.

Most of the men of the company were assigned ground duty. They were the ones who went on the riffs and the ambush patrols, and many of them slept in hammocks. Their hammocks would be as close to the ground as they could hang them and still have clearance. They usually dug out a depression below the hammock, so it was even slightly lower than ground level. The depression doubled as a foxhole in case of an action.

The most ingenious part of sleeping in a hammock was being able to stretch a poncho over the top and stay dry. The hood in the center of the poncho was tied to prevent leaks, and snap links were fastened to the hammock where it was tied off. When it rained, the water would run down the cord or rope that tied the hammock off, and when it reached the snap link, it dripped to the ground instead of running onto the hammock. The technique was dry and efficient. There had been no need for this setup during the dry season, but yesterday's rain shower had some of the men making advance preparations.

When the men were out on a patrol, hammocks weren't often used. Our company didn't like to carry ponchos on a patrol either, because they were shiny when they were wet. That left the poncho liner, which doubled as padding against your back in your rucksack. A few of the men carried air mattresses. They weren't heavy or cumbersome, and they added a nice degree of comfort.

I located Sergeant Hawkins, and he and I searched the other side of the perimeter for Sergeant Lee. We found him working on a foxhole between his first and second tracks. It appeared that he intended to set up a hammock. I knew that he wouldn't be using it tonight, since he was leading the west-side ambush patrol.

There were two other sergeants in first platoon, and one squad was led by a specialist four. Third platoon also had one track that was led by a spec four. If the company got through this mission, I would take it upon myself to submit the paper work to get each of the specialists acting as squad leaders promoted to E-5 sergeant.

Sergeant Lee was always doing more than his share. Instead of sending either of the other two sergeants on the night patrol, Sergeant Lee was taking one of them with him and again leading the patrol himself.

Sergeant Pomeroy would begin rotating night ambushes with Sergeant Lee's platoon starting tomorrow. The second platoon had the east side all to themselves, and Sergeant Rios had tonight's ambush. First he was going to the site of the mechanical ambush and tape gas grenades to each of the claymore mines. He would then return to the company perimeter before going back out past the OP guards' position to the ambush site. I habitually checked my watch, and I noted that he needed to get going, or he would run out of time. We didn't want to be moving at dusk or after dark.

Sergeant Lee, Sergeant Hawkins, and I had our discussion about the night ambush locations. They agreed with me that we needed to move the ambush locations. We would try to avoid being predictable. Since there was already a trail flagged to the OP's position, a patrol could return to the company perimeter quickly if the need arose.

Sergeant Rios and the patrol were leaving the perimeter and would be gone for nearly two hours or longer. Instead of following the edge of the jungle, he would follow a more direct route to the mechanical ambush.

I watched the patrol's departure until they switched to their stealth mode a short distance into the rubber trees. I turned to my next task. It was good to be busy, because I hadn't thought about our predicament for a while. It appeared that I was going to be occupied for some time to come.

Sergeant Pomeroy had talked with Sergeant Moore and had some ideas for improving our security.

His first suggestion proved to be outstanding. "We can put up the RPG screens without having to drive any stakes. Since every track except the mortar platoon's is parked between a row of trees, the chain-link wire fencing can be tied to the trees."

"That's a great idea. I was feeling almost naked without the screens up." I was nodding my approval.

"Sergeant Moore and I are going to add more trip flares and noise-makers to the outside of the perimeter. We can double, triple, even quadruple the number of warning devices."

I was pleased with what I was hearing, but I didn't have time to question him as he continued expanding the idea.

"We'll add more each day inside the current fifty-meter field, and we'll extend the security outward. And we plan to vary the tripping mechanisms so that a number of the devices will be loose-wire setups along with the tight-wire flares already in place."

"Thank you, Sergeant. If you think of anything else that'll help, I want to hear it."

Like laying a minefield, they were keeping a map of the location of each device. They had a separate map for each platoon that emphasized the area that radiated from that platoon's position.

As Sergeant Pomeroy was just finishing with what he had to tell me, another member of his platoon showed up carrying a claymore mine bag. They waited with me as Sergeant Moore came across the perimeter, also carrying a claymore mine bag. Both bags were filled with flares and trip wire.

I had Andy radio the OPs to tell them that there were going to be men working outside the perimeter.

Andy and I would gather Ron and go from track to track helping place the RPG screens as quietly as possible.

So far, the whole company collectively had been as quiet as a small patrol in the jungle. Except for when we rolled in with engines running, there hadn't been a sound that had escaped from the company area. I was still hoping that the trees and vegetation had covered the sound of a single APC at a time idling into position. I wouldn't have believed that a mechanized company could be so quiet. It showed beyond a shadow of doubt that all of the members of Bravo Company were serious about staying alive.

I often felt that the men assigned to a mechanized company had a false sense of security, mainly due to the tremendous firepower that APCs possessed. In most cases the men could afford to be noisy. They all but dared Charlie to take them on. When they were with their tracks, their APCs were like security blankets.

I couldn't have imagined what I was witnessing. Once again I was struck with how quiet we were being. Normally there would be some clanking, banging, and music. That was what was missing most. There had been no music playing loud since we had been in place. It was true that I had seen men with transistor radios and ear jacks in their ears. The men themselves had self-imposed a ban on music being played openly.

Every track had a number of transistor radios, as well as cassette players. Music was very important, and in every platoon there were country-music lovers and hard-rock lovers. Often the music clashed and could be heard at the same time, but when the men were away from their tracks, everything was different. Noise discipline was critical and strictly enforced. No one was daring Charlie when the men were on the ground and away from the security of their APCs.

I was beginning to fully realize the effort the men were putting forth. They weren't doing it for me, but they were depending on me to make good decisions. It was hard to believe that eighty-two men from all walks of life could come together and work so well toward a common goal.

From the first moment that I had thought about it, I had waffled back and forth about the idea of running fake patrols. At one point I had totally dismissed the idea, but here I was, and it was happening. The tremendous responsibility of keeping everyone alive was beginning to weigh on me. I had committed myself, but I still had doubts. I needed to stay busy, because there was a second thought that kept reoccurring. We were due for some action, and that meant enemy contact.

Sergeant Rios interrupted my thoughts as he radioed that he was over halfway to the site of the mechanical ambush that had been set to detonate when a unit of VC or NVA troops showed up. I was aware that an hour had gone by quickly. I also noticed that I hadn't been pulling my weight.

The RPG screens had been quietly lifted from two-thirds of the company tracks and just as quietly unrolled. Everything was progressing as I stepped in to assist in lowering a screen to the ground. We had just placed the screen on the ground when we heard another helicopter. This one was headed in the other direction on the same line; however, this time the flight path was farther south, and it was going to pass directly over us. Before I could see it, I was aware that I was standing alone in the open. Everyone else had moved to the side of a track or into the edge of the trees. I had been taken by surprise, so with as much casualness as I could muster, I edged to the nearest tree until the helicopter passed. Once the helicopter was out of sight, even though we could still hear it, everyone stepped out and resumed the task of erecting the RPG screens. The mortar platoon's tracks were parked in the open, so was staying out of sight that important? As I searched the area of the mortar platoon's tracks, nobody was moving around, and nobody was in the open. The few men I could see were sitting on the shady side of the tracks with their backs against the tracks.

For me this was the clincher that the entire company had bought in to plan A.

We were finishing up with second platoon's last two tracks. The RPG screens were on the ground and unrolled, and they had only to be strapped to the trees in front of the tracks when the radio crackled. It was Sergeant Rios again. He had armed the mechanical ambush with the gas grenades and had spent some extra time camouflaging the mines and the trip wire. He had also replaced the battery and raised the trip wire to waist high. He was on his way back, so I signed out and headed for the command track. I wanted to write some things down before I forgot them.

As I crossed the perimeter I was scanning the sky. It looked as if it might be raining far to the southeast, and it could be coming our way. There were also darkened clouds to the north of us. I decided to tough it out at least one more night. I wasn't ready to string my hammock yet. The only difference today was that I would pull on my poncho when it began to rain. I continued to scan the sky. If and when the monsoons finally hit, it could rain steadily for a day or more. I felt fortunate that I was stationed in the south. I had heard stories about the weather in the highlands up north. There the rain could sock in for up to a week, grounding all air support. When the rains finally did arrive, we could look forward to high winds and lots and lots of mud.

Charlie didn't seem to like the severe weather any more than we did. During a storm was the most likely time to get a break from the war; however, when we were in the field, we had to stay alert just in case Charlie ever figured out that he could get a lot closer to us during bad weather.

As I approached the command track, I glanced at my watch. It was 1730 and coming up on 1800. I tipped up an empty ammo can, sat down, and wrote down several things that I wanted to discuss with the NCOs when we had our daily meeting.

Sergeant Rios should be back anytime now. He would have just enough time to eat and head out for his night ambush patrol.

It was time to eat, but I remembered that all that was left in our picked-over case of C-rations was ham and lima beans. I just couldn't stand the thought of another can of ham and claymores in the same day. I was ready to tell Ron and Andy that it was time to open another case of C-rations. If and when we ever left this site, I would puncture the remaining ham and claymores and bury them. Besides, we needed the toilet paper.

Every company logger site needed a latrine. It wasn't a problem, since we had been doing it the same for some time. Eighty-three men needed a place to go. In fact, we had two latrines. We dug two slit trenches that were about ten feet long to start with, and they were over a foot deep.

The latrines at this location were placed to either side of the mortar platoon and went all the way to the edge of the rubber trees.

All a person needed to do was straddle the trench and do his thing. Next, he sprinkled some lye and covered that portion of the trench with some dirt. The longer the company remained in one place, the longer the trench became. As the trench was being filled in from one end, the open end continued to be dug going away from the perimeter. You could pee almost anywhere. Most men used the area directly in front of their track. Using the slit-trench type of latrine kept the odor at a minimum, even during the hottest days. The strategy was to dig it deep and keep it filled in.

After my proposal to open a new case of C-rations, Ron had a better idea. He reminded Andy and me that there were still some of Captain Cooper's LURP rations left.

The thought of the freeze-dried LURPs made me even hungrier. Ron produced an open case of LURPs that had five remaining meals. He was reading what each meal was. There were no ham and claymores here; however, if I had to guess, the army probably had a LURP ham-and-lima-bean meal. What could the army have been thinking? Millions of men in the military and not a single one that could possibly like ham and lima beans.

I was handed a chicken and rice, and this time we were able to heat the water to soak the freeze-dried mixture. The LURP rations were truly a treat. I drank unsweetened Kool-Aid that I mixed with my canteen water. The water had an awful chemical taste that was particularly disgusting to me, so I had my wife send me packets of Kool-Aid with her letters. The current flavor was grape.

I kept the extra Kool-Aid packs in my personal ammo can. The ammo can was watertight and contained all of my letter-writing supplies, salt and pepper, a small bottle of steak sauce, a small bottle of hot sauce, a camera, extra film, plenty of extra pens and pencils, some photographs, and over one hundred dollars in cash. The money was the military currency called MPC. I normally wouldn't have that much cash except that for each stand-down I would buy an eighty-case pallet of beer and sodas to go along with the steaks, which was a stand-down tradition.

As we ate our LURPs, the conversation was on the weather. Were we going to get wet or not? I was beginning to think not, but it was possible that we could get rained on later tonight. We could see it raining to our south. The larger butte in the basin was getting a good soaking as we ate, and it was raining to the north at the same time. It was easy to determine which clouds carried rain by how dark they were, but as I checked the direction that the weather was coming from, I could see broken patches of blue sky. It was early for the sky to be clearing for the night, but it appeared to be doing just that.

As I looked around the perimeter, I could see Sergeant Rios inspecting the night ambush patrol. Each member of the patrol was looking over another patrol member's equipment to make sure that nothing was loose or dangling that could catch on something or make noise. By now they would have already done the count of munitions and equipment they were taking with them.

A ninety-degree swivel of my head and I was observing Sergeant Lee and his patrol going through exactly the same procedures.

The starlight scopes had worked well last night. I was feeling very fortunate to have them available. All four starlight scopes had been used throughout the night. The batteries had been changed, and each one was ready to go for another night.

We would soon be into our second night of the mission. So far, fingers crossed, knock on wood, nothing had happened, but the probability that something would happen was growing with each passing hour. If the company could just make it through the night, we could then worry about tomorrow. Not that there weren't plans already in place for tomorrow, because there were. The riff was planned, and I was working on the script. Sergeant Hawkins and I would go over the script in the morning. We did have plans. We just couldn't afford to worry about them yet. Everyone was truly living in the moment.

After the sun had set and the last light was fading, I noticed that the sky had cleared considerably. Some stars were beginning to twinkle, and the moon was a little higher tonight.

Our company meeting with the NCOs had been brief. There were no questions, and the fake patrol was approved.

All of the radio calls had been made to the FSB and to battalion headquarters. I had given the artillery at FSB Georgia some new predetermined target coordinates. The FSB also had the coordinates of each of the ambush patrols.

The company was beginning to settle in, but not comfortably. There was absolutely no sound. Insects were the only things that could be heard, and they were becoming increasingly annoying. After the brief rain shower of the day before, there were already noticeably more mosquitoes. Clouds of the biting insects were hovering under the rubber trees. Even so, some of the men had been shirtless during the day. Ron kept track of the medical supplies, and he had informed me before we left the FSB that the company had enough of the daily malaria pills to last a month, and there were just as many of the weekly pills.

I was only too aware of the fact that before we got out of here, there was going to be a huge drain on the company's supply of insect repellant. The little one- or two-ounce plastic atomizer bottles easily fit into a pocket, and they had more uses than turning female mosquitoes away. The female mosquito was the only one that bit and thus the only one that carried malaria. My favorite use of the repellent was to get rid of leeches that had attached themselves to my skin. When I found a leech gorging itself on my blood, all it took was one small squirt, and the leech immediately let go and writhed to the ground. I don't know how the leeches did it, but they could get under your clothing and attach themselves without your feeling them. If you saw leeches on the ground or on the vegetation, you needed to periodically strip down and check for them. I didn't know whether the repellent was an antiseptic, but I usually gave a second stinging squirt at the drops of blood running from the leech's bite and then moved on.

I was trying to force myself to relax. I was concentrating on slowing my breathing as I sat in my jeep seat on top of the track in the dark. It was already time for my radio watch, and I hadn't even dozed. Andy made sure that I was fully awake before turning the radios over to me. It would be Ron's turn next, and the company situation reports were still at ten minutes after the hour.

As I sat there in the jeep seat with the radio braced against the TC hatch, I patted my hand along my right leg until I located my M-16. OK, I was ready now. The calls that I made on the radio were hardly noticed. After all, there wasn't much to say.

I couldn't help but wonder what the higher-ups were thinking about us. Since we hadn't provided them with any action yet, what would they do? What moves would they make? How were they going to mess with us?

It was finally time to wake Ron. He was asleep on the bench inside the track. Once again our driver and TC were with the third platoon. I returned to the jeep seat as Ron took up his position on the other side of the track. I rolled in my poncho liner and didn't remember a thing until Andy was gently shaking me awake. It was time for my last early-morning radio watch. I tried to wriggle around and stretch my muscles. I had some stiffness and aches.

The first thought that hit me was that we had almost made it through another night. Now I could start worrying about making it through the day. The day's riff was all ready to go. It was scripted and would be a probe into the west side of the basin. The patrol was to go five hundred meters (half a klick) west along the edge of the jungle before turning south into the jungle. The patrol would then cloverleaf to the west and eventually back to the north and return to the company after entering the rubber trees. I was trying to think of something to add to the script that might satisfy battalion enough so that they wouldn't put any extra pressure on us to find anything.

I wasn't having any luck coming up with any ideas that satisfied me. Anything out of the ordinary might set off the wrong alarm. All I could think of was trail sign, the existence of a trail network, fresh and older cuttings, footprints in the soil, an old campsite, or maybe some discarded equipment. I had pretty much decided to go with the script that I already had without anything added. Today's script had the patrol cutting brush all the way, and they wouldn't have enough time to go as far as originally planned. I had a whole day to think of something that I could incorporate into tomorrow's script.

The first signs of light were just starting to show. Another thought occurred to me. I hadn't heard the FSB with a single fire mission since we had been here. I switched my thoughts to the most important issues. As soon as it was light enough, I was going to have a cup of cocoa, and I would then sit down with Sergeant Hawkins and go over the script for the day's riff.

19

As soon as it was as light as it would get without the sun above the horizon, one of mortar platoon's men came looking for me. He was a blond, baby-faced kid, and he was animated and anxious for me to follow him back to the mortar platoon area. There was something that I had to see. I couldn't get over how young he looked. He might have been the youngest in the company. He certainly looked the part.

I followed him around the mortar platoon's tracks to a position where we were looking out over the basin. He was staring in the direction of the larger butte. Almost the entire basin was enveloped in a thin veil of fog. The fog formed a thin layer, and most of the fog was at the level of the tops of the jungle trees. It appeared that the fog layer extended below the treetop level and down into the jungle.

He hadn't said anything since we had arrived at this spot. He turned and looked at me quizzically and then pointed at the butte. What did he want me to see? What was he looking at? I sure couldn't see anything. I was about to say something as I turned and looked back at him again, and he must have seen the confusion on my face.

"Smoke. Don't you see it? Look at the right side of the butte."

I could see it now. There were two—no, three—thin, wispy columns of smoke rising straight up. The wind currents were nonexistent, and the atmospheric conditions were absolutely perfect, or we wouldn't have been able to see the smoke trails.

After watching for less than a minute, I sent the young man to summon Sergeant Finley and then round up any of the other NCOs he could find quickly. The thin smoke trails that reached into the sky were hard to see, since they were so faint. As soon as the sun rose, we would no longer be able to see them.

As I waited for the others to arrive, I was sure that I had pinpointed the source of the smoke trails. They were just behind the edge of the butte that was visible to us. I was positive that the smoke trails originated from the section of the butte where Rock and I had noticed some changes in the vegetation; most notably, what we thought might be a lack of undergrowth.

The smoke trails had to originate from enemy campfires.

I was intently studying the smoke trails and pointing them out as the men began arriving, and Sergeant Finley exclaimed, "There's another one!"

At that same instant, a sliver of sunlight made its appearance, radiating over the horizon. Sergeant Finley had seen another smoke trail coming from the east side of the smaller butte, but because of the arrival of the sun, all of the smoke trails were now invisible.

No one at that moment was thinking at any length about future consequences involving the company. We could only have guessed, and most likely guessed wrong. What we now had was a target, and we were going to rain as much pee on that spot as we possibly could. But it needed to happen fast. I sprinted back to the command track for a map. The map that I had used for the reconnaissance flights had all of the information that I needed. I had even written the coordinates in the margin.

Andy alerted the FSB to prepare for a fire mission on our command. I didn't want them firing yet, not until I could find out what else was available, so while Andy was on the radio to the FSB, I called battalion headquarters to inform them of what we had. Whoever was on the radio for battalion was beginning to annoy me. He wanted more information about what I had seen, such as target description, the exact location of the target, our company location, the proximity of other troops, and on and on. I was finally able to convince him that I was on a high spot and had an unobstructed view of the target area. I would be able to adjust artillery and direct gunships. I was then able to explain that FSB Georgia was on standby.

He gave me the call sign for an artillery battery of 175s located somewhere near Vung Tau and promised to scramble some gunships from Xuan Loc.

I asked him for permission to start the fire mission as soon as I contacted the battery of 175s. In the middle of his giving the OK for the fire mission, he abruptly stopped me. "Hold on a second."

What kind of radio procedure was this?

He soon came back with information that the navy had two "fast movers" (jets) in the air less than two hundred miles away. They had already been contacted and would be on station within minutes. I was given the jets' call sign, and they had already been given my call sign and radio frequency. I was to contact them just as soon as I heard them.

I had the eight-digit coordinates of the spot on the butte ready.

The instant the fast movers showed up, I remembered Sergeant Finley's observation of the smoke trail coming from the smaller butte. That would have to wait a little longer now.

I gave the jet pilot the coordinates and suggested a north-south pass that veered to the northeast. The two jets came directly over our position as they made a long turn to the south. They had made their turn, and I could see them coming north at a much lower altitude and heading straight for the butte. They made their pass and pulled up as they turned to the east and back to the south again. They had gone directly over the spot that I had called in, and nothing had happened. Just then the pilot contacted me, and I could see the colored smoke drifting up through the trees. It was red smoke. The smoke that I was observing was at the base of the butte a little to the south of the intended target. I gave the pilot the target correction by telling him that the target was just to the north of the smoke. It sounded like the pilot was chuckling. The smoke's exact placement had been his intention all along.

The sound was deafening as I looked to the south awaiting the jets' second pass over the butte. Here they came. They were two tiny dots that were growing larger very quickly. There was a sound on the radio that sounded like "Feel the heat." The sound waves felt like wind as the jets made their second pass and were climbing and turning east as they reestablished their formation. After following the jets' paths, I turned my attention back to the butte. The jets' second pass over the target produced a completely different result. The entire back side of the butte was engulfed in a thick, billowy cloud of black smoke. I don't know what I had expected, but the jets had dropped napalm canisters on the target.

Andy was reporting to battalion headquarters that the jets were leaving. They had just flown over our company position at altitude heading back toward the coast. The pilot I had talked to called me on my radio as they did one last flyover. "Have a nice day" was all that he said before they were soon out of sight.

Battalion had already given their OK for the fire missions for the two artillery batteries that had been waiting on standby. I hurriedly asked Sergeant Finley to change the 105s at Georgia to target the little butte where he had seen a smoke trail. He was preparing to adjust fire to the smaller butte while I was on the radio with the 175 battery. The first 175 artillery shot was out of the tube and on its way. It exploded right where I wanted, so I gave them a fire for effect. I moved the exploding sheaf, where the six artillery rounds landed simultaneously, first to the west and then north and south up and down the back side of the butte. At last the 175 fire mission ended, but they would remain on standby until I informed them that they could stand down.

Sergeant Finley was probably the best in the company at adjusting artillery fire. He had those 105s working over the smaller butte very thoroughly.

When the fire mission for the 105s was over, they also remained on standby.

The gunships showed up next, and two teams had been called up. Sergeant Lee directed one of the gunship teams, which happened to be a pair of cobra helicopters. The cobras worked over the smaller butte while Sergeant Moore directed a pair of Huey hogs around the north side of the larger butte.

I was scouting on my map for the enemy's possible escape routes for another fire mission to target when Andy handed me his radio mike with a message from battalion. I took the mike and was speaking directly to Lieutenant Colonel Dumford. He told me to patrol to the east of our logger site and set up a blocking force in the valley leading to the north of the butte.

Since the action had started, I hadn't had time to think about today's riff, which was already scripted. Well, I could forget the fake patrol for now. I would comply with the colonel's order and send a twelve-man patrol to act as a blocking force. However, I wasn't going to send the patrol all the way into the bottom of the valley. The patrol could establish themselves at the edge of the rubber trees and a little ways down the slope and listen from the top. What battalion didn't know was that we already had a mechanical ambush in an excellent blocking position.

It seemed as if only a few minutes had passed, and then I was on the radio with the 175 battery with two more targets. The areas west of the butte and north of the butte contained stream beds. I described both targets as possible escape routes and asked that impacting artillery rounds be walked up the streambed for two hundred meters. I shifted my position in front of the mortar platoon so I could adjust fire. As it turned out, I didn't have to work very hard. All my directives seemed to be "Right on target" or "Move fifty more mikes"—meters—"to the November"—north—followed again by "Right on target."

An artillery battery always referenced the location of the person directing the fire mission. That way the person directing the fire could say right or left, add or drop, in order to place the rounds where they were wanted. However, I was so far away that I could use the cardinal directions on the map to adjust the fire. The artillery people were OK with that once they learned my location.

By the time the fire missions were over, the blocking force was almost in position. Smoke had drifted into every corner of the basin. The radio talk had ceased, and it was just after eight thirty, or, to be exact, 0835. There had been a lot of action in a little over two and a half hours. Battalion had ordered the blocking mission, and we would comply. I could only wonder what would happen next. We might have stirred up a hornet's nest, or, in this case, an NVA regiment. It was probably just a matter of time before our company was in contact. If we had done as much damage this morning as I hoped we had, it might take a while for it all to register and Charlie to regroup.

The twelve-man patrol was in place, and they were the primary focus of everyone in the company. The action in the basin and the surprise orders from the battalion commander had canceled our planned riff.

In the early-morning quiet of my radio watch, I had worried that we might not be able to give battalion enough to think about. They were overloaded with stimulus and information to process. How would they come back at Bravo Company now? The order to set up a blocking force that had come from the battalion commander was starting to eat into my thoughts. I couldn't let Bravo Company be commanded from battalion headquarters. We were here on the ground, and they were in Long Binh.

Sooner or later, probably sooner, someone would have to be sent into the basin to assess the damage, and Bravo Company was the most logical choice.

Today was February 22. It had been six days since my birthday, six days as the acting company commander. I felt I was changing. I just hoped that it didn't show. My main goal was keeping everyone alive, and that goal had become an obsession. My plan, the one I had hatched in a fit of anger, was on the line again. After this morning's action, I was wondering if the plan to run fake patrols could still work. I recalled the battalion meeting at the FSB and how I felt after receiving the mission orders.

It was still early in the day, and there was a lot of work to do yet.

Sergeant Moore was leading the blocking force, and in the event they had movement, I wanted the patrol to try to avoid detection and contact if at all possible. Let Charlie go on by and run into the mechanical ambush. We had the mechanical ambushes coordinates, so if it blew, we could get the artillery on them again.

Sergeant Finley and the mortar platoon were on standby in the event that the patrol needed close support. First and third platoons had a reaction force ready to go if the patrol got into contact.

After the early-morning action, things slowed down. I wanted to stay busy, but the most pressing business was to wait. I moved to the command track with Andy in tow. The radios were silent, and I was feeling tired. The thought crossed my mind that maybe I could catch a quick nap. After the rush from the morning's excitement, if I was ever going to be able to sleep, it should be now, while everything was on the downswing. I was asking Andy if he could think of any reason why I couldn't get some brief rest when Sergeant Pomeroy showed up and wanted to talk about his night ambush.

Sergeant Pomeroy had me functioning at a higher level again. His scheduled night ambush was to be on the west side of the perimeter. He was inquiring about taking the ninety-millimeter recoilless rifle with three flechette rounds.

Of course I would OK the use of the recoilless rifle. Even so, Sergeant Pomeroy was prepared to argue for its use. He was going to be only two hundred meters or less from the company perimeter. He had talked it over with his patrol members, and they didn't mind carrying the extra rounds. I assured him that it was a done deal.

Andy produced the commander's throne. He opened the folding lounge and patted it. I took that as my signal to get some rest. I hardly remember sitting down, and I don't remember leaning back. I was asleep almost instantly.

Both Andy and Ron had become protective of me, and both kept a close watch on me. I could be confident that they would allow me to get as much rest as possible. They would awaken me only if they absolutely had to; otherwise, they would wait until I awoke on my own. It had been a while since I had gotten some quality rest. I didn't need to sleep long, but I needed the rest in order to recharge.

I awoke to the sound of helicopters. When I opened my eyes, there was immediate recognition. There was no fogginess or hesitation to get oriented. Not often, but once in a while, a person can awaken from a deep sleep to full consciousness, and I had just done it. I hadn't yet located the helicopters, but it didn't take long to have them positioned out over the basin.

I might be fully awake, but my muscles and the rest of my body weren't responding. I struggled to get out of the chair and was able to steady myself by placing my hand on the side of the track. The center of the clearing was devoid of any men. The sounds of the helicopters had sent them to the fringes of the perimeter and the cover of the trees.

I climbed to the top of the track. Once on top I reached out at arm's length to touch the tree trunk that was next to me. I was able to comfortably maintain my balance as I watched and studied the helicopters.

There were three helicopters. Two were a gunship team. Hueys that had been converted from carrying troops to armament and served as gunships were called hogs. The Huey proved to be a versatile aircraft because of the variety of weapons that it could employ. The hogs could carry rocket pods, a belt-fed grenade launcher, and miniguns, in different combinations.

They were flying quite high and doing lazy circles. Above the hogs was the third Huey, which remained out of synch with the two hogs.

The helicopters were fascinating to watch. I was waiting for them to dive down to treetop level and expend some ammunition. The longer I watched, the more I anticipated the gunship's attack, but it never came. They were working their way farther south, and I was remembering the reconnaissance flights that Rock and I had flown in the south sector of the basin. There was a much better chance of catching Charlie out in the open down there.

I was losing interest in the helicopters when I noticed that Sergeant Pomeroy was standing below me on the ground and motioning, so I hopped down to hear what he had to say. He wasn't overly concerned or seemingly excited to any degree, but he had my attention with what he had to say. The OP guards in front of his position had just reported that they had movement to the west in the rubber trees. I had questions, and so did Sergeant Pomeroy. He had just gotten off of the radio with them and had told them that he and one other person were on their way out to their position. That other person was going to be me. Andy was informed, and in seconds we were following the flagged path to the OP's position. I was able to secure my M-16 and a loose bandolier of ammunition without stopping. The two men at the observation post were each sitting next to a tree, a row apart. A radio was next to one of them, so I headed for the radio while Sergeant Pomeroy headed for the other. Neither man seemed excited as I sat down to question the man with the radio.

He told me that they had just changed guard and had only been there for about ten minutes when he saw definite movement to the west. He was trying to tell how far away it was in meters but gave up and started counting rows of trees. He finally gave up trying to establish the exact distance and placed the movement at the very edge of our sight line. He said that he was watching the jungle line when he saw the movement in his peripheral vision, and when he turned for a better look, there were two hunched-over shapes disappearing. As near as he could tell, they were headed north and maybe northwest a little.

As I studied the terrain under the rubber trees in the direction of the movement, I noticed a couple of dips and slight ridges between us and where the sighting supposedly took place. Then he was talking again after thinking for a short time. This time he mentioned that there had been several people running, and he had seen them run across at least two rows of trees before they were out of sight. He thought he had seen people running upright. He was pretty sure they were human, but he wasn't 100 percent sure. He was equally sure that what he had seen wasn't animals.

It was too bad that he had been looking in the wrong direction to start with. If what he had seen was human, he had only caught the tail end, so we didn't know how many there actually were.

The other guy hadn't seen a thing. He had been watching straight ahead to the north. The four of us gathered at the tree where the radio was and went through the briefing again for Sergeant Pomeroy. I then decided to wait another twenty minutes before returning to the perimeter.

It was not an unusual occurrence for an observation post guard to be alerted. Everywhere we went there were animals, sometimes civilians, and sometimes even Charlie. It was a safe bet to assume that every OP after this and everyone on the perimeter would be focusing just a little harder.

An uneventful twenty minutes passed, and Sergeant Pomeroy and I retraced our steps back to the perimeter. After my earlier nap, I was feeling much better. I would see if I could talk Andy or even Ron into getting some rest.

Andy was waiting for us. I told him that I would monitor the radios for a few hours so he could catch up as I had. Andy was in agreement, but first he wanted to inform me that Alpha Company had been ordered to move more to the east. That would put them right on the road south of the FSB. It sounded to me as if they would be very close to where Rock and I had done our decoy. After the events of this morning, there was no need to warn them. It was becoming evident that battalion was messing with more than just Bravo Company.

The twelve-man patrol was into their sixth hour in position. It was going to mean a tight schedule for both of tonight's ambush patrols, but I was going to wait until 1700 to call them back. So far, the patrol's regular reports indicated that everything was remaining quiet around them. There was a brief time for concern when the two Huey hogs circled close to their position on one of the passes. Sergeant Moore knew that the patrol was short of their position, and they should have been over a hundred meters farther east, at the bottom of the valley.

Andy was getting a good rest now. There was some radio chatter, but for our area, it remained quiet. It was all typical for the time of day. There was the occasional helicopter passing over to the north of us. The FSB had been quiet since this morning, and I was faced with the same dilemma as yesterday. Should I open a can of ham and claymores, or should I open a new case of C-rations? Then it occurred to me that it had already been settled. I could open a new case, and when we left this place, I would celebrate by puncturing the remaining cans of ham and lima beans and burying them.

20

Daylight on the twenty-second of February would soon be slipping away. It was 1700 and time to call the twelve-man blocking force back. Some of the men on the patrol would also be going on night ambush patrols. With so few men in the company, everyone was overworked. The drivers and the TCs were volunteering for patrols. The problem was that if we ever got to the point where we needed to use the drivers and TCs away from their tracks, the perimeter security would be shorthanded. Everyone had a job, and everyone was needed. By now the command-track driver and TC were permanent fixtures in third platoon, and they would work even harder tonight with Sergeant Pomeroy and third platoon covering one of the night ambushes. First platoon was also going to sub in for third platoon where they were needed for perimeter guard duty.

Sergeant Lee and first platoon needed a break—not that tonight would give them much, but tomorrow night it would be Sergeant Lee's turn again for a night ambush patrol.

Second platoon had the most people and the most NCOs, but they were covering the entire east side all by themselves.

Before the second platoon's twelve-man patrol returned, I needed to decide on the next day's riff that we were going to fake. Running phantom patrols during the day by now had become almost a necessity to keep from burning everyone out. I still had today's script, which hadn't been used. I had it in front of me, and it didn't take long to figure out that it could work with some major modifications.

My first thought was that Sergeant Hawkins couldn't lead the patrol as planned. He was on the twelve-man blocking force, which was still out, and he would be leading the east-side night ambush.

There were a number of reasons for using the script that was already prepared. I could argue in favor of a riff in the area that the script covered. For one, it was the only area of the basin that wasn't disrupted today. Another reason for going west was the OP's sighting of someone leaving that area.

I was almost certain that if I scheduled a riff to the west, battalion would get more involved with trying to run the company from their office. I didn't want to antagonize our battalion headquarters, so I needed to prepare a riff to the east. It was inevitable that we would be expected to explore the valley toward the larger of the two buttes. It was worth giving some thought to planning a riff to the east. If I could come up with the right scripted patrol, and if we could pull this one off convincingly, maybe we could get battalion to back off a little. Normally I wouldn't have any problem with following orders, even dangerous orders, but the battalion leadership was going against an infantry leader's strongest rule: Don't ask someone to do something that you yourself wouldn't do. It was so obvious that our company had been hung out to dry. I would need a lot more information before I would be able to change my mind about how our company was being used. The infantry motto is Follow Me. I didn't see anyone taking the lead, and our company was being dangled right in front of the enemy. Even though the job was becoming more difficult each day, I was becoming more convinced than ever that I had chosen the right course of action.

Sergeant Moore called on the radio to report that the blocking force was entering the perimeter. I had to act quickly so the men would have time to eat and prepare for their next patrol. It was time to gather the platoon leaders for a quick meeting. By now there were no secrets and everyone was welcome to attend, and there were usually several other NCOs present, along with some of the third-platoon members, whose track was parked next to the command track.

When the daily meeting was underway, the first thing I talked about was perimeter security. The next item was the night ambushes, so everyone would know the locations and who was on them. Since we had been camped in the clearing in the rubber trees, the next item was the following day's riff, or what amounted to preparing a script for a fake patrol. They all knew that we had a script ready to go, so I went through all of my steps and all of the reasons why we needed to prepare another script. Everyone was in agreement with me. We did some brainstorming and found that it was more difficult to come up with a convincing script. I was thinking that I would lead an actual patrol and go halfway, which would put the patrol in the bottom of the valley. Once I was there, we could hide and call it in, or we could continue. I told the group what I was thinking and was immediately surprised by their responses. They all reacted and began talking at the same time. They wanted me to back off, at least for a while yet.

Sergeant Finley spoke for the group. "It isn't time to stick our necks out."

Sergeant Lee said, "Write another script, and if for any reason the script could be compromised or won't work, we would go with the one we already have. The only change would be to change Sergeant Hawkins's name to mine."

Everyone seemed more relieved than satisfied as we reached agreement, and we adjourned so the patrols could be inspected and be on their way.

I was trying to come up with a script for tomorrow. Getting started wasn't the problem. I needed to know what the bottom of the valley was like. I would have to speak with Sergeant Rios about what the terrain and vegetation were like in the area of the mechanical ambush. I almost had myself convinced that the basin was safe to explore after the damage the jets, artillery, and gunships had done. Two thoughts kept me from abandoning the fake patrols and switching to the real thing. First of all, and foremost, there was no indication that anyone had left the basin. It was likely that Charlie or the NVA regulars knew that someone would eventually come to inspect the damage, and they would be waiting.

A second and equally important reason for continuing the fake patrols was the company's lack of manpower. We were so understaffed that if we ran day riffs the way battalion wanted them scheduled, some of the men would have to be patrolling and awake for over twenty-four hours straight. It is too easy to make a mistake when you are physically spent, sleep deprived, and mentally drained. We needed the daytime to rest so we could be at peak efficiency at night. Even without the day riffs, I was feeling the strain, and the men were getting less sleep than they were used to. This morning's action and having to send the blocking force out upset our rotation and planned rest periods.

The fake patrols were not only keeping the men alive, but they were needed in order to provide just enough rest so that the men could continue to function at a high level. The men's attitude and mental health were just as important as their physical well-being. I seemed to be the only one in the company who was bothered by the concept of running phantom patrols. Deep down I couldn't shake the fact that I knew it was wrong, and Sergeant Moore's comment about me going to LBJ if we ever got caught kept the memory fresh in my thoughts.

I refocused in order to continue trying to script a patrol to the east and south that would drop into the jungle valley that led to the larger butte. I was working overtime trying to put a believable story on paper. As I wrote, I studied the map. There had to be trails in the bottom of the drainage; there just had to be. The patrol would cut brush as they entered the valley until the undergrowth opened up. They then had to find a trail. It would be an old one. After locating a trail, the patrol would move back up the west slope a ways so they were off the trail but could still observe it. They would sit and wait, then move a short distance and sit and wait again. I would have them run out of time and have to turn back by angling uphill to the rubber trees without backtracking. OK, I had it scripted. All that was left was to fill in the call signs, and we were good to go.

I now had two prepared scripts ready. It was a nice feeling to be a little ahead of the game.

This was the time of day when the company perimeter seemed to be the busiest. The night ambush patrols were getting inspected and preparing for their departures. One-third of the company was fixing their dinner or eating. One-third was on guard duty, and the other third was getting ready to patrol. The OPs were included in this group. There was no set time to eat, but the patrolling schedule had a bearing on the available time, and the men were aware that they couldn't all be eating at the same time.

Andy and Ron had already eaten, so that left me. I opened a can of apricots and a cold can of pork and beans and drank sour Kool-Aid. I ate as slowly as I could in order to make the meal last as long as possible. I paused between bites and tried to recall the events of the day. The day had been filled with a lot of action, but most importantly, the company was still intact. How much longer could we hold out with no casualties and remain in one piece? How many more days would the company be in place?

I was aware that I had developed a pattern in my thinking. During the early-morning hours when I was on radio watch, my thinking was more positive. In the early morning, I was planning the day to come and following the breaking of dawn and the increasing daylight. The cup of coffee or cocoa that I looked forward to had also become a daily ritual.

It was between the times that the night ambush patrols left the perimeter and midnight that I had my darkest thoughts. This was the time that I second-guessed myself and had my greatest doubts. I conjured up too many what-if scenarios. It was evident that I did most of my thinking in the morning and most of my worrying at night. With that realization I vowed to keep my thoughts tonight on a more positive level.

Ron was assisting Andy as they prepared for the night by placing the radios on top of the track behind the TC hatch. That position had become the best place for the three of us to be able to reach them because the handsets could extend to each of our jeep seats.

It was getting close to sunset, and soon the sun would be slipping below the horizon. The company was making last-minute preparations for the night security. Not a person or a single piece of equipment that could be seen was out of place. It would take only one mistake, one lapse in judgment, or one person to fall asleep on guard duty, and the entire company could be in jeopardy.

I was a little worried about third platoon being able to uphold their sector of the perimeter tonight with Sergeant Pomeroy out on ambush patrol. This thought occurred to me when Sergeant Pomeroy picked up the recoilless rifle and the ammunition for it.

The sun was now setting, but best of all, we were going to be dry for another night. The afternoon clouds had been fewer today and hadn't thickened to produce any showers in the area. I was searching for the moon and hoping that it would be a little larger tonight. I wanted it to be waxing and not waning.

I had waited until now to call the fire support base. I had more than the usual predetermined targets to call in tonight. I was going to request three different fire missions throughout the night. I wanted to put the artillery on each of the buttes and a third barrage in the valley just to the north of the larger butte.

I gave the FSB the exact location of each of the night ambush patrols that were outside the perimeter and some predetermined targets for each site. I then conveyed the information for the three fire missions into the basin. I scheduled the first fire mission to be directed to the smaller butte and to commence at 2200 hours. The one on the larger butte was scheduled for midnight, or 2400 hours, and the one in the valley was set for 0200 hours. There wasn't a word of protest or any questions. I was sure that the request would be approved. At last, with little left to do, it was time to settle in for the night.

Both ambush patrols left the perimeter before I called for the fire missions, but they had already been briefed at our evening meeting. When the first barrage started at 2200, each patrol called the company to report instead of waiting for us to call them. They were obviously nervous and at a high state of alertness. The next report went as scheduled at ten minutes after the hour, and they waited for Andy to call them this time.

My next radio watch wouldn't be until 0100, so I was adjusting my position for maximum comfort when I heard a new sound above the hum of the insects, which were mainly mosquitoes. I could barely hear it, but somewhere off to the northeast, a firefight was taking place. It was difficult to judge how far away the firefight was since the rubber trees and vegetation absorbed much of the sound. I was convinced the fight could actually be quite close to our location. I could just make out the sounds of small-arms fire and the larger explosions of what must be mortars. Then an artillery battery opened up. There was the familiar one shot at a time while the shots were adjusted to the target, and then the full battery firing when the target had been pin-pointed and the command for fire for effect was given. I was almost sure that the battery firing that fire mission was the same 175 battery that we had used that morning. The direction of the sound of the outgoing seemed right.

Andy was resting and I was monitoring the radio, so he wasn't scanning the frequencies and searching for information about what was going on near our position. When it was his turn to take over, he would somehow come up with the information.

Twenty-three hundred hours soon arrived, and Ron was awake and there to take over. I didn't have to leave my seat. All I had to do was slink down, cover my arms and shoulders with the poncho liner, and try to doze. I soon realized that I wasn't tired. The day nap had rejuvenated my body. I couldn't sleep, so I studied the stars. I couldn't see any that I recognized. I was trying to relax, and my mind was clear. So far, I wasn't thinking negative thoughts. I would concentrate on relaxing, and perhaps I might be able to sleep a little.

When I had first climbed to the top of the track, it had still been light, and I had liberally applied insect repellent to my exposed skin, namely my face and hands. At the moment I was covered in mosquitoes. I couldn't see my face, but my hands were almost totally dark with solid mosquitoes, but I wasn't feeling any bites. These must be all males. "OK, guys, I'll try not to slap you."

The serenity of the moment changed in an instant. There was a brilliant flash of light that was instantaneously followed the echoing roar of a large explosion. It happened in front of me, slightly to the left of where I was facing. The blast was straight out from third platoon's position. As the echoing of the explosion died away, I knew exactly what it was. Sergeant Pomeroy's mechanical ambush had been set off.

The area under the rubber trees where the mechanical ambush had been set wasn't returning to the quiet of the night. There was noise, and what I was hearing was a first. I could hear a dog yipping in pain, and another was howling. This was a new and unexpected phenomenon. The sounds that the dogs were making kept up, but they were moving north, away from us. It was several minutes before they were out of hearing and the area was quiet again.

At last it was totally quiet; in fact, it was very quiet. The insects had ceased their hum, and the other night noises had stopped. Every eye in the company was focused in front of their position. The mechanical was just far enough away and in a depression, so there was no reason to sweep the area with fire from our perimeter. No one had twitched as we all sat in silence.

Andy and I were now on the ground, each of us with a radio. Andy called the night ambushes, starting with Sergeant Pomeroy, to inform them what had happened and to find out if they had seen anything. Sergeant Pomeroy's ambush was in the rubber trees not far from our perimeter and the closest to the mechanical. His patrol hadn't observed anything. He commented that the mechanical was more to the north of his position and around a corner to the east. While Andy was informing the ambush patrols, I had the fire support base on the radio. All I said after I identified myself was "fire mission." I gave them the coordinates and the direction from my position to the target as well as the distance. The target was due north of my position, and the distance was over two hundred meters. I planned to move the exploding artillery rounds quickly to the north in the direction that the sound of the dogs had gone.

Andy had Sergeant Finley on his radio and was preparing the mortar platoon to fire illumination rounds out to the sides of our perimeter and over the mechanical's position.

I adjusted a second round from the artillery battery farther to the north and east before I gave the fire for effect and then kept moving the exploding rounds farther and farther away from our position. I was trying to walk the sheaf along the depression as it angled away from the company.

When the fire mission ended, four of the mortar platoon's parachute flares were still in the sky, and they were drifting to the northwest. There was no wind on the ground, so I was surprised by how fast they were moving. The flares had been positioned quite a ways out from our position. Two of the flares were drifting over where the artillery had landed, but they weren't helping our visual of the area at all. The drifting flares were creating long, shimmering shadows under the rubber tress that seemed to move and dance as the flares drifted to the northwest and eventually burned out.

When it was dark and quiet again, I called each of the ambush patrols to let them know what I knew. I found out that each of the patrols had heard the dogs, but neither had seen or heard anything else.

The call to battalion lasted a lot longer. They must have thought I was in a dayroom in the rear with nothing else to do, because I couldn't get them off of the horn. They kept asking question after question as I was alternating talking to two different people and replaying the incident a couple of times for each of them before I was finally able to sign off.

Andy and I then skirted the entire perimeter and talked to the men at each track. I wanted the company on 100 percent alert for the next hour. I was sure they would take the alert to two or three hours. It would be some time before anyone would be able to sleep.

By the time we reached the second platoon, we could hear another distant firefight to the south. I could almost be sure it was Alpha Company that was in contact. I wanted to listen to the radio in order to confirm my suspicions. I even wanted to go directly over to the mortar platoon's location so I could view the southwest for tracers, but first I would finish reporting to the second platoon.

By the time Andy and I had finished our tour of the company perimeter, it was quiet in the south. I was convinced that the latest firefight had involved Alpha Company. The artillery at the FSB hadn't been used, but I distinctly heard the mortars. I made the assumption that the mortars were Alpha Company's and not Charlie's.

The radio that I still carried with me sounded with my call sign. I answered the call from the FSB as the artillery was ready to fire the second fire mission that I had called in earlier. "Shot out." Now the larger butte was getting blasted again. I couldn't help but smile in the dark as we all listened to the sound of the outgoing at the fire support base and the sound of the louder explosions on the butte. The targeted area was slightly closer to our position than the FSB was, as I remembered without looking at the map.

My radio watch wasn't due for another hour. It was going to be a while before anyone in the company would be able to sleep. It was just after midnight; we had blown one of our mechanical ambushes, and there had been two firefights within earshot of our position. There seemed to be a lot going on around us.

I couldn't begin to predict what was going to come next during the rest of the night. The men would come down fast as daylight approached, and fatigue was going to affect all of us during the day.

While I had the chance, I was trying to think ahead. I was going to go with Sergeant Pomeroy to check out the site of the blown mechanical just after daylight. I, for one, wasn't feeling any of the letdown effects after an adrenaline high yet, but I knew it was coming. I was sorting through all that had happened and was trying to make some sense of it all.

When Andy had the time, I would have him find out about the two firefights we had heard. I could bet that he would have the information without my having to ask. The other thing that I was thinking about was time. I planned to be with Sergeant Pomeroy's patrol to search the area of the mechanical. When I returned from the site of the mechanical, one of the planned riffs needed to be underway. It was going to be a tight schedule, and I couldn't see a time when I could get any rest. At least the scripts were already prepared, and we just had to choose one.

There hadn't been any excitement for over an hour. It was my turn to monitor the radios, and I had been given a lot to think about. I was recalling the events of the blown mechanical ambush. The sound of the dogs was a confusing factor. Had they been wild dogs? I hadn't heard of any wild dogs or packs since I had been in-country. All of the dogs that I had seen had been near population centers, base camps, and rarely, but once in a while, a fire support base such as Georgia.

Had the dogs that were hanging around the FSB followed us hoping for a handout? This was highly unlikely because the dogs would have shown up much sooner. Judging by the time that the mechanical had blown and the location of the mechanical, all pointed to Charlie using dogs to clear his path. Wild dogs, camp dogs, or Charlie's dogs—hopefully, there would be a clue when we searched the site at daylight.

I began analyzing the day's coming events, starting with a search of the area of the mechanical ambush. At first I hadn't been thinking realistically. It was going to take much more time than I had initially considered, and now I had another idea. The patrol would check out the blown mechanical and would then continue to riff north into the rubber and cloverleaf back to the company perimeter. My idea was to do a quick reconnaissance of the area and return to the company area, where the rest of the patrol would be scripted. That would mean I would need to prepare a third script.

I had two scripts waiting, and now we would have another. Well, it would have to wait until daylight. I was sure that I could have it ready by 0700. At 0700 a patrol led by Sergeant Pomeroy, since it was his mechanical, would go check out the site.

When it was almost time for my assigned turn at the radio to be over, I was still keyed up. The next call from the FSB would end my watch, and I was looking forward to the valley north of the larger butte being pounded for ten minutes.

As I waited, I was fascinated by some fireflies in front of the track. I thought the lights blinking on and off might be a VC patrol out in the rubber trees until I was able to fix the lights' position at five to ten feet. It was a plausible idea, because Charlie was known to use flashlights with painted-over lenses that emitted a tiny pinhole of light that could appear to be a firefly. I was relieved that it was a false alarm at the recognition that the lights were only fireflies. My heart had raced and was slowing down again. I assumed that everyone in the company was as edgy as I was.

Part of my job since being assigned to Bravo Company as an NCO was paying attention to all that was happening around me so I could better serve my platoon. There was a difference now. That same responsibility was multiplied by four, to include the entire company. All of my waking time, 100 percent of it, was devoted to avoiding mistakes and being prepared. I was feeling the weight of the added responsibility. I was behind in my letter writing. My wife, my mom and dad, and my aunts in Minnesota might worry why the usual timely letter hadn't arrived in the mail. The last thing that I wanted to do was worry any of them unnecessarily, but the letter writing would have to be a lower priority for now. I would catch up sometime in the future. I could write all day on the next stand-down if I needed to.

I was brought out of my trancelike thoughts when the fire support base called to announce the third planned fire mission. My watch was over at 0400. I didn't have to wake Ron. He was adjusting his poncho liner as the first round of shots left the FSB. These explosions were quite a bit closer to us than the first two fire missions had been. I just scooted down a little lower in the jeep seat and listened.

I must have been really out, because the next thing I remembered was Andy waking me for the 0400 radio watch. At 0410 the ambush patrols gave the usual two squelch replies.

Knowing that a cup of coffee or cocoa and the sun's warmth weren't that far off, I was ready to organize the events that would likely take place today. As soon as it was light enough, I would knock out the new script. I would have it ready to go over with the NCOs before we left to check out the mechanical.

The blown mechanical was the second order of business and the most pressing. I was going to be with Sergeant Pomeroy's patrol when he checked it out.

The third thing was the details of the riff into the rubber trees. At this point I was thinking that we really should follow this one up with an actual patrol. I was trying to count heads and remember who had already been on patrol and who had done the night ambushes. The blown mechanical was throwing off our patrol rotations. The men were being pushed hard, so I decided that we would sit tight on this patrol and talk our way through it inside the safety of the company perimeter. After a sleepless night, I would allow the men to get some rest.

21

The insect and jungle noises were becoming softer now. The sounds were still there, but they weren't as loud. I assumed the insects were quieter because of the coolness of the morning. The arrival of the sun would bring everything back to full power. I was searching the eastern sky for the first signs of light as one sound piped up and became louder than all of the rest. I had heard this sound only a few times before, and to my knowledge, this was the first time in this area. Maybe it had been making its call, and it just hadn't registered with me yet. In my own defense, my thoughts had been occupied by things other than wildlife calls. The sound built to a crescendo for a second time. It began as a throaty, deep, guttural sound and tapered off to a surprisingly clear "fuck you." The *oo* sound in the "you" was extended for another measure. There in the trees at the western edge of the perimeter, between the mortar platoon and first platoon, was a fuck-you lizard. I had been told that a lizard made the sound, but I had yet to see one of the creatures. This was an English-speaking animal in an Asian country, and it was taunting me.

Soon after the lizard became silent, a thin veil of light began to widen in the eastern sky. I started writing the new script. This patrol would be different because I was going to be with it and would be reporting to the company. Another tricky part of this patrol was that Andy or Sergeant Moore would have to relay information to battalion, and I worried that battalion could surprise them with an off-the-wall request or order. In the script, we would reset the mechanical and angle to the northeast. If we walked all day, we would still be in the rubber plantation, so I needed to establish a return time. Realistically this should be a longer riff. If the patrol left the site of the mechanical at around 0800 and patrolled until noon, the circle back would make the return trip longer. Based on company history, a patrol returning much after 1700 was considered late. Nevertheless, I chose to have the patrol return between 1630 and 1700. Maybe my subconscious remembered the dogs leaving to the north when the mechanical blew, but whatever the reasons, I wrote that after patrolling to the northeast, the patrol would circle to the west for their return trip back to the company.

It was barely light, and I was ahead of schedule, as I had just finished the script. Andy had a message for me that battalion was on the radio and wanted to talk to me. Sometimes it was hard to sort out the calls from battalion. Much of the time, depending on who took the call, I didn't know the origin of the call. Lieutenant Duff sometimes used the battalion frequency to contact our company. He was at the FSB, and battalion headquarters was in Long Binh. As it turned out, this wasn't Lieutenant Duff. The call sign was one that I didn't recognize. The person on the other end of the radio wanted to know if we had already scouted the area of the blown mechanical. I advised the other end of the radio that I had a patrol organized and ready to depart as soon as our conversation was over.

I was beginning to be upset by battalion's meddling in the running of the company when the voice at the other end stated that he was an intelligence officer, and he wanted to know everything that I could tell him about the blown mechanical. This I would be more than happy to comply with. He was rattling off some dos and don'ts about how to methodically search an area. None of what he had to say was new information. He added that he would be personally monitoring our company radio frequency as we patrolled and searched the area. He requested that he be constantly updated.

I took the time to tell him about hearing the dogs after the claymores blew. The men in the perimeter and I had heard only two dogs, but the ambush patrol that was to the west of the logger site all swore they had heard more. Until now I had forgotten that bit of information, which Sergeant Pomeroy had passed to me last night. The intelligence officer would have something to think about until we actually left the perimeter to patrol to the site.

The ambush patrols were returning. Sergeant Finley was standing by; since he had helped set the mechanical ambush, he automatically assumed that he would be going with the patrol. That was OK with me, but his line number wasn't part of the original makeup of the patrol. I would call it in and add him to the patrol.

Sergeant Moore and two riflemen from second platoon carried fresh claymores for the new mechanical that was going to be put in to replace the blown one. The three of them waited with Sergeant Finley.

Sergeant Pomeroy and the returning patrol came from behind first platoon where they had just entered the perimeter. Of the six-man patrol, three of the men angled for their tracks, and Sergeant Pomeroy, his RTO, and one rifleman lined out straight to our group. The RTO and the rifleman were carrying the three flechette rounds, and Sergeant Pomeroy had the recoilless rifle. Andy, Sergeant Moore, and I relieved them of their burden and placed the recoilless rifle and the ammunition inside the command track.

One more thing and we would be ready. Before we left the perimeter, I wanted to go over the morning schedule with the remaining NCOs. It didn't take long to explain the new scripted patrol and the reasons behind it. With no questions or opposition, it was time to get on with finding out what had set off the mechanical. I cautioned everyone that battalion was listening to our company frequency, and that piece of information needed to be passed on to all of the members of the company.

At last I was ready, and we could find out what had actually taken place a couple of hundred meters just to the north of our perimeter at a little after midnight. I was thinking that we were getting a late start, but as I examined my watch, I was relieved to see that it was only 0715.

The OPs were already in place at daylight. Our patrol was going to follow the path to the OPs' position and then turn toward the mechanical ambush location. I radioed the remaining platoons that we were leaving the perimeter. At the same time, I wondered how many sets of ears were listening at battalion headquarters.

When the patrol turned away from the OP's position, everyone spread out and gave away more distance to the next person.

Sergeant Pomeroy was on point, with another man from third platoon walking slack. They were followed by the third platoon's RTO. The men were spaced six to eight meters apart. Sergeant Moore and another member of second platoon were four rows of rubber trees out to the left side. The other member of second platoon was four rows of trees out to the right side. I was in the center of the formation a little farther back, with Andy behind me. Sergeant Finley followed at another ten meters behind Andy and acted as rear security.

It didn't take long to reach the dip or depression, and then Sergeant Pomeroy led us right down the middle toward the location of the mechanical. When Sergeant Pomeroy stopped the formation, Andy and I moved forward to his position. Everyone got down on one knee. Sergeant Finley remained looking back the way we had come, and Sergeant Moore and his men were on the high ground watching out to the sides.

No one said a word. Each of us was studying the area in front of us. Starting twenty meters to the front, the low vegetation and grass had been laid flat in the fanned-out direction of a claymore blast. Judging from the blast patterns, the area in the depression had been well covered with the interlocking fire of the three claymores. Each claymore had been placed next to a tree and sighted away and down the depression. The placement of the trip wire was at the south end, while the kill zone was down the depression to the northeast. The set-up was designed to take the first person in line and anyone following for up to sixty meters.

Sergeant Pomeroy approached me and leaned over and whispered, "I suspended a loose trip wire all the way across the row of trees, and it was set thirty inches off of the ground. A dog should have been able to pass under the wire without setting it off."

I was mulling over what he had just told me as I got Sergeant Moore's attention to move the flank security up even with us. Sergeant Pomeroy was studying the area where the trip wire had been placed. He returned with the battery that he had used. He had found it still on the ground behind the tree where it had originally been placed.

I radioed the intelligence officer that I had spoken to earlier to inform him that we were at the site and had located the battery and the position of the trip wire. We were gathering the information, and I would call back in zero thirty mikes.

The trip wire caused us more confusion. The wire was there, but it was in the wrong position. Sergeant Pomeroy went over the original placement. From the battery, the trip wire was attached behind the short loop of bare wire that was connected to the battery. The trip wire went up the tree trunk, over a small branch, and then strung across the row to the opposite tree. When a person or animal ran into the wire, it pulled the two bared loops of electrical wire together, completing the circuit that fired the blasting caps and set off the claymores.

The trip wire had been hit hard, as the loops were elongated and tight together. The trip wire had also broken loose from the tree that it had been anchored to across from the battery. The wire lay on the ground angling across the depression, but it was on the north side instead of the south side. The mechanical was set with the intention that someone would be coming toward the company from the north, but all of the clues indicated that the mechanical had been tripped by someone or something coming from the south and heading away from the perimeter. It was also apparent that a person coming from the south and hitting the trip wire on the perimeter side away from the middle of the depression could escape being wounded by the blast.

I hadn't known what we would find at the site, but I had expected to find something. So far, there was absolutely nothing. We reorganized everyone on line and began sweeping the area. We covered the area down the middle of the depression, then the sides, and finally the area on top. We covered the area outside the blast up to fifty meters from the kill zone, and still we found nothing. We went over some of the areas again and again but came up negative.

When we could do no more, a new four-claymore mechanical was set fifty meters farther down the depression. The patrol was reformed to return to the perimeter, but before we moved out, I radioed the intelligence officer. It had been more than thirty minutes, and I could tell by the way he identified himself that he wasn't happy. I reported what we had found regarding the position of the trip wire. I had nothing else to report except my theories. He kept insisting that there had to be a blood trail. Without going into all of the details of the design of the mechanical because of the time it would take, I tried to convince him that we had covered the area thoroughly looking for blood and anything else. He finally signed out after I told him that we were going to cloverleaf the area and search for a trail beyond the blast site.

It was time to start the fake patrol. Everyone with the patrol was keyed up, but fatigue was beginning to show on the faces of the men. Since we hadn't found anything, there would be less guilt on my part. The twist on this patrol was that I was leading it, with Sergeant Pomeroy attached. Sergeant Finley had been added to the patrol's roster, and I would be reporting to Sergeant Lee at the logger site. I reported that we were still on site and searching. In actuality, we were entering the perimeter. I positioned myself at the rear of my track, where I could see Sergeant Lee at his track. Sergeant Pomeroy's track was next to mine, and he would be doing half of the reports.

As I was reviewing the script, I was confident that it would work, except the time sequences were off. Everything had happened earlier than I had planned for when I had written it. I gathered Sergeant Pomeroy and headed for Sergeant Lee's position. I explained a simple solution in order to correct the discrepancy. The patrol would simply continue to search the area of the mechanical until the scripted time to line out to the northeast arrived. It wouldn't be long now; another forty minutes, and everything would be back on schedule.

Before forty minutes passed, battalion called me. I was in a tricky situation. Battalion wanted me to report to them regularly throughout the day. I had to inform them that I was on patrol and couldn't keep an open mike. They could get their report from Sergeant Lee. I used his line number and gave them his call sign. This was all on the company frequency as I looked over at Sergeant Lee at his track. He had heard and gave me a thumbs-up. Seconds later I listened to Sergeant Lee receive the same message from battalion headquarters. They wanted an updated progress report every two hours until further notice. That meant that there would be a report at noon, 1400, 1600, and 1800 hours. If they still wanted a report after 1800, I would be back and able to make that one and any future reports. Sergeant Lee had three of the battalion reports to look forward to.

Finally the script was back on schedule. The phantom patrol was moving slowly northeast, following the depression. My map was in my lap, and I was closely studying the patrol's route, which I had traced in pencil. When I had written the script, I had overlooked a mention of where the artillery rounds had landed. I recalled that none had landed in the depression. Most of the rounds had impacted to the northeast. I didn't want to change anything at this point. Besides, the patrol was moving beyond the area of the artillery strike.

I did get creative by having Andy radio the FSB to inquire about the possibility of other troops or civilians in the area. If either was present, we should have already been informed. The report from the FSB was negative, which meant it was just us and Charlie in the area.

The OPs were out, and the company remained on 50 percent alert. The other 50 percent were getting much-needed rest. I caught myself yawning. Let's make it through today. Then we will worry about tonight. I was worried about how battalion might react. It was their job to keep track of the companies, and I didn't have a problem with regular reports. What worried me the most, and what I objected to, was when they tried to give directives that disrupted the way we operated. I was hiding a lot from them, and I was the one who was leading them on.

I was so impressed with the company's noise discipline. Since we had been here, the only sound that had come from the company was the mortar platoon firing illumination last night, and that had taken place at the same time that the 105s were firing from the FSB. It's hard enough to judge the direction and distance of the low thumping sounds of outgoing mortar rounds when there aren't any other distracting sounds, and our mortars had been concealed by the artillery fire mission.

It was a little before noon, and battalion headquarters was calling Sergeant Lee on our company frequency. They wanted to know the current location of the patrol. I was holding up my map and pointing to the top margin, where I had written coordinates along the route. It would soon be time to change direction. Sergeant Lee followed my lead perfectly. He told whoever was on the other end that he didn't have the exact location since the patrol was moving, but the patrol should be in the vicinity of... he rattled off a six-digit coordinate. In ten minutes, I would radio that the patrol was almost at a slightly different set of coordinates. At that point the patrol would start circling to the west.

I could see Sergeant Lee opening a can of C-rations. I would wait until he finished eating before I radioed that the patrol had changed direction. It was just after 1300, and Sergeant Pomeroy would call in the 1400 report.

Andy had news about the firefight that had taken place early last night to the northeast. A platoon of straight-leg infantry was pulling security for a unit of Australian engineers that was maintaining the road from Highway 1 to Vung Tau. They had caught a group of NVA regulars crossing the road.

I was interested, but it was time to call Sergeant Lee. Besides, battalion was listening and anticipating my call to Sergeant Lee. Andy had more news and was holding a hand up, signaling me to wait. I shook my head and pointed in the direction of Sergeant Lee. I tried to indicate with my thumb and index finger, "Just a second." Andy let out a long, exaggerated sigh, signaling me to go ahead.

Sergeant Lee was waving at me to let me know that it was time. I radioed that we hadn't found anything and were going to look farther to the west before we would be on our way back. There were three and a half hours to go before the fake patrol would be back. Sergeant Pomeroy was going to call in the next two reports. That gave me more than a couple of hours to lay out the company's strategy for tonight.

Andy was ready to finish the report about what had happened around us last night. He said that he would get back to how he found out about the Australian engineers in a moment. The firefight to the south wasn't Alpha Company at all. There were a number of small villages in the area to the west and south toward the delta. This explained all the rice paddies and other agricultural activity in the vicinity. A unit of local militia or regional forces had caught some NVA regulars moving through the area. The Ruff Puffs (South Vietnamese regional forces) had spotted the NVA troops skirting a wood line. The mortars had belonged to the Ruff Puffs. Andy added that a MAC-V advisor working with the Ruff Puffs was wounded. Andy had gotten the information by listening in on Alpha Company reporting to an intelligence officer at battalion headquarters.

I knew that guy. It was most likely the same intelligence officer who had called me early this morning.

The information about the other firefight, where the NVA troops were crossing the road, had come from our company clerk in Long Binh, who had gotten the information from one of his buddies who worked in the battalion headquarters.

It was early in the afternoon. As I looked around the company, I noticed three things that stood out. First, there was a man on top of every other track sitting and watching out into the rubber trees. Second, there were men lying in the shade on stretchers or suspended in low-slung hammocks. The rest of the company—those who weren't resting or watching—was cleaning their weapons and equipment. One group had their rucksacks laid out and were cleaning their extra ammunition. The mortar platoon was also cleaning their tubes.

I spread out my map to work. It was earlier than usual for me to have the opportunity to make preparations. I made some notes for discussion at the evening meeting. I wanted to organize the night ambush patrols. It had been the company policy ever since I had been with the company to have two night ambushes, and that wasn't going to change. I would continue with two six-man patrols, with one deployed on each side of our perimeter. The patrols alternated between the edge of the jungle and out in the rubber trees. I knew the men were being careful to police the sites before they left to return in the mornings. My other thought had to do with alternating the ambush sites. Was that too predictable? Tonight we would be out in the rubber again.

I heard a distant helicopter crossing the now-familiar north-to-southeast route, headed toward the Pacific Ocean. Clouds were beginning to build and bunch up. It was still too early to tell whether we would get rain. I was only too aware that we had been lucky the last two nights.

Not long after I had joined Bravo Company, the southern part of Vietnam was hit by a typhoon. At the time, the company was working in Tay Ninh Province, and I was out on one of the night ambushes. The rain started in the afternoon, and it was raining hard as we left the company area. I remembered that the wind just kept increasing. Being in that storm was every bit as scary as being shot at. The wind and rain lasted all night and into the next morning, when the typhoon subsided to a really bad storm. Many times when I noticed the clouds building, I had flashbacks of the typhoon. The men who had to be out on patrol during that storm would remember the storm of '69 for a long time to come.

I was sorting out options for the phantom patrol that would take place on the twenty-fourth of February. I had two scripts prepared and waiting. Either script would work, but I couldn't predict what might happen between now and tomorrow morning, so I would have to wait and see. The way things had gone so far, each new day had produced its own set of surprises. The company was still intact, and it would be nice if all the action and excitement would taper off.

I was still contemplating which script I should use for tomorrow when I noticed Sergeant Pomeroy calling Sergeant Lee. That was my cue that I had thirty minutes before I radioed that the patrol was headed back to the perimeter. Once that call was made, the NCOs would meet to make preparations to survive the night. Make it through the night. Make it through the day. Make it through the night. It was a simple strategy.

Andy was smiling at me.

"What?"

"Battalion wants Alpha Company to move again, and Alpha doesn't want to move."

I understood completely. It was way too late in the day to be moving an entire mechanized company.

"Someone at battalion headquarters must have their head up their ass."

"You got that right." Andy had another interesting bit of information. "Battalion is moving Charlie Company across the road to our side. They're going to be loggered up in the rubber trees east of our last logger site. Charlie Company's CO—that would be Captain Sorenson—confirmed that they would move first thing in the morning."

Our battalion headquarters had some busy minds.

Looking at my map, I put my finger on our position. I traced my finger to the FSB that was directly to the east. I then located the area that I thought Alpha Company was being sent to, and then to the north where Charlie Company was going to be. We were surrounded to the north, west, and south. Our only open side was to the east. I could guess that battalion would make that our area of responsibility. It appeared that we were still the bait, and there were any number of ways that battalion could go with their thinking now.

I had no choice but to continue doing what I was doing. Bravo Company would survive. We weren't going to show any weaknesses.

More and more, the idea that we were being watched was creeping into my consciousness.

It was time to call in and end today's phantom patrol. It was after 1630 when I made the call to Sergeant Lee that we had the perimeter in sight and would be arriving soon. The west-side OP then called to say that he had the patrol in sight. When I stood up to stretch the kinks out, the first large drops of rain began to fall. Ponchos were coming out quickly. The company was much better prepared this time.

22

I could see a wall of water coming across the basin directly toward our location. It is a scientific fact that warm air holds more moisture than cool air. Here in this part of tropical Asia, the warm air extends from the ground to quite high altitudes. It was warm when the rain began. I would guess that the temperature was well over ninety degrees while it was raining. Usually the temperature dropped five or ten degrees after it started raining, but today it remained very warm.

Two of the men from second platoon had seen the rain coming and were waiting on the ramps of their tracks, each with his shirt off and a bar of soap in his hand. It is hard for people back in my part of the world to imagine a downpour intense enough to rinse off a layer of soap, but we regularly experienced it.

The next thing that happened was a sight that I will always remember. When the full force of the downpour hit the company perimeter, the wall of water bisected the company diagonally north and south. The east side of the perimeter was literally a solid sheet of water, and the west side was still in the sunshine. I had heard men talk about being inside a building with it raining on one side and the sun shining on the other side. Now it was happening right in our logger site.

By the time the rain had moved far enough to the west to engulf the entire company, it was evident that this was not going to be a light shower that would quickly pass. It was raining for as far as I could see, which wasn't far, as I faced the direction the weather was coming from. The intense downpour greatly reduced the visibility. I could no longer view the entire basin; in fact, I couldn't even see the larger butte.

There were some gusts of wind with the rain, and once again I remembered the typhoon of '69. A loose poncho was blowing across the perimeter, coming from second platoon and headed for third platoon. A member of second platoon, one of the shirtless bathers, was chasing the poncho down.

Most of the men had pulled on a poncho and were next to their tracks. Some of the men hadn't bothered with a poncho, and a few others were huddled inside their tracks. The OPs hadn't had a chance to get their ponchos. The company was still at a high level of alertness in spite of the rain.

The amount of rain falling would bring on another concern. The company was going to have to deal with mud. We had been in place long enough that the ground, especially around the tracks, had been worn to the bare earth. Where the bare soil was exposed, mud would form. It was going to be a huge challenge for the company to keep equipment clean and functioning. As I moved around the track, I noticed that this mud was particularly sticky. Our life was about to take on another dimension. Along with fighting the war, we would also be fighting the mud. The mud meant a whole different set of problems. Fortunately, those of us remaining with Bravo Company were seasoned and had dealt with mud before.

The rain eased up considerably, but it continued to fall. It had been raining for the better part of an hour with no letup in sight. I needed to have my NCO meeting. I sent Ron to round up the platoon leaders and pass the word to the other NCOs that they were welcome, but it wasn't mandatory for them. I could tell that Ron was antsy and needed something to do.

The sky had started to lighten up to the south. I could see the larger butte now, and there was even a small patch of blue beyond the butte. As I looked to the east, the direction the weather was coming from, there were no breaks to be seen. It was going to continue to rain for a while.

The meeting with the NCOs went smoothly. It was reminiscent of each of the previous evening meetings. The same subjects were discussed in the same order. There were no changes in duties or schedules. Perimeter security, the night ambush patrols, and the next day's planned phantom patrol were the topics of the meeting. By now all the NCOs knew that there were two scripts that had yet to be used.

With all of the action and excitement of the last few days, there had been a need to meet in the mornings also, and most of the NCOs favored continuing to meet in the morning as long as we were running the phantom patrols.

All around the perimeter, the men were eating in shifts as equipment was checked and extra batteries laid out for the radios. The men who were assigned to one of the ambush patrols were getting their gear together, but they were keeping it much more compact this evening, since it was still raining. Even in the rain, each seemingly minor task had been done many times before and in the same way each time. Efficiency was the desired result of all of the repeated practices. In order to be efficient, each task needed to become routine. This was particularly true of how Bravo Company ran their night ambush patrols. Each member of the patrol was responsible for certain equipment. When the patrol moved, all of the members moved the same way. Each member had an assigned place in line. The arrangement of the patrol members at an ambush site varied, but it wasn't random. Usually the same members were placed next to each other to facilitate guard duty and capitalize on individual strengths.

I was standing next to the radio when it sounded with a call from battalion headquarters. This was one of the rare times that Andy was beyond reach of a radio, but he was taking his turn eating a can of C-rations and sipping a warm soda.

It was 1815, and the person on the radio wanted detailed information regarding the day's patrol north into the rubber trees. I gave a brief summary of the mechanical going off, the presence of the dogs, what was discovered at the ambush site, and the negative results of the patrol. There really wasn't much else to report.

The person I was talking to wasn't the same intelligence officer I had talked to earlier in the day. I guessed that this was a lower-ranking person who had been given the assignment of getting a report from us. It seemed apparent that the person I was talking to had been given a list of questions and had been told to write everything down. The questions kept coming, and if I gave any answer at all, I had to wait while he wrote it down. Did the patrol discover any sign? Did they discover anything at all out of the ordinary? Did they find any evidence of human activity? Did they discover any paths, trails, roads, or travel routes? When it seemed as if the questions would never end, the conversation finally did conclude, and they were out.

The call from battalion had me thinking. It was unusual and irregular to receive such a call, and I was becoming suspicious. Had he been fishing for something? Did he know something that I didn't? Then I was struck with fear. The patrol had been one of the phantom patrols. Had I been discovered? I searched my memory, frantically trying to uncover any mistake that I might have made. Had anything been said that would make battalion think that we weren't doing what we were saying we were doing? I pictured myself being escorted by MPs to the gates of LBJ. I had Sergeant Moore to thank for making the comment about LBJ. I probably would never have made that association had it not been for Sergeant Moore. He might have been joking, but it was my neck that was sticking out, and this wasn't the first time that LBJ had entered my thoughts since Sergeant Moore's innocent comment.

Whatever battalion was thinking, or whatever they had discovered, was going to have to wait. It wouldn't be much longer, and it would be getting dark. Nightfall would come sooner today because of the cloud cover. I was wondering if it would ever stop raining tonight and clear off. It was getting closer to 1900, and the rain was continuing in a steady downpour. I was momentarily encouraged when it appeared to be lighter in the west, but the east was still consistently dark, and that was where the weather was coming from. 1900 hours was the time when the company went on a higher alert, and 1900 hours was when I took my position on top of the track with the radios. It was surprisingly warm yet for as long as it had been raining, so I opted for the top of the track instead of the cramped quarters inside.

I was finally climbing to the top of the track. I was wearing my poncho with my boonie hat inside the hood, and I had my poncho liner folded in my left arm under the poncho. The poncho liner was mostly dry, and I was sure that I would need it before the night was over. Before I climbed up, I placed my M-16 between the jeep seat and the TC hatch. Andy had fashioned a cover for the radios out of a torn poncho. We would keep the radios dry for as long as we could.

I was now up to the task, and the task at hand was to make it through the night, and when morning arrived, the next task would be getting through the day.

It continued to remain quite warm for as much rain as we were getting. Even as wet as I was, I wasn't uncomfortable at this point.

Darkness arrived early. There was solid cloud cover, but the rain had stopped. I had heard that in the highlands in the middle of Vietnam and in the mountains up north, it could rain for weeks at a time. I couldn't imagine a week of solid rain.

As I sat in the inky darkness, the dominant sound had been the raindrops striking the various surfaces, but currently the sound of the raindrops had given way to the sound of thousands of insects humming, buzzing, and clicking. Mosquitoes were buzzing everywhere. Where had they been when it was raining? I didn't need to hunt for my repellent. It was in its usual place in my left breast pocket. I hefted the repellent in my right hand and then shook the plastic bottle. I guessed the bottle to be over half full, and at that point I was sure that I would be able to use all of it before the night was over.

After a rain like the one we had just experienced, there would be leeches in the jungle and all along the edge of the rubber trees where the plantation ended and the jungle began. Repellent would become as important as any other piece of equipment.

Earlier today Ron had done an inventory of the amount of repellent in the company. The mortar platoon had the most left, and if other platoons began to run low, they could get more from Sergeant Finley's crew. Ron estimated that the company had enough repellent for more than two weeks of heavy use. The malaria pills turned out to be a different matter. Ron was very upset. When he had informed me back at the FSB that we had a month's supply of each of the malaria pills, he had been working with the FSB medics. When we departed he had received a package from them that he assumed included all of his requests, but it hadn't included the order of malaria pills that he had asked for. Each person in the company took a daily pill, and this was supposed to prevent one type of malaria. Each person also took a weekly pill every Monday, and that provided immunity for another stain of malaria.

Ron had an exact count of the malaria pills and knew to the day when each would run out. The daily pills would last for a week and four days. The weekly pill would be gone after next Monday. Today was Tuesday, the twenty-third of February. The only reason that I knew it was a Tuesday was that I had taken my weekly malaria pill yesterday, and that pill was always taken on Monday all over Vietnam by every member of the US military. The only reason that I knew that the date was the twenty-third was that my birthday had been on the previous Tuesday. I kept better track of the date than the day of the week. After all, I had a reminder every Monday when it was time to take the weekly malaria pill.

I had been thinking about insects, repellent, and malaria pills, and Andy was interrupting me, wanting to find out if I had called in any fire missions for tonight. I had given the FSB the positions of the ambush patrols and the usual predetermined targets.

Andy was satisfied with my answer and had started to ask another question when, as if on cue, there was a fire mission to the south or southwest, and Andy forgot his question. He was fumbling with a second radio that he was tuning to the FSB's frequency. I kept expecting anything to the south of the FSB to involve Alpha Company, but the FSB had someone else on the radio. I could only guess that it was a MAC-V advisor adjusting artillery for the ARVN unit that he was assigned to.

When the guns were silent, Andy couldn't remember what he was going to ask me. There was a change of sound to our front. I strained to listen for a number of seconds before it registered that it was raining again, and a moment later, the drops were landing on me. It had been a long time since I had experienced a night as dark as this one.

I finished my turn at the radio, and Ron took over. My next watch would be at 0100 hours. The last rain shower had been just that and hadn't lasted long. I could see a few stars peeking through breaks in the clouds. I closed my eyes and wondered if I would sleep. When I awoke it was after midnight, and I had to pee. Ron had gone below to sleep on the bench, and Andy was at the radios. I shed the poncho and the poncho liner as quietly as I could. It had cooled off considerably, and I could feel the chill in the air. I climbed down and moved to the front of the driver's hatch and aimed at an angle out away from the track. The stream of urine hitting the ground was unusually loud above the sound of the insects.

When I returned to my seat, I was wide awake and cold, but I felt much better. I carefully tried to fold the crinkly poncho and wedge it under my seat while opting for just the poncho liner. I settled in, wondering how long it was going to take before I would be comfortably warm again.

The dread of something bad happening was becoming more of a reality. First we had discovered the smoke trails on the buttes. Then one of our mechanical ambushes had blown. I didn't think I was superstitious, but if things happened in threes, the company could expect more to come.

There was less than forty minutes to go before I relieved Andy for his two-hour rest. It was the twenty-fourth of February. How long had I been a company commander? How long would it be before I was replaced? It seemed likely that I would be relieved when this mission was over. Unfortunately, the mission might not be over until we made contact with the NVA regiment that was supposed to be near. If that was the case, there might not be a Bravo Company to command.

As frustrating as it was, all I could do was to continue with the course of action that I had chosen. I needed to look a little deeper and take a closer look at myself. When I had first come to Vietnam, I wasn't any different than I had been as a high school student, a college student, or an elementary teacher. At each stage of my life, I had been positive and tried to be a good citizen. I had taken pride in my accomplishments, and I participated in life with enthusiasm.

In high school I was just smart enough that I didn't have to study very hard to get by. Most of my time was spent on sports and having fun. College wasn't any different until I met my wife, and then school became more important.

Now my life was no longer pleasant or fun. I was all too aware that the exuberance, the ambition, and the competitiveness that I called on to complete a task was currently lacking. I felt that I couldn't afford any added emotion or action. Everything that I said or did was calculated, planned, and deliberate.

I worried and I planned. I worried and I reacted. I wasn't aware of what I had given up. I simply assumed that when this was over, my life would be back to normal. Yet a toll was being taken, because every action had such serious consequences.

At last Andy was signaling me that it was my turn to monitor the radios. I called each ambush patrol and got the anticipated two squelches. I then did the same for each platoon within the perimeter and then called battalion to give them their report.

The call to battalion triggered some thoughts. I could only guess how they might harass the company tomorrow. The hour of radio watch passed quite quickly. Each time I checked my watch, more time had elapsed than I had imagined. When 0200 arrived, I awakened Ron. We each got comfortably wrapped in our poncho liners. I was more relaxed and was looking forward to dozing until it was time for my last watch.

I was sitting with my eyes closed and enjoying the sensation of warmth that I was feeling around my torso. I was listening to Ron as he went through the patrols' and platoons' call signs. After he had finished with the company, he was ready to report to battalion. Without having to look, I knew that it was 0215. I was willing myself to relax as I slid farther down into the jeep seat and covered my arms and shoulders with the poncho liner.

The sound of an explosion jolted me straight up in my seat. It took a moment for me to clear the fog from my brain and realize that the blast wasn't in or near the perimeter. I had been asleep, and I was having trouble getting myself oriented. The explosion had been so loud, yet it wasn't artillery. The sound had come from the east. I fumbled with a light under the poncho in order to check the time. It was 0228, and I remembered that I had been awake at 0215. The sound, the explosion, and the ambush patrol all registered at the same time. By now it had taken a half a minute for me to be fully functioning.

I spoke to Ron. "Check the second platoon 'bush."

Less than a minute had passed since the explosion, and the radios were still silent.

Ron called Sergeant Hawkins's patrol and asked them to press squelch twice if they had a negative situation. Only one squelch came back.

I asked Ron for the radio. Andy was standing beside the track with the artillery on line. I could be assured that Sergeant Finley was on standby and had the mortar tubes ready to fire.

I hesitated only briefly before I called the patrol back and asked them to press squelch twice if they couldn't talk. The response came back with the sound of just one squelch. I was momentarily confused, and then the patrol was calling me. Sergeant Hawkins was whispering into the mike, and every syllable was a hiss.

The mechanical ambush with the gas grenades had blown. Sergeant Hawkins estimated the patrol to be two hundred meters from the site. He had been looking in the direction of the mechanical when it had blown. He had seen the flash, heard the explosion, and then heard shouting, coughing, and gagging. He was using the starlight scope to view the area and could still see movement at the edge of the jungle.

I quickly informed Sergeant Hawkins that artillery was on its way. The location of the mechanical was already registered with the artillery. I planned to put the first rounds on the mechanical ambush site and quickly move the strike south in the valley toward the butte. I was still on the radio with Sergeant Hawkins when I gave him the "shot out" from artillery. Sergeant Hawkins informed me that the first round had landed a little long and was beyond the 'bush site. I gave the artillery a drop fifty, right fifty, and fire for effect. I was preparing to walk the artillery south down the center of the valley.

Andy was holding the radio that I was using to adjust the artillery, and I had that mike to my left ear. I had another mike to my right ear, and it was connected to the radio that I was using to talk with Sergeant Hawkins. The artillery was landing in the valley, and Sergeant Hawkins was still seeing people running back and forth at the edge of the jungle.

Andy asked, "What about illumination?"

All I could say was "Not yet."

I wasn't ready for illumination. I was afraid that it would backfire and reveal the patrol's position. I was going to hold off on illumination until Sergeant Hawkins requested it.

By now several minutes had elapsed, and Sergeant Hawkins could no longer see movement. The artillery was 150 meters down the valley from the site of the mechanical. The radio that I had pressed to my right ear sounded without a call sign or identification. What I heard was "Cease fire, cease fire, cease fire" in rapid succession.

I relayed the same cease-fire message into the mike at my left ear.

The fire mission was silent. Now Sergeant Hawkins reported that an artillery round had exploded less than one hundred meters from the patrol just to the southeast. The artillery battery had given us a short round. This was particularly unnerving since the shots were coming directly over the company. After the information was relayed to the FSB, the fire mission resumed. I don't know if they were only firing five guns or what corrections had been made, but there were no more short rounds.

I kept the artillery working for fifteen minutes, waited thirty minutes, and then started over. After the initial reaction, I now had time to think and analyze the company's next moves. The amount of movement that Sergeant Hawkins had reported made me think that a large force had set off the mechanical ambush. How many had escaped? The ones who had been seen at the edge of the jungle had avoided the blast. What were they going to do now?

I was considering a number of options that I could follow when battalion was on the radio. This was poor timing on their part. I wasn't ready to report because this wasn't over yet.

I warned them that I could only give them a partial report and then proceeded to tell them only what they had already heard on the radio. I finally had to put some urgency into my voice. I informed them that I had a patrol on the ground in place near the ambush site, and the patrol had confirmed hearing voices and had visual sightings. I informed them that I was busy and had pressing things to attend to.

By the time I was finally able to get off of the horn with battalion, it was after 0300 and almost time for my last radio watch. With the lull in the action, I took the time to circle the perimeter and talk with each track. The level of concern was high, as you might imagine, and I had the feeling that this incident wasn't over yet. As I went from track to track, I had to clean the mud from my boots several times.

When I returned to the command track, I was five minutes late for my watch. I was embarrassed and told Andy that I would make it up to him. He just laughed and waved me off. He was sure that things had already evened out, since I had let him rest several times in the past few days.

I was beginning to think that I was going crazy. I was convinced that every time Charlie made his presence known, time slowed down. This could be the Miller theory of combat relativity, but I didn't have time to amuse myself at this point. In fact, I could find no humor in any of the situations that the company had faced lately. I had always appreciated humor, and most of the time an adverse situation could produce some private thoughts that I considered funny. Battalion was always giving me cause to think, but nothing was coming across as humorous. I needed to shake myself. We hadn't gotten through the night yet.

I never made it back to the jeep seat for my last radio watch of the night. The stars had come out, and I couldn't remember whether the sky was clear when the mechanical blew. I was sitting on an ammo can near the rear of the track with the radio that was tuned to the company frequency. The radio tuned to the battalion frequency was above me, on top of the track. What I needed was privacy. I was shaking, and it wasn't from the cold or from fear. I was fighting hard to get control. If I had to get up and move to another location in a hurry, I wasn't sure that I could do it. The source of my agitation became clear when I thought about the day's plan. The night's action had changed things again. A patrol would be organized to check out the blown mechanical, and that was going to be an actual patrol. Yesterday by this time, I pretty much had an idea of what I was going to do.

Currently, I was afraid of making a mistake, and that fear almost had me paralyzed. I absolutely couldn't afford a single bad decision. The fate of the company and all of the uncertainty surrounding our situation was getting to me. I was down, I was depressed, and I was worried. I had to think my way out of this fast.

After carefully analyzing my current state, I concluded that the phantom patrols and the fear of getting caught was the source of my worry. I could rationalize my way out of this now. There was pride in the fact that the company remained in one piece, and that was due in part to the phantom patrols. I was the only one the army could go after if my scheme was ever discovered. I would be the one prosecuted, given a dishonorable discharge, and sent to jail. Was it treason to disobey the order that I had been given? A person could be shot for treason.

I had regained my composure. I had a company to run, and the men depended on me more than ever. I had thought through my anxiety; however, it took a little longer before I stopped shaking inside and some more time before I dared to stand up.

I didn't remember calling in the situation reports, but I had done it. I checked my watch in the early-morning light. It was almost 0500 and my duty would soon be over, but the most important duty was yet to come, with little time left. In less than an hour, I had to decide how the company would proceed through the day.

I was getting an idea. I was going to go with Sergeant Hawkins and Sergeant Rios to search the area around the blown mechanical. I had a feeling that this patrol might take some time. In the event that we made it back to the perimeter with enough time left, we would use the script of the riff to the east.

With that decided, we would try to make it through the day. I felt a surge of relief. It was time to concentrate on the patrol to the site of the mechanical, and this time I expected to find something.

It was getting light quickly, and I wasn't ready yet to meet with the NCOs. Ron had taken over the radios, and Andy was heating water for all three of us to use. Our driver and TC were back from helping third platoon. At last I was busy and had something to do. I handed Andy my canteen cup and said, "Surprise me," as I needed to speak with Sergeant Rios. I found him close by, only a track away. I gave him a verbal patrol order for the number of personnel and equipment that we would need. Just two more things had to happen before we could leave the perimeter. One, Sergeant Hawkins had to return from the night ambush patrol. We needed him because of what he had seen last night, and he was also familiar with the placement of the mechanical. Sergeant Rios would go because he had also helped set the ambush, and he was the one who had incorporated the gas grenades. The second thing that needed to happen was the NCO meeting this morning. This was going to be an important one, and everyone needed to be informed.

At last I was ready for coffee. I was confident that I had prepared well, and the company was ready to tackle the day. There was nervous excitement throughout the company. Men were volunteering to go on the patrol to check out the gas mechanical. I planned to stick with second platoon for the patrol, but first and third platoons would be the reaction force should we get into contact. Second platoon had been my platoon, and these were the men I had worked with many times before. These were the men I would choose to be on a patrol with.

I had forgotten all about the likelihood that battalion headquarters would find a way to interfere. The current call on the radio was my reminder. It turned out to be the same intelligence officer from the day before, and he wanted to run our company from his desk in Long Binh. He was ordering me to get the patrol moving. I explained as patiently as I could that we had to wait until the night ambush patrols returned. He quickly changed tactics and insisted that the nearest ambush patrol check out the site. Again I had to explain that our company SOP was to have the people who set the mechanical present when it was checked out, and neither of the night ambush patrols had the person who had set the mechanical with them. That was untrue, since Sergeant Hawkins had been in on the original placement.

We went around and around, but he got nowhere. I knew I would win this argument, because I was here and he wasn't. I must have finally worn him down, because he was resorting to asking instead of telling. In the end, the agreement was the same as that of the previous day. I would keep him informed every step of the way. He would know what we were doing when we were doing it.

His call had been a reminder that there would probably be more to come from battalion before the day was over. I knew by now that I could count on battalion headquarters' undivided interference.

Sergeant Hawkins had returned, and the other ambush patrol was just entering the perimeter. As soon as they had a chance to shed their gear, we would have the NCO meeting. Today I expected questions, and everyone—that is, all of the company's NCOs—were present. Sergeant Hawkins was the last to arrive. He was still wearing his rucksack and had a claymore bag. He was ready to go back.

I briefed the group about the patrol that was going to the site of the mechanical. Once we had a chance to search the area, we would decide whether to reset the mechanical at that location. Sergeant Lee would be the person we would be reporting to at the perimeter. Sergeant Moore and Sergeant Pomeroy would have a reactionary force ready to come to our aid in the event that we got into contact.

I was having another thought. "If someone is waiting for us at the site to ambush us, just drive the second platoon tracks straight at us.

"It goes without saying, Sergeant Finley, your mortars are on standby.

"Everyone, be aware that battalion, and who knows who else, is listening to our company frequency.

"If everything goes well and by chance we are able to return early, Sergeant Lee and I might be scripting a continuation of the patrol."

It was time to inspect the patrol and be on our way.

23

The patrol was ready, and the men seemed anxious to get started. Sergeant Rios had the point with Ness, and Tommy was walking slack. Tommy was followed by his assistant gunner, with Sergeant Rios next in line. Andy and I were in the middle of the formation, and we were followed by Sergeant Hawkins, Bey, and two riflemen from his squad.

Everyone was inspected for the required smoke grenades, fragmentation grenades, extra machine gun ammo, and C-4. The patrol also carried four claymores, a battery, some trip wire, tape, and gas grenades so we could replace the mechanical that had blown.

The last thing that a patrol did before leaving the perimeter was check for noise coming from their equipment. At this point, the men of the patrol were checking one another for anything that was loose and could make noise, flop, or get hooked on the vegetation. Each of us would jump up and down on both feet, jarring the gear to see if anything rattled or bumped. If the bouncing produced any noise or anything loose was found, the source would be searched out and the process repeated until all equipment was compact and quiet. The men had done this so many times that there rarely was a problem.

Sergeant Rios and Tommy were inspecting each other, and it was Tommy's turn to check his sergeant's equipment. Sergeant Rios bounced up and down on both feet, and Tommy stopped him and said that he could hear something in the rucksack.

Sergeant Rios didn't understand what Tommy had said. Sergeant Rios was bilingual and spoke English and Spanish. Tommy, on the other hand, was from Mississippi and spoke with a pronounced Southern accent.

"Tommy"—Sergeant Rios was gesturing by tipping his head back—"stop gargling peanut butter, and spit it out so I can understand you."

Tommy was patting the sergeant's rucksack while he replied. "You damn Yankees are the ones that talk funny. I can't understand y'all. I'm the ones that talks right." The "right" was pronounced "rat."

I was caught a little off guard by their friendly bantering. It had been a while since anything had been funny, and I caught myself smiling.

We were just about ready; in fact, we were moving slowly in the direction of the trail that led out through the perimeter security. Sergeant Rios had quickly repacked his rucksack and had Tommy's approval, but Tommy had to get the last word in. "You Yankees! At least I can say 'foke' the same way y'all do, so, foke you!"

It was just as humorous that Tommy was calling Sergeant Rios a Yankee. He was obviously of Latin descent, but to Tommy everyone not born in the South was a Yankee.

The line numbers of the patrol were called in to battalion, and the platoons remaining in the perimeter were notified of our departure. The OPs were called and alerted that we were on our way. I called battalion again using the intelligence officer's call sign. I was surprised to hear a different voice on the other end of the line, so I informed the new voice that the patrol was on their way, and all of battalion's calls needed to be directed through Sergeant Moore. I gave his call sign and his line number without using his name.

The people in the rear area never ceased to amaze me. Once again the new voice wanted a direct line to me throughout the patrol. What was wrong with the people at battalion headquarters? They were flaunting their incredible stupidity.

It was time to end this conversation. "I am on a patrol in hostile territory. I will not have an open mike. I'm out!" With that the radio was shut off. I could guess that right now, Ralph—that is, Sergeant Moore—was being bothered by the same person.

When the patrol reached the observation post, everyone took a knee, and Andy and I went forward. We would spend some time just observing the area. The OP position was about 150 meters from the perimeter, and the edge of the rubber trees wasn't that much farther. It was a little more than 200 meters to where Sergeant Hawkins's patrol had been last night and had observed the mechanical's location after it had blown.

The OP position was ideal. From where we were, the land under the rubber trees sloped gradually downward toward the jungle edge and the valley, and there was good vision for 360 degrees.

Sergeant Hawkins was pointing out the position of his ambush site. He had set up a couple of hundred meters farther out and fifty meters to the north. When we were ready to move, that would be our next stop. From there we would be able to observe the site of the blown ambush.

There was a fallen rubber tree where the artillery short round had landed. The short round had exploded a little to our right and less than 100 meters to our front.

I wasn't ready to continue just yet. I wanted to take in everything visually before moving on. I looked back toward the company. The 150 meters looking back wasn't as clear as the view to the front. My view of the company was obstructed by grass and other low-growth vegetation. From where I was looking, I didn't have a single unobstructed view of the company. I knew where each track was parked, yet it took some concentrated searching to be able to pick them out.

The view down the hill to the east away from the company was more open, mainly due to the slope. Still, the edge of the jungle was just out of view, so we moved the patrol to the location of Sergeant Hawkins's night ambush.

When we reached the spot, the men formed a tight circle, and Sergeant Hawkins and I moved to the east side where we could see the jungle. I remembered that Sergeant Hawkins was using the starlight scope when he saw the movement back and forth at the edge of the rubber and the jungle. From here the jungle was still at the limit of our vision. The starlight's magnification had been a definite advantage. Now was a good time to ask Sergeant Hawkins the questions that I had in mind.

The first question that I had for him was, had the sky been clear? He couldn't remember, and that was bothering him. He started backtracking in order to jog his memory. When he had arrived at this spot, it was raining hard. Later the rain had slacked off, but it kept coming down. Then sometime after midnight it had stopped, but it had remained cloudy for a while. It was after the 'bush had blown and things had settled down that he remembered stars being out, but he still wasn't sure whether the sky had cleared earlier.

I tried to help him by taking a different tack. "When you viewed the movement through the starlight scope, how clear was the picture?"

He answered immediately, "Real fuzzy."

That meant that it had been cloudy. That meant that it had been very, very dark.

"Tell me again about the movement."

Sergeant Hawkins positioned himself so that he was facing in the direction of the mechanical. He was staring and squinting. He finally recalled first seeing two people moving to his left and heading north at a run. They had been a row or two out in the rubber trees when he had gotten the scope on them. They had appeared to be carrying weapons. After the first two were out of sight, he looked back and could see more people coming up out of the jungle and into the rubber. He hadn't been able to get an exact count, but he put the number at a dozen to fifteen. The entire time that there were people in view, he could hear coughing and gagging. The second group had milled around for some time before they disappeared. He was certain that they had headed north.

I asked if he could find the spots where he had seen the movement again without going to them in a straight line. I wanted to circle to the south and approach the site along the edge of the jungle. Bey would need to check for booby traps.

Sergeant Hawkins nodded.

We were now ready to move out. We had just spent the better part of an hour viewing the area from the OP position and then the night ambush patrol's position.

Even though we had left the perimeter earlier today than we had yesterday, we were in no hurry. Yesterday by this time, we had already been at the site and were searching. I remembered being disappointed when we couldn't find anything at all. I had expected to find something. The above-ground, shape-charged blast of a claymore mine can be absolutely devastating and almost always produces results.

Today was going to be different. For one thing, my expectations were even higher than yesterday. I knew that we were going to find something at this site, and I wouldn't be satisfied with yesterday's results all over again. This situation and this patrol had a whole different feel to it.

I called the company to inform them that we were moving up. I purposely ignored battalion and the intelligence officer for the moment. They had already heard my call to the company.

The patrol was alert and moving well. We spread out and circled to the north instead of the south. I had changed my mind after further studying the terrain. The higher ground was to the north, and I concluded that approaching from that side offered a better view into the valley. When we were eventually close enough to view the site of the mechanical, we would also have better vision of the surrounding area by coming at it from an angle.

We made the circle to our left and were now headed slightly downhill. We were lined up with the ravine where the mechanical had been set, and just ahead of us at the edge of the jungle was the original spot where Sergeant Rios had peered into the jungle and seen the trail coming up out of the valley.

Ness was walking point and was the first to reach the edge of the jungle just above where the mechanical had been set. He palmed his hand to the side to halt the patrol. What he did next I had never seen him do before. Keeping his hand and arm to the side, he slowly waved his hand up and down and began backing up. He continued to face forward as he backed up to Tommy's position. He didn't stop when he reached Tommy, but they both then still facing the front moved slowly backward. They retreated all the way back to the assistant gunner and Sergeant Rios's position before they stopped.

I was more curious than confused. I waited for Sergeant Rios to motion me forward. Tommy and the assistant gunner moved several paces forward and knelt down facing the jungle. Ness told us that when he had reached the edge of the jungle where he could see down toward the ambush site, he had smelled gas, and according to him it had been quite strong. This pause gave us a good opportunity to allow Bey to scout the immediate area for booby traps and sign.

It was getting close to midmorning. The sun was out and beginning to dry off any surface moisture left by the recent rain. The action of the sun was causing the air currents to rise, and the ravine was acting as a funnel coming up out of the valley. Gas residue left over from the blast was being carried by the rising air.

While Bey searched the area along the edge of the jungle, he was accompanied by Ness and Sergeant Hawkins. I used the pause in the action to call battalion. I tried to make the call routine. All I had to report was that we were at the site and in the process of establishing security. The intelligence officer was talking quite fast and insisting on maintaining an open mike so that he could get a continuous report. That wasn't going to happen. I merely said that I would call him back as soon as we checked the position of the trip wire, and I gave him an "out."

I got a whiff of gas. Still kneeling, I grabbed the right side of my sweat towel and pulled it from under the rucksack strap and held the corner over my nose and mouth for the men close by to see. Everyone except Bey carried a sweat towel. The towel was rolled or folded and worn around the neck with the ends tucked under the rucksack straps for extra padding. The towel had a number of uses. The most obvious use of the towel was wiping sweat from your face or clearing your eyes, but other important uses included cleaning your weapon. It could also be dampened and worn around your neck or draped over your head in order to keep cool during the heat of the day. As long as you carried a towel with you, other uses made themselves available.

Two men were directed to remain fifty meters up the slope in the rubber trees where they could observe anyone approaching along the edge of the jungle from the south or the north. They would also have the best view into the rubber trees in any direction.

Bey was sticking close to Sergeant Hawkins as they waited at the edge of the jungle where the ravine ended and the rubber trees began. I moved toward Sergeant Hawkins to see if he and Bey had found anything. Sergeant Hawkins was smiling at me as I approached him. I didn't have to guess. I knew he had something.

The rest of the patrol was getting into position to provide security for Sergeant Rios and Ness while they inspected the area of the trip wire. We moved up once more. I could smell the gas, but I didn't think it was that bad. I could imagine that there would be pockets where the smell would be stronger.

Sergeant Hawkins was still waiting for me when Tommy's assistant gunner went to the ground. He was clutching his nose and mouth with his sweat towel and trying to suppress his coughing and gagging. He had just run into one of the stronger pockets of gas. He was doing a good job of suppressing the sound. It was barely audible, and the insects, birds, and other jungle sounds were helping to mask his muffled sounds. Tommy, I noticed was only a few meters from the assistant gunner, and he seemed unaffected. Some people might be more sensitive to the gas than others. I moved to the side of the coughing-gagging soldier and helped him away from the immediate area. He was trying to say he was sorry, but each time he tried to speak, the coughing fit started all over. I motioned for him not to talk and pointed him up the hill to join the two men already on security.

I turned my attention back to the jungle where the ambush had gone off. The jungle was naturally thinner here, and there was much less undergrowth. The area of the ravine appeared to have been cleared of brush and trees at one time. Tall grass covered almost a quarter of an acre on our side of the ravine. There were small patches of brush and some small trees that had started to take over the grassy slope. The brush and small trees were thicker near the bottom of the ravine where the ravine blended into the wall of jungle. From here you couldn't tell where the ravine entered the valley, and the mechanical had been set under the taller trees in this location. I could see Sergeant Rios's and Ness's heads and shoulders as they intently poked around below me. Tommy had moved down the slope and into the jungle just above them in order to provide security.

I directed my attention to the jungle around the area where the ambush had gone off. The jungle vegetation above Tommy, Sergeant Rios, and Ness was a mat of hanging and broken branches where an artillery shell had landed. The leaves on the dangling foliage were beginning to wilt.

Sergeant Hawkins and Bey could wait no longer, and they started for me. I walked to meet them. The look on the sergeant's face confirmed what I already knew. He had something. He approached to within a half a step and whispered his message. It wasn't unexpected news, but there was still a surprise. He and Bey had found blood as soon as they had reached the edge of the jungle. They had been alerted to the presence of the blood before the assistant gunner had inhaled the gas. The surprise was in the amount of blood that was visible. Sergeant Hawkins was eager to show me what he had found so I could confirm it. I pulled out my notepad to begin recording. He said there was a lot of blood. The blood trail was six to ten feet wide, and there was blood on the ground and on the vegetation at chest height. More than a few people had lost blood as they left the area. He was speculating that the amount of sign left indicated that many more people were headed north than the few he had viewed through the starlight scope.

I sent Sergeant Hawkins and Bey back to work the trail thirty meters farther to the north or until it turned back into the jungle. He and Bey were adamant that there were at least six different blood trails and probably more. I wrote it all down.

I was ready to call battalion. I gave them the blood trail information and promised to get back with more information as soon as we had the rest of the area searched. The call went smoothly for a change. They indicated that they were on standby and awaiting the next report.

Sergeant Hawkins and Bey returned from following the blood trail to the north to where it turned back into the jungle. The three of us moved back to the south in order to cover Sergeant Rios, Ness, and Tommy. They were harder to see because they were searching farther down in the valley.

Depending on what Sergeant Rios and Ness found, I planned to follow the blood trail to the north for a ways. If we found a body, battalion would most likely send someone to observe and record. I didn't want battalion to get involved, because their presence would mean that the fate of the company would be out of my hands.

We had been here for some time, and I was becoming impatient. I was anxious to know what Sergeant Rios and Ness had found. Now that my mind had done some wondering, it was becoming harder to wait. I thought about moving down into the ravine to assist in the search, but at this point it might send the wrong message. They knew what they were doing, and their search would be thorough. There was nothing that I should do differently. We were following company SOP set forth by Captain Cooper. I needed to stay out of the way and let the men do their jobs.

Once again I reminded myself that I was the decider, and there were some important decisions to be made in the very near future. Then I realized that I wasn't alone. I looked at Andy, then Sergeant Hawkins, and even Bey, who was hard to read. They, too, appeared impatient.

We were following the two searchers' progress from above while Tommy covered them from below. Frequently we could see one of them reach into his breast pocket for his insect repellent and then unbutton his shirt, pull up his sleeve, or drop his trousers to squirt off a leech. Yesterday's rain had the leeches moving. On top of the rain, this had to be a particularly infested area, judging by the number of times Sergeant Rios and Ness were reaching for their repellent.

They turned around and headed back up the ravine, searching on a different track.

I looked at my watch again. It was the third time that I had checked the time in the last five minutes. Our patrol was spread out, and our security was being tested. I had the radios turned off temporarily so we could finish clearing the area without interruption. I could see both Sergeant Rios and Ness at the same time, and each of them was carrying items besides his weapons. They were finding what the enemy had left behind after fleeing the area. I could only imagine what Sergeant Moore was going through back at the company perimeter. I could guess that battalion would really be riding him for information. Just a little longer, and soon enough, I would be able to report our findings. Then I could predict that battalion would go nuts.

I thought I recognized one of the items that Ness was carrying, and I was still feeling some consternation for Sergeant Moore, who had to deal with battalion command.

This had been a trail ambush set with four claymores. Each of the company's NCOs was proficient at setting mechanical ambushes, but Sergeant Rios seemed to enjoy it the most. He put extra time and effort into camouflaging the mines, trip wire, and battery. He was meticulous in directing the blast of each mine to interlock with the next for maximum coverage of the area.

As I watched and waited, I was aware that the search would soon be completed. I was replaying the radio conversation that I had with Sergeant Hawkins right after the mechanical had blown. I walked the five meters that separated me from Sergeant Hawkins. "Doug," I said, "last night you said that you could hear voices. You said, human voices."

"That's correct. I was too far away to understand anything, but they were definitely voices. I guess it was yelling."

I was of the opinion that the gas grenades that had been incorporated into the mechanical had been an unexpected surprise. The gas grenades had to have contributed to the confusion.

The three men were coming up the ravine, with Tommy in the rear. As they approached, we moved out of the sun and into the rubber trees a couple of rows. Each of them carried something besides his weapon.

We could all see what Tommy had. He had hooked a lone sandal over the barrel of his machine gun. It was a tire-tread, inner-tube-strap Ho Chi Min sandal. "I couldn't find the other one."

Ness produced two AK-47 magazines. Each had ammunition in it. He next produced a canvas bag that contained medical supplies that included syringes, pills, tubes, jars, and bandages.

Sergeant Rios had another set of items. The first thing that he produced was some old rags. On closer examination they turned out to be old bandages. There were several different sizes and shapes, but most notably, they were used. "There are some more of these on the ground down there."

The next item came out of the left cargo pocket of his trousers. It was a five-round link of fifty-one-caliber ammunition. From the right pocket, he carefully palmed a chi com grenade with a string fuse. The last item was already on the ground in front of us. The NVA pith helmet had captured everyone's attention, and it was just what I had seen earlier while they were still searching.

Sergeant Rios said, "We covered the area really well. We couldn't have missed much else, but the battery is missing. I found the trip wire, but the battery is gone."

I checked and double checked my notes. I now had some questions for Sergeant Rios and Ness. "Did you find blood?"

"There was no blood at the trip wire, but we found blood at about ten feet on each side of the trip wire. There was a lot more blood on the downhill side."

"What can you tell me about the trail sign?"

"There were a lot of people involved. The trail was torn up pretty good. Whoever was below the trip wire went downhill and turned east, angling uphill, but I only went about seventy-five meters. Some of them came north right up the center of the ravine. Oh! I almost forgot, there were tire tracks, like bicycle tracks."

"Ness, do you have anything to add?"

"Nope. I think Sarge covered everything."

"Tommy, how about you? Do you have anything to add?"

"I found the sandal halfway up the hill, like whoever was wearing it was headed straight for the rubber trees."

By now I had acquired several pages of notes to report. The one thing that I had expected to hear hadn't transpired. There were no bodies. We had found enough blood that I was convinced that there were bodies somewhere, and most likely close by.

I was almost ready to call in the report, but there were a couple of things bothering me. The enemy was good at picking up after an action, and they had gotten all of the people out of the area. But they had still left some things behind, and I attributed that to the lingering gas. The missing battery was a mystery. I couldn't imagine the battery being found in the dark right after the blast. However, what if the area was swept just after daylight? There still could have been enough gas around to prevent them from doing a thorough job.

I started the process of reporting by calling Sergeant Moore and telling him to go up on battalion's frequency to hear what we found. I then informed him that as soon as the report was concluded, the patrol was going to continue to follow the blood trail and develop the situation. I wanted to ask how the last several hours had been, but I dared not.

I was thinking that it was a waste of time to go to the battalion frequency, since I knew they were listening to our every move, but I got the intelligence officer on the horn and went through my notes sequentially. It took a lot of time to go over everything that I had. It was the longest radio conversation that I ever had. When I finished the report, I confirmed that we were going to follow the blood trail. I was surprised that there weren't more questions.

The patrol reformed, and we were going to pursue what Sergeant Hawkins and Bey had found. I radioed the company that we were following a trail to the north. I expected the trail to eventually circle back to the south and head back toward the butte. Ness was the point, and as soon as he started along the jungle following the blood, he stopped and motioned to me. He commented that this was only a small fraction of the amount of blood going south and east. The drops that he was following were the size of a nail head, with an occasional drop the size of a dime. The bent and broken grass and bushes all pointed north. There was no mistaking the direction of travel.

We arrived at the spot where Sergeant Hawkins and Bey had turned around. Bey came forward with Ness, and we continued into the jungle. We intersected the main trail coming up the valley, and there were fresh tracks made since it had rained. The trail continued straight north. It didn't turn back to the east or south, as I had expected it to. The blood was no longer red, but it had dried black and was much harder to see in the shade.

Bey was on point now, since we were on a trail. I knew without looking at my map that the valley would get narrower and narrower as it continued in the direction that we were headed. It finally tapered into nothing, and the open rubber plantation was all that was left. That could be only a few hundred meters farther.

I wanted to know what Bey was thinking, so I stopped the patrol. I talked to him in our broken English and signs that we used when he and I communicated. When I asked if the VC were here, he just smiled. He pointed to the northeast and said, "VC go. Beaucoup VC go away. VC go."

It hardly seemed worth going on at this point. It was early afternoon, and there wasn't a lot of time left. I decided to continue to the north and circle back to the west at some point and return to the company through the rubber trees. I was curious to see if the blood trail led out into the rubber trees. We went another hundred meters, and the blood was getting harder to find. It couldn't be much farther, and we would be out of jungle. The terrain was getting steeper when Andy signaled me to stop. Everyone went to a knee, and I reached for the receiver. I couldn't begin to guess what this was going to be about.

I identified myself and was shocked to speechlessness.

24

Battalion had taken it upon themselves to send us a tracking dog team to follow the blood trails. It was afternoon and getting late to start a new mission. Plus, we had already followed the trail to the north. That left the trail to the southeast, which hadn't been explored yet. There wasn't a lot we could do today, so the dog team would have to spend the night in the perimeter.

I was informed that the dog team was already in the air and on their way. That produced another problem. The nearest LZ was the company perimeter, and we were several hours away. If we hurried we could be there in around two hours. We were still in hostile territory, and if we hurried, we would be sacrificing our safety.

Battalion was calling me back. When I had first received the news, I was so shocked that I needed time to think things through, so I had told them to "wait one." It had been more than a minute since I had received the news, and now they were back. I identified myself and asked where we were going to pick them up. I knew that the dog team would have to be dropped off at the company area. I was going to convey to them that we couldn't link up much before 1600 hours.

Battalion came back and ordered our patrol to return to the mechanical ambush site. The dog team was headed there. I then informed the person on the radio that there wasn't an LZ at the ambush site. The helicopter crew would have to use a penetrator to unload the dog team, or we would have to drop some rubber trees, which would take time.

When battalion came back again, there was a different person on the horn. His map showed the grassy-brushy area between the jungle and the rubber trees. I called back to warn him that the grassy area was a steep slope and not suitable as an LZ.

I had no choice. It was an order.

I reluctantly informed the patrol of what had just happened. We reformed and headed up to the rubber trees so we could move faster. We no sooner started up the hill than I heard a helicopter. It was a Huey.

It was the dog team, all right, and the pilot had our company frequency and was calling. I answered and told him that we were on our way to the site. He would need to circle until we could get into position. I added that he should inspect the site since it might not be suitable.

We moved quickly, but it still took over thirty-five minutes to get to the site. As we moved into the site, we set up security, and I made the call that we were in position. Sergeant Rios threw out a green smoke canister. The smoke was identified, and the pilot brought the helicopter to a hover overhead. I warned the pilot about the ground sloping away, but he didn't seem worried.

The helicopter was hovering with its nose pointed toward the rubber trees as it slowly inched its way downward. When the fronts of the skids were just a couple of feet off of the ground, Sergeant Rios, who was in the edge of the rubber and had been guiding the helicopter's descent, stopped the helicopter's progress.

I had been keeping an eye on the rotors, specifically the tail rotor, to make sure it wouldn't become a brush cutter. The next thing I noticed was a shadow just before a dog flew out of the helicopter. The dog was a German shepherd, and it landed in the grass on the slope. The dog had dropped about six feet from the bottom of the skid to the ground, which made it closer to eight feet from the cargo deck.

After the dog surprised me, I looked up to see where it had come from, and a man standing on the skid was just initiating his jump as he left the skid. He was in the air, arms flailing as he fell. I noticed that he was wearing a pack. He should have thrown the pack ahead of the jump.

I didn't know where the dog was, but the man landed and rolled down hill. The helicopter was up and leaving. And the man was yelling.

I was the first to get to him. His head was downhill, and he was thrashing about. I got to the downhill side of his head and clamped my hand over his mouth. His thrashing intensified. Two members of the patrol arrived, and each took an arm and held on. I hadn't noticed yet who was helping me, but we almost had the dog handler subdued. I was bent over him whispering in his ear repeatedly, "Shut up! Shut up!"

His thrashing subsided, and I started to remove my hand from over his mouth. I had barely relaxed my grip when he yelled, "My leg!"

My hand was back over his mouth, and I clamped it even tighter now. I bent close to his ear once more and whispered, "Too loud!"

He was looking up at us, his eyes erratically darting from one of us to the next. His eyes were open wide. They were a deep blue and full of pain and fear.

Sergeant Rios joined us with the medical bag that we carried when a medic wasn't assigned to the patrol.

The dog handler was not able to remain still or keep from thrashing about. He was in a terrible position to try to treat him. He was lying across the hill and angling downward with his head at the lowest point. I scanned his upper body and then his legs. It was right there to see. His right leg was broken just at the top of his boot. It looked as if both bones were broken, by the slight angle of his foot. I tried several times to ask if there were any other injuries beside his leg, and each time I saw the terrified look on his face I was reluctant to remove my hand from his mouth. I asked a fourth time, and this time he shook his head definitely no.

Without looking up at Sergeant Rios I said, "Give him morphine."

The morphine that we carried was in a tube, not a syringe. It was like a tube of glue or a small tube of toothpaste with a needle mounted on top. The cap came off of the needle without hesitation, and Sergeant Rios plunged the needle into the left thigh right through his trousers. The dog handler jumped and jerked, stiffened, and started to fight us again. Sergeant Rios was having a hard time squeezing the tube to get the morphine into the injured soldier's system because of all of the movement.

After twenty or thirty seconds, he wasn't fighting us as hard, and by the time a minute had passed, he was starting to relax. Now we had to get him to the top of the slope to the shade of the rubber trees and some level ground.

Andy got in position on the uphill side, and together, he and I angled up the slope. We each had a grip under one of his arms, and once we started moving, it was easy. We made the top and dragged him to the shade.

When we got him to the shade, I noticed that his leg had straightened out. I was pretty sure that he didn't have a compound fracture, but there was no way that we were going to remove his boot to find out.

Wouldn't you know it! While Andy was helping to drag the dog handler to the top of the slope, battalion headquarters had called. Sergeant Hawkins was on the radio, and I could tell he was anxious to let someone else take over.

The radio went to Andy first while Sergeant Hawkins filled me in on what they wanted. They had originally wanted a status report on the dog team and were inquiring as to when we would be moving. Sergeant Hawkins had told them about the trouble we were having and had tried to stall. Andy was doing more listening than talking. He finally rolled his eyes and handed the mike to me. I was thinking about the dog. The dog was nowhere in sight. The man was lying on his back with his rucksack still on and bunched to one side. That left him looking as uncomfortable as could be. He was blinking and staring at the sky. Andy, using the other radio, had contact with the pilot again. He had made it almost back to his base at Xuan Loc when Andy had finally reached him. He didn't want to come back. He was low on fuel. There was no way he could land at our site, and he didn't have a jungle penetrator to lower from a hover. I was next to Andy and listening to the whole conversation while battalion had me on hold. I told Andy that we had some C-4 plastic explosives and would blow down some rubber trees, but the pilot had already signed off.

"Get a dust-off."

Andy was on it. A dust-off would be on the way, and they would come up on our frequency when they got close.

Where was the dog?

Sergeant Rios and Andy stayed with the injured handler, and I went to the other members of the patrol, who had spread out for security. They all knew where the dog was and where it had been.

After the dog had been thrown from the helicopter, it ran directly up the slope and into the rubber trees. As it headed away from the helicopter, it ignored the men in the patrol until it located Bey. The dog went after Bey, and Sergeant Hawkins and Ness were able to help Bey up a tree while they scared the dog away. The dog circled the tree that Bey was in and milled around the immediate area for a while until it located the blood trail. The dog found the blood trail coming out of the ravine. The men saw the dog going back and forth several times before disappearing into the jungle where we had followed the trail. The dog had just reappeared in the rubber trees and was lying down watching Bey from about forty meters away.

The dust-off was on the radio, and I explained the situation. I gave the pilot the nature of the injury, that morphine had been administered, and the fact that there was a dog involved. I looked around, and the dog was in the same place.

The dust-off had a penetrator with a seat harness. This pilot admitted that he had never picked up a dog team before, but he knew how it was done. The dog would lie across the handler's lap while a hoist was used.

The dust-off pilot then informed me that a gunship team would soon catch up with him and be able to provide security during the pickup.

I figured that we had about ten minutes before the dust-off would be on station for the extraction. It sounded like he would be using the penetrator. If he could hover at the edge of the rubber trees, it would only be fifteen or twenty feet to the helicopter.

I could see Andy gesturing as he was talking to someone on the radio. I needed to know what was going on, so I hurried to his side. He stuck out the mike and said, "It's battalion."

I identified myself and listened. The person on the other end was talking fast and was furious. He was blaming me for allowing the dog team to be compromised. Those were the words that he used. Not once did he mention the injury to the handler. He was clear on one thing. The dog needed to come back with the handler. He made it sound as if the dog was more important than the handler. There was barely any mention of the injured handler. His main concern was for the dog.

I was ready to give this guy a piece of my mind.

We had been told that we were getting a tracking team, and from what I knew about how the army used dogs, a tracking team meant Labrador retrievers or golden retrievers. From what I had heard, a tracking team consisted of two dogs.

What they had actually sent us was an attack dog that was used to walk trails and scent out booby traps and alert to enemy soldiers. I was saving my knowledge of dog teams for the last part of what I was going to say.

I calmly began my side of the conversation. "We have an incapacitated handler. We have a dog that no one can get near and is trying to attack our Kit Carson scout. I don't know the dog's name or what commands it responds to. Until I can get some information from the handler or anyone else, no one in my patrol is going near that dog."

I had to pause for a breath. "Now, the dust-off will be here in a few minutes, and I need information. If I can't get it from the handler, then you need to have it ready. I'm in a hurry, and I need the radio for the dust-off. I'm out.

"Andy, can you handle the dust-off?"

"I'm on it."

I went over to the handler and knelt down. "What is the dog's name?"

The morphine was working. "His name's Duke."

"What commands does he respond to?"

"The usual—sit, stay, come, heel, and halt." The handler was trying to roll on his side. I put my hands on his chest to keep him from turning. The rucksack was still smashed behind him, and he hadn't changed position since Andy and I had deposited him.

Andy interrupted. "The dust-off is here."

"Have them circle." It was all that I could think to say.

I unsnapped the quick-release strap on the rucksack and pulled it out from under the handler. I then fluffed it up and tucked it under his head. He was mumbling something, and I couldn't hear. Andy caught it immediately and reached for the side pocket of the rucksack. He unzipped the upper pocket on the left side of the rucksack and produced a plastic bag of dog treats. The handler then reached into the cargo pocket of his trousers and handed me a leash.

I could hear several helicopters and knew that the gunships had arrived.

With the leash and the treats, I started for the dog. Ness walked beside me. As we walked, he reached out his hand for the treats and the leash. "I raise dogs in the world. Let me try."

I turned the two items over to Ness. He had heard. He knew the dog's name and the commands. Ness was moving ahead of me and requesting that I stay back, and be sure to keep Bey out of sight.

The helicopters were circling wide and high. They were aware that we were trying to catch a dog.

We were all watching Ness approach Duke. No one was looking out to the sides for security. I started pointing, and heads turned away. I too was scanning the area for anything that might have changed or any movement.

After clearing the security thoughts from my brain, I visually scouted the best place for the helicopter to hover for the pickup. The injured handler's current location was as good as any place.

I turned back toward Ness and was relieved to see that he had the dog on the leash and was walking him toward the handler.

In the meantime, Andy and Sergeant Rios had moved the dog handler into a sitting position with his back to a tree. His rucksack was beside him. I could see the morphine tube, which had been stuck in the lapel of his fatigue jacket and fastened in place with the cap placed back over the needle point.

My gaze turned back to Ness. Ness was the picture of confidence, but Duke was very nervous. The dog's entire body was quivering. Every muscle was twitching as it walked with Ness. Ness was continually speaking softly to the dog and being as reassuring as possible. When they reached the handler, he spoke to Duke, and the dog seemed to respond. Ness held on to the leash. Duke was responding to the handler, and he was able to get the dog to sit. Duke, however, continued to have the shakes.

We were ready for the dust-off. I took the radio from Andy. The plan was that Ness, Sergeant Rios, and Andy would get the handler and the dog in the sling while I maneuvered the helicopter into position. Its skids were at the treetop level. This would not be a long lift. It appeared to be closer to fifteen feet than twenty feet from the ground to the helicopter. This should be a piece of cake.

The longer the Huey hovered, the more agitated the dog became. The handler had a hand on the dog's collar, and Ness was kneeling with both arms around Duke's shoulders. Here came the penetrator with the harness seat. Sergeant Rios and Andy started dragging the handler toward the harness. Ness tried to follow with Duke.

Instantly I knew that this wasn't going to work. There would be no way the handler could manage the dog by himself once he was strapped into the harness seat. I told the pilot to abort. Pull the penetrator up and give us a chance to become better prepared. I had expected the pilot to be upset, but he seemed fine and relayed that he would be ready for a second try as soon as we were.

As the helicopter pulled up and away to begin circling again, I explained what I wanted to do. First we would sedate the dog with morphine, since that was all we had. Then we would fashion a bag to place Duke in and tie it to the dog handler and the hoist.

Sergeant Rios handed Ness a tube of morphine. The handler had the dog lying down. Ness didn't hesitate. As soon as the cap came off of the tube, he jabbed the needle into the dog's hip. Duke yipped and snapped at Ness. Ness must have done this before, because he had anticipated the dog's attack. He had shielded the morphine tube in his right hand with his left hand. The dog viciously bit Ness's left hand repeatedly four or five times in quick succession. The dog was snarling as Ness finally pulled away. "I didn't give him all of it. He isn't as big as one of us."

It didn't take long for the morphine to have an effect. Duke had quit twitching, and his eyes had a glazed-over look.

I needed two fatigue shirts. One came from Sergeant Rios and the other from Ness. Everything in their shirt pockets went into the cargo pockets of their pants.

When I took the shirts from them, Sergeant Rios noticed a huge leech attached to Ness's back. This wasn't the little inch size that we were used to seeing. This one had been in place for a while. I couldn't believe that we were admiring the leech. Sergeant Rios, with his repellent in hand, held off until we had all seen it before he gave a quick squirt, and the leech dropped to the ground to be crushed under Ness's foot. The blood ran down his back and into his pants. He ignored the blood for a while before reaching back to blot it with his sweat towel.

I hurriedly buttoned the two shirts together, forming a large bag. I planned to place the dog in the bag with the open bottom ends of the shirts facing the handler. With the dog in the bag and on the handler's lap, the four arms of the shirts could be tied to the harness.

"Call the dust-off back."

This time everything went smoothly. Duke was as limp as a noodle, but the bag held. My biggest worry was that the dog would slide out of the bag and off of the handler's lap before either of them could be hauled into the cargo bay of the helicopter.

At last the dust-off was up and gone, taking the gunship escort that had circled continuously during the ordeal with it.

All the patrol, especially Bey, was a bit traumatized by all that had taken place. I asked Ness about his bandaged hand. The bite was serious and had produced a couple of jagged tears. I would be sure to have Ron take a look at the bite when we returned to the company area.

I moved the patrol to the top of the hill, in the rubber. We would sit in place for a while before we returned. It was late in the afternoon, but a fifteen-minute break was welcome. By staying in place and continuing the patrol, I had an excuse not to talk on the radio. I did need to call Sergeant Moore to get the night ambushes ready because we were going to be late getting back.

We formed a tighter-than-usual circle, with Andy and me in the center. Bey was still shaken, and no one could blame him. I hadn't seen it, but the dog would have taken him on if Sergeant Hawkins and Ness hadn't blocked the dog's path and gotten Bey up a tree. I was glad that they hadn't shot the dog right then. After the lecture that I had received over the radio, I couldn't imagine what would have happened to me if Duke had been killed.

Duke had been trained to go after Charlie, and since the Bey and the VC were both Vietnamese, how could the dog be expected to make the distinction?

It had been a while since I had checked the time. It was clouding up, and I was thinking that it was probably going to rain. The dog team had arrived around 1300, probably a little later. It was now 1657, and we were still a ways away from the company perimeter. I needed to call Sergeant Moore, and he too had been waiting for me as I whispered my call sign into the mike. He had wanted to tell me not to worry, that everything was taken care of. The night patrols were set, as was the perimeter security. I finished up by telling him that we had policed up the area and we would be returning to his location soon.

In reality I planned to remain where we were for another five minutes. It would take over thirty minutes to reach the company from here. I sat back to enjoy the moment. I was listening to the insects and following the billowing clouds in the sky. I had a lot to think about and plan for, but I was going to put it off for as long as I could. What a day this had been so far!

25

It was after 1700 hours, and we had just left the spot where we had rested. I was feeling completely drained as I radioed that we were approaching the OP position.

Again I was amazed that as open as the terrain under the rubber trees appeared, I couldn't see the two men at the OP guard site. I knew exactly where they were, and it wasn't until I was inside fifty meters that I could finally pick them out. On the other hand, they could see us in the spot where we had been resting.

There was no reason for me to be in a hurry, even though the patrol was returning late. I had a good idea of what awaited me once I entered the company perimeter, but I couldn't help myself. I just couldn't wait as I started going over in my mind what I was going to cover at the NCO meeting.

It had been such a strange day up to this point, and it wasn't over yet. I recognized the feeling of coming down off an emotional high. When I got to the company and my track, I would counter the oncoming depression with a double-strong cup of coffee. That was one of the few things that I could actually look forward to.

As we entered the company perimeter, I was still thinking about the up-coming NCO meeting. It would have to take place very soon. I anticipated that the meeting would go smoothly and that the company would be well prepared for the night. What worried me the most was wondering what battalion headquarters was planning.

My relationship and the company's relationship with battalion command had changed when I had attended the tactical meeting at the fire support base, and it only had gotten worse after the realization that we were being sacrificed. Now that relationship had entered a new phase.

When the battalion command took a good look at what Bravo Company had accomplished in the last few days, they would have to conclude that we had done everything that was expected. As far as they knew, Bravo had complied with all aspects of the mission orders. I would never be 100 percent sure that battalion command had no clue that I had opposed them. I desperately wanted to keep them from gaining any insight. I also realized that by design, I had set myself up to be the only person who could take responsibility for failing to carry out the mission as ordered.

The NCO meeting had been rescheduled, and the night ambush patrols would have just enough time to get set up before it was too dark. I relieved Sergeant Moore, who returned to second platoon in order to prepare for one of the nighttime patrols. The company was running itself. Only when something out of the ordinary happened did the men look for leadership in order to take direction. They had always been up to the task.

I opened my notepad to jot down some notes for the meeting. My notepad was getting thin. I was burning old pages every morning when I made my coffee. It was apparent that I would need a new notepad by tomorrow or the next day.

Tomorrow was going to be the Twenty-Fifth of February, and it was only a few hours away.

I found a medium-sized plastic bag that had come out of some packing box or container. Almost everything from ammunition to food had a layer of plastic to seal out moisture, so there were always plastic bags available. I placed all of the items that were found at the site of the mechanical into the bag except the NVA pith helmet. I would stick to the usual procedure at the meeting and go over the perimeter security first, followed by the night ambush patrols, and then on to plans for tomorrow's riff. After that I would go over what we had found at the ambush site. That part of the meeting was optional.

It was a good thing that I was reviewing my notes. I almost overlooked another important topic that had to go with the first couple of items on the agenda. Sergeant Rios had brought to my attention when we were resting before our return to the perimeter that we hadn't reset the mechanical. Fortunately, I wrote it down when he mentioned it. After giving the dog and the handler their sendoff, Sergeant Rios had suggested setting a mechanical on the slope of the hill in view of the OP position. I was still thinking this over. I tended to think that the mechanicals should cover areas that we couldn't see. The night ambushes were going to be at the edge of the jungle tonight, and Sergeant Moore would set a mechanical to protect his position. I could wait until tomorrow to decide the placement of another mechanical.

It was after 1800 hours and getting close to meeting time, because the sergeants began showing up. Sergeant Pomeroy had been sitting on an ammo can since I had returned and didn't need to move. The rest of the NCOs assumed different positions, with some standing, some sitting, some squatting, and others leaning against the track.

The first thing out of my mouth was "If we're lucky, it won't rain tonight."

Now we were on to the subject of perimeter security. Sergeant Pomeroy reported that he and Sergeant Moore were still expanding the warning devices beyond the perimeter. In fact, they had installed some four-foot-high trip wires with flares set to go off in the trees.

Nothing had changed since we had been here except that different people alternated between perimeter guard duty and night ambush patrols. It seemed unimaginable to me, but we had established a routine amid everything that was happening. Had we been here that long? As I looked over the sergeants, who stared back at me as they took notes, it struck me that each of the men sat or stood in the same spot at each meeting. I thought back to yesterday's meeting and the day before. Sergeant Pomeroy was sitting on the same ammo can, Sergeant Finley was leaning against the track in the same spot, Sergeant Lee was standing next to Sergeant Pomeroy, and all of second platoon were together. Andy and Ron were sitting on top of the track. Had I taken a picture, it would have been the same for at least three days in a row. This was a sure sign that we had been here for a while.

The night ambush patrols were covered next, and there wasn't much to be said. Everyone knew the routine and the locations. The rotation of the night ambush patrols consisted of three NCOs alternating on the east side of the perimeter and two NCOs alternating nights on the other side.

The subject of resetting the mechanical ambush was covered quicker than I had anticipated. All agreed to wait until we found the right spot, since it would be left in place and not picked up and moved each day.

The NCOs on the ambush patrols were excused, and I was ready to report our findings at the site of the mechanical. I went through a quick description of what I thought happened. It had been quite a large group that had been ambushed. I estimated from the amount of trail sign that there had to be more than twenty and maybe as many as fifty. I looked to Sergeant Rios and Sergeant Hawkins for verification. Sergeant Rios confirmed that it had been a large group and gave an even higher estimate. The trip wire had been set to cover more of the downhill portion of the kill zone. Sergeant Rios stated that more people had bailed to the southeast than had gone north. He then gave me some information that I hadn't gotten earlier. The main trail didn't come up the ravine to the rubber trees. That had been just a small fork. The main trail continued inside the cover of the jungle as it went north. It made sense now. When we had followed the blood trail back into the jungle, we had intersected the main trail coming up the valley. If more people had headed south after the blast, then my estimate was way off. There could have been a hundred or more, and only a fraction of a unit of that size would have been inside the mechanical's kill zone. I was certain now that they hadn't been coming after us, but instead they were more likely fleeing the area. If they had been coming for us, there were much better routes.

The fact remained that they had come back sometime between the time of the blast and early daylight to retrieve bodies and equipment. The gas grenades had prevented them from doing a thorough job.

I showed the men the contents of the plastic bag. The bandages were old and no doubt a result of the napalm strike, the gunships, and the artillery the morning that we discovered the smoke trails. I showed them the first-aid kit, the AK magazines, and finally the fifty-one-caliber linked ammunition. I balanced the NVA helmet on one finger for display. The helmet drew some soft whistles, as did the fifty-one-caliber ammunition. I had just upped the company's insurance policy. There would be no complacency around the company tonight.

There was still one thing to cover, and that was the scripted riff. We were back to the east-side script, with a riff into the valley. Sergeant Hawkins would lead the patrol that was scheduled to depart the perimeter at 0800 hours. We confirmed that he and I would get together around 0700 and review the script. Everyone was warned again that there were a lot of ears tuned to our company radio frequency.

Earlier, Sergeant Moore told me that battalion had him going back and forth, and up and down on the radio all day. He was referring to changing radio frequencies. They would call him and then say to go to another frequency and call them back. It was a game that the armchair soldiers played to remind you that they were in charge of the war.

Before the meeting finally ended, I reminded the group to tell everyone that I planned to use the artillery all night.

The clouds were solid, and it was probably going to rain. It was just one more thing to worry about. It was also going to be dark soon, and darker than usual because of the cloud cover. I wasn't feeling hungry, yet I felt that I should eat something. I went over to our track's open case of C-rations and began pawing through the meals. Most of the meals had been torn apart, and various cans were strewn about. I found a can of apricots and some crackers and peanut butter. I had been looking for pork and beans, but this was just as good.

Andy and Ron hadn't moved from the top of the track. I moved to stand next to Andy while I ate.

With a mouth full of apricots, I listened as Andy confided to me. "I was able to call Top just after we got back. He says he's worried about us. We're big news in the rear."

I had thought that we were doing a good job of lying low and staying off of the main radar screen. From what Top had told Andy, it was just the opposite.

Andy bent over and tilted his head toward me in order to get a little closer and spoke just above a whisper. "There was a lot of stuff to tell Top, but y'all know I couldn't with all them REMFs listen'n in."

"I'm sure that Top understands.

"Before we try to get comfortable, remind me at 0800 to call in some artillery missions for tonight."

I remained standing where I was and finished eating in silence. I wiped my plastic spoon on my shirttail and put it back in my left breast pocket. I stepped to the rear of the track with the empty cans and slipped them into the box that served as a garbage container. The garbage box was under the corner of the ramp, and all of the cans would be stomped flat and the garbage burned when we left the site. That was the way that it was supposed to work, and it played out that way when we had a planned departure. When the company has to leave in a hurry, as they did on the morning of the sixteenth of February, the garbage boxes were left in place.

Charlie liked to use C-ration cans for booby traps. A grenade fit neatly into a C-ration can. Charlie would attach a can to a tree, pull the pin on the grenade, and slide the grenade into the can. He then attached trip wire or fishing line to the grenade and ran it across the trail. An animal or person walking from either direction on the trail would hit the trip wire and pull the grenade from the can. The handle on the grenade would pop open as soon as the grenade cleared the can. A person then had seconds to dive for cover. Charlie got more sophisticated by unscrewing the handle from the grenade and replacing the delayed fuse with one that didn't delay. That way the grenade exploded as soon as it cleared the can.

Punji stakes often accompanied this type of booby trap. Sharpened bamboo stakes that were dipped in human feces in order to speed infection were hidden along the edge of the trail. When the grenade was pulled from the can and everyone dove for cover, they were diving on the sharpened stakes.

That was the best reason for rendering the cans unusable. Fortunately, we had Bey, who was really good at discovering the booby traps before we accidentally set them off.

After I discarded the cans from my meal, I decided to visit each track to assess how the men were holding together. My first stop was the mortar platoon. I spent about five minutes at each track. I had used up twenty minutes, and I still had three platoons to go. I would have to talk to a couple of tracks at a time. I had time yet to visit second platoon before I had to call in the fire missions. I would take care of the routine radio messages and the artillery fire missions before visiting first and third platoons.

The mortar platoon was always upbeat. If they had a complaint, it was that they weren't getting to use their mortar tubes enough.

I still thought of second platoon as my platoon. These were the guys I had broken in with. These were the guys I had worked with. These were the guys I knew best. I could level with them, and they would always give me an honest answer. I asked how they were holding up. Was there anything in particular that was bothering them? Were they getting enough rest? Were they able to maintain the pace? Did they have any advice for me? The questions were open ended, but I felt that I needed to ask them. Everything was fine. No one offered any suggestions, and this told me a lot. Their lack of answers spoke volumes. There should have been some off-the-wall comments and some attempted jokes. The men were nervous, fidgety, and worried. I couldn't blame them. I was feeling the same way. I was able to speak with twenty-three men of second platoon at the same time. This was the company's largest platoon, and I was struck by how few men were present. There were only six men and Bey missing, since they were out on patrol.

I now had more to think about on my way back to the command track. It was almost 2000 hours, and Andy and Ron were still on top of the track. Andy changed the frequency on the radio at his side and handed me the handset so I could call in the fire missions that I wanted during the night. The battery was already doing a fire mission for Alpha Company at 2200, so I scheduled the first of my fire missions for 2300. I gave them some coordinates that we had used before as a starting point. I wanted to target the trail in the valley north of the larger butte. I described the target as a trail running north and south that troops were using at night. The artillery would automatically move the impacting rounds up and down the valley. They could fire all six guns so that the rounds landed in a line instead of a circle or all on the same point.

My second target was the area between our position and the butte. I wanted the artillery to work the jungle on this side of the butte. So far, this area had remained untouched. The time that I gave for the mission to begin was 0100 hours. I would be on radio watch and could observe.

I was still standing next to Andy and handed the mike back. The fire missions were set. I took some time to review past fire missions, and I realized that there was only one area of the basin that hadn't been explored by artillery fire. I had been using my map when I had called for the fire missions, but I didn't need to study it with any intensity. A huge section of the basin that covered over a third of its total area formed a triangle between the smaller butte, the company's position, and the fire support base. This untouched area now raised my concern. Originally the area had been overlooked, but it had my attention because battalion's next move could be to explore this section of the basin.

The more I studied the area on the map, the more concerned I became. The trail system in this area could very likely run east-west instead of north-south. The small streams indicated on the map all flowed east and then south. I hadn't been alerted earlier because of all of the action that had me focusing on the area of the larger butte.

My thoughts were electrically charged because I was developing a couple of ideas at the same time. I chose to focus on the mechanical that had blown and the dogs that had run off. It had been tripped by someone or something headed north, away from the company. This scenario wasn't as confusing anymore. Charlie was coming out of the jungle between us and the fire support base. Another thing that occurred to me was the sighting by the OP on guard duty. He hadn't been taken seriously, but I didn't doubt him now.

When we had loggered at the fire support base, we had riffed the edge of the rubber trees and jungle in this direction, and Sergeant Lee had gone from here back toward the FSB. The riffs had overlapped, and no prominent trails were discovered. We had a mechanical ambush set in the largest and most likely ravine or gully that cut into the basin. Sergeant Lee had checked the mechanical twice since it was set, and no new sign had been discovered.

Charlie must have a way to exit the basin to our west closer to the FSB. There were just enough dips and rolls to create enough variation in the terrain to hide movement. The day after tomorrow, I planned to have the riff focus on the untouched triangle. We would then be able to come up with a reason to pepper the area with artillery. It looked as if neither of the prepared scripts would be wasted.

Battalion headquarters called and appeared to just be nosy. We had given them plenty to think about in the last few days. I was convinced that their expectations of the company hadn't been very high, but here we were, and we were still in one piece. I concluded that as long as we remained unscathed, they would continue to test us.

It seems that every call from battalion headquarters was an adventure, and it was happening again. It was an unusual request for them to be asking for the coordinates of our ambush patrols at this hour, especially since they had already been called in to Lieutenant Duff at the FSB. I knew not to give those coordinates openly over the radio. This wasn't for a fire mission. A gunship didn't need them to mark their location. Charlie had radios too, and we knew that he listened to us. So I decoded the coordinates of each ambush location with my spinning wheel. A spinning wheel was a simple device that allowed you to send a decoded message. The term "I shack" meant that the following message over the radio was decoded.

I should have guessed. The person on the other end wasn't prepared and had to get back to me. He had the information, but he obviously didn't have a spinning wheel to be able to decipher the message at his end. I was glad that this wasn't an important LZ landing or supply drop. After several more minutes had passed, I got conformation that my message was received. I honestly wasn't trying to make life miserable for them. I was doing what I was trained to do. I wanted to be off of their radar. It seemed that the harder I tried to get them to forget about me and Bravo Company, the more prominent we became.

I wanted to talk to Sergeant Pomeroy about my latest theory and thoughts about enemy movement on the west side of our perimeter. Sergeant Pomeroy's track was right next to the command track, and I was able to locate him in seconds. He was writing a letter and taking advantage of the last moments of daylight. I waited and planned to let him finish, but he noticed me eyeing him and set his pen and paper down. I apologized for being so obvious.

I explained what was on my mind, and he seriously considered each fact. He agreed completely and retrieved his pen and paper. He tore a clean sheet from the pad and sketched for me how he had placed the claymores in the mechanical. We were going over old ground, but if Charlie was following the dogs and coming from the southwest, the blast most likely would have missed them.

I couldn't help but think that if gas grenades had been incorporated into Sergeant Pomeroy's mechanical, we would have heard voices, coughing, and/or gagging, even if they were untouched by the blast.

The sergeant's eyes were downcast, and his posture slumped. I hadn't meant it as criticism and told him so. I told him not to feel bad. The gas grenades were my call. He had set a defensive ambush, and that was exactly what we had wanted at the time. We both agreed that we would like a do-over on that mechanical ambush.

I returned to my track and climbed to my jeep seat with my poncho liner and M-16. It was still light, but not for long. The clouds had filled in solid, but we hadn't gotten any rain yet. I was hoping to stay dry.

Andy alerted me to the radio. He had a radio tuned to the FSB's frequency. It sounded like Lieutenant Duff calling battalion headquarters. He was giving a report of a sighting just to the north of the FSB. A lone Huey had been ferrying some personnel back to the FSB and caught a group of VC crossing the road and headed west. The sighting had taken place just moments earlier, and they had come from our side of the road. It had been only a couple of klicks away. Lieutenant Duff was off of the radio, and the sound of artillery had taken over. Unless Charlie was pinned down, the artillery would only have the effect of keeping him moving. I could picture the enemy unit running through the wait-a-minute vines.

This bit of information needed to be passed on to the rest of the company by word of mouth. I didn't want battalion to hear us on the company frequency any more than necessary, so I carried the news to first and third platoons while Ron went to second and mortar platoons. This would be all that was needed to give the men an edge for alertness tonight.

By the time I returned, I was wondering if the sighting was really VC or formally trained NVA regulars.

There didn't seem to be any rhyme or reason to where and when sightings happened to occur. This most recent sighting fit with what Sergeant Pomeroy and I had been discussing a short time ago. The troops seen crossing the road had most likely come out of the basin from the area of the triangle formed by the little butte, our position, and the FSB, but I could think of one more possibility. What if the blood trail that we had followed to the north this morning had turned west once the trail was out of the jungle? The time frame fit, and if that was the case, we hadn't been that far behind when we had been on their trail.

I trusted Bey on this one more than my hunches, but I continued to explore the idea. The rubber plantation narrowed like an hourglass not far to the north of us. It would be less than two klicks to the west to an isolated patch of jungle. The patch of jungle covered a large enough area to hide a sizable force. It was at least one square klick in size. This section of jungle was on our side of the road leading to the FSB, and it began just to the north of the FSB. The more I thought about it, the more likely it seemed to me that the sighting could have been the clean-up committee at our ambush site. They would have had enough time to sweep the ambush site at daylight and then be at the road crossing where they had been seen. I now wondered if that had been the route that the original group had been taking when they had tripped the mechanical.

Charlie Company had been deployed another couple of klicks to the north of us. The VC had ways of knowing where we were and could avoid us when they wanted to.

It was almost dark now, and there were no lights or noise coming from the company. Clouds of insects, most of them mosquitoes, were hovering under the rubber trees. A whole case of bug repellent had been passed out just before the ambush patrols had left.

The throaty call of the talking lizard was coming from the same area where I had first heard it. Now everyone in the perimeter would hear its taunting cry. I couldn't help but think that it would be fun to catch one of the lizards and take it back to the world as a pet. I could picture my "fuck you" lizard being more popular than a parrot with a large vocabulary.

With the onset of darkness, the insects were revving up, but everything else was slowing down, including me. I was tired, muscle and joint tired, but not sleepy. There was too much at stake to be able to afford a letdown. We had been at this location for too long. There was a lot happening around us. Some of the action had been initiated by us through our mechanical ambushes. Nevertheless, we were right smack in the middle of the action. It was only a matter of time before Charlie came after us. I could only guess that Charlie had been waiting for us to come looking for him in the basin on his turf during daylight hours. In that situation it wouldn't matter how stealthy and quiet we could be; Charlie would have a huge advantage. At the moment, I was feeling more and more like a piece of bait being dangled in front of the enemy.

I was surer than ever that we were being watched. I meticulously planned to avoid any patterns that could be observed. Tomorrow night I would change the night ambush patrol sites. Rotating between the jungle edge and out in the rubber would be noticeable and had become predictable. I needed to make it more random.

I did a quick check with Andy and Ron and positioned myself to be comfortable in order to test the possibility of an early nap, and that was all it took. I was awakened by the sound of outgoing artillery at 2200 hours. Andy was awake and wouldn't give up the radio. He went through the situation reports and reported to the FSB.

I was fully awake and ready for the fire mission that I had scheduled to take place at 2300 hours. The valley where the phantom patrol was going to take place in the morning was being well peppered. The rest of the hour was uneventful, and I turned the radios over to Ron. I didn't think it was possible, and I don't know how it happened, but I fell asleep again. This time I was awakened by the sound of the second fire mission that I had requested. These explosions were much louder, since they were in a direct line between us and the larger butte and were much closer to our position.

I had no problem getting Andy to give up the radios this time. During the day he had done everything that I had done, and he was on the same sleep schedule. It was his turn at last, and before the fire mission was over, he was breathing heavily. The fire mission concluded, and the rest of the watch passed uneventfully.

I had to climb down to wake Ron, who was sleeping on the bench inside. The driver and TC had their own cozy sleeping arrangements in third platoon's tracks. After making sure Ron was fully awake, I took the time to relieve myself before climbing back to the jeep seat. The next radio watch would be the start of a new day. I was thinking, just make it through the night, and then...

I was half thinking and half dreaming as I woke myself to full consciousness with my thoughts alone. It had been a realistic dream. I was aware that the company had dodged a huge bullet today. If the dog handler hadn't broken his leg, he would now probably be attached to the company for the remainder of the mission, and that would make it much harder for us to control our own destiny. At this point I didn't want an outsider observing the company.

We had been trailing an enemy unit that was much larger than our own. The dog team probably would have led us beyond the range that a reaction force could come to our aid. If and when we made it back to the company's logger site, our mode of operations had to change. The dog handler would have been like an observer. I shuddered at the thought. I then remembered how pissed off I had been over the whole situation when he had broken his leg. And Ness—he should get a medal. When the dog had bitten Ness, the bite broke the skin in a couple of jagged tears and may have even broken bones in his hand. Ness was to be part of Sergeant Moore's night ambush, but he was ordered to remain behind because of his swollen, bandaged hand. Ron had concerns that the bite was already infected.

As I reflected on the whole situation, it had been pure luck that things had happened the way that they did. Ron had been amused that we had actually used morphine on the dog. That had been the only way that I could think of to sedate the dog so we could control it. Ness had been more concerned for the dog than the handler had been; however, in his defense, the guy had been given a shot of morphine.

That whole mess was over. Battalion had screwed up, and we had lucked out.

I was adjusting my poncho liner and looking at stars. I was sure that the way I felt now would make it hard to get back to sleep, and I was assuming that I would be awake at 0400 hours for my last watch. The next thing that I remembered was Andy gently shaking me awake. I had gone to sleep in a hurry and had slept soundly. It was harder to wake up this time. I rubbed my eyes and decided that I needed to stand up. Only after standing and wobbling back and forth was I able to ask Andy if anything had happened.

"Naw, it's been quiet." Andy was just as tired as me.

I propped the radio against the front of my jeep seat and stood on the ground next to the track with my poncho liner draped around my shoulders. By standing, I assured myself of staying awake. At 0110 I went through the motions of getting two squelches from each patrol and each platoon and reported to the FSB. So far everyone was doing well. Hopefully, I was doing as well as everyone else.

I knew that I still had a few things to sort out before daylight, and then I had to meet with Sergeant Hawkins. At the same time, I should have a short NCO meeting to outline the day.

One change that I wanted to make today was to add a third person to each of the OP positions. When the company had been in hot areas before, Captain Cooper had upped the customary two-man OPs to three men. This certainly qualified as a hot AO. The longer we were here, the tighter our security needed to get.

Over the past few days, when it wasn't raining all of the company weapons had been cleaned and oiled. The track-mounted fifty-caliber machine guns and the track-mounted sixties had all been gone over and thoroughly cleaned and oiled. Ammunition was stacked and ready. We had three tripod-mounted fifty-caliber machine guns on the ground with a poncho over each one to keep them dry. There were more machine guns than riflemen in the event that our perimeter was attacked. Sergeant Pomeroy had called dibs on the recoilless rifle and vowed to deploy it where it would do the most good. Harlan was going to be his assistant and hump the ammo. Each platoon had a couple of M-79 grenadiers; however, the M-79s would be discarded in favor of a heavy machine gun. There was no doubt that we could bring some pee on Charlie. We didn't have very many men, but we had firepower.

I wasn't going to spend time worrying about the perimeter. Sergeant Moore and Sergeant Pomeroy were taking care of it. I needed to concentrate on today's script. So far, I saw the script as the key to making it through the day. What I didn't know and couldn't predict was what battalion would cook up to make our lives more difficult. I could expect them to come up with something, and so far, every move that they had made had been a surprise. I had finally figured them out. I would expect them to surprise me.

It was getting light in the east, and I was almost sure that I was ready to start the day. I couldn't wait to get the night patrols inside the perimeter, tighten up the daytime security, and be sure that everyone was on the same page. The morning NCO meeting would unify everyone's thoughts.

In a few more minutes, it would be light enough for coffee. I enjoyed my coffee and cocoa, but it seemed even more important today.

Today was the twenty-fifth of February. This would be my ninth day as acting company commander. The battalion command, brigade command, or whosever idea it was to send Bravo Company here had to be surprised that we were still here and in one piece.

It had been more than three days since I had thought about the consequences of my actions being discovered. I had been too busy to fret or worry about myself. All my attention had been focused on making the right decisions. I was still the decider.

26

I had taken my first sip of coffee and was enjoying the inner warmth as well as the outer warmth of the first rays of sun. There was the sound of outgoing from the fire support base. They were single rounds, so someone was adjusting fire. Shot three was out and on the way. Shot four was fired, and after a short pause, a fifth single shot was fired. Whoever was adjusting fire was having trouble getting the artillery on target. I had jumped the gun, as the next sound was all six guns firing for effect. During a fire for effect, it wasn't six guns shooting at once and then a pause and six guns shooting as one again. Each gun crew loaded and fired as fast as they could. The result was one continuous sound of outgoing.

I was ready for a second cup of coffee as I relaxed in the warmth. Andy had a report on the fire mission that we were listening to. The artillery was firing for Alpha Company. One of the night patrols had remained in place after daylight and had caught some enemy troops moving across an open area.

It was time to regroup and begin preparing for the day. The two-man OP positions were already manned and in place. On the next guard change, there would be three men at each OP site.

I could see Sergeant Hawkins carrying his canteen cup and headed my way. I searched for and quickly found the watertight ammo can that held my personal items. I opened it and withdrew the notepad that had the script that I wanted.

I opted to not have a third cup of coffee as Sergeant Hawkins and I each sat on an ammo can to go through the script. With only a few minor changes, we agreed that the written account would work just fine. I was anxious to get this one out of the way and burn the script.

I passed the word for a quick NCO meeting, and in a short minute, they were all there. Sergeant Moore and Sergeant Lee had just returned and hadn't shed all of their gear yet. The first thing that I covered was our perimeter security and how I wanted to avoid any appearances of routine. I elaborated on expanding the OP guard duty to three people, and NCOs could also cover. I also wanted the times for the OP guard duty rescheduled. They needed to be staggered and of different durations, and we needed to make sure that the guard duty didn't change exactly on the hour. My suggestion was to have the OP guard duties range from one hour and forty minutes to two hours and ten minutes. That was just a suggestion. The platoons could decide how they would vary the times for the guard duties. I cautioned the platoon leaders to be sure that none of the men on today's patrol were scheduled for an OP duty.

Next I wanted to discuss the locations of the night ambushes. We varied the schedule for the ambushes, but the locations were still the same—either the edge of the jungle or out in the rubber trees.

The men had a lot of suggestions, but what was most interesting was the concern for the east side of the perimeter. Almost to a man, they thought that the greatest threat of an attack was from the east side of the perimeter. Only Sergeant Pomeroy and I were in agreement that the threat from the east or the west was equal. We both kept quiet and listened as the discussion continued. There was consensus on the east-side ambush location. The night ambush would be moved farther to the north in the rubber trees. There was good vision, and with the starlight scope they would be able to see almost all the way to the jungle to the south. It was decided to place a mechanical at the edge of the jungle in the area of the past ambush sites. It was a good plan and would work for a couple of nights; however, eventually we would have to expand our night ambushes farther and farther from the company perimeter.

The west-side ambush plan took less time and less discussion. The west-side night ambush was going to be moved farther into the rubber trees and farther away from the company perimeter. Tonight's patrol was going to leave early. They were going to angle out into the rubber trees and then circle back to the mechanical, disarm it, and move it farther to the west. The patrol was then going to set up in the rubber trees where the edge of the jungle could be observed. This was Sergeant Lee's idea. Since he had set the mechanical, he was the one to disarm it, and it was his turn for the ambush patrol. Sergeant Pomeroy made a slight protest about spreading the duties evenly, but it had already been settled. Sergeant Pomeroy suggested that the battery be replaced, and the meeting was just about over.

I no longer needed to caution the company about noise discipline during the phantom patrols; however, I did need to caution them to be aware of battalion orders coming down that could alter what we were doing. I had confidence that the company could adjust to just about any situation after what had happened with the dog and its handler.

The NCOs were dismissed, and they quickly dispersed. Sergeant Hawkins and I had some time yet before we began our fake patrol. I heard helicopters to the north, so I lingered near the radios until they passed. They were following the now-familiar route to the southwest. I was hoping the entire time as the helicopters were approaching that it wasn't a surprise from battalion command, and as soon as I was sure that the helicopters were headed somewhere besides our location, I breathed a sigh of relief.

Was I just being cautious, or was I being paranoid? I was again analyzing myself, and this time I judged my behavior to be more paranoid. The fact that I hadn't heard from battalion headquarters was making me jumpy.

Sergeant Hawkins was signaling me from the back of his track that it was almost time to begin the patrol. He was only two tracks over. It was 0755, and the patrol was to start at 0800. I radioed battalion command to inform them that we were sending a patrol into the valley north of the butte to work their way south toward the butte.

The call to battalion went well, and that surprised me. They didn't give me any advice. In fact, there was a relaxed attitude, as if they weren't even interested. Now I really was confused. I had anticipated that they would try to manipulate the patrol, and I had been prepared to counter anything that might cause deviation from the script. I had finally gotten through to someone who wasn't testing me.

Sergeant Hawkins's nine-man patrol with Bey was about to be on their way, and I received the call that they were leaving the perimeter. A few minutes later, I could hear a formation of what sounded like maybe a half dozen helicopters passing over to the north and heading east. Sergeant Hawkins was waving at me and pointing up. He then radioed that the patrol could hear helicopters, and he wanted to know if there were going to be other troops in the area. I radioed back that I would find out and get back to him ASAP. It was a nice bit of ad-libbing. Andy followed up with the call to battalion for the requested information.

Battalion answered after a pause that there were no friendly troops, ARVN or US, in the area.

My next move was to alert the fire support base that we had a patrol on the ground. Things were progressing smoothly. I was feeling a little more confident now that we had started, and it would soon be 0900 hours. The script called for four more conversations with Sergeant Hawkins or his RTO, and the patrol would be headed back. On the way back, the patrol was going to be extended so that they would actually return to the perimeter at 1550 hours.

The phantom patrols gave everyone in the company a chance to get some much-needed rest and relax a little. Most of the men used part of the time to clean their weapons and maintain their gear. Most of the time was spent on the weapons, and the time wasn't wasted. It had become apparent the phantom patrols weren't giving the company a break. Without the phantom patrols, there would be no time for maintenance of equipment and gear. The drivers and TCs were doing most of the OP guard duty during the day. Everyone was contributing.

I was aware that I was probably the only one in the company who wasn't benefitting from the time provided by the phantom patrols. The stress was building, and it was becoming harder and harder not to show how I was feeling. Not a single day had gone by since we had left the fire support base that I hadn't thought about the consequences of what I was doing. Sergeant Moore had joked about me going to Long Binh Jail. The thought of being sent to LBJ was now a reoccurring nightmare. The idea that I might get caught was occupying way too much of my time. Worrying about getting caught was counterproductive and took away from things that needed my attention. I really didn't want to go to jail. My life would be over. I was in Vietnam, and I was an infantry NCO. My chances of survival and returning to the world were not that good to begin with. There was a good chance that I could be killed or wounded anyway. Now I had upped the odds. I could die from a bullet or go to LBJ. If it was going to happen, I would prefer the bullet over LBJ. At least a bullet didn't disgrace you.

I was brought back to reality when Sergeant Hawkins radioed that the patrol had entered the jungle and was descending the slope into the valley and headed in a southeasterly direction. I was temporarily snapped out of my funk, and after the quick correspondence, we were both signed out with one hour remaining until our next conversation.

My mind had cleared, and I was looking around the company. I frequently scanned the perimeter in order to assess the men's attitude. So far everyone in the company was aware of what I was doing by running the phantom patrols, and no one seemed to care. They all accepted the plan and even embraced it. I thought back and remembered thinking that there was only a fifty-fifty chance that it would work when I presented the idea to the NCOs. I had given the plan less than a fifty-fifty chance after the NCOs had talked it over with their platoons.

Each time I planned a phantom patrol and it was underway, I played this game with myself, and today was no different. I was second-guessing myself again, and, if anything, the feelings were stronger. How could eighty-two people keep the phantom patrols a secret? I was thinking that I needed to prepare myself to go to jail. It was just a matter of time, but it hadn't happened yet. How long would it take before someone got pissed off at me and spill his guts? What had I been thinking?

Today was the twenty-fifth of February, and it was turning out to be my hardest day since I had taken over the company. During my entire life,

I can't remember being so obsessed with negative thoughts. I had never been a doom-and-gloom thinker. What was happening to me?

There had been no action last night, and today was progressing smoothly. It would soon be noon. I should be in a much more celebratory mood, but I felt just the opposite. I was considering my fate, and I was convinced that at some point, I would be found out.

What if I did make it back to the world? Could I still get caught? In my mind, the odds that I would be found out were probably even higher once I left Vietnam. It was more likely that people would relax and talk as time passed. It wouldn't matter whether I was still in the army or out of the army. If they found out, they would come after me.

Sergeant Finley distracted me by coming to the command track to visit. It was an ongoing thing with anyone from the mortar platoon. He was concerned that his platoon wasn't getting to fire their tubes enough. He was worried that they would be out of practice. Sergeant Finley wasn't complaining. He was just talking. They drilled regularly with dry-fire practices.

Sergeant Finley was in a mood to talk, and I was content to listen. He was reflecting on the company's good fortune, and he was right. Things had fallen into place. It was more than a coincidence that we hadn't been probed or even mortared. He kept talking, and he had me thinking more positively. It was evident as he talked that he had given our situation a lot of thought. He too suspected that Charlie was watching our every move, and the company hadn't shown any weaknesses. Charlie had to know that our perimeter security was tight. He had to see the night ambush patrols leaving and returning, and he had to be impressed with the noise discipline. To me that was the most impressive attribute that we presented to Charlie. Another thing that Sergeant Finley pointed out was that Charlie had no way of knowing how many men we had. Everyone continued to lay low and be quiet. That alone had to have Charlie guessing and somewhat baffled. There had been no lapses in the company's alertness.

I was feeling better; and it was noon, because Sergeant Hawkins was calling to report a lot of artillery damage. He then deviated from the script, saying that he was looking at what appeared to be bicycle tracks. His ad lib made me nervous, so as soon as he signed out, I headed over to his track with Sergeant Finley in tow. I wasn't upset. I just didn't want to alert battalion with any extra stimulus.

Sergeant Hawkins was apologetic, but he didn't need to be. He was remembering the tracks that we had seen at the site of the blown mechanical ambush. The blown mechanical was only a klick to the north of where he was supposed to be now.

I told Sergeant Hawkins that it was a good idea to tie in the tracks that we knew were there, but let's stick to the script and get this over with as planned.

As we walked back to the command track, Sergeant Finley was pumping me up again. He was saying how impressed he was with how I was handling the mission. He also verbalized that the phantom patrols had been necessary, and he felt that they had played a big part in contributing to the company's morale.

These comments coming from Sergeant Finley meant a lot to me. Sergeant Finley had a college education, with a bachelor's degree from Boston College. He had been practicing for the LSAT test, which would get him enrolled in a law school. However, he wasn't looking at just any law school. He really wanted to qualify for Columbia University's law school. Unfortunately, he had been drafted before he had an opportunity to take the LSAT and become enrolled.

Sergeant Finley was also a "shake and bake" product of Fort Benning, GA. As we talked, he surprised me by saying that he wasn't sure he wanted to go to law school and become an attorney when he returned to the world. He thought that he would like to do some traveling first. He had always wanted to go to Europe.

I was about to ask where he would get the money when Sergeant Hawkins called to say that the patrol was turning around to head back. They were going to explore the valley a little farther to the north before turning west and returning to the company.

The phantom patrol would soon be over, and then it would be time to make preparations for the night. I needed to start thinking about what needed to be covered in the evening NCO meeting. The night ambushes were already covered. Tonight's meeting would focus on perimeter security. I had to assume that Charlie would eventually come to us.

Sergeant Finley must have been thinking ahead also when he remarked, "We've been in one place for a long time now. Somebody has to be thinking about moving us."

"I agree."

"This is the sixth day already. There must be some SOP somewhere. I can't remember being loggered in the same place for much more than a week."

I was remembering past missions. "You're right. We usually spend only four or five days in an area. There's a reason for that—because it only takes four or five days to riff the surrounding area."

"That's right, but that was also when we had enough men in the company to send out two or three patrols a day.

I think we might be going to move real soon."

He was so adamant, so positive that we would have to move soon, that I couldn't help but agree with him and hope that he was right.

"You know what?" I said. "The only area that hasn't been covered by us so far is the west corner of the basin toward the fire support base. Once that area has been covered, we'll be retracing our steps. If they're waiting for that last area to get covered, I've got news for them. That area has already been scripted and is on deck for tomorrow's riff."

"Don't give battalion headquarters too much credit. We hope they're looking at a map and will realize where we've been, but don't count on it." This was Sergeant Finley's first negative comment of the afternoon.

"It just occurred to me that once we've covered all the areas that are reachable from this site, I can inform battalion to let them know that we might be done here."

"That sounds good to me." Sergeant Finley was even more upbeat.

With tonight's ambush patrols already planned, all I needed to do was concentrate on the perimeter security. Sergeant Finley had gotten me back on track and in a positive mood again. He excused himself and headed back to his platoon.

It was 1405, and Sergeant Hawkins's RTO checked in to say that they were moving slowly. They had to cut trail, and they were going to be late returning.

Sergeant Finley had been with me for several hours, and his support had saved me from my own gloomy thoughts. At last I had some time to myself. I found the captain's throne and set it up in the shade. It felt good to just sit. I cleared my thoughts and just sat and listened. The only sounds were insects and an occasional bird or sound from the jungle.

Sergeant Hawkins's RTO called at 1510 to say that they were turning west toward the rubber trees, but it was too steep and they would have to traverse to the north before climbing up and out of the jungle.

In another hour and a half, the day would be covered, and I was aware that most of the planning for the night was done. I would, of course, solicit ideas from the NCOs at the evening meeting just before the ambush patrols left. That reminded me that the meeting had to be earlier tonight, since Sergeant Lee had to leave earlier in order to move the west-side mechanical closer to the FSB. I needed to bring the phantom patrol back a little earlier than was written into the script, so I walked over to Sergeant Hawkins's track. Both he and his RTO were reading paperbacks. After a brief explanation, Sergeant Hawkins had his pen out and made the notation on his copy of the script. The patrol would call in at 1658 and enter the perimeter at 1706.

I reminded him that the meeting would be at 1706. I would have the word passed to the rest of the NCOs.

"Roger" was all he said, and he was back to his book.

"Could you tell the rest of second platoon, and I will cover the rest of the company?"

"Roger."

With that, I excused myself and started around the company perimeter to inform the rest of the NCOs of the meeting time. I figured I had just enough time, and I was also checking the perimeter for fields of view. I was hoping to be able to predict where a probe might come from.

After giving Sergeant Finley the meeting time, I crossed to first platoon to notify Sergeant Lee. I wasn't surprised to find him going over the patrol order with the men he was taking with him.

When I reached the third platoon, I found Sergeant Pomeroy and all three of the third-platoon TCs wiping down the two tripod-mounted fifty-caliber machine guns that were on the ground between the tracks.

Each platoon had been notified, and I was back at the command track with some time to spare. I was thinking ahead about the possibility of getting the third platoon's fourth track back in the company. It was still in Long Binh being repaired. If we ever got it back, there were no men to man it. Most of the APCs had only four or five men now, and that included the drivers and TCs.

Sergeant Hawkins was waving at me, so I gave him thumbs-up. He radioed right away at 1653 that he had reached the rubber and could see the perimeter. He was going to break for zero five and then return to the company.

By now I should have been feeling really good. The script had worked well, and we were almost through with another day. All I could think of was "Let's keep it going. Just get through this day and move on."

I was back to sitting in the Captain's throne when Sergeant Hawkins called to say that the patrol was entering the perimeter. Andy took the call because I was preparing for the NCO meeting.

So far, this day had been too easy. After the last three days of battalion trying to run the company from Long Binh, I couldn't help but wonder where they had been all day. They were being way too quiet. Were they leaving us alone, or was there something yet to come? I was willing to bet that we would hear from battalion before the day was over.

The NCOs showed up at the mortar platoon's position a little early. The meeting was brief; it took only twenty minutes to cover the night security, a quick review of the night ambushes, and the plan for the next day's riff. Everyone approved the plan. On the twenty-sixth of February, we would run a fake patrol into the basin to the west. Sergeant Pomeroy and Sergeant Rios would be in the script. I wanted to make this an actual patrol, and some of the phantom patrols should have taken place on the ground, but we didn't have the manpower. It hadn't been possible.

As I returned to monitor the radios, because I still expected battalion to call, I was keyed up with anticipation that something was about to happen. Sergeant Lee was leaving the perimeter, and Andy handled his departure. Second platoon's ambush patrol wouldn't be leaving yet, since they didn't have as far to go.

As I lounged in the captain's throne, I was aware that I wasn't hungry. I had used the chair more today than all of the previous days combined. I checked the weather. It was hot, as hot as it could get before it would start to cool. There were fluffy clouds covering 50 percent of the sky, but it didn't look as if we would be getting any rain tonight. Things could change quickly, so I would keep my poncho handy.

I was feeling the need to do something, but I couldn't think of anything that hadn't already been covered. The feeling that something was about to happen was currently getting stronger and stronger. I finally attributed my uneasiness to the fact that battalion command still hadn't called. I couldn't even attempt to speculate what might be on their minds.

27

I was aware of the time when I noticed the second platoon getting ready to leave for their night ambush patrol. I had just lost an hour. I was sure that I hadn't dozed. In fact, I knew that I hadn't drifted off. I had spent the time watching the clouds and listening to the sounds.

I still wasn't hungry as Andy took the call from the departing patrol.

Andy had no sooner signed off when battalion command called. Ron heard it too. All three of us stiffened, and in a rare moment, Andy allowed them to repeat the call a second time before answering. He must have been as stunned as I. It seemed highly unusual for them to be calling now. It was too late to move the company to a new location. Besides, we had two patrols out. I was straining to think of a reason for them to be calling at this time of the day.

Andy wasn't saying much. He was listening intently. Both Ron and I were moving closer to Andy and the radio, trying to pick up on the conversation, but by the time we were close enough to hear everything, Andy was saying, "Out."

Andy just turned and stared at us for a long time before he spoke. "We're gett'n a new CO tomorrow. And we're to be prepared to move."

This was the last thing that I had expected to hear from battalion, and for the moment, I was speechless.

When I finally recovered enough to talk, I said, "OK, Andy, who is it going to be?"

"They didn't say who. They just said a company commander would be arriving tomorrow."

I continued to question Andy. "Did they say what time?"

"Yah, he's supposed to be here at 1000 hours."

"Did they say anything about the move?"

"Nope, just be ready to move."

The news caught all of us off guard, and it was taking a while to sink in. All three of us were silent and thinking. I was feeling uneasy and a bit confused. This was the news that I had been hoping for and waiting for, but there was an unknown that hadn't been included in my thoughts until now. Who was our new company commander going to be, and what was he going to be like? Captain Travis Cooper had been one of a kind. It was hard to believe that anyone could follow Captain Cooper and do as well.

The questions were building in my mind, and almost every question was a comparison to Captain Cooper. Would the new CO be knowledgeable? Had he been in-country, or was he an FNG? Was he gung ho or more laid back? I had many more questions, but they couldn't be answered now. I would just have to wait and see. Some of the questions would be answered as soon as we knew who it was going to be.

Everything had changed in an instant. I needed to have another meeting, and it had to be right away, before it got dark. The patrols that were out would be told as soon as they returned in the morning. After the last sit rep, I would have them pick up the mechanical ambushes and bring them in when they returned.

I now had more to think about besides getting through the night. I was hoping that the night would pass quickly and we would be into the morning daylight. I knew though, that it was more likely to be a rough night. It was going to be extra hard to get any naps or sleep because of the news that had just come over the radio. I turned to look at Andy. He and Ron hadn't moved or spoken. Each was mulling over his own thoughts.

I spoke quietly to Andy. "See if you can find out who the new CO is going to be. I don't know how you can do that, since you won't be able to get a name over the radio."

"I'll see if'n I can get hold of Top. He'd surely know."

"I would like one more favor. See if you can pin down the exact time that the new CO will arrive."

"I'll get on it, but I might not have what y'all want until morning."

"Just do what you can. Thanks."

The company had been operating without an officer for ten days. Ten days is long enough to establish habits and routines. Any combat unit develops close ties among its members, but our company had gone a step beyond that. We now had a shared secret.

Sergeant Pomeroy must have noticed Ron, Andy, and my body language and guessed that something was up, because he showed up at my side. I quietly told him the news and was able to keep any emotion out of my report. Like us, his reaction was sober concern. After some more conversation, because Sergeant Pomeroy had the same questions for Andy that I had, he and Ron left to round up the NCOs who remained inside the company perimeter.

In a matter of minutes, all the company's sergeants minus the three who were out on patrol were gathered at the rear of the command track.

To a man, they all reacted in the same way. Each took the news just as solemnly as Sergeant Pomeroy, Andy, Ron, and I had.

I paused to let the news sink in and give each man time to think. I then gave a short speech. I hadn't foreseen this moment and had little idea of what I was going to say. Our phantom patrols were going to come to an end, and my main concern was to keep them a secret.

I slowly began. "When the new CO arrives tomorrow, the phantom patrols are over. It will be back to business as usual. We are going to have to do more than just protect ourselves. We will be back to hunting Charlie during the day again. Everyone has to know what is going to happen tomorrow. I will see that the ambush patrols are told as soon as they get back, and I will have them pick up the mechanicals on their way in."

I paused for questions, and when there were none, I asked for comments. Several of the men wanted to say something. Mostly they wanted to know what to say to the rest of the men.

"Tell them everything that I just told you. As soon as I know who the new CO is going to be, you will too. My biggest concern is how we can convey that what we did here has to be a secret."

We were having the discussion at the rear of the command track and right next to a third-platoon track. The NCO meetings were open to anyone, and the third-platoon members assigned to the track parked next to the command track had witnessed most of the meetings. Everyone was silent when Harlan, who had been listening the entire time, spoke up. "Sarge, have everyone drink to not tell. That's what we done at my sister's wedding. You know, everyone drank to them being married and all, and that the marriage would last. There's a word for it."

Sergeant Finley answered right away. "It's called a toast. That's it. We will toast to never tell."

There was more input, and several men confirmed that a toast would be the best way. It would be like making a promise.

Another ten minutes passed, and we had come to some agreement. Sergeant Pomeroy and Sergeant Moore would meet the patrols when they returned in the morning and give them the news. I would do the ceremonial toast with the six men going out on OP duty at daylight. That way, every single person would be included. At 0800 the rest of the company would all meet in the center of the perimeter and do the toast. It was settled.

As the meeting broke up, I was aware of the time. Today seemed to be going faster than normal. Maybe the earth was rotating faster. Anyway, the sun was setting, and the darkness was on its way. The moon was going to be between three-quarters and full tonight. Hopefully there wouldn't be many clouds.

The sergeants had dispersed, leaving Ron, Andy, and me together. I could see small groups of men gathered and talking as the news of a new CO spread. I didn't see any animation or anything that appeared to be frustration. Everyone heard the news and with little or no reaction went back to what they were doing.

A can of soda sounded good to me, and there was just enough light to still be able to read the labels. I found a warm orange soda, but I couldn't find a B-52 can opener, so I improvised with my P-38. With the P-38 I made two narrow slits on each side of the can. Then I twirled the tip of my knife in one of the slits in order to make the hole bigger for the drinking portal.

Andy and Ron were both climbing to the top of the track. Our driver and TC were still with third platoon for guard duty. I hesitated for a moment to decide whether I wanted to sit in the Captain's throne while I drank my soda or sit in the jeep seat on top of the track with Ron and Andy. It was an easy decision, and I climbed to the top of the track.

As soon as I was seated in the jeep seat, I felt a wave of relief. I realized that the feeling wouldn't last long, but here I was sitting comfortably and drinking a soda as the last threads of light lingered in the west. The temperature was perfect, and it looked as if we might not get rained on.

The three of us sat in silence while the radios chattered with more air traffic than usual. It was much easier to listen to the war than to be directly involved in it. We could hear an artillery barrage going on far to the northwest. Our fire support base had been quiet for some time now. I could hear the faint sound of helicopters somewhere to the north. They were too far away to identify the type of helicopter by the sound they made.

This moment was as close to being stress free and clear headed as I had been before my birthday. If I let myself relax totally, I would fall asleep, and I wasn't ready for that yet.

The night had descended and darkness had arrived, and once again I was struck with how fast the clock was moving. It seemed as if every time I looked at my watch expecting to note the passing of five minutes, the time had been stretched to thirty minutes.

28

Andy was getting situation reports from each of the patrols and each platoon. The battalion radio was still chattering, but at least they weren't bothering us. After the reports were in and we had settled back to listen to the battalion frequency at the lowest audible volume, the person on the other end said something about an action up the dial on a higher frequency. Andy was on it right away. He was closer to the radio and had heard better than Ron and I had.

A leg unit with a call sign that I didn't recognize was in contact. They had to be reasonably close, or we wouldn't have been able to hear them. A "seven" was telling a "six" to get off of the net. There was another high command involved in the conversation. After a few minutes, we were able to sort out what we thought was happening.

A patrol, mostly likely a platoon-sized unit, that was going to come in for a stand-down the next day had pooled all of their claymores and set up a huge mechanical ambush, and the mechanical had blown. Three men had left their position to go check out the blown ambush in the dark, and at least two different people were trying to turn them around. The main body of the patrol was apparently some distance from the mechanical, because the three men had been moving for a while now. Every time that they spoke on the radio, they were still moving toward the site of the mechanical.

A new voice entered the conversation and was calling the three men on the ground. We knew there were three men on their way to the site of the mechanical because the new person on the radio was using their line numbers. Judging by the call sign, the current person talking to the three was a battalion or even a brigade commander. The three men had stopped and were arguing or pleading to be able to continue. Those three men had balls. The fact that they were running around in the dark meant that they were either very brave or very stupid; probably a little of both.

This was like listening to a ball game on the radio. I wanted to know the results of the blown giant mechanical ambush and what the three men on the ground would find. They were standing up to several officers who were now ordering them to turn back.

The next voice on the radio was identified as one of the three, and he was saying, "We are here. We can smell it. Let us take a look. Don't make us go back now."

The command voice reluctantly gave the OK, with a sprinkling of "Watch yourself" and "Be careful."

The radio was momentarily silent, and all three of us were waiting with anticipation for the next call. I could imagine that a lot of REMFs were also listening in tonight. Flipper had once told me that he and his clerk buddies listened to the line companies and searched the radio for units that were in contact. For example, Flipper monitored our battalion frequency, and if one of our units or patrols was in contact, he would pass the radio frequency and information on to his friends in other battalions and companies.

The radio crackled, and the awaited call was coming back. I recognized the voice that had pleaded with the higher-ups to be able to search the area of the mechanical, and he had a report to make. He started with "We have a count." There was a pause that added suspense to the report. All three of us—Ron, Andy, and I—were on edge with anticipation.

He continued. "I report. One Victor Charlie…" Now there was another pause. It was just a short pause as he blurted out, "Rabbit."

I did a number of gyrations to keep myself from laughing out loud, and I noticed Ron and Andy doing the same. The guy had a clever sense of humor. It had been such a tense and serious moment, with probably half of the rear area tuned to the radio. At least the people in the rear area were where they could laugh out loud. I thought of the three men on the ground and hoped for their sake that the commanders who had ordered them back also had a sense of humor.

Enough time had lapsed while we were listening to the report of the VC rabbit that it was time for me to get the next situation reports.

We had made it through another day and already had a good start on the night. I didn't wish that the night would be uneventful. I didn't want to jinx our situation. I had only thirty more minutes, and it would be Ron's turn at the radio.

I was worrying again. This wasn't the intense worry that I had gone through earlier during the mission. This time it was about the new CO. What was he going to be like? The company functioned well. Most of the men were in the last half or third of their tours, and I was in that group myself. If the new CO was new to Vietnam, then the company was probably in for trouble. I could be sure that I wasn't the only one in the company who was worried. There was nothing that I could do. The army had made its decision, and we would all find out tomorrow.

The night was cooling off, and the moon was nearly full and very bright. The starlight scopes would work well tonight. As I viewed the area directly in front of the track, the shadows cast in the rows of trees from the extra bright moon shimmered and danced. At the hint of any movement at all, my senses went on full alert, but it was just my own mind and eyes that made the shadows appear to move.

Soon it was Ron's turn for the radios, and it was time to roll in my poncho liner in an attempt to trap some body heat. I had felt tired earlier, but I was absolutely wired and wide awake as I adjusted my position. I tried to focus my thoughts to my life back in the world. I missed teaching, and I planned to return to being an elementary teacher if and when I ever got back. However, I was here in Vietnam, and my thoughts returned to the present. The coming day was a complete unknown. I had to be ready for the unexpected, and the new CO was an added unknown factor.

I had given up trying to picture my former life back in the world and began to reflect on my current situation. I had been pretty gung ho when I arrived in Vietnam. Once it became evident that I was going to Vietnam, I tried to get as much as I could from the training stateside. As I sat and considered my situation, I realized that I didn't feel gung ho now. I didn't have the enthusiasm for life that had been part of my personality. Life for me now was different. The eighty-two lives of the men of Bravo Company had become as important as my own life. How much of myself was I willing to sacrifice? I tried to be philosophical and recall the recent past to analyze whether I could have done anything differently that would produce better results.

I was shackled and standing at the main gate to Long Binh Jail. I was looking up at the sign that said, "Welcome to LBJ." Andy was gently shaking me awake. I didn't think that my eyes were even closed, and I was having a hard time bringing myself back to reality. As consciousness slowly returned, I first thought that something had happened. It was a relief to finally discover that it was 0100 and time for my turn at the radios.

At last I was fully awake. The air was quite cool, and I was chilled to the point that my teeth were chattering. I had perspiration beads on my face, and that moisture was making me colder. I longed for a cup of coffee. I didn't want it for the caffeine, but for the warmth.

Andy waited until he was sure that I was completely awake and said, "Y'all were dreaming, and it wasn't a pleasant dream."

I looked Andy in the eyes. The moonlight lit up his face, and his trademark smile was absent. His expression was one of genuine concern. I anticipated that he was going to ask me next if I was OK, so I beat him to it.

"I'm fine. I'll be OK. Yes, I had a bad dream. I must have eaten something that caused it."

Andy didn't want to let it go yet. "Y'all were talking in your sleep. It wasn't very loud, and y'all were hard to understand most of the time, but I heard 'Welcome to LBJ' as clear as a bell."

"I don't remember." I immediately felt guilty for lying, but it ended the uncomfortable conversation.

Andy was wrapping his poncho liner around his shoulders and making minor body adjustments as he tried to make himself as comfortable as possible.

I was thinking that we were more than halfway through the night. With the moon as bright as it was, this would be a good night for travel. I was sure that somewhere nearby, Charlie was on the move.

During my hour of radio watch, everything stayed calm for both ambush patrols and the company perimeter. It was time to wake Ron, who had taken to sleeping on the bench inside the track. When I reached the ground, I took time to relieve myself of some of the orange soda.

Like me earlier, Ron proved to have a hard time waking up. I stayed with him for almost fifteen minutes before he waved me off, indicating that he was OK.

I was still cold as I settled into the jeep seat, which had become my favorite place to sleep. I dried my face again with my sweat towel and draped the towel over the top of my head so that it covered the back of my neck and ears for more warmth. It took a little longer to get the poncho liner in position to stop any drafts from stealing warmth. I was convinced that Vietnam was one of the coldest places that I had ever been. The air temperature wouldn't bear me out, but my body wasn't lying to me.

I was wide awake and thinking once again about the events of the coming day and the arrival of a new CO. It dawned on me that Andy had said to be ready to move. That was definitely good news. We were overdue to be hit or probed by Charlie. We were just as likely to be mortared. I had a strong feeling that the company was being watched. Since being in Vietnam, this was the first time that I could remember having this thought as part of my consciousness. Sometimes, such as now, it could be really strong, and as I got busy with something, the feeling would ebb or even disappear, but it always came back.

When the company pulled out tomorrow, I would volunteer for a stay-behind ambush. If we really were being watched, Charlie would come and look through our garbage after we left.

I had convinced myself early on that this would be a good site for a stay-behind. We had a ninety-millimeter recoilless rifle with flechette rounds. It would be nice to be able to stay in one spot for a couple of days without moving. There would be nothing to do but wait. The idea of a stay-behind was becoming a better and better idea.

I considered myself an active person. I didn't have a lot of patience. In fact, I had to work at being patient. So why was I looking forward to being immobile and stuck in one place for a period of days? I was projecting the stay-behind ambush as a short vacation from the current pressures of the job. I really was looking forward to being on a stay-behind. I was equally convinced that a stay-behind at this site would produce results.

Things once taken for granted had become more important. For example, I had never thought much about being comfortable, but now I took extra pains and put extra effort into being comfortable. I found that when I was comfortable, I could concentrate more on the job at hand. Water was another issue for me. I craved and even dreamed about a cool drink of water without the heavy chemical taste. Temperature control was another issue. When I first arrived in Vietnam, the heat during the day was almost unbearable, but lately I seemed to have adjusted to it. I even looked forward to it, but the cool nights were getting worse. I would have liked very much to be warmer at night. And TV—I missed watching sports on TV. When I made it back home, all that I would need to be happy would be comfort; temperature control; cool, clean water; and a TV for watching sports.

The sound of distant helicopters jolted me back to the present. At first I thought they might be headed our way, but the sound gradually faded. I noticed Andy was at the radios, so I checked my watch to see how long it would be until my turn at 0400. I had only twenty-five minutes. I couldn't reason why the last twenty hours had passed so quickly.

In just a few more hours, the company would be preparing to receive a new CO and packing up to move. It was going to be a busy day, and I needed to start preparing myself and the company for the transition of command. I couldn't count how many times my memory had flashed back to the sixteenth of February, the day that I was assigned command of Bravo Company, and once again I was reviewing the events that led to the present. It had all started when the company was called to react to the sniper fire at fire support base Georgia and entered an unmarked friendly minefield. The minefield was supposedly marked with a single wire strand bordering the minefield, but the vegetation had grown up to the point that most of the warning markers hanging from the wire were hidden in the growth.

We had been left in the minefield overnight. I still thought that we could have backed the tracks out. Knowing now what the engineers found when they cleared the paths, backing the tracks out would have saved a lot of time. We wouldn't have been waiting for the engineers' late arrival, even though they had a legitimate excuse. Still, it caused unnecessary consternation within the company.

As soon as we were set up outside the fire support base, the artillery lieutenant showed up to assign our company guard duty so the artillery could have the night off. Just thinking about the lieutenant's formal military posturing and his condescending manner made me just as angry now. It was a good thing that the run-in with the artillery lieutenant happened when it did, because if it happened now, I would have argued with him and probably have been in a lot of trouble.

Then I received the biggest shock and surprise of my life when I attended the tactical meeting at the fire support base. Not being able to speak or ask questions seemed so absurd. Then being verbally reprimanded by the battalion commander and the whole scenario surrounding the mission orders continued to make me angry every time I thought about it.

Andy was interrupting me. It was 0400 and my turn at the radios. Recognizing that I was awake, he waved and turned away to climb down off of the track.

I didn't wonder if he would return to his jeep seat, or if he was going to go somewhere else, or if he was just going to relieve himself. My thoughts shifted instantly back to the tactical meeting at the fire support base. My anger had been based on how I was being treated and how unfair it was for the company. A few days later, I had a chance to be upset with myself when I finally figured out what battalion had in mind for the company.

I couldn't hold back the smile that was forming on my face as I prepared to call for the situation reports. We had beaten the odds, and we were still in one piece. It looked as if we might make it out of here and be on to a new mission and a new AO sometime today. This was exactly what I had wanted to happen.

As I called for the sit reps, all stations except the mortar platoon returned the call with the customary two squelches. I climbed down and headed for the mortar platoon area. I found two men seated on the ground with a radio. Their backs were up against the track, and they were facing out overlooking the basin. They were awake and startled by my appearance. All that was wrong was that the radio had been turned off to save the battery, and they hadn't remembered to turn it back on.

I accepted their apology and gave them a grin to let them know that they weren't in any trouble.

I returned to the command track and climbed back into the jeep seat. As I adjusted the poncho liner, I felt a draft of cold air. When I had gotten down to visit the mortar platoon, I had forgotten to be cold, but there was no mistaking the fact that I was cold now.

I realized that I had found the right people to advise me. After the battalion commander issued the orders, he had us leaving the next day. Thank goodness for Major Anderson. He had gotten us out of the ridiculous guard duty, and he had given us a couple of more days to prepare. I can't forget Lieutenant Duff. He had really come through for us. The recon pilot was another person I would remember.

There had been a fair amount of luck involved that allowed the company to remain intact. The atmospheric conditions that revealed the smoke trails in the basin to us were a stroke of luck. The jet strike, the gunships, and the artillery all working over the basin had caused Charlie and his NVA buddies to scatter.

Our mechanical ambushes had blown two nights in a row, and I could now appreciate the effects of the gas grenades that we had incorporated into the mechanical. The blood trails and the heavy tracks that had gone north leading out of the basin were proof that we had put everything in motion when we targeted the smoke columns.

Sergeant Pomeroy and I had put together a scenario that explained how the mechanical out front had come up empty. Charlie most likely had been circling the company from the west and going to the east. The more I thought about what had happened and the surrounding terrain, the surer I was that we were being watched from the west side of our perimeter.

When battalion sent the dog tracking team to assist us, I was sure that disaster loomed on several fronts. Instead of sending a tracking team, they sent an attack dog, and they picked the LZ against my advice. The dog handler broke his leg when he jumped out of the helicopter. Everything about that incident went wrong. It took a while to realize that luck again played a part when the handler broke his leg.

I was back to the present and looking for the first signs of daylight. I couldn't hide the fact that I was nervous and jumpy. I couldn't wait to get out of here. As I scanned the east, my eyes could barely make out the top of the larger butte. I flinched at the sound of a single explosion that came from the south. It hadn't been artillery. There had been one explosion and then nothing. It most likely had been a mechanical ambush. It had been loud enough, and I could guess that it was one of Alpha Company's patrols that had set the mechanical ambush.

As it began to get light, I started thinking about making it through the day. The first thing that I needed to do was have the toast with the men going out to the observation posts. Then I would burn the script of the riff to the west that had been planned for today.

The day was progressing smoothly. The night ambush patrols had returned and had brought the mechanicals back with them. They had been met as they entered the perimeter with the news of the new CO and the fact that we would be moving. Sergeant Moore and Sergeant Pomeroy would pick up the mechanical out front and the claymores and trip flares right after the toast.

I was waiting for and expecting an emotional letdown. The toast had been completed, and I now sat in the captain's throne that Andy had set up for me. Ten days ago I had become twenty-six years old. For ten days I had been Bravo Company's commander. "Has it only been ten days? It seems like it has been so much longer."

I had one thought that wouldn't let go: the toast that we had shared to keep a secret was a solemn promise. I could only wait and worry. Only a short time had passed since the toast had taken place, and I was already wondering how long it would be before I would stop worrying.

29

I must have dozed off, because I had an urge to rub my eyes, and I was staring skyward at overhead tree branches. The sun had moved, and part of my body was now out of the shade. I was somewhat confused, because I had been dreaming and it was taking a while to sort out what was part of the dream and what was reality. I had slept soundly, and it was taking a while to shake off the stiffness and get the cobwebs out of my head. I dropped my gaze so that I was looking at the mortar platoon's tracks. I slowly and shakily stood and slid the chair back into the shade and sat back down. It was taking longer than usual for me to awaken and be able to function. As I awakened in stages, I noticed Andy slouched in a jeep seat out of the corner of my eye. He had the radio propped next to him with the mike cord draped over his shoulder and the handset resting on his chest.

Andy had his head turned and was watching me. I was noticing him blink, and before I could say anything, he spoke. "I've got some news for y'all, but it isn't everything that you asked me to get. I know who the new CO is going to be, but I don't know when he's going to get here. I tried to get hold of Top, but Top wasn't around, so I talked to Flipper. I don't know why I don't go to Flipper first when I need information. It seems that Flipper is the one that keeps Top informed."

Flipper was our company clerk, and very few of us knew his real name. Flipper was the equivalent of Radar O'Reilly on the TV series *M*A*S*H*.

There sat Andy with his infectious grin, and he kept on talking. I wanted to interrupt him, but he was thinking that I needed more time to fully wake up. "You know that you were snoring?"

I was embarrassed, because, first of all, I didn't want to get caught sleeping, and second, I didn't want to be heard snoring. A loud sleeper couldn't be tolerated on a patrol.

Finally I couldn't wait any longer. "Andy, you're killing me. Who is it?"

"Oh, sorry. I'm not messing with y'all." And then he quickly added, "It's Lieutenant Maxwell of the recon platoon."

Then we were interrupted by some not-too-distant cracks of thunder, but this wasn't thunder. I knew exactly what it was. It was the fire support base on a fire mission. I waited as I subconsciously counted seconds. When I got to six, I heard the faint sound of the detonation. The fire mission was to the south, and given the time of day, midmorning, I was guessing that a patrol on a day riff had made contact. Charlie generally wasn't out and about during the day, but we were actively looking for him.

I spoke to Andy. "Lieutenant Maxwell is an interesting choice. We could probably do a lot worse. He has been in-country for a while. He knows the battalion and how it operates. He has a lot of experience on the ground. The only thing that worries me is that he might be too gung ho or aggressive."

Andy didn't answer, and the fire mission continued as the outgoing interval and volume picked up. The battery was into the fire-for-effect phase of the fire mission, and the artillery was giving Charlie everything they had. Then the plug was pulled, like pulling the plug on a loud boom box, and it suddenly became quiet again.

Soon there was the sound of helicopters in the distance. They were following the road south to the FSB and continuing on to the south. Each make or model of helicopter was of a different shape and size and had a different source of power. That meant that each produced its own unique sound. The sounds that I was hearing were not the sounds of Hueys. I identified the sounds as that of a pair of cobra gunships. The cobras flew in pairs and had a higher and faster-pitched rotor sound than that of the Hueys.

Alpha Company was somewhere in the area to the south, and I couldn't help but wonder if we had caused some of the enemy troops to be flushed in their direction. I was guessing about what had brought on the fire mission. Knowing what was going on around you helped to keep you sharp, and staying sharp was the key to staying alive. Guessing was also how rumors got started, and Vietnam was one giant rumor mill.

Andy said, "That's Alpha Company in contact. It sounds like they ran into a pretty big element. As soon as the gunships clear, there's more artillery on the way."

The radio was just far enough away that I could hear it crackle, and I could hear the excited voices of men in combat yelling above the sound of shooting and explosions. A firefight was incredibly loud. It was truly deafening, and when you added artillery and gunships, you were lucky to hear yourself yelling into the radio.

As I listened to Alpha Company, I couldn't help but think that we had had something to do with all of the action going on around us. I thought of where Alpha Company was. They were smack in the middle of an east-west infiltration route that was south of Saigon and north of the delta. Starting with the northern edge of the U Minh Forest on the Cambodian border and the south side of the Parrot's Beak, there were strips of jungle that provided cover and concealment all the way to the Pacific Ocean. Once you were close to the ocean, there was heavy jungle bordering the coastal plain continuing for miles to the north. There was jungle all the way to Cam Ranh Bay and beyond. Where we were, there was plenty of jungle with a lot of room to hide in, and there was a patchwork of original French rubber plantations in the area scattered over thousands of acres. The land along the coastal plain was more open, with rice paddies and a maze of dikes that separated the paddies. The coastal plain was a ready food source for the VC and infiltrating NVA soldiers from the north.

Alpha Company was still working the area of the contact, and the helicopter traffic had picked up measurably to the west, following the road south to the FSB and on south from there to the area of the contact. The FSB artillery had completed two more fire missions, and things were beginning to quiet down.

Lieutenant Maxwell was late. It was 1050, so maybe he was having trouble getting a ride with all of the action Alpha Company was having. I was sure that couldn't be, because there had to be plenty of rides available. Something else was keeping him. I began to wonder how much longer I would be the acting company commander. I was feeling impatient, but it wasn't nearly as hard waiting for the new CO as it had been waiting for the news that I was going to be relieved.

Time passed, and Lieutenant Maxwell was well overdue. I had no control over when he would finally arrive, so I started wondering and speculating as to why he might be late. What if I had somehow been found out? Would Lieutenant Maxwell be taking over the company, with me going back to the rear on the helicopter that brought him here, being escorted by MPs on my way to LBJ? It was a thought that I couldn't stop worrying about. Damn Ralph for mentioning it! If the reason that he was late wasn't because an escort of MPs needed to be rounded up, then I had another worry. Would the men of Bravo be able to move on and not mention what had happened the last few days? There were just a few flakes in the company, and they were able to do their job. I was aware that beyond second platoon and now Andy and Ron, I really didn't know any of the others that well.

During the past ten days, I had been aware that I was nervous and jittery, but what I was feeling now was a new experience and uncharacteristic of past worries. The feeling of guilt was consuming me. I had no tolerance or patience. I realized that this was out of character since my civilian teaching job had demanded that I have patience. I reasoned that my wild and random thoughts were occurring only because Lieutenant Maxwell was overdue.

What if the recon platoon had to react to Alpha Company? It could be several more days before we got our new CO. This certainly hadn't played out the way that Captain Sorenson had predicted.

We had been told that we were going to move to a new AO today, but I was out of the loop now. Lieutenant Maxwell had those orders, so what if he couldn't take command today? I needed to be prepared, which meant that I needed to have some contingency plans. I went back to work as company commander. Damn army.

Plan A would cover orders that had us staying put. If we had to spend another night here, we would still have tight security. I actually thought that this was the most likely option if the lieutenant was delayed. Lieutenant Maxwell could simply join the company the next day. I would have the company ready for plan A.

Plan B was needed in case we got orders to move to the new AO. I needed to check maps and plan the order of march for our departure. I would have it ready for the lieutenant, and if he didn't show and we still had to move, we would be ready.

Plan C covered anything else that could happen. We could be ordered back to the fire support base, or we could be sent to Long Binh for a stand-down. That would be the preferred option, but it was also the least likely to happen.

It was getting later, and I was sure that we would soon know which plan we would be following. Whichever plan battalion chose, we would comply. I was just hoping to get the orders sooner rather than later. I couldn't wait any longer to meet with the company chain of command to discuss the options of each plan. It was after 1300 hours, and it was beginning to look as if I would be the company commander a little longer. I was over my jitters now that I was busy planning. I was writing down the details of each plan.

I really wanted to do a stay-behind ambush. When I considered all of the action around us and the fact that we had blown two mechanicals, Charlie had to have a fix on our position. After we left, the VC would show up at this site to go through our trash for anything that they could use. If we stuck around, they were just as likely to show up to inflict some casualties. Lieutenant Maxwell had to be here so I could volunteer for the stay-behind. Moving the company without the new CO meant that there wouldn't be a stay-behind ambush. I was remembering that Captain Cooper's last words of advice were for me to keep the company together.

Andy startled me as he jumped down from the top of the APC and landed next to the Captain's throne. "He's coming. ETA is in zero five mikes." That ended some of my worries. It would be over in five minutes.

I grabbed a purple smoke grenade as Andy was hoisting the radio onto his back. We weren't hurrying as we walked to the center of the perimeter where the helicopter would land.

Around the perimeter, word spread quickly. The first ones to see us walking knew that the wait was almost over. There were no outward signs or hints of excitement, nor were there any signs of anxiety or consternation. The transition was going to be routine. The new CO would have to earn the men's respect. Captain Cooper had left some big shoes to be filled. This was in no way going to be a special event for the men of the company.

I heard the LOH long before I saw it and wondered if Rock was the pilot. I knew it was an LOH by the sound. My eyes were now on Andy, who had radio contact with the pilot. He soon said to me, "Pop smoke." The egg-shaped helicopter had just come into view overhead. I pulled the pin on the can of purple smoke and held the can in my hand as I directed the smoke away from the center of the perimeter. Wind wasn't a factor as the pilot and Andy went through the routine of authenticating the correct color of the smoke. The pilot identified grape and brought the helicopter down for a smooth landing.

I noticed with some disappointment that the pilot wasn't Rock as the LOH slowly lowered its hover until it barely touched the ground. The door opened before the skids touched, and a slender man carrying a rucksack in one hand and an M-16 in the other jumped clear. His fatigues were worn and faded. He bent at the waist and hurried toward Andy and me as we were quickly stepping backward to get away from the turning rotors and the draft created by them.

The pilot wasted no time. His passenger hadn't yet reached Andy and me, and the LOH was hovering, rising, and turning all at once as it took off and headed west, in the direction of the FSB.

Lieutenant Maxwell stood in front of me as I said, "Sir, welcome to Bravo Company." I then added, "We are genuinely glad to see you."

The lieutenant didn't look like the person I had imagined. This was especially true now that I had a close-up view of him. I had seen him several times before in passing. I had seen him once in Long Binh when we were on a stand-down. He was talking with Captain Cooper, and Captain Cooper introduced me. I had seen him one other time, at Xuan Loc, when our company was refueling the APCs. And, of course, he had been at the tactical meeting at FSB Georgia.

He wore dark horn-rimmed glasses, and he looked more like a student than a soldier. He was a West Point graduate, he had already been promoted to first lieutenant, and he could very well make captain even though this was his first tour. His hair was light brown with a few lighter streaks that were almost blond. In addition to the color of his hair, I noted that it was longer than I thought it should be, especially since he was an officer. He wore a mustache that needed some trimming, and he had a two- or three-day growth on his beard. He was quite handsome, with deep-set dark-blue eyes that had an unmistakable sparkle. His stare conveyed a heightened sense of alertness, and he seemed to take in everything around him. If appearances and first impressions were all that mattered, then Lieutenant Maxwell was going to be all right.

No time had elapsed since I had welcomed him. It was his turn, and he came directly to the point. "I would like to meet with each platoon as the first order of business. Then I need to brief the platoon leaders on movement to a new AO."

So without hesitation, Andy and I led him toward the mortar platoon. On the way, I introduced Andy as his RTO, and he smiled at Andy and made an effort to shake his hand. The lieutenant confided to me before we reached the mortar platoon. "I've heard really good things about you, sergeant, and equally good things about Bravo Company. I'm going to need your help and input. We'll be spending some time together in the very near future."

We reached the mortar platoon's tracks, and I introduced the lieutenant to Sergeant Finley, who had already passed the word for his platoon to gather between the first and second tracks.

The lieutenant spoke to the mortar platoon for only about five minutes. "I'm really sorry about what happened to your company outside fire support base Georgia. I knew Travis from battalion meetings." He was referring to Travis Cooper, Captain Travis Cooper, who was our CO before the minefield fiasco.

I couldn't suppress a shiver at the mention of battalion meetings. An overload of emotions swept over me as the memory of the TOC meeting that I had recently attended came flooding back. Once again I was reminded of my dislike and distrust of Elmer Dumford. I believed that Lieutenant Colonel Dumford had intentionally planned to sacrifice Bravo Company in order to further his own career.

Our new company commander continued. "I will do my best to maintain the company's integrity and reputation that you and Captain Cooper have built."

To me that meant that he didn't plan to change much.

He finished with "I believe in sharing and delegating responsibility. Anyone that has any problems or complaints, I need to know. Try to follow the chain of command and you will get answers, but I can't guarantee satisfaction. I plan to know each of you personally very soon."

And so it went with first, second, and third platoons. The lieutenant's speech was different enough at each location to know that it hadn't been rehearsed or planned prior to his arrival.

I explained to the lieutenant that it was time to change both of the observation posts, and I summoned the six replacements who were already scheduled and waiting at the ready. The lieutenant asked a series of quick questions so he would know where each OP was and who was returning and who was leaving the perimeter. He then indicated to the six who were leaving that it wouldn't be a full duty cycle. We would be leaving as soon as he could meet with all of the platoon leaders. He then told the men going on duty to send the men they were relieving to the command track so he could also meet them.

I was learning a lot about the lieutenant, and I especially appreciated his not referring to me as the acting company commander or the NCOs as acting platoon leaders. Since his arrival, things were happening fast. While all the introductions were taking place and he was speaking to each of the platoons, he spent the in-between time visiting with Andy. I also noticed that he kept Andy close by at every stop.

The change of command, so far, was falling into place far better than I had expected, or even hoped for. The lieutenant seemed to genuinely care about the men and the company. He was making all the right moves.

At last it was my turn to speak with the lieutenant. We wouldn't be having a friendly chat. I had a report to give. I showed him my security plan. I explained the rotation and order of night ambush patrols and day riffs, with emphasis on our shortage of manpower. I covered how the company rotated the order of march when it was on the move and how it would fall today when we headed for the new AO. I also tried to indicate some company SOPs that he might not be aware of.

I liked his eagerness to absorb everything. I also liked the way he spoke to the men. He seemed to have the knowledge, positive attitude, and ability to command. I was becoming more confident by the minute that he was going to be a good fit for our company.

It took less than thirty minutes for our meeting to conclude. He thanked me and shook my hand. The new CO then asked to see all the platoon leaders so he could fill us in on the next AO and give us the marching orders.

The men on OP duty were summoned back, and we were on our way, with me in my jeep seat on the number-one second-platoon track. My platoon was second in the order of march. First platoon was point, followed by the command track. The mortar platoon followed us, and the third platoon was the rear security.

I was relieved that we were finally on our way. The new AO was to the north and west of the fire support base. We would be working a rubber plantation that was close to where Charlie Company was on the night of the sixteenth of February. Apparently the lieutenant was very familiar with the area from when he was with the recon platoon.

We were going to stop off at the fire support base to take on fuel; get a clean change of fatigues; and get a resupply of food, water, malaria pills, and insect repellent. However, the most important purpose for the stop would be to pick up our mail.

We would be out of the fire support base and on our way just forty minutes after arriving. That was certainly fine with me. I had bad memories of the place, and I didn't want to spend any more time there than I had to.

While riding to the FSB, my most-feared thoughts came to the forefront. Don't tell. Don't anyone tell. What if some lifer wants to hand out medals for the mission? I seriously doubted that it would happen, but it was possible. I remembered the lone helicopter that was escorted by a gunship team. I had since learned that it had been the brigade XO who had flown over the basin. He would put himself in for a medal, so he would want someone on the ground to get a medal in order to justify his. That was how the system worked.

There was no way that any of us could accept any awards. I was the one who usually wrote people up for medals. Captain Cooper had asked me to do the writing as a favor when the company was in Cambodia and he was busy. I had done it ever since. However, there were two people who needed to be singled out: the second-platoon medic, Marcos Ramirez, for his actions at the minefield, and Ness, for dealing with the medevac of the dog and the dog handler. I didn't want to have to lie about an award.

When we reached the FSB, I had a chance to see Lieutenant Duff again, and I thanked him for all the support that he had provided the company. I brought up the subject of awards with him and explained Ness's and Marcos Ramirez's situations. He agreed with me that they both warranted awards, and he added some news that I hadn't heard about. Captain Cooper had already put Marcos Ramirez in for a silver star, and this pleased me very much.

After leaving the FSB, we were speeding north on the same road that we had come south on so many days before, and it wasn't nearly as dusty as the first trip had been. When I thought that we might be getting close to Highway One, we turned left into a grove of rubber trees all in precise rows just wide enough for the APCs to pass. We were off the dirt trail that served as a road. The main road had been swept for mines that morning by the engineers. This was still an ongoing everyday occurrence before traffic was allowed to and from the FSB. However, the side roads were not cleared. Each APC followed exactly in the tracks of the APC in front of it. If the lead APC happened to miss a mine, then so would every APC that followed. Staying in exactly the same track as the APC ahead of yours was called tracking. If a driver had trouble tracking, he wasn't allowed to be a driver.

We came to a steep ravine and turned north until we came to a series of three dikes that crossed the ravine to the west. The ravine wasn't so steep or as deep here. We probably could have continued north and gone around the top of the ravine, missing it entirely, but we crossed at the dikes. We didn't take the first dike, which appeared to be the main trail or access road. It showed the most travel and use. Instead we crossed on the second dike after first platoon had checked it out on foot before bringing their tracks across and then the rest of the company.

Within minutes of crossing the dike, we came to a large clearing in the middle of the infinite rows of rubber trees. The clearing was at least three or four acres in size. It didn't appear that rubber trees had ever been planted here. Grass was tall, at least waist high in the center of the clearing, where it received the most sunlight. Around the edges of the clearing, the grass was noticeably shorter.

Our arrival at the clearing meant that were had officially begun a new mission in a new AO.

30

We were soon loggered up, and I was busy planning since my platoon was scheduled for a night ambush patrol. I wanted to leave early enough to be able to set up while it was still light.

The night ambush patrols at the last AO had not been faked. They had been real, even though they were a little closer in. They set up and worked just like the one I was going to lead tonight.

We quickly ate and hoisted our gear. Art, my RTO, called Andy for a commo check. The radio was working fine, and Art showed me the extra battery. I then did a quick inspection of everyone's equipment before we checked one another for loose or noisy gear. As soon as the check was complete, we would be ready to depart the perimeter.

There were eight of us, an average-size patrol for our company, with two more men than we had been running for the past eight days. What made this patrol unique was that we had two 60 gunners. Tommy was in his element, and Richard was the other 60 gunner. After each was assigned an assistant gunner, that was half of the patrol. The assistant gunners helped feed the belted 7.62 rounds into the gun and helped direct the shots. I thought of assistant gunners as glorified mules, because they carried extra ammunition for the machine guns. As long as they wanted to do it, I didn't mind, because it gave us a lot of extra firepower. After the 60 machine gun teams, the remaining four included Art, my RTO; two riflemen who were along to carry extra equipment; and me.

Everyone carried extra machine-gun ammunition and had a Poncho Villa–style cross-chest belt of the 60 ammo, as well as a waist belt. Tommy was almost giddy as he hopped from one foot to the other while I proceeded with my inspection.

In addition to the extra machine gun ammunition, the other four of us, including Art, had extra batteries, an extra antenna for the radio, extra smoke grenades, fragmentation grenades, hand-fired parachute flares, and claymore mines. I had placed four gas grenades into my rucksack along with some tape. We would be prepared. It felt good to be back with my platoon and leading a patrol.

I had everyone in the patrol wait for me while I hurried over to the command track. It was an unplanned visit, but I wanted to be informed about the status of the stay-behind ambush. I had volunteered for the stay-behind, but Lieutenant Maxwell said that he couldn't spare me at that time. He really liked the idea, so Sergeant Lee and two other men hid when the company left the site. I couldn't actually believe that I was envious of Sergeant Lee getting the stay-behind. I had a strong gut feeling that the stay-behind was going to produce results.

The lieutenant and I picked a spot for our night ambush five hundred meters to the southeast. The big ravine that we had skirted and crossed to get to the company logger site was a possible travel route for Charlie. To the south and east, the ravine widened considerably, and there was a series of finger ridges that sloped upward and eventually reached the elevation of the rubber trees. We were headed to that spot on the map. I was hoping to locate some trails entering or leaving the rubber trees. Tonight's ambush was going to be on top at the edge of the rubber trees. If that didn't produce, we would drop into the ravine and set up an ambush in the bottom.

The lieutenant had gotten my attention when he emphasized that the recon platoon had marked a lot of sign indicating troop movement in the area. He included that they had gotten into contact twice, but he didn't volunteer whether the contact was initiated by the recon platoon or if it was random.

We could move quickly through the rubber trees because there were no wait-a-minute vines or underbrush to slow us down; plus, the visibility was good. Even so, we kept our pace at a slow-motion walk, as we were tensely listening and watching. We were spaced a long six to eight meters apart and walking single file. The patrol was organized from the front to the rear. The point man was Ness, who was still wearing a bandage on the hand that the dog had bitten. Even though he was walking point, he was one of the riflemen who were loaded down with extra equipment. Ness had a full share of fragmentation grenades, smoke grenades, and extra 60 ammunition, but nothing dangled or hindered his movement in any way.

Following Ness was Tommy walking slack with his M-60 machine gun. Tommy had modified his machine gun to make it shorter and lighter. The gun hung from a strap around his neck that left the gun suspended parallel to the ground with his hands free to direct it. A short belt of thirty to fifty rounds was loaded, and the loose end was draped over his left arm, where he gripped the hand guard around the barrel. His right hand was always ready where it gripped the gun behind the trigger. Tommy's assistant gunner followed him and was assigned left security. His eyes continuously searched to the left as we moved ever so slowly along.

I was next in line, and I had assigned myself the right-side security. The right side of the patrol as we moved was all open under the rubber trees. This gave me a chance to quickly glance around as we moved. Art, my RTO, was behind me, and he was followed by Richard, the other 60 gunner. Behind Richard was Stinky, his assistant gunner. Norm brought up the rear. He was the last in line, so he was the rear security, which meant that he walked backward and sideways most of the time.

After we had gotten a fair distance from the perimeter with the company still in sight, it was as if the entire patrol automatically shifted into a slower gear. At less than two hundred meters from the perimeter, the patrol was on 100 percent alert. What was simply amazing was that it happened to each member of the patrol at the same time without a word being spoken. The eight-man patrol acted like one living body.

Our movement was practiced and deliberate. We used hand signals and other subtle ways to communicate silently. Spitting could indicate a change in direction. Holding your arm out to the side and scratching it could also mean a change in direction. Patting your butt meant that you were taking a break.

Most companies had their own system of signals. Except for radio communication, voices were rarely used, and when they were used, they were hushed whispers, even on the radio.

The open terrain under the rubber trees allowed for easy travel, and we made good time. When we arrived at the spot on the map where we had been headed, it was easily recognizable. The first finger ridge that we came to appeared to have a small, lightly used trail leading down its spine and into the ravine below. A second ridge fifty meters farther was smaller and only went out thirty meters before it dropped off steeply to the bottom of the larger ravine. This second finger ridge was more thickly foliated and was full of wait-a-minute vines with stickers and thorns.

Judging by the view of the treetops, the ravine widened into a valley with a flat bottom as it snaked south. From the map I knew that the bottom of the valley was over three hundred feet below my current position. A third finger ridge that curved south into the valley had my attention. It was a hundred meters beyond where I was standing, and it looked promising. I made a decision on how I was going to organize the ambush, but first I needed to scout the third ridge where it intersected the rubber trees.

I left five men at the second ridge and took Norm and Ness with me to scout the top of the third ridge. The ridge was about fifty meters wide and flat on top. We could find no defined trails, but it was much more open on top. Ness explored down the spine of the ridge thirty meters and reported a major trail leading up, but there hadn't been any recent use. This confirmed my thinking that this ridge was a good corridor for movement into and out of the jungle valley.

I had a brief discussion with Norm and Ness. Mostly they listened while I talked, and in the end we were all in agreement that we would set the mechanical on the ridge where we were, and the patrol would set up on the second ridge. From the second ridge, we could observe the first ridge and out into the rubber trees.

I was feeling fortunate. Usually the jungle or lay of the land didn't present you with simple or easy decisions on where to place your ambush. It was with a true sense of excitement that I produced three gas grenades and the tape to fasten the grenades to the claymores that were to be deployed in the mechanical. Ten minutes later, the three of us were approaching the others. I explained to the remaining five members of the patrol that I had decided to set a mechanical on the third finger ridge because of its distance from us. We would be able to cover the first ridge with interlocking fire lanes.

Everything was ready, and we were all in place just as the daylight started to fade. As soon as the radio watch was set, I called in some predetermined artillery targets. Our mortar platoon was ready with illumination rounds and the HE (high explosive) rounds if we needed them.

We would be on 50 percent alert until midnight, and then we would drop to 25 percent alert. That way there would always be two people awake at the same time. I usually scheduled my watch with Art, and I made sure we had the 0330 to 0430 watch. The early-morning guard duties when it was the coldest seemed to be the least popular, and that suited me fine. I preferred to be awake at that time.

The company had scheduled its situation reports on the hour, so we staggered the times for our guard duty to begin on the half hour and run for one hour. You didn't want to be away from the radio awakening the next person when the call came.

I was really keyed up, but I was also hoping that the night would be uneventful. And so it went. We spent a quiet night, and I actually slept between guard duties. We picked up the mechanical ambush and cleaned up the area, trying to leave no trace that we had been there.

We were headed back, and as we were approaching the company perimeter, the tension was fading and the patrol's movements started to relax. The men were coming down off a self-imposed adrenaline high of an ambush patrol. Often the emotional roller-coaster ride caused from anticipation seemed worse than when an ambush was actually blown. I radioed that we were coming in, and we were immediately given the OK. One of the OP guards had already seen us approaching and radioed that we were returning.

As we entered the perimeter, the other seven members of the patrol turned toward second platoon to unload and clean their gear and to get something to eat and try to unwind.

I continued across the perimeter toward the command track. I needed to give Lieutenant Maxwell a debriefing of the patrol, and I couldn't wait for news of the stay-behind. When I reached the command track, Andy greeted me with the information I sought without my having to ask for it. The stay-behind was still in place.

The rest of the day was boring and uneventful. My platoon pulled daytime security since we had done one of the night ambushes. Lieutenant Maxwell went with third platoon on a riff to the north. They planned to stay entirely in the rubber trees and were scouting for civilians who might be working in this part of the plantation as well as signs of the enemy. Apparently it was a long hike, since they didn't get back until 1700 hours.

First platoon was doing a night ambush, and second platoon was scheduled for the day riff the next morning. Everything seemed to be progressing at a normal pace. The company was operating as it had when Captain Cooper was commanding. The word "normal" bothered me. "Normal" shouldn't be used to describe anything in or about Vietnam. Vietnam wasn't normal. I needed to come up with a suitable synonym.

The night was uneventful again except for the outgoing artillery in the distance. At one point, around 2300 hours, several men on guard duty at several locations around the perimeter thought they heard mortars to the west. That didn't include me. I was sleeping at 2300.

The next day, our riff was to the west. The lieutenant and Andy were with us. I could assume the lieutenant planned to lead the day riffs. We were going to check out a deserted hamlet at the edge of the rubber. It took several hours to get there, especially since we had to negotiate two steep ravines with the usual wait-a-minute vines. The leeches and red ants helped to keep the pace slow. There seemed to be more of the pests in and around this rubber plantation. Each of us carried insect repellant, and whenever we entered the jungle, such as when we had to cross one of the ravines, we got to use the repellent.

At the bottom of the second ravine was a waist-deep muddy brown creek. The problem was, at first, that we didn't know how deep it was. When we came to the creek, we paused and listened for several minutes. There were a lot of jungle sounds. The loudest sounds were that of insects, followed by birds, and there were even some monkeys moving high in the trees overhead. Ness had just stepped into the creek to check the depth to cross when everyone tensed and froze in place. The sound that we all heard was that of a chicken. The clucking of a hen was coming from the top of the ravine straight above us. It was common knowledge that the VC kept chickens at their bunker complexes and camps for food.

We hesitated for several minutes, with Ness still in the water. When some time had passed and we didn't hear it again, the lieutenant gave the signal to cross the creek and angle up the slope of the ravine to our right. I was walking slack for Ness, so I was the next one to cross the creek, and I was followed by Bey. Bey had actually begged to be included in the patrol. I had upset him when I hadn't taken him with me on the previous night's ambush.

The sound of the chicken had Bey ready, and the rest of us were tense with anticipation. Ness slowly—one step at a time and pause—climbed toward the top of the ravine. We continued to traverse upward to the right until we were at the edge of the rubber trees again. The lieutenant and the rest of the patrol came to the top and dispersed to the right of our position, remaining concealed at the edge of the ravine where they could see into the rubber trees.

I motioned to the lieutenant that Ness, Bey, and I would move to our left and check out the area where we had heard the chicken. Without being asked, Bey took over the point, followed by Ness and me. We moved only fifteen meters to where we could see around the corner of some jungle vegetation. We could now see at least several hundred meters along the edge of the ravine and farther out into the rubber trees. There was nothing there. Not a chicken was in sight, so we returned to report to the lieutenant.

I had heard somewhere that this was the part of the world where chickens were first domesticated. It might be that there were a few wild ones around yet.

The hamlet that we were searching for was close. According to the lieutenant, it was right in front of us, just on the other side of a slight rise in the rubber trees. Ness and Bey moved out, side by side about twelve feet apart, and when we got to the top of the rise, we could see the edge of the jungle and the abandoned hamlet. We skirted south through the rubber trees to a cluster of waist-high brush and sat down to listen and observe.

There were six thatched pole buildings. This was more than I expected. I was used to seeing just two or three buildings way out here at the edge of the jungle. The hamlets that I had previously come across consisted of just one or two families barely eking out a living off the land. As I studied the structures, I was struck by how well the buildings had been maintained. Someone was using this site. I looked around, and everyone was wide eyed and alert. They had obviously noticed the same details that I had, and they had come to the same conclusions. There might not have been anyone there now, but the buildings were being used. Bey was our canary in the mine. I watched him, and it was evident that he suspected that there had to be VC in the area. He had finished studying the buildings and was intently looking everywhere but at the buildings.

We spread out our formation a bit and settled in to wait and see if anyone would show up. After almost three hours in the same spot, we were ready to head back to the company. We took a different route back by circling to the north. Even though it was quite a bit farther on the map, it proved to be easier going and faster.

The next day I could look forward to a shorter day riff and then another night ambush. I would be sure to include Bey. Lieutenant Maxwell wouldn't be going with me on my riff; instead, he was going with Sergeant Pomeroy again off in another direction.

We returned to the company area, and there was still no word from the stay-behind. I was wondering how long the lieutenant was going to leave Sergeant Lee there.

Time was passing quickly. The night went by without any glitches, and it was time to get ready for my day riff. My patrol was to scout the company's back trail to where we had come west from the road to the fire support base. I was to specifically check for booby traps and "signs of passing or human activity," as the lieutenant put it. Bey would be an important part of this patrol.

The patrol went smoothly. We couldn't find any evidence that anyone had been snooping around our back trail. If we had found anything, that would have been the site of the night ambush.

When I returned to the company area, I decided on my back-up location for the night ambush. I planned to return to the site of our first ambush. The lieutenant wasn't back yet from his riff with third platoon, but he radioed for me to go ahead if I wanted to get started. He ended the conversation quickly, which had me thinking that his patrol might be into something.

Back at second platoon's area, the preparations were the same as they had been on the first evening of our arrival, except that Sergeant Hawkins (Ness's squad leader) and Bey would be going. Norm was dropped from the original patrol so he could assist with perimeter guard duty. Sergeant Hawkins would take up the rear security.

We were set up in the same location and waiting for it to get dark. I could hear a helicopter approaching. It was coming south, but it was on our side of the road. I caught a glimpse of the Huey as it circled over our location. It was landing at the company logger site. There was nothing on the radio. They were apparently using another frequency. I had Art go to the battalion frequency, and I was able to put together enough information to know that the lieutenant and Sergeant Pomeroy had two prisoners. I was feeling left out. I should have known what was happening. I didn't know any of the circumstances. Had there been a firefight? If there had been a firefight, artillery or mortar support hadn't been called for.

The helicopter had picked up the prisoners and was leaving. I could imagine the excitement at the company, but it was time for us to settle in for the night.

For us it was another quiet night. It was daylight, and we were on our way back to the company. This morning I wanted a cup of cocoa, and I planned to fix it before I reported to the lieutenant.

When you are busy, time does go by more quickly, and I was busy. As hard as I was working, I couldn't shake the thoughts of the past two weeks. I tried to reassure myself over and over that I had done the right thing. I had kept everyone alive, and that was most important. Nothing else mattered.

I was beginning to wonder whether I was going crazy. On last night's patrol, I had been awakened for guard duty in a sweat. The air had been cold, and once I was awake, I couldn't get warm again. I was awake and shivering until daylight, when I could move around. When I was awakened, I had been dreaming about being in LBJ.

Now, back inside the company perimeter, I was heating water for my cocoa and making plans for another day riff, and there was Andy. "You startled me. You need to whistle or snap your fingers or something."

Andy was practically jumping up and down with excitement. I assumed he was going to tell me about the captured prisoners. This was as animated as I had ever seen him. He wasn't going to wait to start talking. His voice was lacking his distinctive Texas drawl because he was speaking so fast. "The stay-behind blew their 'bush just after daylight. Seven NVA troops walked in and started poking around. They got them all, and one of them was an officer. Sergeant Lee is hoping to be back with us by tonight."

I followed Andy back to the command track with my cocoa to give the lieutenant my debriefing. I got through the report quickly, and I excused myself to visit with Andy to be brought up to date on yesterday's action. We stepped to the rear of the command track toward the center of the perimeter to be in the warmth of the sun.

"Tell me about Sergeant Pomeroy's patrol."

Andy was talking faster than I had ever heard him speak. "The patrol walked right up on them. The two VC were in a shallow ravine taking a break. Their AKs were leaning against a tree away from them, and the patrol had them surrounded. It was as easy as pie."

I returned to my track and climbed to my jeep seat on top of the track to think. A lot was happening, but the news of the stay-behind was the best possible news. It mattered now. This was the news that I had needed. I hadn't known what to expect or how I would react, but this might give me some closure. There had been an NVA unit in the area, and it didn't take any imagination to realize that we had been the bait. This confirmed that I had done the right thing. I had saved lives and with a stroke of luck was able to inflict damage, although the amount of damage might be difficult to prove.

I couldn't wait to talk to Sergeant Lee when he returned to the company.

That evening, Sergeant Lee returned. He was able to hitch a ride on a Huey on its way back to Xuan Loc from the fire support base. As soon as he squared things with his platoon, he came looking for me with an unexpected message.

It had taken three days and three nights for anyone to show up. He kept stressing how boring it was lying still for that long. He had expected to be called back much sooner.

It had been light for over an hour when they saw them coming from the west along the edge of the rubber trees. He was set up on the east side of the old perimeter on the slope just behind where the latrine had been. "They were nonchalant and talking. They weren't being careful at all. They walked right into the clearing and were standing in a tight group. They made it easy for us."

What he said next took me by surprise.

"As soon as we blew the 'bush, we stayed in place to let things quiet down. That's when I called the fire support base to report, and in minutes we could hear helicopters. A leg unit was already in the air in our area and was reacting to our ambush. The reaction unit was the first of the Twenty-Seventh, or the First Wolfhounds. They came from Xuan Loc, where they had been camped at the helipad for two weeks waiting to react to anyone in contact in the area.

"But that's not all. I talked to a staff sergeant who knew you. His name was Larry Sydow, and he said for me to say hello. He told me that his company was waiting as a reaction force specifically for our company."

31

I was indeed getting short. I had no idea that the "early out" to go back to school to work on a master's degree had gone through. My wife Kate had submitted the paper work to the army shortly after I had arrived in Vietnam, and she kept up the correspondence and made sure that the army was provided with the necessary documents that proved that I was enrolled in a master's program for spring term of 1971. I was going to be out of the army and be able to leave Vietnam after eleven months in-country.

On March 26, a call came over the radio. The line number mentioned happened to be mine. The platoon was to get me to an LZ where I could be picked up by helicopter. The problem was that the nearest LZ was over a half a klick away, and the men weren't at all happy about having to move so far in the heat of the day. Even though we moved slowly, it required a lot of energy to stay tense and alert. We were still in Charlie's backyard and had to be ready for the unexpected. The men's irritation was getting to me.

The radio message had been confusing and more than a little upsetting. The company had changed the way it operated, and I was eight days into a twelve-day ambush patrol. On the sixteenth of February, it had been my turn to visit men in the hospital, and now it was a little over a month later, and it was due to be my turn again. Anyway, that was my assumption. But how stupid was it to be taking me out of the field in the middle of a mission? Why couldn't they factor in where I was and what I was currently doing? Why couldn't they call me on my downtime between patrols?

This was like being taken out of a close football game for some minor equipment repair. You had been contributing to your team's success, but now you had to stand on the sidelines and watch. So, like complaining to a coach, I called Lieutenant Maxwell to get the order rescinded. I was confident that the lieutenant would see things my way and get me out of whatever it was. To my surprise, all the lieutenant said was that I had to go. Now I was pissed off! I didn't want to be separated from my platoon. Damn army.

After I was picked up, we flew to the new fire support base that the company was now working out of. As the helicopter approached the landing pad, I noticed Top standing back from the pad. I could think of only one reason why Top would be meeting me. His presence only confirmed what I was now sure of. I was going to visit men in the hospital.

When I reached Top, he didn't wait to greet me. He was in a hurry and began talking as he turned and walked away. I hurried my pace to keep up so I could hear what he was saying, and I was waiting for an opportunity to let him have it.

"Come with me. We have to catch a ride to Long Binh." He paused and seemed to pick up the pace. "I'm not letting you out of my sight. You're going home tomorrow."

I had heard him, but it hadn't registered. I was pissed off and focusing on telling him what was on my mind for pulling me out of the field in the middle of a mission. It took a half dozen steps before I came to a complete stop. He walked on for a ways and then turned to look at me. Neither of us spoke until I finally managed, "What?"

Top started walking again. "You're staying with me tonight. You'll get a haircut and a shave without the massage...you got that?" He didn't wait for an answer. "You'll take a shower and put on clean fatigues. In the morning, I'm personally taking you to Bien Hoa. Your flight leaves at 1100 hours. I know you don't have any questions, so let's be on our way."

I didn't know what to expect, how I should feel, or even how I should act, so I just kept quiet. Everything was so sudden. This was a dream that I didn't want to wake up from. There was one thought playing over and over like a broken record—I was going home.

We rode in Top's jeep, escorted by a platoon of Black Horse APCs. When Top and I arrived at the company's rear area in Long Binh, I was in for one more surprise. We stopped at the company dayroom so Top could check in with Flipper, the company clerk. I followed Top into the office and was met just inside the door.

"Are you Sergeant Miller? They said you would eventually show up here."

I recognized this guy, but I couldn't place him. He wore a baseball-style soft cap instead of the more popular jungle cap, better known as a boonie cap. He had a large, bushy mustache. It was much more than army regulations allowed. He was dressed in clean fatigues. The shirt and trousers were the unfaded, just-out-of-the-box variety that the FNGs and REMFs wore. His boots were also recognizable, because they were not the standard REMF boots. They were worn and scuffed. In fact, they looked just like my boots.

The man addressing me could see the confusion on my face, so he apologized and proceeded to introduce himself. His name was Sergeant Quinn; just call me Quinn. He followed up the self-introduction with the fact that he was a reporter for the *Stars and Stripes* and that he would like to interview me.

I was still trying to place him. The name seemed vaguely familiar, and I was also becoming suspiciously nervous. I had more than a gut feeling that I knew what this was about.

He finally got around to saying that he was originally from Alpha Company and we had met when he was returning from R&, and our company was here on a stand-down. I was still having a hard time placing him when he added that he had gone to the NCO club with five of us, and I had been one of them.

I remembered now. On the way to the NCO club, our group decided to follow Sergeant Moore's advice and take a short cut to the club by weaving our way through the maze of hooches and barracks that housed the REMFs.

On the way, our group split going around one of the buildings. Three of the sergeants went around the left side of the building, and three of us went around the building to the right. Sergeant Doug Hawkins, Sergeant

Bernie Rios, and I rounded the corner of the building and were confronted with the sight of three REMFs taking pictures of one another.

It is hard to convey just how disgusting this sight was. Through their photographs, they were trying to portray that they were in actual combat. In reality these three slept in clean sheets every night. They had maid service, and they probably even had air conditioning.

The three REMFs were taking turns lying prone on a little patch of green grass and posing with a brand-new M-16 rifle that had to have been checked out of a company arms room. The rifle was the newest and most updated version of the M-16, and it was better than any that we had for use in the field. The rifle added an extra sting to our building disgust.

It would be an understatement to say that these guys were shocked to see us. Sergeant Rios didn't hesitate. With more than a little fury and cat-quick speed, he closed the distance to the one who was posing and deftly grabbed the rifle out of his hands. The REMF didn't have time to protest or get a better grip on the rifle. Sergeant Hawkins and I blocked the other two so they couldn't retreat.

Bernie took over. "You want your girlfriends in the world to know that you're fighting a war, so you need to make it real." He picked up a handful of dirt and began rubbing it on the rifle. He poured some dirt down the muzzle. He opened the dust cover, and, after checking to make sure it wasn't loaded, he sprinkled some dirt into the chamber.

"You need to do the same thing to your clothes that I'm doing to this rifle." Sergeant Rios stared at the REMF on the ground. He had barely moved.

By now the three REMFs were really scared. The one on the ground was actually slowly rubbing dirt on his arms and legs. Sergeant Rios was on a roll.

Sergeant Hawkins, not wanting to be left out, turned to the other two. "What about you guys?"

"Here. Give me that." He reached for the camera with blurring speed. He had the camera in his hand before the REMF could react to protect it. "I'll take his picture"—he gestured to the man still on the ground—"while you guys get ready. Lucky for you that we came along, or your pictures might not be believable. How embarrassing would that be?"

Sergeant Hawkins had the camera, and Sergeant Rios was helping to pose the man on the ground. Then Doug snapped a couple of pictures, opened the camera, and pulled the film out, exposing it. Then he dropped the film to the ground. He made a show of being extra careful as he handed the camera back to the person he had taken it from.

We had all three of the REMFs close to tears. Sergeant Rios had one last comment. "You get that rifle clean before you turn it back in. It's a lot nicer than anything that we have."

As if that were all of the fun that we could have, we continued toward the NCO club. When we arrived at the club, we were able to provide the night's entertainment with the story of our encounter. We all got absolutely shit-faced that evening. I especially remember paying for it when we had to pull out for a new AO at daylight.

I was only half listening as Quinn was saying that he didn't want to spend his last five months in the army doing spit and polish stateside, so he had extended his tour for five months to work for the *Stars and Stripes*. He had studied journalism before he was drafted.

Top finally interrupted us, saying that I had just enough time for a haircut before they kicked all of the civilians off of the base for the night.

Smiling, Quinn said that he'd be right there waiting when I got back.

Quinn's presence was something that I hadn't anticipated, and it was certainly something that I didn't want.

Top was true to his word. He went with me and kept me in sight. The haircut went quickly, and the Vietnamese barbers were very thorough. I naturally turned down a chance to have my nose hair and ear hair trimmed. When we returned to the company orderly room, Quinn was waiting. He was drinking a cup of coffee and joking with Flipper. They were both having a good laugh when Top and I walked in.

Quinn started right away. "Sergeant Miller, I'm writing a story about you and your company from February twentieth until February twenty-sixth. I need for you to tell some of the details about what specifically happened."

There it was. I was momentarily frozen, and for the time being, I couldn't speak. I was actually trembling inside, and every ounce of my conscious being was directed toward making me act, look, and sound calm.

After a long silence, I decided to test my voice. "That's old news. It's been over a month since that happened. The story has already been in the *Stars and Stripes*." That was all I dared say until I regrouped my thoughts again.

Quinn immediately countered. "A company without officers was kicking ass all across South Vietnam and was single-handedly responsible for bringing down a North Vietnamese regiment. That NVA unit was legendary until you and your company took them on. This isn't a news story. It's a feature story. You and your company did what no one else had been able to do, and I want to be the one to write it."

All I could think of was that I needed to put an end to this. "Listen to me. The navy jets, the cobras, the Huey hogs, and the artillery are the ones that did the damage. We just happened to be in the area. Intelligence already knew the NVA were there. They had them pinpointed. Don't give us the credit."

I had to pause for breath. I was close to hyperventilating. "You know how the army keeps score. They can't give a body count to the navy, artillery, or even gunships as long as there is a leg unit in the area."

I continued with what I had silently rehearsed while I was getting my hair cut. "Think about it, Quinn. There were no awards or citations given for that mission. The deeper you dig, the less interesting it will be."

I paused for effect in order to study Quinn more closely. I felt more confident as I noticed that he had quit taking notes. The open notepad on his lap was blank. I didn't want his next utterance to be a question, so I spoke again. "If I were you, I would look into Charlie Company of our battalion. There's your story. They're a magnet for finding VC. They're always running into something."

I knew I had won. Quinn looked utterly baffled. He was speaking with less confidence. "So far, you're the first person I've been able to interview. No one could have more information than you. Major Anderson declined to be interviewed, but he referred me to you. I talked to Lieutenant Duff, and he answered a few questions, and again, I was referred to you. Everyone I've talked to has said that I needed to see you. Now I just don't know. It seemed like such a good idea, but it looks like I've come to a dead end. Maybe I'll see Charlie Company."

Top was staring at me transfixed as Quinn excused himself and unceremoniously left.

Then Top started in. "That's the biggest bunch of bullshit that I've ever heard. Either you're way too modest, or you're hiding something, and either way, none of that crap that you just spewed was what I was told. I know that you turned down an Army Accommodation medal and a Bronze Star for service." Top paused and then added, "You're being way too modest."

Top's respect for me had been elevated when I had downplayed the events of that mission. All I was doing was taking care of damage control in order to keep myself out of jail. It made sense that no one wanted to talk about the mission. The battalion officers also had a secret. They would never want it known how they had set Bravo Company up for that mission. So far, no one outside of the other eighty-two members of Bravo Company knew the exact nature of the events of that mission and how they had really played out. Top's comment about hiding something had been too close for comfort, and it had me worrying when I should have been celebrating.

The next morning Top dropped me off at the Bien Hoa air terminal, and just like that, I was on my way back to the world and home.

32

The freedom flight landed in Oakland, California. I had left Vietnam at eleven o'clock on the morning of March 27, and after crossing the International Date Line, I landed in Oakland at one o'clock in the morning on March 27. Along with the rest of the men on the flight, I was ushered into a large warehouse or hangar complex that had been converted by the army to handle men returning from Vietnam.

Most of the men returning had time yet to serve in the army and were being reassigned to their next duty station. Since I was getting out of the army, it was going to take longer for my paper work to be processed. In fact, it took most of two days of going from station to station with no scheduled breaks before I was able to complete the ordeal. At each station there was a long line, and at each station it took forever before it was my turn to be whisked through and directed to the next long line.

At night things slowed down, and I don't know why, because the flights kept coming day and night. The only thing that changed at night was that the lines got longer.

I had spent the entire time since I had arrived processing through the medical stations. There were no windows, and it was hard to know whether it was day or night. Occasionally an outside door would open and I would have a hint as to the time of day. I thought it was afternoon, and I still had more medical stations to go. The first thing I had done was a blood draw so I could be checked for infectious diseases. As near as I could tell, I had at least two more medical stops. One of the stations was the psychological evaluation, and I didn't think that it would be very demanding. The other station, I hoped, was the last of the medical stops, and it was the doctor's interview where your entire medical records were gone through. I expected that station to take the most time.

The line at the psychological evaluation station was extra long. I could see twenty or thirty men shifting their weight from one foot to the other as they waited to move up a spot. I couldn't see how many more were in line around the corner of the partition that led into the cubicles where the interviews took place. All of the lines had moved slowly, but this one was even slower. The men moved up one step at a time and then waited several minutes before advancing another step. There was a steady stream of men taking their place at the end of each line. I had been at this for over twenty-four hours since my arrival. This was classic army. Hurry up and wait.

I had eaten a couple of doughnuts and had drunk a cup of juice and some water. The food snacks were strategically placed so that you had to give up your spot in line to get something to eat or drink and then return to the end of the line. I was obviously tired. My legs were aching and weary from standing on concrete since I had gotten here.

I had plenty of time as I stood in line, and fatigue was getting the best of me. I thought, "Why not?" There were two men behind me in line. I didn't say anything, because I didn't care. I scratched my left arm as I moved to my left. It was an ingrained habit that indicated a change in direction. I covered the ten feet to the concrete wall and slid down to the floor with my back against the wall. I was only able to catnap in five- or ten-minute blocks of time. Then the shuffling of the line would wake me. I would adjust my body position and doze again. This was how I had learned to sleep in Vietnam, and I wasn't aware that my sleep habits could change now. I wasn't even aware that my sleep habits had been different before the army. There was no thought about changing anything. I was still living in the moment. I had to make an effort to remind myself where I was each time I awoke. Every time I opened my eyes from the light sleep, it took some time to realize that I wasn't in Vietnam. I didn't have to plan for tomorrow. There would be no more riffs or night ambushes. I would just take things as they came and let them happen.

After a couple of hours of on-and-off napping, I came fully awake. This was a different feeling. I craved a cup of coffee or cocoa even though I was aware of my surroundings and where I was. I merely got to my feet and shuffled to the back of the line. I wasn't surprised to see two other men dozing against the wall as I had done, and I recognized one of the sleeping men as having been on the same flight from Bien Hoa.

When I finally got to the front of the line, I was led into one of several cubicles. Sitting behind a table that served as a desk was a captain in an army uniform. I can't explain why, but I was immediately suspicious of this captain. When I spoke to answer his questions, I always began with "Sir." He told me that it wasn't necessary for me to call him sir, but I ignored him and continued to do so. I thought the questions were ridiculously absurd. It took most of ten minutes before the captain initialed a form in my military folder, handed the folder back to me, and directed me to the next station.

And so the processing out of the army continued. It was boring, tiring, and lacked anything that would make it memorable. It was uncomfortable inside the huge building. There were no windows, and I had given up trying to keep track of the day and the night. The artificial light was bothering me, and I didn't know why. My watch had been an important piece of equipment just a few days ago, but now it seemed worthless. I wasn't able to keep close track of the time, and what's more, I didn't care. I was content to nap on the concrete floor, stand in line, and blindly go with the flow.

I had made it back to the world, but my mind was still in Vietnam. My mind refused to give in and come home. I was constantly thinking about the men I had left behind, and that was how I viewed it. I wasn't there to help them any longer. I had been plucked from my platoon in the middle of a mission, and I didn't know why. I hadn't been able to even say goodbye. I vividly remembered events from the past year. I couldn't begin to focus on the future. The future was far too abstract.

The next-to-last station was finance, where I would learn if the army owed me any money. When it was my turn, I met with one of the clerks. I handed him the manila folder that I had carried from station to station. It was the sum of my military career. The clerk took the folder and began making notes as he spoke. He might have been speaking to me, but he seemed to be talking more to himself. He was mumbling about R&R, leaves, and other leave time, and something about unused leave. He finally concluded that the army owed me $143. I formally reported to the officer in the cubicle next to the clerk and received my pay in cash.

At the last out-processing stop, I was able to shower, shave, and brush my teeth before being tailor-fitted with a new set of dress greens. All the ribbons, awards, and individual and unit citations were appropriately placed on the jacket.

Once I was dressed, with my discharge papers neatly folded and placed in the inside breast pocket of the jacket, I headed for the door. It took a while to find a door that led outside. I finally exited and was standing on a sidewalk looking for a taxi to take me across the bay to the airport.

The street noise was having a negative effect on me. It was so loud. I was actually looking for a place to hide when I was interrupted by a deep voice from behind me. "Sergeant, can I assist you?" When I turned to find the voice, I was looking into the friendly eyes of an E-7 sergeant first class (SFC).

"I need to get to the airport," I said.

The SFC motioned me to follow as he said, "Follow me." It is sometimes funny what crosses your mind in different situations. "Follow me" was the infantry motto, and one of the first things that I noticed was that the SFC was wearing a CIB (combat infantry badge). The senior sergeant led me back into the building, across it, and out a side door.

"There's your ride, sergeant."

A Huey was just warming up. The door slid open as I thanked the sergeant. I then bent forward and hurried toward the waiting helicopter. Two other passengers, both officers, scooted over to make room for me on the rear seat.

The helicopter lifted, and we were on our way. However, this helicopter had its doors on, and they were closed. No door gunners sat in the rear cubbies. My feet were not resting on the skids so that I could be one of the first ones off. The crew chief wasn't going to say, "Pull your feet in. We're going to go over ninety."

On March 26 I was on an ambush patrol in the jungle of Vietnam. I arrived in Oakland, California, a little after one o'clock in the morning on March 27. I left the processing center on the morning of March 29 with my discharge papers. I was out of the army.

On March 31 I was sitting in an eight o'clock class at Western Oregon University. One of the students sitting next to me in that first early-morning class remarked that I had a great tan. He wanted to know if I had been skiing.

33

Coming home wasn't as easy as I had thought it would be. I had expected to pick up where I had left off and continue my teaching career. I was going to school, and that was keeping me busy, but something was missing.

The course work that I was taking would have been interesting to me at one time. Now the classes were monotonous and mundane. It was hard to stick to a task and see it to completion. I even had trouble watching a sporting event on TV to the end. There was little to smile about, but I kept plugging away.

It had been sixteen days since I had left Vietnam. It was Thursday, and I picked up the mail on my way home from class. There was a letter from Dennis Finley. I sat down at the kitchen table and just stared at the letter for a long time before I slit it open with my pocketknife. As I was opening the letter, I sensed that it contained bad news. When I pulled the folded pages from the envelope, I took extra time to smooth and flatten them on the table.

The dread of bad news filled my entire being. I only read the first paragraph, and I couldn't go on. Second platoon had been hurt badly.

I sat stoically with tears running down my cheeks and beginning to puddle on the table. I wasn't sobbing or shaking. I just couldn't control the tears that kept forming. I had no idea how long I sat before I was able to return to the letter.

Three days after I had left them, the second platoon was headed for an LZ to get picked up at the end of the mission, and they walked into a VC bunker complex. Bey spotted an artillery shell hanging in a tree. He climbed up to investigate and discovered an electrical wire leading away. With no time to escape, he tried to bite through the wire. The artillery shell was a command-detonated booby trap, and it was set off by the VC in the bunker complex.

Bey was killed instantly, along with Ness, who had been on point with Bey. Tommy was the next in line, and he was severely wounded along with his assistant gunner. A number of men behind Tommy and Richard were also wounded by the blast. Ralph Moore and Art had been in that group.

I hadn't finished reading the first page, and I had to pause again. I was numb and had been jolted to the core. I picked a point on the wall and stared. I had no sense of time passing. I just sat and stared at the spot on the wall until I could continue.

The rest of the platoon was able to pull Tommy, Richard, Ralph, and Art back to a safe location and get them medevaced. Bey and Ness had to be picked up the next day after the site had been bombarded by artillery and gunships. The final result of that action was two KIA and nine wounded. First and third platoons had to return to that site in the jungle to retrieve Ness and Bey.

I was already having trouble adjusting to civilian life, but the letter from Sergeant Finley was a huge setback. I finished the school term by merely going through the motions. I learned little, and the planned master's degree took a back seat. However, I did land a teaching job that was to begin in September.

I had been back from Vietnam for several months now, and I had developed problems that I didn't fully comprehend. I had mood swings that left me deeply depressed. Nightmares were common, and I had developed some phobias. I had several reoccurring nightmares, and all of them were about Vietnam. One of my phobias was a fear of bright lights. Lights scared me, and I preferred to be in the dark. Loud noises had the same affect, and everything was intensified at night. I had developed claustrophobia to the point that I couldn't sleep with the bedroom door closed. I panicked in elevators or driving through tunnels.

Those first months after returning from Vietnam had me behaving in other ways that weren't productive. Having lived with men for the past two years, I chose to spend time with men. Strength and toughness along with strong language had been normal to me. I wasn't even aware of this behavior until my wife pointed it out.

My wife, Kate, saved me. She was my rock. She was more aware of my actions than I was. She was there for me. She woke me from the nightmares. She talked me through the phobias when I was on the verge of panic. Kate was able to communicate with me, and her voice was soothing and therapeutic. All this time I thought that I was "normal" and doing fine, but ask Kate. She told me much later in our lives that "I was as loony as they come." She stood by me and was the force behind my recovery.

I was able to return to being a teacher, a job that I thoroughly enjoyed. My life mission was to immerse myself in my family and my job and try to forget. It was a noble effort to try to forget, but I discovered over the decades that the memories might be dormant for a while, yet they are always there.

My Vietnam experience was like a Shakespearean tragedy. The relief came at the end when it was over.

"Wars are won and lost, and at some point they always end; but for those who were there, it is never forgotten."

Epilogue

A year and seven months had gone by since I had returned from Vietnam. The men of Bravo Company had dispersed and were becoming harder to find. I exchanged several letters with Dennis Finley, and he seemed to know more about what happened to the men we had served with.

Sergeant Lee was still in the army. He had been promoted to staff sergeant and was stationed at Scoffield Barracks, home to the Twenty-Fifth Division, in Hawaii.

Sergeant Pomeroy headed for Alaska when he was discharged. He was currently running a charter fishing boat out of Homer.

Sergeant Hawkins's whereabouts was unknown. He had talked about going to college, and I had to think that he was currently a student at some university.

Sergeant Rios had a blasting cap explode in his face. He lost the sight in his left eye, which ended his dream of playing professional baseball. He was in college in Arizona studying to be a teacher so he could coach high school baseball.

Sergeant Moore's wounds were severe enough that he was sent home. While he was recovering, he was living at home and helping on the family farm near Longmont, Colorado.

Richard died of complications from his wounds nine months after being wounded.

Tommy was 100 disabled and was living in a veteran's care facility somewhere in the South.

Art called me on Christmas. He seemed to be happy and was doing fine. He had recently married and had a farm in Iowa.

Ness's mother wrote me a very touching letter. She wanted to thank me for being Ness's friend, as she noted that I had been mentioned in most of the letters that she received from him. All that she had left were two medals for valor and a flag.

Dennis Finley didn't go to law school. His last letter was from Italy. He had applied for a position teaching English at an Italian university.

I was a teacher, a job that I thoroughly enjoyed. I planned to teach until I could retire.

Glossary

AO—Area of operations. The area a particular combat unit was assigned to operate in.

ARVN—Army of the Republic of Vietnam. The abbreviation was frequently used to refer to individual soldiers of that army.

beaucoup—French word for many. Used by the Vietnamese in their language. Many times pronounced *boo coo.*

C-4—Plastic explosive used for a variety of demolition assignments.

Charlie—A nickname for the Viet Cong. It came from the phonetic alphabet for VC, Victor Charlie. The names Chuck and Mr. Charles were also used. The NVA were also referred to as Charlie.

Chiew Hoi—The government of Vietnam's program to persuade VC to defect.

CO—Commanding officer. At the company level, the CO was usually a captain. The CO was also referred to as the company commander.

CP—The command post. The CO's position or location on the ground or his APC.

day riff (or riff)—A patrol on the ground walking. Generally, a search-and-destroy mission.

DEROS—Date of estimated return from overseas. The date when a soldier's tour was over.

di di (di di mau)—Vietnamese for "go away quickly."

dust-off—The call sign for medevac aircraft. The call sign originated with the Fifty-Seventh Med Detachment and later became used by all medevac aircraft.

fire base (fire support base, or FSB)—A small base camp for artillery. The place where an artillery unit supports the infantry.

FNG—Fucking new guy. Term used to refer to those newly arrived in Vietnam.

FO—Forward observer. Generally an artillery officer assigned to the infantry for the purpose of coordinating their artillery support.

Hoi chanh—A VC defector.

KIA—Killed in action.

Kit Carson scout—A hoi chanh who was trained to serve and fight alongside US units.

Klick—A slang term for kilometer, or one thousand meters.

LBJ—Long Binh Jail. The army's maximum-security prison in Vietnam.

logger site—A company-sized encampment that provided a temporary base for combat operations.

LOH (loche, or loach)—A light observation helicopter.

LP—Listening post. Nighttime guard duty.

LRPs (lurps)—Long-range patrol. Also, the rations they ate, which were freeze-dried meals.

MAC-V—Military Assistance Command-Vietnam. The US military advisory group.

medevac—A medical evacuation helicopter. Early on in radio transmissions, the code "medevac" meant the patient was Vietnamese ("dust-off" meant he was American).

NVA—North Vietnamese Army.

OCS—Officer Candidate School. Located at Fort Benning, Georgia.

OP—Observation post. Security measure for small emplacements.

REMFs—Rear echelon motherfuckers. A term used to describe support personnel who did not see combat. While it was recognized that their jobs were necessary, the attitude of some REMFs earned them disrespect.

RTO—Radio telephone operator. The soldier who carried and operated the PRC-25 backpack radio.

short—The term for little time left on one's tour. When a soldier was within thirty days of his DEROS, he was considered short.

straight leg—The term used to identify nonmechanized infantry troops.

stand-down—A combat unit's return to a secure area to refit and resupply.

ti ti—Vietnamese term for small, tiny, or diminutive.

TOC—Tactical operations command.

XO—Executive officer. The second-in-command of a unit.

About the Author

Resting after a rlff

Larry Sydow served in the Vietnam War with the US Army's Twenty-Fifth Infantry Division in the early 1970s. After leaving Vietnam, Sydow received his master's degree in education. He is an advocate for veterans and a Vietnam-era historian who speaks about his personal experiences in Vietnam to US history classes in the Pacific Northwest.

Now retired from his teaching career, Sydow engages in professional sport fishing and has started his own business, which allows him to travel throughout the western half of the United States leading fishing seminars.

Sydow is the proud father of two sons who have families of their own. He enjoys spending time with his four grandchildren and passing down his love of the outdoors. Sydow lives with his wife, Jean, in Salem, Oregon. For more information about his work, he invites you to contact him at larrysydow7@gmail.com.